DEATH AND CONSPIRACY

SEELEY JAMES

Published by

Machined Media

12402 N 68th St

Scottsdale, AZ 85254

DEATH AND CONSPIRACY released September 24th, 2019

Print ISBN: 9781732238893

ePub ISBN: 9781732238886

Distribution Print ISBN: 9781733346702

Sabel Security #7 version 2.42

Formatting: BB eBooks

Cover Design: Jeroen ten berge

ACKNOWLEDGMENTS

My heartfelt thanks to the beta readers and supporters who made this book the best book possible.

- Certified StoryGrid Editor Leslie Watts whose brilliant coaching and critical diagnosis turned this book from just another great thriller into the greatest masterpiece of all time. Probably. Visit her website https://writership.com/
- Extraordinary Editor and Idea man: Lance Charnes, author of the highly acclaimed *Doha 12, SOUTH, THE COLLLECTION, STEALING GHOSTS and CHASING CLAY*. If you like beautifully written art heists, visit http://wombatgroup.com
- Medical Advisor and Character Diviner: Dr. Louis Kirby, famed neurologist and author of *Shadow of Eden*. http://louiskirby.com Without his help, the ending would've been a snoozer.
- Amazing Editor: Mary Maddox, horror and dark fantasy novelist, and author of the Daemon World Series and the fantastic thriller, DARK ROOM. http://marymaddox.com

A special thanks to my wife whose support, despite being a tad reluctant, has gone above and beyond the call of duty. Last but not least, my children, Nicole, Amelia, and Christopher, ranging from age twenty to forty-six, who have kept my imagination fresh and full of ideas.

ONCE YOU READ THIS BOOK, YOU'LL WANT MORE!

JOIN THE VIP LIST:
SEELEYJAMES.COM/VIP

You'll get updates on the next book, deleted scenes, the occasional drawing, and fun things. And you get stories about how the series was created.

BOOKS BY SEELEY JAMES IN ORDER:
SABEL ORIGINS: THE GENEVA DECISION
SABEL ORIGINS: BRING IT
SABEL SECURITY #1: ELEMENT 42
SABEL SECURITY #2: DEATH & DARK MONEY
SABEL SECURITY #3: DEATH & THE DAMNED
SABEL SECURITY #4: DEATH & TREASON
SABEL SECURITY #5: DEATH & SECRETS
SABEL SECURITY #6: DEATH & VENGEANCE

FOR MY SON
and future conscience of corporate America
Christopher

CHAPTER 1

BRADY BLED OUT RIGHT WHERE he dropped, slumped against the bed with his knees bent and his feet against the wall of the tiny room. Ace stared at the blood. On the other side of Brady, Diego did the same. More blood poured out than Ace had ever seen before. It flowed down Brady's chest and onto the floor where it pooled around his butt. They kept watching as his face faded to lifeless gray. Then they couldn't look anymore.

Ace wiped the razor on Brady's shirt, folded it, and slipped it back in his pocket.

"Had to be done," Ace said.

"*Si,*" his partner replied.

Ace looked up at the small window, canted into the attic roof. He pulled the thin curtain and peered through the gap. Four feet of sheet-metal roofing separated them from their nearest neighbor. In Paris, cheap hotels huddled together like homeless people around a barrel fire.

He checked their surroundings. Nothing moved. No lights. No sounds.

"Clear." Ace nodded. "Nobody's up at this hour."

Diego nodded. Their eyes dropped to Brady again.

"Hell." Ace tugged at his beard. "We'll deal with it. How much did he tell them?"

Diego fished Brady's phone out of the mess, wiped it with his shirttail, and checked. In his thick Spanish accent, he said, "He say not knowing *destino*, ehm, destination."

"Turn that thing off. They could trace it."

Diego checked the nightstand and found a sewing kit. Using the needle, he pushed the SIM card out.

They looked at Brady again. Then at each other.

"Should we abort?" Ace asked. "What am I thinking. Everyone's counting on us. We recalibrate, that's all. We got this."

"*Si*, we got this." Diego nodded. "We walk instead. Much traffic anyway."

"We use the alternate. We can make it work."

"No difference. We die before hour of lunch anyway."

"Don't be saying that shit." Ace pushed Diego's shoulder. "We go in, spray some lead, run for the river. On foot, that's all. Extra thirty seconds. We got this."

Diego looked down at Brady's blood spattered down his shirt and pants. "I shower."

He handed the phone and SIM card to Ace and slid into the tiny bathroom.

"Yeah, I'll put it on a delivery truck," Ace said to himself. "They'll chase it all over town."

Ace grabbed the duffle bag of their old clothes.

"Hey, give me your stuff." He knocked on the bathroom door and opened it. Diego stood staring at a pocket-sized picture of a pretty girl with short hair. Ace said, "Hey, gimme that too. No trace, remember?"

Diego kissed the girl's picture, then handed it and his clothes to his partner. He said, "Go fast. They find us. Day terminate, ehm, before we commence."

"Just get in the damn shower." Ace regretted his sharp tone the instant he said it. With only hours to go, this was a time for unity. "For ROSGEO."

He held out his fist.

Diego observed him for a moment, apparently forgiving him as he did. Then he bumped Ace's fist. "*Para el* ROSGEO."

Ace marched through the hall and creaked down the worn, ancient stairway to the lobby. Outside, he started looking for an unlocked delivery vehicle. The streets were empty. The scent of baking pastries wafted his way. So did the smell of garbage as he passed trashcans set out for pickup. Which meant there had to be a garbage truck somewhere nearby. He kept walking.

The tension in the back of his mind came to the fore as he strode down the cobblestones. He couldn't believe Brady was a snitch. How had that gotten past everyone? Maybe someone in the leadership knew about him. Maybe there was another traitor in their ranks who'd protected Brady. He pushed it out of his mind. Useless to ponder that question at this point. When he and Diego returned, hailed as heroes, they'd ask questions then. And there would be hell to pay.

He concentrated on the task at hand. Everyone was counting on them to put things in motion. They had a contingency plan in case Brady didn't show. They always knew the car would be risky. Cops. Blockades. Breakdowns. They'd just do it on foot. No problem.

He visualized their secondary route. He could see the scene as if he were a bird just over their shoulders. They walk into the narthex, calm and easy. They shed the tan overcoats. Now they're raising their rifles, flipping the switch to full auto, down the center aisle, firing left and right and behind. All the time, keeping a wary eye out for hero-wannabes. Put people down quickly. The magazines run dry. Toss the empty rifles. They shout their phrases for the survivors to remember and fear. They run out through the north transept. Dumping the second overcoat, the black one, they run hard across the sidewalk. A right on Rue Saint-Sulpice, left on Rue Mabillon, through the little mall, walking now, crossing Boulevard Saint Germain, to Rue de Seine. From there, five hundred yards to the river on a sunny spring morning. Their man waits in a red boat. They step aboard. Done.

Should they save time by skipping the overcoat ruse? Nah. People see men in tan come in, they see men in black do the shooting, they see men in t-shirts leaving. The key to survival is not looking like the guys who killed a hundred people.

A hundred people. Ace liked that. They'd be at the top of the list. Above Oslo. Above Christchurch.

Ace came out of his meditation and looked around. No garbage trucks. A street sweeper the size of a Mini Cooper rounded the corner ahead of him. It moved as slowly as an old lady with a walker.

He put the SIM card back in Brady's phone and turned it back on. He

3

lifted the flap on the back of the sweeper as he rounded it. Without breaking stride, he tossed in Brady's phone and watched it drive away. Two blocks later, he dumped the duffel full of their old clothes and their phones in a dumpster. He took a circuitous route, checking for anyone following or watching. He was clean by the time he got back.

Diego leaned against the window. He had his gear on. His rifle was neatly concealed inside the tan overcoat, the black coat underneath that. He fingered a string of beads and mumbled to himself in Spanish.

Ace's overcoats and rifle lay on the bed. Diego had set it all out for him. Nice, but with six hours to go, he didn't feel like suiting up.

"Where'd you think we're going, huh?" Ace waved his hands in the air. "You think we're gonna walk around like that until it's time?"

Diego nodded at the gear. "No stay here." Then he looked at Brady and sniffed.

Ace checked out the corpse. Brady smelled like shit. Literally. He'd forgotten, dead people crap their pants when they die.

Diego held out his fist. "ROSGEO *por siempre*."

Ace knew his partner was right. If they were committed to the cause, staying in the room was a risk that could jeopardize the mission. He bumped Diego's fist. "ROSGEO forever."

CHAPTER 2

SOMETHING WENT WRONG WITH MY girlfriend.

I trudged along the stone-paved streets at dawn wearing my blue jeans and black leather jacket over a t-shirt that read, "That which does not kill me—should run." I was thinking things over. There were no real indicators I could put my finger on, but when I said we should step out for coffee, Jenny offered to join me "later." Something in her tone of voice. Something in her distant gaze.

What happened? Last night we were thirsty for each other. I did my Julius Caesar impression, *Vini, Vidi, Vici.* She channeled the Whore of Babylon. Laughter and romping ensued.

This morning, she was different.

A shop lady dragged a stand filled with bouquets onto the sidewalk in front of her store. Figuring flowers might perk Jenny up, I picked one. The lady took one look at my face, smiled, and told me they were free for lovers. At least, I think that's what she said. I studied Arabic and Pashto to get through my eight tours of duty in Iraq and Afghanistan. French never came up. I thanked her, sniffed the bouquet, and kept strolling.

We'd had a storybook romance, the kind you read about in romance novels. If you read that kind of thing. Which I don't. So, I guess it was how I imagined a storybook romance goes. I'd saved her mother's life, which led to Jenny getting a pardon. As soon as she got out of prison, she came to my house to say thank you in person. Come to think of it, that doesn't sound like a storybook romance at all. Anyway. One thing led to another. Two weeks later, I invited her for a getaway weekend. I was thinking something like a bed-and-breakfast in the Shenandoah Valley.

Cozy and affordable and nearby.

Then I made the mistake of telling my boss, Pia Sabel, about my plans. She thought Jenny Jenkins would prefer Paris. After all, Jenny's the daughter of Bobby Jenkins, the billionaire drug lord—I mean, founder of Jenkins Pharmaceuticals. Since no one can say no to Ms. Sabel, especially when she insists on paying and providing a private jet, the next thing I knew we were in Paris, staying in the Hotel Lutetia on the Left Bank.

It turned out Jenny had been to Paris so many times it was like going to Walgreens. Her dad rented out Napoleon's Tomb for her ninth birthday. For my ninth, Dad filled a barn bin with dried soybeans so we could jump in them. Things are different for farm boys in Iowa.

There was an upside. Instead of going to see the fire damage at Notre Dame or visiting the Louvre, she wanted to spend the entire trip in bed. I was fine with that.

Then this morning happened.

My brain came back to the street in front of me. Two men hauled tables and chairs out of a café and placed them on the sidewalk. I put my flowers on a table and dropped into a wicker chair. One of the men said something about not being open yet, but the other guy pulled him away.

I said, *What did I do wrong? I made sure she was satisfied several times over. Wait. She wasn't faking it, was she?*

Mercury, winged messenger of the Roman gods, pulled up a chair next to me. *If she be faking an orgasm when you're going downtown like a Detroit rapper, who is she cheating?*

Sometimes it's nice to have a god you can chat with. Most of them are invisible and mute. I enjoy our little chats. Sometimes. But every now and then, the diagnosis of my Army psychiatrists rolls through my head like a thunderstorm. "PTSD-induced schizophrenia," they said. Yeah. Well. What do they know? The guys who served with me in combat considered me divinely inspired.

Mercury first came to my aid in a battle where a company of Iraqi Republican Guards had pinned down a Marine platoon. I'd been separated from my Army Ranger unit and had snuck through the combat zone lost, scared, and confused. Then, with Mercury whispering in my ear, telling me where to aim, I took out half the Iraqis attacking the Marines and scattered the rest. The Marines loved me. I got medals. From then on, my heavenly powers on the battlefield made me the soldier's soldier. Everybody wanted to transfer to my platoon.

All Mercury wanted was to return to his former glory. Just kick Christianity to the curb and reinstate the whole Roman pantheon. No problem. After fifteen hundred years, he and his buddies were done with living on food stamps and desperate for a reunion tour.

I said, *Is it me? Too much of a socio-economic divide?*

Mercury leaned in. *You want a woman like that, brutha? Really want a woman like that? Then you gotta think like a Caesar.*

I said, *I'm her master and commander in the bedroom.*

Sheeyit, dawg. Mercury rolled his eyes and leaned back. (Did I mention he's black? He cites the Judeo-Christian Bible, where it says God made man in His image. Mercury points out that the Great Leap Forward happened in Southern Africa. There were no white people in Southern Africa in the days of Adam and Eve. Therefore, all gods are black. Yeah, took me a while too—but facts are facts.) *I'm talking real Caesar, not just another white dude whipping out some cheap leather gear in a hotel room. I'm talking invading nations, burning villages, raping, pillaging...*

And that's where I tune him out. Certain aspects of civilized behavior have changed a good deal since he whispered in the ears of the rich and powerful.

I texted Jenny that I was waiting for her at the *Café de la Mairie*. She didn't reply.

Ever listen to some old guy go on about winning the state championship back in high school? Try spending an hour listening to a used god talk about the good ol' days when Julius Caesar defeated the official Roman Army under Pompey—not because he should but because he could.

Mercury said, *And that's how Julius Caesar became emperor. The lesson here is: Kill everyone who defies you.*

I said, *How'd that work out for ol' Julius in the end?*

The streets began to fill with enough vehicles to start the rhythmic honking cycles peculiar to big cities. It sounded a lot like that Broadway tune by George Gershwin. What was it called? "An American in ..." somewhere.

There were no texts from Jenny on my phone when I checked for the three hundredth time. I sent her a picture of the menu and asked if she wanted me to order for her. No response.

Mercury said, *There they go again. Those two clowns been circling the block all morning, dressed like Siberians.*

I had a croissant with jam and a coffee. Alone.

Are you listening to me, homie?

Mercury's supposed to be the god of eloquence, but tutoring William Shakespeare four hundred years ago didn't work out for his resurrection, so he tried channeling inner-city kids. He thinks he sounds like Dr. Dre, but he comes off more like Eminem will in forty years. Desperately dated.

I'm telling you, Mercury said, *those two are your ticket to fame. You kill them, and the press will love you. Glory will be ours!*

Having lost track of which two people he wanted me to kill, I said, *Jenny doesn't care about glory.*

The sun rose higher in the sky. The waiter brought more coffee. People going places began to fill the sidewalk. Singles, couples, families. It was Sunday, and many of them were filing into one big-ass church across the street.

Mercury said, *What's the big deal about this here girl has you so distracted, brutha?*

I said, *Remember when I rescued her mom from the assassins? Back when she was an admiral. The brass tends to expect a concierge rescue. But not Admiral Wilkes. She fought and ran and knocked out bad guys like a superhero. That woman was determined to get out of there. I was impressed. When Jenny showed up, I realized the apple didn't fall far from the tree. She was just as determined and driven as her mom. A woman like that, you can build a life together. A real partnership. We could grow old without the flame dying out.*

Mercury said, *Determined? Driven? You really want a woman like that, dude? Nothing but trouble if you ask me. In my day, women didn't read, they didn't vote, they didn't talk back. We had a good thing going and y'all messed it up.*

My phone's screen was blank. Still no word from Jenny.

I said, *Maybe she needs something more than just sex?*

Mercury said, *What else is there?*

I dunno, I said. *Like therapy or something. She had a traumatic year. Maybe she needs help with her mental health.*

Mercury said, *What would you know about mental health?*

The waiter brought a vase for my bouquet. It was wilting. I gave him a nod. *"Merci."*

Pretty much the extent of my French vocabulary.

I was stuck. If I went back now, I'd look insecure, worried. If I kept my cool, acted unconcerned, maybe she'd come around. Maybe she'd text me back.

Ugh. I hate playing games. Unless I win.

See here now, bro. You need to take down those terrorists with the two coats. Mercury nodded at the men he'd pointed out earlier. *You can be a hero again.*

I said, *What makes you think they're terrorists?*

Mercury said, *They radiate hate.*

Across the lane was a large, open plaza. In the center stood a massive chunk of marble with statues of ancient Frenchmen in niches surrounded by water splashing from a central fountain. The Frenchmen were probably important at some point in the history of the area, but now they were just a backdrop for selfies.

Two guys stood next to the fountain. They stole glances at the cathedral doors. They had black hair and beards. One had a swarthy, Mediterranean look. The other looked distinctly American. They kept their heads down, their hands shoved in their coat pockets. Their overcoats were heavy enough for winter, but it was a sunny spring day.

Maybe Jenny was worried about the paparazzi. We'd been swarmed outside our hotel. Again later when we went out to dinner. Neither of us is a celebrity, but her divorced parents are minor tabloid material. Jenkins Pharma sold a questionable number of opiates, and her mom is now the Vice President of the United States. Which is why there'd been plenty of controversy over Jenny's pardon.

The paparazzi couldn't be it. I'd shared Ms. Sabel's advice for dealing with tabloid photographers with Jenny. Ms. Sabel told me to smile for the cameras because (a) they hate that, and (b) they'll print it anyway so you may as well look good. Jenny still hated them.

I thought about going to church. I checked the name of the one across the street. *Église Saint-Sulpice.* I invited Jenny in a text. We hadn't discussed religion, and she didn't seem the type, but if she was mad at me, where better to work things out? She was the kind of woman worth working things out for. The kind worth having an intimate relationship with. Someone you could tell all your secrets to. Or is it, someone to whom you could tell all your secrets? I never get that stuff right. Maybe she didn't like my grammar.

Mercury grabbed my hair and pulled my head up out of my phone. He pointed at the two guys. *Quit thinking about getting laid and ask yourself the million-dollar question: why two coats?*

Shoplifters wear overcoats. It gives them room for all their stolen merchandise. So do mass shooters. Coats cover weapons.

The shorter guy fiddled with a string of beads. Sweat dripped from his forehead. He mumbled to himself. The American looked calmer, yet significantly more agitated than your average churchgoer. My military training included a good deal about recognizing terrorists. They often say prayers. They're often quite nervous. They often sulk to avoid notice.

Either these two were sinners in desperate need of redemption … or they were terrorists.

I found myself crossing the street, heading for the fountain. At the same time, the two men headed for the church. As he pushed off, the short guy tossed his beads into the water.

It was a wide plaza, and they had a shorter distance. I changed course to intercept them. Being unarmed put me at a disadvantage. But they had the terrorist's tunnel vision. Their eyes remained glued to the entrance. Nothing around them mattered anymore.

A few people in nice clothes funneled up the steps and filed through the massive front door, each taking a bulletin from the greeters. None of them wore more than a light sport coat.

The overcoat guys slowed and hung back. When the funnel cleared, the greeters at the door waited. The overcoat guys trotted up the steps and entered without taking the offered bulletin. Without a bulletin, they would have no idea which hymns to sing. Definitely terrorists.

I bounded up the steps, full throttle.

CHAPTER 3

THEY WERE SHEDDING THEIR COATS as I transitioned from the bright daylight to the dark interior. My vision was off, but I could sense they had rifles out and raised. I jumped and tackled the shorter guy. My arms wrapped around his back and slammed his elbows to his chest. The move drove the rifle stock under his arm and jerked the muzzle of his weapon upward just as he fired on full auto. His bullets hit the ceiling.

He yelled a loud curse that ended when his face hit the marble floor. Our combined body weight drove him in hard enough to leave a dent.

His partner wheeled around and leveled a Beretta AR70/90 at my head. An automatic rifle used by the Italian military that's capable of firing over 600 NATO rounds per minute. NATO bullets are high-velocity rounds that tumble on impact, destroying all bone and tissue on their way through the human body. They're designed to kill an enemy without requiring a direct hit.

I stuck my knee in my victim's butt, grabbed his shirt collar, and yanked him back hard. His backbone cracked as it bent backward. The man's body shielded mine. His partner froze for a second.

Rapid, panicked exits weren't a high priority for seventeenth century church builders. Worse, the nave didn't have fixed pews like modern churches. It had wooden chairs. When everyone started screaming and scrambling for the exits, they turned over chairs and crushed into each other. They gridlocked the space in seconds.

The guy in my grip tried to shake me off. I held firm. He pulled the trigger again, sending a spray tinkling through a stained-glass window high in the vaulted ceiling. He yelled, *"Allahu akbar!"*

He tried to fire again. I fought and managed to wrestle the barrel under his chin. He panted and squirmed.

"Let him go," the other guy shouted in perfect English.

I said, "Drop your weapon or die."

The guy in my grip tried to repeat *God is the greatest* in Arabic again. His accent was terrible. I pulled harder on his collar, cranking his backbone farther to maximize his pain. He stopped.

The American's eyes shot around the room. The crowd had stumbled and fallen, people and chairs sprawled in every direction. Some folks desperately reached for the elderly and the children, compounding the problem by blocking the narrow aisles for the quick.

The American's eyes came back to me, filled with hate and anger. "Turn him loose, or I let you both have it."

"I'm a former Ranger. I can kill you before you can blink. Drop the weapon. NOW."

I could see the gears in his head turning while he thought it over. He came to the wrong conclusion. He turned to the crowd pinned against the stone walls. A third of them found protection behind the thick stone arches. The rest were exposed. He raised his rifle.

With an extra-hard yank on my victim's collar, I freed the muzzle and wrapped my hand around his. His finger was still inside the trigger guard. I squeezed. Three poorly aimed bullets fired off. My worst fear, hitting an innocent civilian, didn't happen. My best hope, killing the American, didn't happen either. Instead, the bullets clanged off the organ pipes at the far end of the church. The metal vibrated with dissonance.

Shrieks and screams reached a fever pitch. Worshippers squeezed behind the pillars. The children's piercing cries rose like a descant to the adult howls.

The American's furious eyes swung back to me over the iron sights of his Beretta. The muzzle pointed directly at me; his finger squeezed. I pressed my victim's finger and tried to roll. Rounds spewed from both weapons. The American's bullets struck my human shield with a wet slap, exiting with the crunch of broken ribs.

My aim had improved—considering I wasn't the one holding the rifle. A couple of my rounds missed but three of them hit and put the American on the ground.

14

Dropping the carcass in my grip, I pried his Beretta from his dying hands. I staggered to my feet and trained the AR70/90 at the American. He didn't move, but he held his weapon close. I approached cautiously, expecting a trick.

The congregation had stopped screaming. There were plenty of kids still crying. Their wails reverberated in the stone chamber. Parents huddled over, shielding the little ones with their bodies. No one wanted to face the danger or see a bullet coming.

I kicked the rifle away from the American. He made no attempt to hold on. I stepped closer and saw the back of his skull lying ten feet down the center aisle.

I flipped the Beretta's safety on. I turned to the people on the left. "It's OK. You're safe. No more danger."

Slowly, people began to peep around the stone pillars. What just happened wasn't clear to them. They looked at me, then at the gore, and then back at me, and back at the gore.

Mercury twisted his head to examine the American. *Whooee, dawg! We're gonna be famous now. You saved a whole bunch of Christians from these ... these ... what are these guys?*

I said, *I don't know. That guy was trying to speak Arabic but it's not his first language.*

Whatever they are, I can't wait to tell Jesus about this. Oh brutha, he's gonna owe me big time.

You mean He isn't here? I looked around the ancient church filled with sacred art.

Mercury looked at me like I'd farted. *You serious right now, homie? You think he hangs in a place like this? He's all about lepers and hookers and homeless people.* Mercury looked to the ceiling. *I had me nicer places than this back in Rome, y'know. And I stayed in them all the time, too. None of this associating-with-losers bullshit. Gotta be available to your peeps, right?*

An angry official shouted behind me. His tone caught me by surprise. I didn't need to speak the language to realize what was going down. The AR70/90 was still in my hands. To the first responders, I had every appearance of being an active shooter. The shouts continued, two or three guys yelling at me simultaneously. The faithful started wailing again. With any luck, some of them would defuse the situation by explaining my heroic acts. If they saw anything from behind the stone arches.

It occurred to me that I could explain things in a reasonable tone. The police might understand, lift me on their shoulders, and carry me outside to a hero's welcome.

Or, none of them spoke English and I could get shot by a nervous cop.

Surrendering has its advantages. Like, living until lunchtime.

I spread my arms out wide, lowered my knees until the rifle butt touched the marble, then gently laid down the weapon. I raised my hands slowly, knitted my fingers, and put them on top of my head. My knees touched the floor as many booted footsteps rushed in behind me.

The police were not gentle. They tackled me, forcing my face to the floor. My hands were yanked behind me. Cuffs snapped on my wrists. Shackles clicked around my ankles. Someone grabbed me by the hair and yanked my head up. An angry face met mine, shouting French insults and swear words. Spittle flew from his lips, landing in my eye and covering my cheek.

A well-dressed, handsome lady ran to my aid. She spewed what sounded to me like a lengthy rebuke at the officer.

Then she spat on me.

At first, I thought she must have been spitting on the other American and missed. Then she kicked me. She shouted, *"Va te faire foutre!"*

It was a phrase I wasn't familiar with, but given her tone and delivery, I figured it meant, *Go fuck yourself.*

Swearing in church. What has the world come to? Then I realized, the worshippers had huddled together, seeking cover behind the supports and shielding each other. Not the best vantage point for observing what was going on in the nave. They misunderstood what had transpired.

A young couple came to my defense. I think. They appeared to be arguing with some of the cops and the old lady. They were all pushed back to the sides.

The cop dropped my head on the marble like a melon. Only a thin layer of blood cushioned my fall.

Mercury got on his hands and knees and lowered his face to the floor. *How did you manage to mess this one up, dawg? Couldn't drop the rifle before the cops showed up?*

I said, *I secured the area.*

All she saw was you and a weapon. Mercury stood and dusted his hands. *Well, they're gonna give you the Marie Antoinette treatment, so I gotta find someone else to evangelize for me. Good luck, homie. It's been nice.*

WAIT! Aren't you going to help me? Can't you get me out of this?

"Américain?" the cop asked. "Get you out? Most certainly."

Two guys grabbed my arms and yanked me to my feet. A fist landed on my right cheek.

I made no move to defend myself. More punches landed in my breadbasket. After the man in charge finished with me, they swung me around and dragged me outside. Other officers pushed the so-called Christians back and taped off the area around the bodies. As we exited the building, I looked up at a clock over the front door. A video camera sat on top of it.

I said, "Tell me that thing's on."

CHAPTER 4

THEY SHOVED ME INTO THE sliding door of an ambulance. A medic approached. I stole a glance at the *Café de la Mairie* across the street. I'd left my phone and bouquet over there, not to mention a small bill for breakfast. I wondered if Jenny had arrived. A quick scan of the guests told me no. With my luck, she probably texted me while I was busy doing my hero-not-hero schtick.

The cop in charge blasted a few questions my way. I could tell they were questions because his voice went higher at the end of each rant, along with his furry eyebrows. He was heavy for a Frenchman with a thick, gray mustache and a paunch. The men around him snickered. The medic pushed them aside, opened his ambulance, and grabbed gloves. He peeled my jacket down to the cuffs.

"I'm not hurt," I said.

"We must check just the same," the medic said with a light accent and a bit of a lilt. He craned over his shoulder at the big cop. "Major Pavard, our suspect speaks English, you know."

Major Pavard, my inquisitor, grunted.

The medic lifted my t-shirt and raised his brow, the way women do, when he saw my abs. "*Quoi.* We are working out most regular, no?"

"Thanks. My boss was a world-class athlete. She insists we stay in shape. What's with Major Pavard?"

He said, "Pavard speaks the English—when he wants to. He thinks only of French dominance. Turn around."

I complied and lifted my cuffed hands.

After a second, he dropped my shirt and turned me back to face him. "All the bullets flying, yet you are not wounded?"

"Aside from Pavard throwing a few punches, no."

"We must check for the internal injuries."

"I don't have any. I'm fine."

The guy leaned in close enough for me to smell his fancy cologne. "We are stalling. Pavard's superior comes this way soon. A more civilized man."

When I'm in France, I can never tell which guys are gay. Not that I care. I'd rather not waste their time. I'm a friendly Midwesterner from a small town, an attitude that is sometimes mistaken for interest. I've ended up in a couple of awkward situations.

"Would you mind wiping the blood off my face?" I asked. "My girlfriend is supposed to meet me in a few. I don't want to look like a serial killer."

His attitude changed dramatically at the reference to Jenny. He sounded a bit huffy when he said, "Of course. Right away."

Mercury looked over the medic's shoulder. *Aw, dawg. Rude to brush the guy off like that. Benoît here dances at the Moulin Rouge on his days off. You might want to catch his act.*

Not my style, I said. *I thought you dumped me. Again.*

That was before Lieutenant Colonel Hugo took an interest in our exploits. Mercury slapped my shoulder and nodded at a newly arrived officer who was making a grand entrance. *Guy like him might turn your fortunes around, get things going. With the right presentation, we could put you on a path to Caesar-hood.*

The ranks of cops surrounding me broke their shoulder-to-shoulder formation. Two guys walked through the line. One was a thin, middle-aged Frenchman wearing a military uniform with the bearing of a king. The other was a short, wiry, bald guy with a piercing gaze, business casual khakis, and a blue button-down. The king-guy held a tablet under his arm.

Pavard met them with a scowl. The king-guy made a formal introduction in French. The only part I recognized was *Lieutenant Colonel.* The king-guy held out his tablet, but Pavard waved it away. Pavard stroked his mustache as he drooped an inch. He backed up and said something to his men. One of them trotted to me and removed my cuffs and shackles.

Benoît wiped the last traces of blood off my forehead, dried it, brushed my short hair back, and looked me over. He broke a smile. "Well. Are you not the most important of men?"

"Most of the time, I'm the only one who thinks so."

"If your girlfriend does not think so, I can show you the best side of Paris."

"I'll keep that in mind." I shook his hand. "Thanks for your help, Benoît."

After the shock that I knew his name wore off, he tucked a card in my pocket and pushed me out of his ambulance.

The king-guy stood directly in front of me. The short, bald guy kept back a yard, his piercing eyes never leaving mine. Pavard's officers kept a loose circle around us, as much to keep the press and onlookers away as to keep me from running.

"You are in France for what purpose?" the king-guy asked.

"To kill bad guys," I said.

"You are going to IDC, yes?" the Hugo asked.

"Sorry, Hugo, I don't know what IDC means." I stole another glance at the *Café de la Mairie*. No Jenny.

He ignored my use of his name. "You have been in contact with IBÖ?"

He and the bald guy leaned in forming a tight triangle with me.

I said, "No idea what you're talking about."

"Come now, Mr. Stearne. We know you are connected with *Identitäre Bewegung Österreich*."

"That German or something?"

"Austrian. Perhaps you know them in English as *Identitarian Movement Austria*."

I tossed my hands up. "You looked me up. You know my record. You've reviewed the church video, which means you know I saved fifty lives in there." I pointed at the cathedral. "You're testing me for some reason. Why not just talk to me?"

The bald guy turned away to hide a smile growing across his face.

"I am asking questions," Hugo said in a commanding voice. "You are answering. Are you contacting Free Origins, Birth Right, or Fair Heritage while you are in Paris?"

"I'm done answering questions." I used my commanding voice. "I want a lawyer."

Uh. Dude. Mercury leaned around the Frenchman. *This is France, not the USA. There is no 'I wanna lawyer' trick. They can question you for three days before giving you food and water. And this guy is ready to go there.*

"You are working for Sabel Security, yes?" Hugo asked. He and his sidekick backed up a step, giving us all a little air.

"I'm on vacation," I answered.

"And you are the specialist of security for Pia Sabel, correct?"

"Yes."

"And she sends you to Europe for the Identity Defense Conference, oui?" His slip into French indicated his annoyance with my reluctant answers.

"No."

He crossed his arms and leaned back. "Do enlighten me, Mr. Stearne. Why did Ms. Sabel send her chief of operations special to Paris?"

His accent was getting thicker. He pronounced special as *spess-ee-ahl* and Paris as *Par-ee*. Must have been very annoyed with me.

"She liked how I handled a recent operation and gifted me a little romantic getaway with my girlfriend."

"Girlfriend?" His eyes narrowed. "Her name is …?"

"Jenny Jenkins." I scanned the café for her again. No Jenny. I sighed.

"Jenny Jenkins? A most familiar name." Hugo looked pensive and scratched his chin. Then he wagged his finger at me. "Ah. The recent controversy of the American president? She murdered a man, oui? She is the woman pardoned under questionable circumstances. This Jenny Jenkins?"

"Yeah." I ran my fingers through my hair. It didn't feel good when people brought up her past. I mean, ever since she stuck a pistol in a guy's eye socket and pulled the trigger, everybody thinks she's gone bad.

Hugo turned to the bald guy, who shrugged.

"Look, if you're not going to give me a medal, then I'm outta here."

I hooked a finger in my jacket and tossed it over my shoulder. With a push off my back foot, I started forward.

And stepped directly into Hugo's hand.

"Why do you make assumptions that we have reviewed your record?" he asked.

"You're a high-ranking GIGN officer, or something close to it. You brought a CIA guy from the embassy with you." I gave the bald guy a nod; he scowled right back at me. "You have the video on that tablet in your hand. You offered to show Pavard, but he refused to question you because of your rank. Pavard had me released right away. That means you know what went down in the church. If I cared, I'd ask about your interest in all those things you asked me about. But I don't. So, may I go—sir?"

Hugo stared at me, still pressing his hand in my chest while he thought about what I'd said. "How do you know *Groupe d'intervention de la Gendarmerie nationale*, GIGN?"

"You guys handle terrorist attacks like this one and the intelligence on the groups that sponsor them," I said to impress him. It didn't work. He waited for an answer to his question. "We studied your handling of the Air France 8969 hijacking in Ranger School. Takes some balls to mount an operation like that and stick the landing."

Confusion twisted Hugo's face. He turned to the bald guy and said something in French. The bald guy answered him in flawless French. Hugo faced me again.

"Ah, 'stick the landing' is a good thing." He gave me the faintest smile of all time. "We are releasing you into the custody of your embassy representative. You are not to leave Paris until our investigation is complete."

"What?" My voice goes high when I'm pissed. "Turning me over to the CIA instead of thanking me? What is this?"

"This—" he moved his hand to my shoulder and squeezed the way my dad does when he's proud of me "—is a favor you will do for France. And it is your only alternative to being Pavard's guest for several days. Your embassy's representative will explain."

With a more genuine smile and a twinkle in his eye, he walked away, leaving me face-to-face with a pissed-off bald guy.

CHAPTER 5

"I'M ZACK AMES, AGRICULTURAL ATTACHÉ for the Foreign Agriculture Service." He put out a hand while trying to drill a hole in my head with his gaze.

"Agriculture? Really?" I looked at his hand without reciprocating. His name brought a memory of him back to the surface. Even though we'd never met, I knew about Zack Ames. "You're CIA. Why are you here?"

He tightened up his eyes and mouth and spoke through clenched teeth. "Agricultural attaché."

"Sticking with it, huh? OK, test question. I take the corn head off my combine and put on the draper. Why?" I leaned over him. At six-one, I had enough height to cast a shadow on his face. The physical menace didn't intimidate him in the least.

But the question did. He stammered.

"I'll give you a hint," I said. "It's late September when I change the heads."

He stuttered but couldn't come up with anything.

"Time's up." I stuck a finger in his chest and pushed him back a step. "Corn heads are used to harvest corn. Drapers are used for wheat. If you'd ever set foot on a farm, you'd know that. Agricultural attaché, my ass. You analyze terrorist threats as a liaison to the GIGN. You knew this shooting was about to happen, and were supposed to stop it, but you blew it."

"What makes you say that?" His face betrayed him. I'd nailed it.

"Not ready to level with me? Want to debate Case versus Deere?" I waited while he considered bluffing his way through. "They're the Chevy and Ford of farm equipment."

"Look." Ames huffed and glanced away. "Your record's impressive. You've got a Distinguished Service Cross and a bunch of Bronze Stars from your time with the Rangers, so I'm going to tell you the truth. But this goes nowhere. Nowhere. Not to Pia Sabel. Not even Jenny Jenkins. Got me?"

I glanced at the café. My waiter stood by my table, looking at the things I'd left behind. "Talk to me while we walk."

"Wait a second." He lifted his chin as if daring me to punch him. "You're in my custody. We're going where I want."

"You want a cup of coffee, Zack." I crossed the street. My memory of Zack Ames returned to me in bits and pieces until I stitched it all together.

"First, you have to level with me." He trotted to catch up. "Have you heard of the Identitarian Movement?"

"No." I waved to the waiter. He spotted me and smiled.

Ames stopped talking as we neared my old table. I ordered coffees and croissants for both of us. God only knows how the French live on a single pastry for breakfast. Maybe that's why they're all thin. I looked around. No one nearby had a belly hanging over their belt. Huh.

I sat down and checked my phone. Nothing from Jenny.

I looked at Ames. "Tell me about this identity thing, or I jump bail on you."

There was a text from Ms. Sabel. She asked what happened. It was five in the morning back in Washington, DC. I guessed her life-long insomnia had not improved in my absence. Her sixth sense for trouble hadn't dulled, either. I texted back about taking down a couple terrorists before breakfast. I put the phone down and rolled my hand for the short guy to start talking.

Zack Ames said, "There are a bunch of small, right-wing political parties in the European Union. They've been moving ever further to the right over the last three to four years. They're xenophobes who want to retreat into a Balkanized economy circa 1912. Brexit is the mainstream version. All of that is just political opinion, neither right nor wrong.

"But a more sinister side developed around the immigration issue. There are legitimate arguments one can make about immigration based on how many new people a society can absorb. Racist views often creep into the arguments. Anti-immigration is not automatically racist. It's often a concern about unemployment rates and financial burden. But the controversy gives cover to the more vehement racists. Some splinter groups gave up on democracy and openly advocate violence. The political parties distanced themselves from the violent factions a while back, stranding and isolating the outliers.

"Not long ago, some of the more radical groups reached out to each other. But it's been a shaky marriage because they hate everyone. The Greek splinter groups denigrated the Jews, Muslims, Asians, Blacks, and Italians. The Italians hate the same groups and include the French. The French include the Germans, and the Germans include the Spanish. And so it goes. About a year ago, they realized there was strength in a united front. They decided to form a union. The irony that they were advocating leaving the EU to form an EU of their own was lost on them."

"Idiots are a dime a dozen," I said. "How's that my problem?"

"I'm getting to that." Zack looked around to check for eavesdroppers.

When he was satisfied, he said, "The danger began when they banded together to advocate violence against their common enemies. They attracted donations and amassed a significant fund from wealthy backers. A large meeting of the leaders and activists took place last year in Kraków. People came from all over the world. One guy left the meeting and shot up a synagogue. Another guy left and defaced a mosque."

"Sounds like some guys who need to be in jail. What's Europol doing about it?"

"They don't have anything actionable." Zack gave me an impatient glance. "Let me finish."

Our coffees and croissants arrived. Zack stopped talking while the waiter was near.

When his idea of danger passed, Ames went on. "We didn't get much intel on the meeting in Kraków. The new regime in Poland is not friendly to the US intel community. We know the Identitarians fought over strategy and split into three distinct groups. They were antagonistic toward each other. They fought in the streets and several young men were arrested. One attendee came to the authorities in Slovakia,

SEELEY JAMES

disgusted with the more violent direction the groups were taking, and told them what was going on. But he'd left the sessions early and didn't know the details. The Slovaks came to believe a large-scale attack had been planned at that meeting. They think it's coming down soon. Maybe this month. Trouble is, we have no visibility into that community."

"You don't know where to focus." I finished my coffee. "Why do you believe the Slovaks?"

"Because a large number of attendees went dark after Kraków." Zack gave me a grave look. "Diego and Ace, the codenames used by the two guys you took down, were at that meeting. Those names won't be released publicly. Keep them to yourself. After they left Poland, we tracked them for a while. Ace went back to his home in Lewisburg, Pennsylvania. Diego went back to Málaga, Spain. They dropped off the grid a couple weeks later. We think today was a test run for the main event. Ace and Diego are the tip of the iceberg. We think there's an international group of radicalized racists out there hiding in plain sight. Ace and Diego weren't the only ones to disappear last year—a total of sixty-eight of them from Kraków are smoke in the wind."

"You didn't know these two guys left home until they resurfaced last week in Paris." I put some jam on my croissant and took a big bite. Delicious.

"Worse." Zack sipped his coffee. "Facial recognition didn't catch Ace until he reached Heathrow yesterday morning. He took the Chunnel to Paris in the afternoon. Diego showed up at Orly Airport about the same time."

"You knew they were in town. Why not arrest them?"

"For what?" he asked. "We raised the alarm but didn't know the target. And these guys were good. They arrived in Paris at rush hour, changed looks and clothes, walked in crowds with their heads down, and—"

"You lost them quicker than Osama bin Laden."

"Hey, we found bin Laden."

"Ten years later."

He clenched his coffee mug and let out an angry breath. "What do you have against the Company, Stearne?"

28

"Nine dead soldiers from botched intel." I leaned in to make sure he felt my heat. "When you torture prisoners, they tell you whatever you want to hear. But that's your problem. When you send men into battle based on your unconfirmed fiction, it becomes a crime."

He put his hands up in surrender and shook his head several times while he gathered the guts to reply. "I didn't have anything to do with that."

I leaned back. "Let's pretend the Zack Ames I traced seven years ago was a different guy. You were never at the CIA's Cat's Eye prison in Thailand. You didn't transfer to Cobalt prison in Afghanistan. You weren't the Zack Ames who provided intelligence gleaned from torture for the Battle of Wanat in Nuristan. You're a different guy. OK. Let's play your game that way. What do you want from me, Zack?"

He composed himself. Enough time had passed to justify his war crimes in his head. He could probably pass a polygraph. He sipped his coffee and leaned back in his chair. "We need to find out where the other sixty-five radicals went."

I turned over his words for the real meaning. Tracking terrorists was his job. Killing them was Hugo's. I came along and saw something going down. I acted. Right place, right time. Hugo and Ames benefitted from my actions. But. How did that bring me into Ames's world?

"Why does the CIA want me?" I asked. "Don't you have your own guys for that kind of work?"

"We're in a tight spot." He shook his head with exasperation. "The last administration blew a lot of relationships and devalued the Company. Lots of good people left. We're low on personnel and low on international relationships. You have a Distinguished Service Cross, which speaks volumes about your qualifications. You're our best hope, Jacob."

"Hope for what?" I asked.

Zack drank his coffee.

Mercury pulled up a chair and straddled it. *You don't get it, brutha? He wants you on the inside.*

"Holy shit … You want me to infiltrate these guys?"

Ames said, "A soldier like you could get into their inner circle."

Mercury said, *What could possibly go wrong with a CIA undercover operation? Think of the institutional brilliance they bring to the party: The Bay of Pigs, the Shah of Iran, Allende in Chile, Noriega in Panama, the Chinese Embassy in Kosovo ...*

"How the hell would I get into their inner circle?" I asked.

"There's a conference coming up. The one Hugo mentioned, the Identity Defense Conference. All three suspected groups from Kraków will be there along with a thousand ordinary European and American citizens. There are probably twenty splinter groups among them, but the big three are Free Origins, Birth Right, and Fair Heritage. One of those groups is the one we're interested in; we just don't know which one. Our intel leads us to believe they're in dire need of expertise. You get to know a couple of the leaders and sweet-talk—"

"Whoa!" I nearly fell off my stool. "Expertise? The only thing I'm good at is killing people. You want me to teach potential terrorists how to kill innocent women and children?"

"You don't need to actually teach them." He swirled his coffee in the cup and drained it. "Just get close enough to find out which ones are simply racists and which ones are bent on violence. Hugo's GIGN, acting with local authorities, will move in and take them all down. We need you to uncover three things: which group is planning it, who's in charge, and who or what Ross Gio is."

"No."

"That's not the answer we want, Jacob."

We glared at each other. I gave him my soldier-stare, the one soldiers get after they've been in combat so many times they're not sure if they're dead or alive—and they don't care. Usually, it puts a little fear in people, causes them to back off. Not Ames. He'd experienced his share of high-tension events in the clandestine world and held my gaze. But after a minute, he folded. He dropped his eyes to his croissant.

"We hoped you would sense the importance of this mission," he said. "Hugo didn't want to play hardball. I warned him it would come to this."

"What, you're going to toss me in jail?"

"Worse. Some of the parishioners at Saint-Sulpice had the wrong impression of your actions. You and I know what went down, but they saw an assault rifle in your hand and two dead men. The ones who think you're the monster will be released shortly. They'll be allowed to address the press if they want. The others will be detained for further questioning. The press will not be kind to you, Jacob. You might even lose your job."

Mercury said, *Nice guy, this Zack Ames. You should kick his ass into the street and push him under the first truck that comes along. No. On second thought, grab a 9-mil off one of those cops across the road and shoot him.*

I pulled my phone up and dialed Bianca. I said, *If he wants to play games, I can oblige.*

Bianca Dominguez was an MIT graduate and star at the NSA before Ms. Sabel tapped her for president of Sabel Technologies. Despite having twenty thousand employees reporting to her, she always took my calls. Even when I called before dawn in DC. Because she owed me.

I was the guy who introduced her to her wife a couple years ago.

She answered in a hazy voice. "Jacob, what is it this time?"

I looked over at my CIA buddy. "Can you hack the video system at *Église Saint-Sulpice* in Paris and give it to Emily?"

Bianca's wife, Emily, was a star reporter for the *Post* who once saved my life by shooting a guy in the face. I owed her. She's one of those instinctive journalists. Emily would watch the video and know exactly how to present my case to the public. Bianca promised to have it done in an hour.

I rose and picked up my bouquet for Jenny. "Nice try, Zack. You forgot to mention what happened to the last guy you had inside."

"What're you talking about? What guy inside?"

"I never work with people who lie to me." I leaned down, grabbed his throat hard, and squeezed. "Don't mess with me, Zack Ames. You tracked sixty-eight guys going off the grid after Kraków. I took down two. But you're only looking for sixty-five. That's one man short, Zack." I kept squeezing as I lifted him out of the chair. "He was your undercover guy. He's dead. That's why you didn't know the target. Yet you were only minutes away. If you'd been honest with me, told me you had a problem, I would've been glad to help."

CHAPTER 6

IT WAS ALL I COULD do not to shove people off the sidewalk as I stormed down the boulevard. Zack Ames, Nuristan Zack, an agent who got away with war crimes, asked me to help him. That took some balls.

I wasn't aware of where I was going. Next thing I knew, a bus unloaded what seemed like ten thousand Canadian tourists in front of me. The red maple leaf motif was a dead giveaway. They rounded the bus and held up their phones to take selfies with the Eiffel Tower. Which meant I'd walked off my anger for a couple miles. Before I could get my bearings, another bus pulled up and disgorged what seemed like ten thousand Chinese. Why do people go to the landmarks in a foreign country when they're guaranteed not to encounter any of the country's people or culture there?

I shook my bouquet at the Chinese. "Buy a coffee table book and spend the day in Troyes instead."

I was invisible. They didn't even notice me.

Mercury hooked a thumb in his toga. *Why you unloading on these poor bastards, homie? If they don't get a selfie with the Mona Lisa and the Iron Lady they'll forget they were ever here. You think they'd rather spend their vacation in an authentic sixteenth century village no one's ever heard of? Oh hey, but let me tell you, we had us some good times back in Troyes when it was called Tricassium. That'd be a major stop on the Via Agrippa. It's a shame Tricassium fell on hard times for a thousand years. That's what they get for going Christian. Oh, that reminds me, did I ever tell you how many shrines they built for me on the Via Agrippa?*

I said, *I don't care.*

You what? Mercury said. *Ah. I see. This isn't about tourists or CIA agents. This is about Jenny.*

My personal god sure knew how to throw some butt-hurt into a conversation.

Mercury peered at me. *What d'you see in that girl, anyway?*

I said, *I like the way she fits inside my shoulders when I wrap my arms around her. The way she always looks for a mutually agreeable answer instead of arguing. The times she puts her foot down when something's important to her and doesn't when it's not.*

Mercury said, *She's not pretty enough for you.*

I said, *She's perfect. I wouldn't trade her for Doutzen Kroes. She's in a class of her own. I can't wait to see her again. Why hasn't she texted me back?*

Mercury said, *Why not ask her? Tuck your tail between your legs and go back to the hotel, dawg. Oh wait, I know why. And you know why too. Cause you're getting dumped. Oh my Venus, I'd think you'd be used to that by now.*

I said, *I'm not getting dumped. She just had something to work out, that's all. Maybe she took sick. Or. Maybe she wants to get kinkier. Take it to the next level.*

One thing was for certain; I was dying to see Jenny. I was afraid to look at my phone. What would it mean if she hadn't replied? It was time to bite the bullet and find out. That sent me on a mission back to our suite.

After a couple wrong turns on the crazy streets of Paris, I swirled through the Hotel Lutetia's revolving front doors. The hotel's entrance is a labyrinth of chambers, the first being the concierge. He greeted me with a big smile and a salute.

He said, "Your guests are waiting for you in the Bibliotèque, monsieur."

My stride carried me past his station as his words sank in. What guests? As I stepped into the next chamber, the lobby, the clerk waved to me with a big smile and a glance at my bouquet. She pointed across the small space where a phalanx of people milled about. As the mass of humans looked up from their phones, they began shouting questions at me, mostly in French. As a group, they blocked the elevators and seemed overly aggressive about their enthusiasm. A couple phrases in English came through the tangle of words, "hero of Saint-Sulpice" and "savior of the congregation."

Their flashes flashed, and their questions poured out so fast, I decided to check on my "guests" in the Bibliotèque. The chattering group followed me to the "library," a small room with a handful of books in front of the Bar Josephine. In it was a cameraman with a big lamp in one hand and a video camera in the other.

An attractive middle-aged woman rose from the chair next to him and put out her hand. "Hey there, Jacob. I'm Brynn. Y'all are the toast of Paris today, aren't ya?"

Her deep Southern accent took me by surprise. I shook her hand with a quick and confused glance at the cameraman. My entourage followed, tapping my shoulder and snapping pictures. A few more English questions popped out of the French mesh. "Was this a Sabel Security operation?" Another asked, "How did you spot the terrorists?"

Brynn's smile disappeared. She turned to the others and shouted in French and added a few elaborate Italian hand gestures for good measure. The crowd quieted and retreated. Brynn scowled at the last guy hanging by the entrance. "Go on now, scat."

Mercury beamed from the bar in the next room. *This is it, homeboy! You're about to get interviewed on TV. Don't forget to say something nice about your favorite deities. Jupiter has a lightning bolt for those who fail to honor and praise the gods.*

I stared at him for a moment.

Brynn gently tugged my bicep until I faced her. She looked down at the hunk of muscle in her hand. "Oh my. Um. Emily and I are working together on your story. She said you'd give me an interview for TF1." She smiled.

"Did she?" My voice sounded hollow.

I wanted to find Jenny. I wanted to know why she ghosted on me all morning. I looked over Brynn's shoulder at the empty hallway.

Brynn's voice dropped an octave. "She told me if you were hesitant to remind you that you owe her."

And I did owe Emily. My life. I said, "An interview would be nice. Can I run up to my room to change?"

"Hell no. We have to get edited and posted on the site in five minutes. Those other hounds out there are posting as we speak. These days, a scoop is only a scoop for ninety seconds. Sit down."

Her last statement had a dominating undertone. I plopped into a comfy chair. The cameraman walked a big circle around Brynn. When he found the angle he liked, he turned his flamethrower at her. She produced a microphone out of thin air and posed. The cameraman gave her hand signals to turn left and right in small increments. When he was satisfied, he gave her a thumbs up. Without looking at me, she pointed to a spot that formed a triangle between the three of us. She said, "Stand there. Lose the flowers."

I left my bouquet on the side table, rose, and stood where she wanted.

Staring into the camera lens, she streamed French for thirty seconds. Somewhere in the flow was my name and the church. Then she turned to me and dropped back into an easy Southern drawl. "Major Pavard insists the video is inconclusive and some of the witnesses say you attacked innocent parishioners. Everyone else in the world thinks you're the Hercules of Paris. Can you tell us what happened, Mr. Stearne?"

Before I could answer, she repeated the question in French then stuck the microphone under my bottom lip.

"Yeah. Uh. Well. They… I…"

"*Merde!*" Brynn rolled her eyes.

The sunshine stopped pouring from the cameraman's lamp. I was blinded by darkness.

"I do apologize, Jacob." Brynn was smiling when my vision came back. "Emily forgot to tell me you're slow as molasses. So, let me prep you a bit here. I'm fixin' to ask you some questions about what happened this morning. There's been some confusion going on, and the authorities haven't been helping none."

I said, "Major Pavard got the wrong impression when he arrived on the scene and won't let go of it."

"That sounds about right."

"Didn't Emily get the video released?"

"She did that. But you were damn near underneath the camera, all three of you had your backs to the lens, and the action's a tad confusing. It appears those boys had machine guns out when you tackled the first one. Anyone who looks closely can see one of them aiming his assault rifle at the crowd. But it went by in a blur."

Mercury leaned over the cameraman's shoulder. *Is this for real, bro? You killed two bona fide terrorists, and nobody believes you?*

I said, *Don't worry, she's a friend of Emily's. She'll get the public straightened out.*

At that moment, just over Brynn's shoulder, Jenny appeared— looking like Venus in the flesh.

Brynn was talking, but I couldn't hear her over the sound of angels singing.

Mercury said, *Those aren't angels, dude. Those are the Vestal Virgins praying for your soul.*

I said, *Is that a good thing?*

Mercury nodded. *Sometimes.* Mercury stopped nodding and started shaking his head side-to-side. *Not this time, though.*

Brynn squeezed my bicep again as I started forward. She looked pissed. "Did you hear a word I said?"

"Give me a minute, Brynn. I'll be right back."

"Don't you dare give your first interview to some floozy." Brynn was looking over her shoulder at Jenny when she tightened her grip, then turned her dagger-gaze back to me. "We have to get my interview done and posted right now."

I used my master sergeant voice. "Sit down, Brynn."

She dropped into the nearest chair with frightened eyes. Her cameraman did the same.

I grabbed the bouquet, crossed to Jenny and stopped close enough to hold hands, not close enough for a hug. She made no indication she wanted me closer. Her hands were behind her back. Her face downcast. Behind her was a roller bag. I held the flowers between us.

"I, I…" She glanced up but couldn't hold my gaze.

"You're leaving."

"Yes." She grabbed my arms as if to hold me in place, not letting me get farther away or closer. "It's not you…"

Mercury stood behind her. *Oh dawg. How many times have you heard this refrain? More than 'this little piggy went to market.'*

I said, *Shut up.*

"You bring out the animal in me and … OK, that part is delicious, um, that gladiator outfit and the voice … Listen. I'm just not ready to be an animal again. I don't feel right about it. You're the first man I've been with since the rape and … I'm not ready."

A hundred spears with blades of razor-sharp steel drove deep into my chest. I couldn't breathe.

She let go of me and half-turned to leave. She hesitated.

I said, "Take all the time you need. I'll wait—"

Before I could finish, she looked up. "Don't wait for me, Jacob. I'm not playing a game here. I don't want to be pursued. Quite the opposite. I may not ever be ready for … You're a great guy. You deserve someone less damaged."

She put a finger across my lips and kissed me on the cheek as my heart shattered like a crystal vase dropped from Saint-Jacques Tower. Then she grabbed her roller bag and fast-walked down the hallway.

I said, *You can take me across the Acheron River now. I have nothing to live for.*

Mercury said, *Don't be like that, homes. You're gonna have your heart broken a lot worse'n this many times before you die.*

I said, *Thanks. So helpful.*

Brynn stood at my shoulder, startling me. "Did you just dump Jenny Jenkins? Hoo-boy! We're going to be doing two interviews."

CHAPTER 7

TEN MINUTES AFTER SHE FINISHED an interview that made me look like a hero, Brynn was still begging me to spill about my relationship with heiress and convicted murderer Jenny Jenkins. I refused. Call me old-fashioned, but I think there's something sacred about romance. Even if Jenny's dismissal sounded distinctly unromantic and quite permanent.

Brynn promised the backstory on Jenny would cement my place in history as a real celebrity. I didn't care.

Finally, Brynn gave up. She asked me not to talk to the other reporters. About that time, the hotel manager came in and asked me to talk to the other reporters. He wanted them out of his lobby. We negotiated a twenty-minute head start so Brynn and Emily could post the exclusive interview on their respective websites. And I agreed to address the others in a group and be cagey with my answers. I still owed Emily.

All of that happened. The other reporters loved me. Their enthusiasm and my despondent replies cast me as a casual hero. Killing mass shooters before they mowed down hundreds of worshippers was no big deal in the life of a decorated veteran. Or so I made it sound, but not because that's how I felt about it. Truth was, I never really heard their questions. All I heard was Jenny saying, "I'm not ready."

An hour later, I made it back to my penthouse suite. It was the nicest hotel room I'd ever stayed in. Except. It was empty and quiet.

I made my way to the balcony where the staff had left a bottle of Dom Perignon on ice with two glasses. On the table next to it sat a vase full of flowers larger and nicer than the wilted ones still in my hand. I tossed mine on the empty chair. Beyond the balcony, the golden dome of Les Invalides glowed in the midafternoon sun. In the distance beyond that,

SEELEY JAMES

the Eiffel Tower crammed thousands of tourists into sweaty elevators.

It was a beautiful view on a gorgeous day, yet it did nothing for me. I left.

After wandering for an hour, I began to long for the sound of a human voice and a cold beer.

I walked by a bar called the Junkyard. It sounded like the right place for my mood. It was dark, had a TV playing a soccer game, and only four patrons plus a bartender. Two of the customers watched the soccer game. I pointed at the only draft tap they had. Apparently, France is not big on beer.

The bartender set the foaming glass in front of me but didn't let go. He knitted his brow, tilted his head, looked me over. He smiled and let go of the glass. "*Gratis*, Jacob Stearne."

The others in the room looked over. They raised their glasses and smiled at me. They toasted me in French. Saturn only knows what they were saying. A nice lady about twice my age came over and asked for a selfie in terrible English. After she took hers, the rest lined up. A series of flashes later, I was blind. When my vision cleared, two more glasses of beer waited for me.

Mercury took the stool next to me. *Classic move, dawg. Get dumped, get plowed. You'd make a better redneck than a Caesar. It won't help the shitstorm that's coming your way, but at least you won't feel it when Paris turns on you.*

I waved my arm at my admirers. *Why would Paris turn on me? They love me.*

Mercury said, *You're a bit blank right now, brutha. Getting dumped out like yesterday's bedpan has done clouded your mind. You didn't even notice that movie-star looking guy following you.*

I said, *Probably just a fan too shy to ask for my autograph.*

Mercury said, *Don't listen to me, bro. What could the messenger of the gods possibly be telling you that you don't already know? Damn mortals.*

The game on TV took a halftime break. A newsman came on, and my picture appeared. His voice was in that unmistakable mode of saying, "Stay tuned for this surprising revelation." Sixteen advertisements

40

followed. Then the news guy came back. The inset picture of me was very different. When you're about to kill someone, your face contorts with rage—because you tend not to kill people when you're happy. The picture of me was damn ugly. A parishioner had taken it with a phone. From that angle, I was clearly killing a man who had a rifle pointed at the ground.

The anchor's voice was gruff and getting gruffer. My name came out of his mouth like an f-bomb followed closely by the words *damnés Américains*. Everyone in the room turned to me. The bartender picked up the beers. Someone took a picture of me at a distance. He said something in French that ended with *Twitter*. The others agreed with him. I slid off my stool and wandered back out to the streets.

Mercury walked beside me. *Toldya, young blood.*

I said, *What the hell was that all about?*

Mercury said, *Zack Ames. He said turning him down would be a mistake.*

A car raced down the narrow lane and slammed on its brakes when it passed me. Three men jumped out wearing ski masks. In perfect English, one of them said, "You're Jacob Stearne, the asshole who killed those guys."

I stood still. Antagonizing people when they're wrong is as effective as posting facts on Facebook. Packing my Glock at the small of my back, covered by my jacket, turned out to have been a smart move.

Mercury said, *You thinking of pulling a piece now, homie? Like, killing three more guys on the same day is gonna improve your situation, how?*

I said, *Beats getting killed. But, yeah, I see your point.*

One guy flanked me. The other two spread out by five feet. Shooting all three without hitting innocent bystanders would require more luck than skill. I considered using the razor-sharp knife hidden in my belt buckle but chose to hold it in reserve.

"Two guys exercise their right to bear arms, and you execute them for it?" the leader asked. His dilated eyes bounced around me. He squared his shoulders and faced me. On his forearm was a tattoo the size of a large watch, a thick circle with an equally thick triangle in the middle of it.

My guess was crystal meth. Not exclusive to Americans, but his dilated and darting eyes, combined with the second amendment phrase, summed up his nationality for me. That didn't exactly tie into Zack Ames's warnings about violent racists, but it was suspiciously close.

I kept still.

The flanker took my blindside. They didn't appear armed, so any escalation to hand-to-hand violence would work out in my favor. Three-to-one I could handle. More than that—no matter what they do in the movies—is impossible.

The leader charged me with a right hook.

I raised my elbow and turned to my left fast. The leader's fist glanced off my cheek, while my elbow took out the guy trying to grab me from behind. He went down with a broken orbital socket and a concussion. The leader came back with a couple quick jabs, one of which landed in my throat. The second guy hesitated a beat before jumping in.

My uppercut sent the leader back three steps. It only gave his lieutenant an opening to land four fast blows in my midsection. That took the wind out of me. When I planted a combination on his face, the leader came back with a haymaker aimed at my head.

I ducked in time, but not low enough. His fist hit the back of my skull hard. A church bell rang between my ears.

The second guy recovered enough to try kneeing me in the balls. I twisted just in time. His knee slammed into my hamstring, which sent jolts of electric pain surging through my body.

The third man must've regained his senses because his arm slipped around my neck. He was shorter than me, but stout and had a leverage advantage. He pulled me back, using his belly as a fulcrum. I couldn't breathe much after the throat-punch. With the headlock, I was airless and struggling.

"I hereby sentence you to—" The leader cut off his words as his eyes widened and focused on something behind me. "Hey, we're doing this for you."

I heard a hard thud before the headlock loosened. The guy holding me slumped to the ground. The leader in front of me and his lieutenant had distinctly surprised looks on their faces. A fist flew over my shoulder and slammed into the lieutenant's nose.

I wasted no time in taking advantage of the situation. I slammed my open palm into the underside of the leader's jaw. His head snapped back, he stumbled. The lieutenant took a swing at me as the blur of a man came from behind me and tackled him. The leader came back, telegraphing a right. I twisted, letting his fist skim my back. My elbow came back and caught him in the temple. He landed on the ground in a heap.

My new sidekick turned to me. "You OK?"

He was made of bricks with a chiseled jaw and a fifty-megawatt smile. A wave of black hair topped a sleek fade.

"Fine." I brushed off my jacket sleeve. "Thanks for the assist."

He patted my shoulder as sirens wound up a nearby street. "Anything for a hero—and trust me, you are the hero. I saw the video."

The three masked men got to their hands and knees, spitting blood and shaking some sense into their heads.

"Better beat it, punks," my new friend said to them. He cupped an ear in the direction of the sirens.

The three thugs staggered to their car and took off.

"I know guys like that." The new guy turned to me with that unbeatable smile. "First thing they think of is violence. They don't have anything meaningful in their lives, nothing to make them proud of themselves. People like you piss them off because they know you always do the right thing. They're misdirecting their jealousy."

"OK."

"Gotta run. I'm not a favorite with the locals. You sure you're good?"

"In the last two hours, I've been vilified by the authorities and dumped by my girlfriend." I shook my head. "But otherwise, fine."

"Sucks, brother." He gave me another award-winning grin, squeezed my shoulder, then took off running down the street.

"Hey, what's your name?" I called after him.

But he was around the corner and gone a second later.

Mercury looked at me. *Yo, you believe in random acts of kindness?*

I said, *I do.*

Mercury said, *Do you believe that's what that was?*

I said, *Not for a minute.*

CHAPTER 8

MERCURY STRAIGHTENED HIS TOGA. *May as well keep wandering the streets. Why go back to that first-class crib and drink twelve-year-old Champagne?*

I said, *If the French want to believe that crap Pavard and Hugo are putting out, they can just shoot me now. I don't care anymore.*

Mercury walked alongside me. *Quit yer whining, boy. Everybody gets dumped. Most people dust themselves off and go back for more.*

I said, *Thanks for understanding. Not.*

A mile later, my boss, Pia Sabel, sent a video chat request. A long time ago, she made me confess my relationship with a certain mythological god and—against the advice of her wise and seasoned counselors—determined I was a perfectly normal divinely-guided asset. As far as divinely-guided assets go. There was also the fact that I'd saved her life a couple times, tipping the balance in my favor. In return, she confessed her struggles with reality after her horrific and tragic childhood. We established a sibling relationship from then on. Many others tried to imply that ours had more "benefits" than met the eye because of the special treatment she afforded me. We ignored them. No matter what anyone thought, we were like brother and sister.

I accepted her call.

"Jenny called me." She tucked a loose strand of hair behind her ear. "Do you want to talk about it?"

"No."

"OK, I'll do the talking then. You're probably wondering why she called me. We grew up together, kinda. Her father and mine were besties. She was a bit older. Her parents got divorced when I was about ten. She took her mother's side. I didn't see her much after that. We were never close. But she knows you and I are, so she wanted to make sure I understood what happened."

"I still don't want to talk about it."

"That's OK." Her gray-green eyes never blinked. "I'm calling to let you know you can take all the time you need. Keep the room or move to another hotel. Keep the tickets to the Moulin Rouge. I'd tell you to go out and have fun, but I know that won't happen. I've been there."

I couldn't imagine any sane man dumping a twenty-eight-year-old, world-class athlete, and billionaire. I let it go. "I'd really rather not talk—"

"Just one more thing and I'll change over to the next topic. She's in a bad place, and she's punishing herself. Well. I guess she's punishing you too. Anyway, it's not about you … oh, that's so cliché. Um. But it's true too … actually, it's not, is it? If it's about her, it becomes 'about' you too. OK. I see why you don't want to talk about it. I'll shut up now."

That's what I liked about her.

"What's the next topic?" I asked.

Mercury kept pace beside me. *You know there's a hottie on your tail, dawg. Not more'n two hours since you got dumped like trash in a landfill and you've already attracted a stalker because you're a whack-job-magnet.*

I stopped and checked my reflection in a shop window. Paris streets are busy. There were lots of people behind me. One was a slight young woman in her mid-twenties; the term pixie came to mind. She stopped and looked away when I stopped.

"Congratulations on becoming a hero," Ms. Sabel said. "I understand the President of France is considering receiving you."

"Considering?"

"Maybe you haven't heard, but certain aspects of the situation have yet to be resolved." She never brought up negatives like the authorities lying about me. "I'm sure they'll sort out the narrative and recognize your bravery. Then you can expect a call from the President of France."

"If it's the same to you, I'd rather not. Some haters already showed up. Nothing I can't handle. But an evening with dignitaries will add some pure lunatics to the mix."

"I'll let the ambassador know."

I switched the phone camera to look at myself instead of Ms. Sabel. I raised it a little to see who was following me. To Ms. Sabel I said, "Thanks for the pep talk."

"Sorry it didn't work."

"You get points for trying."

She laughed self-consciously and clicked off.

I held the phone's camera over my shoulder and watched a young woman with hair that reminded me of Tinkerbell from Peter Pan. Only without the bun. And black, not blonde. OK, not a lot like Tinkerbell. But she was small and slight, and her hair was cut short with the same mischievous bangs parted on the side. She wore a ladies' Oxford shirt with the sleeves rolled up and black leggings. She moved like a kitten, a combination of natural grace and youthful awkwardness.

Mercury said, *Do you find it strange that the first two days in Paris all you met were Parisians, then today, freaking Americans are coming out of the Catacombs? What's up with that, bro?*

I said, *I'm not sure. Why don't you tell me?*

Mercury said, *And force you to miss out on exercising your brain? Why don't I tell you everything, like what's beyond the edge of the universe?*

I said, *Wait—what is beyond our universe?*

Mercury laughed so hard he had to bend over and slap his knee. The gods have a nasty sense of humor.

Since I'd been wandering aimlessly, I kept going and made the next four right turns. In any normal city, that would return you to your starting point. Which would prove the pixie was following me. But this was Paris. I was a mile from my original position and lost. Not-Tinkerbell was still following me. In another block, I wound up staring at the *Café de la Mairie*. Back to the scene of the crime. There were other ways to get a look at the young woman.

Mercury said, *Did I tell you she's a hottie? Check her out, brutha. She could take your mind off Jenny tonight.*

I said, *I don't want to take my mind off Jenny.*

But I did want to know why I was being followed. I took a chair at a sidewalk table.

When the woman walked by, I said, "Join me?"

I pushed a chair into her path.

She blushed while she tried to ignore me. She walked around the chair and kept going. A few paces away, she looked over her shoulder to see if I was still watching her. I crooked my finger to beckon her back.

She stopped and thought and stood still and looked at the ground. Her hair moved to reveal a tattoo on her neck. Two old-fashioned skeleton keys crossed with the teeth facing away from each other. She came back and took the chair.

As she adjusted herself and her purse, I took her hand and looked at her fingernails. Not long, not chewed, not shaped, no polish. I dropped her hand and met her gaze. She had a funny look on her face. I had done an odd thing.

She wore no makeup. She didn't need it. A smattering of freckles crossed her nose. No lipstick. No pierced ears. She looked chic in that confident, no-frills Parisian manner.

"The Converse gave you away as 'American,'" I said.

She looked at her scuffed, no-longer-white sneakers. "Next paycheck."

"Are you with the press? Brynn perhaps?"

"Just an admirer." She blushed again. "I don't care what they're saying; I believe you did the right thing. Besides, I'm feeling a little scared in the big city. My brother's gone now and …"

Her voice trailed off and she looked away. A small, frightened young woman far from home.

From her dialect, I placed her as coming from a place somewhere between Fargo and Madison. A stretch settled by Swedes, Germans, and Norwegians who left deep vowels in their English pronunciations.

"Zack Ames. Know him?" I asked.

She didn't blush; she didn't flinch. If it was an act, it was good. So far, her blushes had given her away when she didn't want, which meant the CIA would never put her in a clandestine operation. And that told me she didn't know Zack Ames.

"I saw you on TV and a few minutes later—there you were, walking down the street." She blinked in a poor attempt to look bashful or sexy. "I thought it would be nice to know a guy who protects people."

I was about to call her a liar when a Renault Twingo, a car about the size of my left shoe, shredded to a stop at the curb. Like a clown car, four guys jumped out. I put one hand behind my back, ready to pull my pistol.

Two of the men wore GoPro's strapped to their foreheads. Far too nerdy a look for agents of evil. Another held a recording device with a directional microphone attached. They ran to my table and surrounded me.

"You are Jacob Stearne, oui?" one asked.

Instantly, one of the GoPro guys asked, "Official are saying you overreact. Ehm. You kill-ed two innocent men."

"Which officials said that?" I asked.

"There are the statements of the witnesses," a third man chimed in.

Not to be outdone, the fourth said, "They tell of two tourists, unaware it is illegal to carry weapons in public, yet frightened of the terrorism which plagued our city in the past, who are carrying the weapons for self-protection."

"And fire them on full-auto in a church full of people?" I asked. "If it was self-defense, it was criminal."

The waiter from breakfast came out of the café, shouting in French and shooing the reporters away. They looked at him for a second. Then back at me and continued, unfazed.

"Have you murdered the innocent?" one of them asked.

"They were the opposite of innocent."

"How did you know this?"

Mercury stood behind the pack with his palms raised and a big smile on his face.

I said, *I am not telling them the 'messenger' told me they were terrorists. They'd lock me up, not sacrifice pigeons to you and your pals.*

Mercury looked hurt. *Dude. How many times I gotta tell you? Doves. Not pigeons. Doves.*

I said, *Doesn't matter. They'd lock me up if I told them I get messages from the gods.* I thought for a moment. *Tell me the truth, they were terrorists, right? Zack Ames didn't set me up for this, did he?*

Mercury shook his head. *He don't have that kinda imagination, bro.*

I said, *You got that right.*

The reporters looked at each other, a bit confused. One of them said, "What was it we got right?"

"That they were terrorists. The Beretta AR70/90 is a specialized rifle built for the exclusive use of the Italian military. It's not a personal defense weapon. If you care to look a little deeper into the facts, there are a bunch of other indicators proving they were not there for the bread and wine."

A cop car slammed into the curb. Two men popped out with clubs raised and charged at the reporters. The journalists scattered around their car and jumped in as quickly as they'd jumped out. With a chirp of tires—from the weight, not the horsepower—they sped off.

My new companion looked at me. She said, "Did you kill two innocent men?"

CHAPTER 9

THE COPS CONFERRED WITH THE waiter, who thanked them profusely.

Then everything returned to a tranquil afternoon. Except that a strange woman sat at my table, trying to make eyes at me. And a long-forgotten god wanted me to sex it up with her.

Talk about awkward.

The waiter returned with a bag of complimentary macarons to go. It was a subtle hint. My morning stunt had filled his street with cops and ambulances for hours, killing his business. Now my notoriety was killing what little traffic they were getting in the afternoon.

I thanked him and rose.

Holding out one of the macarons to the young woman, I said, "I just managed to tank a great relationship, so I'm not interested in your fake attempts to seduce me. But I'm feeling a little lonely, so walk with me. Tell me any story you want."

She started to protest, then decided not to. She rose slowly and took the confection as if it were a loaded bear trap. "You're one weird dude."

I said, "Tell me about Minneapolis."

"How'd you know I'm from Minneapolis?"

"All your O's are long. You said, 'I DOH-n't care what the POH-lice say,' which makes you a Minnesotan at a minimum. If you try to deny it, I'll make you say 'donut.'"

"DOHnut." She laughed. "You're from the Midwest?"

"Iowa."

She decided not to lie about her background and prattled on about fleeing a big city full of what she considered hicks. I tuned her out. I didn't care about her childhood or her hometown. I just wanted to hear a human voice talking about something other than me, terrorists, or Jenny.

We strolled across the street to the large plaza. She ate another macaron. I took a bite of mine. I could taste nothing. It may as well have been cardboard.

I tossed it to a nearby pigeon. That was a mistake.

We kicked our way through the arriving flock of birds to the middle of the plaza and arrived at the same fountain where I first spotted the would-be mass shooters.

Mercury jumped in the ground-level basin, toga, sandals, and all. I ignored him. He splashed water my way.

The young lady asked, "What did you mean when you told those guys there were other things about the terrorists?"

"I don't know your name."

"Nema." She held out her hand. "Just Nema. I'm an artist. At least, I want to be an artist. So. I'm going with one name."

Mercury splashed more water. *Pay attention, homie. You never know what people toss into a fountain.*

I recalled the short guy tossing his beads away. I shook her hand, then maneuvered closer to the basin. "What about your family name?"

"Not everyone has a great family," she snarled.

I struck a nerve. I wasn't interested in digging into painful subjects so I changed it. "Is Nema short for something? It sounds like it has a deeper meaning than, say, Marge."

"I based it on Nemain."

"The Celtic goddess of war?" Mercury had drilled so many gods into my head, I swam in them when I slept.

Nema was impressed.

Mercury said, *Don't be thinking about calling on the Celts for help, dawg. They won't treat you right. They're not kind and helpful like me. Besides, we kicked their asses from Gaul to Hibernia. The best gods always win.*

I said, *Is that why ancient Rome turned Christian?*

Aw, now that was low, dude. Just hurtful and low.

He disappeared, as he often does. Where he'd been standing lay a string of beads. I pulled them out and looked them over.

Nema looked them over too. Her brow crinkled. "Do people throw those in there as a religious thing?"

"These belonged to the shooter. The short guy."

"How do you know?"

"I saw him do it. It's one of the signs of a terrorist preparing to attack."

"There are signs?" She swallowed hard as if the morning's events just came into tangible focus.

I'd seen reactions like hers before. If a person wasn't there when I did something heroic, if they only hear about my exploits, they think I'm Superman in the flesh. A larger-than-life guy able to leap tall buildings. At some point, it comes home that I ended someone's life, and everything comes down off the pedestal and becomes as real as road rash.

In Nema's imagination, the raw facts crystalized. The video of me using a man's rifle to blow open his friend's skull was surreal. As the visualization of the brutality and violence sank in, it shocked her.

When you save someone's life, they're grateful. But when you kill others to save them, they become concerned about you. Anyone that explosively violent could easily turn on them by mistake. It takes some coaxing and calmness to convince them otherwise. That's what caused some of the parishioners to misinterpret my actions.

For Nema, standing next to a guy who could kill without hesitation felt dangerous in a bad way. But all that was her problem. I didn't feel like talking her fear levels down.

And that brought up a question. Something was keeping her in front of me despite her revulsion. Figuring out Nema's angle was a nice distraction from figuring out Jenny's.

"That means he's Catholic?" Nema's voice cracked. "So. He really was going in to pray?"

She backed away from me a step and turned a little as if preparing to run. I didn't answer. She never made good on her implied threat to flee.

I counted the beads. I said, "A Catholic rosary has fifty-nine beads. This one has thirty-three."

"How do you know that?"

"Heard it somewhere." One of Mercury's many painfully dull lessons, but I didn't see the need to explain.

"Muslims use prayer beads, right?"

"Theirs have a different kind of tassel on the end." Knowing what she would ask next, I answered. "I spent some time in Iraq and Afghanistan. I've seen a lot of Misbahas."

"What does it mean then?"

"I'm not sure, yet." I gazed across the plaza at the second-largest church in Paris.

"Can I see them?"

"No." I shoved them in my pocket. "They should be evidence."

"Even non-Catholics go to these big touristy churches sometimes. Maybe he wanted to attend mass."

"Then why did he shout, '*Allahu akbar?*'"

She looked around the plaza and up at the church towers. Goosebumps of fear pimpled her skin. She hugged herself. "Can we go now?"

"We?" I struck out across the plaza at a good pace. Not fast enough to make her run, not slow enough to give her time to think about it.

Nema didn't think long. She trotted up and synced to my march. "You said you were lonely. I didn't want to leave you feeling like that."

I watched her as I walked. "Why are you in Paris?"

"Because there're more artists than cab drivers in New York." She held up a hand to stop my obvious question. "If I'm going to starve for my art, why not Paris?"

Mercury walked on the far side of her. *Sounds like a line out of a musical, homie. But let it go. Get to the heart of the matter.*

I said, *Don't worry, I'm about to ask who sent her.*

Mercury looked at me like I was eating a poop sandwich. *Dawg! What is wrong with you? You just got thrown by a thoroughbred; you need to get back in that saddle. And this little filly is practically asking for you to put a bridle on her.*

I considered hitting him, but if he's just a figment of my imagination—like all the doctors kept saying—I'd look pretty stupid swinging at the air. *Not only do you misunderstand me—you're reading*

Nema all wrong.

I watched the young lady in my peripheral vision. She cut glances my way every third step like a pickpocket waiting for the right opportunity. We crossed a small street and wandered down a narrow lane. Every time a scooter passed, she crushed against me and let our contact linger. I didn't push her away.

I asked, "Who sent you to follow me?"

Her glance at me was quick, with sharp and narrowed eyes. "You're not very nice to me."

"Not an answer."

"I saw your picture on the news. I thought you were handsome and, y'know, might be nice." She stopped walking. "Thought I'd feel safe around you. Guess I was wrong."

Mercury said, *D'you hear that bro? The first woman who ever thought you were handsome, and here you are walking away from her.*

I said, *I thought gods knew everything. Watch this.*

Without breaking stride, I raised my voice. "If you want to report back to your handler, you're going to have a hard time doing it standing there like a statue."

Nema ran up behind me. For a second, I thought she might jump on me and start pounding on my shoulders. Women have been known to get that mad at me. Instead, she ran in front of me a few paces, stopped, and wheeled around to face me with fire in her eyes. As I approached, she threw herself at me and grabbed my arms.

Pushing her over would've taken no effort at all with what she weighed. I stopped out of curiosity.

"Who do you think you are, treating me like that?" she said.

"A guy who hates it when a random gay girl tries to flirt with me and won't answer simple questions."

"Who're you calling 'girl?'" She snorted anger through her nose. "I'm almost twenty-six."

With a simple sweep of one arm, I flipped her hands aside and bumped past her. "You skipped 'gay' and 'flirt'—and you still haven't answered my question. You want to hang with me and find out something you can tell your boss, then you need to get real. Tell me the truth."

"Why don't you tell me the truth, huh?" she shouted as I walked away. "Why does it matter that the guy had a rosary?"

CHAPTER 10

NEMA FOLLOWED ME LIKE A lost puppy, a few feet back and unsure whether to get more aggressive or less. Her persistence interested me. She wanted something other than sex. I didn't believe her claim to be a fan. Momentary celebrities often find themselves surrounded by crazies, but she didn't fall in that category. Her moves were too strategic in nature. Someone sent her. She was afraid to fail.

I picked up my pace and turned into a grassy, tree-filled park. She fell behind and tried to make a call. She pecked out a text with her index finger which caused her to fumble her phone several times. Most people under forty grew up with technology and could text a thesis with their thumbs. Nema wasn't one of them.

She sensed me watching her and said, "Chuck does the tech stuff for me."

Then she blushed and didn't bother to explain what she meant.

I hit my usual stride and found a miniature version of the Statue of Liberty. It was three times the size of a normal person and stood on a pedestal big enough to hide behind. While Nema contacted whoever, I slipped behind it to wait.

When she clicked off, she looked around with a touch of panic before setting off in my last known direction.

I popped out from hiding, scaring the wits out of her, and snapped a picture of her. I sent it to Bianca for ID. I asked Nema, "What did he say?"

"He'll meet us here." She stuck her toe in the gravel. "He's not my boss. He's a friend. Associate. We're in a ... club."

"What kind of club?"

"Self-defense." She hesitated again. "Listen, about what you said. You're wrong. I'm not gay."

"I introduced one of my best friends to her wife. Your secret's safe with me."

"It's not that. I don't subscribe to Cosmo-crap, that's all. I'm what the French call a *garçon manqué*. A tomboy."

"Even tomboys wear lipstick and nail polish."

Mercury stroked his chin and nodded his approval. *Say there, dawg. You did call this one. She had me fooled.*

I said, *Any woman who bats her eyelashes at you has you fooled.*

You got that right. The curse of males in every species.

"Look, whatever you're thinking, you're wrong about me." Her mouth tightened up like a drawstring had been pulled. "The guys I hang around with don't play games. So, don't say anything stupid to Lugh, please? By the way, it's pronounced *Lou,* but he spells it like the Celtic warrior-god. I dress plain because I like to, OK?"

"Why did you look at me with a mix of concern and dread? You didn't have the first clue what to do if I took you up on your flirts."

"Promise me you won't say anything."

"Told you once, your secret is safe."

"How many times I gotta tell you? I'm not … gay." She sounded unconvincing.

We watched each other for a long time, standing still. Our only motion was our breathing.

"So why is the rosary a big deal?" she asked.

"It raises questions about the man's intent."

A man hailed Nema and joined us. Average in every way, he could've been an animated mannequin. A featureless face topped a narrow body draped in bland clothes. Unremarkable enough to disappear in a crowd. Anyone that plain had to be an American. I pegged him at late thirties, early forties.

I stuck out my hand, "You must be Lugh."

He looked at my hand before shaking it. "Nice to meet you, Jacob. Quite a brave thing you did this morning. We are in awe."

"We?"

He looked at Nema. "Thank you, my dear. I'll meet you back at the hotel."

First I'm followed for undiscernible reasons by an attractive but odd woman. Then I'm flattered by an anonymous man for no identifiable reason before he dismisses the young lady. My curiosity rose. It was a nice distraction from thinking about Jenny.

"She stays," I said. "You don't dismiss my friends."

The emotions going through his head were as readable as a slideshow in a boring corporate meeting. He didn't like me taking control of the conversation. He didn't like me favoring Nema over him. Which meant he didn't like me. But he needed something, and we both knew it. He sniffed and pulled himself up. "Very well, have it your way."

"What's this little club of yours about, Lugh?" I started walking down the garden path.

Lugh came alongside, Nema trailed behind him. "Technically, we're a civic organization, like neighborhood watch or the Sierra Club. You'd like our group, Jacob."

"When I ask a question, I expect an answer. Simple courtesy."

"If you're the kind of guy who can look to new horizons without being ashamed of your origins, you'll definitely like our group."

"Are you hard of hearing?" I asked.

"I can tell, you're the kind of man who keeps his morals anchored in times of corruption, Jacob. I'm right about that, aren't I?"

Just what I needed, a man who kept up his spiel regardless of the inquiry. I fell back into my earlier mode. Half-listening to the sound of a human voice as long as it wasn't talking about Jenny.

"We're a group of patriots concerned about the traitors in our midst. We like to think of ourselves as men of action. Today's events showed us how ill-prepared we are. When you spotted two mass-shooters about to strike, you didn't sit on your hands, you didn't run for the exits. You jumped them. We want to be more like you, Jacob. We want to take action when action is needed."

Mercury tilted his head. *Ya hear that, dude? He thinks you're a man of action. He's never seen you walk by a TV tuned to Nickelodeon. You get stuck like a man in a tar pit if they're showing SpongeBob.*

Mercury thought for a minute. *Say, ya think these are the guys Zack wants you to infiltrate? That's way too much of a coincidence. Maybe you're destined to be Zack's bitch. Ima check with the Fates to see if Nona is resetting your lifespan.*

I said, *I would never be Zack's ... They could be friends of the guys I took out. Maybe they're looking for revenge.*

Mercury said, *A life or death grudge match. Now that could make for an interesting afternoon. I wonder who would win.*

Lugh was still talking. "If you love America like you love your parents, you'll want to join us, Jacob."

I turned around, looked at Nema, and walked backward. "Is there a short version, or does everyone get the full sales pitch?"

She shrugged. "He's trying to explain our—"

"Shut up," Lugh snapped at her.

"Hey, Lugh." I grabbed his arm and spun him to face me. "Men who treat women badly tend to piss me off."

Lugh glanced at Nema before looking at me. "She needs to know her place."

"My sister dated a guy who showed her no respect in public. Turned out, things were worse in private. I don't let that kinda thing slide anymore. Ya feel me?"

I let go of him. In my experience, bullies escalate violence until someone enforces the Golden Rule on them. I was prepared to teach him all about it.

He stepped back, nursing his arm. "Sorry. I meant no disrespect to you."

We started walking again.

Lugh resumed talking. "Our association is run by a man of vision. He's a man's man. Not one of these feminized men. You'll never find him apologizing for his birthright. He sees the vitality and strength in every man he meets. He leads by example, never by force, but when he must use force, he never holds back. He celebrates human nature rather than regret his position in God's plan. He treats all men with benevolence and instills confidence in us when we most need it. When you meet him, his presence will dominate every thought. He is bringing us all together that we might stand in solidarity, never allowing ourselves or our brothers to be replaced."

Lugh paused. Nema's eyes had wandered while he spoke. She hugged herself.

"You sound like you're in love with him." I punched his shoulder. "Does he have a name?"

Lugh reared back to throw a punch. I gave him my soldier stare, every muscle in my body relaxed as if the threat of death were no more frightening than a gentle breeze. Someone who is utterly unafraid of anything you might do is a terrifying sight. He assessed his chances at survival and unwound his tensed muscles.

But his face still blazed red. "I'm not a homosexual."

The heavy accent on the last word in his statement spoke volumes about his feelings on the topic. I glanced at Nema, who had turned away from us.

"Easy there, Lugh." I put my hands out, palms facing him in a non-threatening gesture. "You were getting a little star-struck about this whatshisname. What was I to think?"

"Well, not that."

"Your bullshit is deep, yet you still haven't asked me what you came here to ask. Does this leader of yours allow you to waste as much of his time as you've wasted of mine?"

Lugh dropped his gaze and gathered his thoughts. "You demonstrated uncanny skills in self-defense today."

"Nema mentioned that's what your group is about." I glanced her way. She'd moved off a ways. "Does your little self-defense group have a name?"

Lugh glared at Nema before answering me. "Free Origins. We want to hire you to teach us self-defense. We can never rise to your level of expertise, but we would like to know how to protect ourselves from active shooters. What happened this morning is becoming commonplace. The Easter bombings in Sri Lanka, the Boston Marathon, the Bastille Day truck ramming in Nice. These are the types of attacks we want to prevent if given a chance. Today, you truly inspired us."

Mercury leaned over Lugh's shoulder. *Strange, isn't it, bro? He left out the attacks by anti-government activists and racists.*

I said, *They didn't kill as many people over the last decade.*

Mercury said, *Before Sri Lanka, their body count was growing faster than anyone else's. From seventy-seven in Oslo to fifty in Christchurch, people who look like you are catching up in the terrorist race. Y'know, homie, there was a time when mortals feared wolves and plagues. Now, the biggest danger in your lives comes from white Christian men.*

I felt sick hearing that.

"What kind of teaching did you have in mind?" I asked Lugh.

"We're going to a conference in a few days. There will be other groups like ours. Birth Right and Fair Heritage will be there, among others. We arranged a shooting range and instructors. Until today, we thought we'd hired the best. Your heroism opened our eyes. Now, we know—we need you."

"You're talking about the Identity Defense Conference?"

Lugh staggered a step in surprise. "You know about it?"

He decided I did and smiled as if we were on the same team.

Mercury walked around Lugh. *Exactly what Zack Ames wanted you to do, get inside IDC. That could work out for you. Everyone hates you in Paris. You disappear for awhile, maybe they'll forget how you killed two innocent Catholics.*

I said, *You were the one who told me the guys in coats were terrorists.*

Mercury said, *Public opinion has changed. What can I say? But if you pull this off for Ames, you might be redeemed. Or you could die. Redeemed or die. Either is better than being the puppy-killer you are now.*

I said, *Why would I die?*

Don't underestimate the evil behind racists, boy. Mercury thought for a moment. *Once you figure out what they're doing, it'll be as dangerous as saying, 'Gimme a match, I gotta check out this here dynamite.' However. If you live through it, you might be Caesar material.*

I said, *But, teaching racists how to kill?*

Mercury said, *Don't worry about that part, bro. All y'all mortals kill each other all the time. It's what we gods bet on when we're bored. Who's gonna kill who?*

I said, *Don't tell me stuff like that. I should go back on my meds.*

I said to Lugh, "Heard something about IDC. Not much, though. What're you paying?"

The question took Lugh by surprise. Nema too. She looked at him, then at me. Lugh said, "We're paying the others five hundred euros for the week."

I gathered my thoughts. I needed a way to determine their game. If I turned them down flat, I would never know their motivations. If these people were legit in wanting my expertise, they would bargain when I named a ridiculous price. If they said yes without dickering, then I would know they were my enemies.

"You get what you pay for." I crossed my arms. "Ten thousand— cash."

Nema's eyes bugged out, then returned to normal.

Lugh choked and swallowed. "That's far too much."

"Twenty times the yahoos you hired because I'm twenty times as good."

Lugh blinked. "Well, we could go as high as two thousand."

"No deal."

He watched me for a long moment. He looked worried. As if someone told him to come back with my expertise but never expected it to cost that much. "How about three?"

He was negotiating. Which helped me believe their story about my expertise. But now I had to get out of it. Spending a few days with a bunch of neo-Nazis was lower on my list than a root canal. I opted for keeping my price too high. They clearly didn't have that much money. "Ten thousand euros. I'm not haggling."

Lugh took a long, deep breath. "I need to check on that."

"You do that, Lugh. When are you planning on leaving?"

"In the morning."

"I'll be at the *Café de la Mairie* at dawn." I walked away at a good clip.

I made it nearly ten yards before he called out to me. I stopped and faced him. Lugh rocked up on his toes. Weak guys do that. They think it makes them look bigger, more imposing. Nema still had her arms crossed as if she were cold.

"Take Nema with you. She ... enjoys your company." He gave her a push in my direction. Then he turned and quickly walked away.

"What did I say about respect, Lugh?" I called after him.

He pretended not to hear me.

Nema stood there with her face down. After a long moment, she took a peek to see if I'd left. I crooked my finger. She slow-walked to me and stared at my shoes.

After a long silence, I put a finger under her chin and lifted it. "I promise you this, Nema: I'm going to break his arm for pimping you out like that."

"He wasn't ... he's just awkward with people is all. He doesn't hear how it sounds. It's not—"

"Shh."

We walked in silence for a while. Past the Senate building and on through narrow cobblestone streets. We turned up a large boulevard and into a more familiar part of town. We crossed the plaza in front of Saint-Sulpice and passed my new favorite café.

"I thought of you as a protector," Nema said. "But I can look after myself with men. I know how they are. They think everything's a transaction. They think if I want something, I have to pay for it with sex. Well. When I said I thought you could protect me, I didn't mean like that."

"Nema." I stopped and stared at her. "We're not all animals. Some men actually have enough confidence to think of women as equals. I'm not interested in you sexually. I'm just ..."

My voice trailed off. I didn't want to say it. I started walking.

"You're lonely," she said. "I get it. Sorry."

We walked another couple blocks in silence. Then I remembered something that could take my mind off Jenny.

I turned to her. "Have you ever been to the Moulin Rouge?"

CHAPTER 11

NEMA WATCHED ME INSTEAD OF the street and almost walked into a lamppost. "Isn't that a titty bar?"

"Is it?" I asked. "I thought it was a musical, like on Broadway. I don't know; a friend gave me tickets."

Mercury leaned over the top of a car. *It's both homie. Like Vegas. Wives can't get their husbands to watch two hours of singing and dancing unless there's half-naked women involved.*

I said, *Why would Ms. Sabel give me tickets to a show like that?*

Mercury said, *Maybe she's not as uptight about sex and nudity as most Americans and figured you'd have fun. And since you have this handy young lady who claims she isn't gay, maybe you will.*

I said, *She's not Jenny.*

"If you want to." She sounded as if she'd been sentenced to hard labor. "What's the dress code?"

I checked my phone. "The e-ticket says, 'Elegant eveningwear, tie not required. No sportswear.'"

We looked ourselves over. Without a fashion sense between us, I was pretty sure we qualified as inelegant sportswear.

"I don't have anything like that," she said.

"You don't have to wear a dress."

"I can wear a dress if I want to." She stuck her chin out. Then pulled back. "I didn't bring any to Paris, that's all."

"I'll buy you an outfit." I tugged Nema's elbow until she met my gaze. "No strings attached. I don't know what Lugh told you to do, but I'm not ready for a new girlfriend—straight, gay, bi, or uncertain. I'm not buying favors. I want the company. That's all."

I let her search my eyes for sincerity. We held a long, deep stare. She decided I was for real.

She pulled away and walked up the street. "I hate shopping."

"We're going to get along fine, then."

I texted the helpdesk at Sabel Security. They answer all my questions. If I ask something they don't know, they make up a convincing answer. They recommended *The Kooples* for edgy fashions. It wasn't far. We went.

The saleslady took one look at us and—in stereotypical French fashion—rolled her eyes and said, "Ugh."

I whipped out the American Express Centurion card entrusted to me by Ms. Sabel. You can't apply for one; they give it only to the uber-wealthy. It's jet black, made of titanium and is recognized by salespeople the world over as held by a customer with more money than brains. Nema watched in silence as the saleslady changed her tune fast. The saleslady turned me over to a guy and led Nema by the arm into the women's section. They disappeared into a mass of brightly colored, flowery prints.

A few thousand of Ms. Sabel's euros later, I wore new slacks, boots, shirt, and blazer. While I waited for Nema, the unmistakable silhouette of a large Navajo caught my eye.

My best friend, Miguel Rodriguez, stood on the sidewalk outside. At six-four and built like a prizefighter, he's easy to spot. He wouldn't stand there by accident. It was a clandestine contact, or he would've come inside. After letting the saleslady know I'd be right back, I wandered outside and eased up next to him.

"Pia sent me." He wasn't a big talker.

"And?"

"You're needed in Úbeda tomorrow. That's in Spain."

Mercury stood on the other side of the big guy and leaned around him. *Guess where they gonna be holding the IDC gathering, bro.*

I said, *He can't be serious. I'm not going there.*

Mercury nodded in Nema's direction, *You already took the bait.*

I said, *I did not ... leave her out of this.*

Mercury said, *And Lugh's busy raising the cash you demanded. In twelve hours, you'll be committed to this trip.*

"I got your six." Miguel nodded across the street at a hooded figure sitting in a café window. "Tania's with me. We're going down there tonight."

"No freaking way." I let my frustration raise my voice. "Ms. Sabel told me I could take all the time I needed."

"You took it. It's been a couple hours." He kept his voice low. "The new president, Charles Williams, reinstated Shikowitz as FBI Director yesterday. He called Pia a few hours ago. They lost an undercover agent this morning. Part of that church attack you unraveled. Oh, by the way—" he turned his stoic Navajo face to me for a second "—nice work. You made us proud of you for a change."

"Thanks."

"Shikowitz wants to know who killed his man Brady. He's short on resources in Europe at the moment. Doesn't have anyone in Paris at all. And the Euros don't know about Brady being undercover. It would complicate things. 'S why he wants us."

"The IDC deal is a CIA operation. Zack Ames is running it. I turned him down."

Miguel snapped a surprised look at me before resuming his cool. "Nuristan Zack?"

"The same."

"That complicates matters." He watched the cars go by. "You'll have to be careful this time."

Mercury said, *Nice friend you have there, dawg. Monster Slayer tells you your next mission is to fight the Four Horsemen of the Apocalypse and his advice is to be careful? Ha! Well, this works out for you then. You're definitely going.*

I said, *We don't even know if there's a connection between the church attack and those groups at IDC. All we know is that Nuristan Zack thought there was. Since when do we think the CIA knows anything? They didn't even sound like terrorist groups. What were they called?*

Mercury patted my shoulder. *Free Origins, Birth Right, and Fair Heritage. Try to keep up here, homie. They ain't gonna call themselves the Minority Hunters Club.*

I said, *I'm calling Ms. Sabel. If she knew Nuristan Zack was—*

Mercury said, *Oh, no you don't. You're not calling Pia-Caesar-Sabel and telling her you're gonna chicken out on her. Jupiter will smite you with a lightning bolt for crossing a real-life Caesar.*

I stared hard at my discarded god while I retrieved my phone and picked Ms. Sabel's number from my contact list. Just before my thumb pressed dial, an explosion rocked a building three doors down. The electrical lines that ran down the outside to the streetlight fastened to the wall buzzed and zapped and fell to the ground in flames. Sparks showered down from the third floor.

Mercury shrugged. *No storm clouds, so he popped the nearest transformer.*

You never know if the gods are messing with you for going against them or taking credit for some random event, but I didn't see any need to test my faith at that particular moment. I eased the phone back into my pocket.

I said, *No harm in going down to southern Spain for a looksee, I suppose.*

"What's the mission?" I asked Miguel.

"The FBI's man was inside a violent group that's plotting a terrorist attack. The guy was so deep undercover they lost contact. He went off the grid in Atlanta, and they didn't hear from him until four this morning. Europol found his body in a hotel near here. Throat sliced with a razor."

"Europol?" The Paris police would handle a murder. Unless Zack got Hugo and the GIGN to step in. But then, pedestrian murders are beneath Hugo's operation. He might call Europol, a group with more resources to handle mundane tasks like handing a body over to the FBI. I said, "Tell Ms. Sabel I'm already on it. I managed an invitation to the big shindig. I'll be going silent on the phone from here on in."

Miguel nodded. "Your girlfriend in there. Bianca ID'd her as Joan Vanrijn, Minneapolis. Don't ask me how to pronounce it, it's way too Anglo for me. Anyway, she dropped out high school. Some kind of trouble that never landed her in jail but cut her relationship with her parents. Her brother went missing six months ago. Hasn't turned up yet. Is she your way into the conference or the reason Jenny dumped you?"

"She's not my girlfriend." I sighed. "Jenny went home before I met Nema. Joan. Whatever."

"Understood. We'll have eyes on you. Any sign of trouble, give us the black power sign." He referred to a raised fist with full arm extension and a slight forward angle. No doubt Tania's idea. With her Latin-African heritage, she'd been leaning toward black-and-proud lately.

"I'm on it. I'm meeting one of their guys at the Café—"

"Lugh. Like the Celtic god. We know. We heard the whole thing from across the street. Long-range directional microphones. We gotcha covered, brother. And if he coughs up the ten grand—" Miguel felt the fabric of my new jacket "—I want new threads."

"Wait a sec," I said. "You and Tania can't go. No way. It's too dangerous. Zack told me they were violent racists."

"Why do you think we want to go?" Miguel asked. "We leave it to you, hell, you'll put it all through the white-man-filter and see nothing wrong."

CHAPTER 12

I QUIZZED NEMA ON THE way to the cabaret. Reticent at first, she told me Lugh treated her badly because he had Asperger Syndrome. I didn't see that. In my estimation, it was a case of asshole excused as Asperger.

Nema never said thank-you for the little black wrap-around dress with black cowboy boots accessorized with a tiny red purse. But she rocked the look. If she ever smiled, she would be a knockout.

When we arrived at the Moulin Rouge, they shuffled us aside, out of the scrum. The manager collected us to give us a grand tour in perfect English. We skipped the pat-down line, standard procedure throughout Paris since the 2015 terrorist attacks. The regular tourists had to give up any large purses and backpacks. I was glad for the royal treatment. I got to keep my Glock.

Backstage, performers wore street clothes and chatted in makeup rooms. The manager showed off the ponies used in one of the acts and the feather-maker's room. Nema and I were both bored by the tour but the manager was so enthusiastic, we feigned interest.

As the manager went on about the shoemaker, Nema whispered, "Are you some kind of rich guy?"

"Not exactly."

Luckily for us, the costume maker kicked us out. There were too many repairs in progress. The manager took us to our seats. The main room was bathed in red light. Really red. As in, hard-to-see-anything red.

A round table for two waited a few inches from the stage, draped in white linen and topped with red roses and an ornate candle. "Our VIP tables are in the balcony, but for friends of Ms. Sabel, we have cleared the front row. I do hope she comes to see us in person sometime."

We glanced around the waist-high stage when we sat. They'd left a small buffer of space between us and the other tables. When the manager left, waiters brought champagne, caviar, and cheese.

"Who is Ms. Sabel?" Nema asked.

"Tell me about your gang, Free Origins. Why do they treat you so badly and yet you stay?"

The regular ticket holders began filing in. Seating was unassigned. They rushed to grab tables near the stage. We were quickly surrounded.

"It's normally a nice bunch of guys." Nema admired her glass of champagne. "We go to shooting ranges and have parties. Paladin is a lot of fun. Those things Lugh said about him are true."

"Who or what is Paladin?" I asked.

"The guy Lugh's in love with." She cracked her real first smile since we'd met, fleeting as it was. "You were right about him in a way. They're not gay, but Lugh worships the ground Paladin walks on."

"Is that the guy's real name or is he named after Charlemagne's twelve paladins? The ones named after Palatine Hill in Rome, where the she-wolf Luna found Romulus and Remus."

"It's just a nickname." Nema stared at me as if I'd grown horns. "How do you know all that stuff?"

"Oh, uh. I was forced to memorize a lot of Roman history."

Waiters appeared with the first course, tiger prawns in basil pesto with caponata, chives and pine nuts.

"You said Free Origins guys were normally nice. What happened?"

"A few months ago," she said, "some of the guys got in arguments, and they've been fighting ever since. Too much testosterone. It makes everyone tense at a time when we're competing with other groups like ours."

"You took the wrong side in the fight?" I asked.

I struck a nerve. Her eyes met mine and grew wide with fear. She sipped champagne to avoid the question.

I said, "And that's why Lugh pimped you out."

"It's not like that." Her fear turned to anger. "You've got me all wrong. I'm not Lugh's bitch. I'm not gay. I'm not anything you think."

"Then what's your story?"

"You did something amazing and I'm in awe." She batted her eyelashes. "Those guys had machine guns. Why would you tackle them unarmed?"

"Someone had to."

For some reason, she didn't like that answer. She frowned as if saving lives regardless of the danger was a foreign concept to her. I guess it is for some people.

The show started with a thunderclap of music and dancing and sequins and sparkles. They kicked and twirled right over our heads. I grabbed my champagne glass to keep it from becoming a casualty. For a long time, we were both spellbound by the spectacle. I've never been a fan of musicals, but when you're close enough to see the dancers' chests heaving to retain enough air for the exertion while maintaining a brilliant smile, you appreciate the effort. It was nothing short of astonishing.

Pace and variety had clearly been perfected over the cabaret's century of operation. The acts came and went, funny ones, loud ones, soft ones, romantic and frenetic in an endless chain of wonder.

At one point, a familiar face appeared dressed as a pirate. He spun in a circle and stopped three feet from me. His eyes met mine—Benoît, my medic at the church. Recognition crossed our faces at the same time. He winked at me in the quarter second he held his pose. On the next beat, he danced away.

Nema was fascinated with the show for a time. Then she went back to eyeballing me as if I were about to do something terrible.

"What was that guy you met in front of the store earlier?" she shouted in my ear.

Mercury danced right off the stage and landed on the floor next to me. *More important, homie, why is she phrasing her question without any humanity in it?*

I said, *What are you talking about?*

She didn't ask who he was, Mercury grinned before slipping between tables and away. *She asked what.*

I turned to Nema. "He was some guy asking about great restaurants."

"He seemed to know you."

"Americans tend to be friendly with each other."

"He wasn't American. He was something else. Not colored, not Asian."

Even though I'd been expecting as much from Lugh, I'd hoped Nema was above that. I said, "He's more American than you and I. He's native."

"How do you know that if you're not friends?"

"No beard, no facial hair."

She leaned back as if I'd solved a puzzle she'd been working on ever since she laid eyes on Miguel. But that made him identifiable at a distance. If she saw him in Spain, my cover would be blown. And Miguel would be in danger.

"Why?" I asked. "You have something against Native Americans?"

Her gaze went back to the stage where ladies danced wearing nothing but a few rhinestones draped across their chests.

I tried to determine if I'd been wrong about her gender preference. She didn't watch the nearly naked ladies with any salacious interest. She was more intent on avoiding my question. She'd been doing a lot of that.

A strange-looking waiter squeezed through the two-inch gap between the stage and our table. He blocked our view of the show for a moment and bent to the floor. Then he scampered away.

The scantily dressed ladies were quite good dancers. I found it impossible to look away. Exceptional poise, posture, and balance.

Mercury popped out from under the table. *Yo. Dude. Quit staring at the boobs while pretending to admire their skill. Did you see that guy pretending to be a waiter put a bomb under your table?*

I lifted the tablecloth and leaned down. The first thing I could make out in the dark space was a partially disassembled flip-phone. A light on it blinked a steady beat. As my eyes adjusted to the dark, I could make out wires running from the phone into the backpack that sat on the floor beneath my feet. The bomber hadn't quite gotten the phone back in the pocket after arming it.

I leapt to my feet, turning the table over and sending our dinner to the floor. The backpack fell over.

I faced the audience. "BOMB! RUN!"

Everyone stared at me. They thought I was part of the show.

I pointed at the backpack. "BOMB!"

One of the dancers saw it and shrieked. Everyone on stage ran out. The music stopped. A mad scramble for the exits erupted. Most of the tourists would get out in time. Being in the center of the room, we would be inside the blast radius if we ran for the exits.

Nema rose slowly, staring at the backpack like a deer staring into oncoming headlights. Then her eyes swept the room.

I grabbed her hand and tugged. She pulled away. She was staring at the waiter who'd left the bomb. He stood by an exit. He wore a wig, eyeglass frames without lenses and a fake beard. He turned and joined the fleeing crowd.

The color drained from Nema's face. I'd rarely seen anyone look so scared and confused and betrayed and hurt at the same time.

I scooped up Nema and jumped onto the stage, figuring our best route was through the shoemaker's room.

We made it three steps before the blast threw us both through a wall.

The wall was a stage prop and gave way easily. It broke our fall. My elbows hit the floor. I landed on top of Nema. Since I cradled her inside my arms, my body shielded her from the debris falling all around us. A steel beam full of spotlights crashed to the floor an inch from the top of my head. The room went dark and filled with reeking smoke.

Cries and screeches surrounded us.

I got to my knees. "Are you all right?"

Nema was dazed. I saw no scratches, but her mind was stuck in shock. She had yet to catch up with what was happening around us. Her eyes darted to one side, then another.

Then it came to her. She let out a wail that nearly broke my eardrums.

Emergency lights snapped on, providing direction despite the thickening smoke.

"We've gotta get out of here!" I rose and pulled her arm and dragged her to a standing position.

Nema looked at me as if I were the devil himself. She pulled out of my grasp.

I waved at the destruction around us. The bomb had been at our feet. When I jumped on stage, the platform negated much of the blast. But the damage to the building was my biggest concern. I heard metal on metal creaking and saw stage scaffolding swaying.

Terrified screams for help came from every direction.

I grabbed her more forcefully and started to pull. Then I saw Benoît, unconscious under the light beam. I let go of Nema and said, "Get outside. I'll find you."

She didn't move. Most people react to an emergency with shock, not urgency. It takes a few minutes for the brain to process everything before the urgency kicks in. Nema was taking longer than most. I couldn't help that. She was on her feet and capable of saving herself. Benoît was not.

I grabbed the steel truss and tugged with both hands. It was really heavy. Then it got lighter. Nema had put her shoulder under the higher end and stood up. Together, we shoved the lights aside. I grabbed one of his hands; she grabbed the other. We got him to his feet. But his brain wasn't functioning yet. I tossed him over my shoulder like a sack of potatoes.

Nema wrapped her arms around me. "I knew you would protect me."

Not a good time for a discussion, but she'd just telegraphed critical information. The bomb was meant for her. She knew it. And she suspected one of her rival gangs.

I shouted over the screams, "Find a way out of here!"

CHAPTER 13

MAJOR PAVARD GAVE UP WHEN Hugo of the GIGN arrived and pulled rank for the second time in a day. Hugo admired Nema for a moment, then told me to enjoy the rest of the evening. He said, "Our mutual friend will be in touch."

There had been no fatalities, but there were a lot of broken bones. Nema's façade was one of the casualties. She hid behind my right shoulder, gripping my bicep like a shield, through the medical checks and the police questioning. Every sound made her jump. Every motion made her flinch.

We caught an Uber after three in the morning. She snuggled under my shoulder.

Mercury craned back from the passenger seat. *Gay, huh, homie? Maybe you misjudged this one.*

I said, *I just saved her life. She's grateful, that's all. I think.*

Mercury said, *She said you don't know anything about her. Five hundred aurei says she's right.*

Never bet with gods. That much I've learned the hard way. They gamble with people's lives, and it never works out well for the mortals.

Too wired when we got to the hotel, we ordered hot fudge sundaes from room service and finished with some kind of dessert wine I'd never heard of. But it was awesome.

Nema toured the penthouse suite before the exhaustion caught up with her. The opulence convinced her I was filthy rich. It didn't make her like me any more or less. She crashed on the sofa at the far end of the suite and purred herself to sleep within seconds.

I staggered through the dining room to the master bedroom and fell face down on the bed. Not long after, someone was scratching at the window.

Miguel stood on the bedroom balcony in the dark. I quietly opened the door and snuck out, hoping not to wake Nema. In the distance, the Eiffel Tower glowed gold. A shadow stood to my right. The shadow made a muffled noise that sounded like a plea for help. A light drizzle began to fall.

I said, "I thought you went to Spain."

"We were on the jet when we heard the news. Tania made them turn around." He sounded rather casual about using Ms. Sabel's third jet. She used to keep it in reserve for my missions. Now she was letting anyone take it for a joyride.

"Aw. You worried about me," I said.

"Tania figured Pia would want us to bring your carcass home."

"Hate to disappoint." I flapped my arms to prove I had life left.

"If I didn't know better, I'd say the gods were on your side."

I rolled my eyes. "Mercury still thinks you're Monster Slayer."

"Maybe I am." He grinned.

"The bomb was professional." His voice dropped to business. "Hastily built with a professional timer and a shaped charge. They meant to minimize casualties beyond the target. Not terrorist stuff. More like an assassination. Sabel Labs offered free expedited services to analyze the materials. That'll take a couple days."

I gave him the rosary the shooter left behind. "Based on the number of beads, he was either Eastern Orthodox or Protestant. Maybe Episcopalian or Anglican. Which is odd for a Spaniard. They look mass-produced, but it's all we have."

Miguel tucked them in his pocket with a nod that said he'd get them analyzed. Then he said, "Oh, hey, brought you something."

He turned to the shadow in the corner and pulled Zack Ames into the dim light. Miguel ripped a strip of duct tape off Ames's mouth but left the man's hands wrapped.

"Fuck you both," Zack said.

Miguel slapped the tape back on. The muffled pleas resumed. Miguel said, "Found him loitering around after the bombing. Figured you'd want to chat before you head off to Spain. Although I thought he'd learned some manners during the ride here."

See here, homes? You be on the top floor. Mercury squeezed between us and leaned over the railing. *Ain't no fire escapes or ladders or stairs outside. He dragged a CIA agent up here. See what I'm saying? The man is not who he says he is. I'm telling you, he's Monster Slayer, son of Changing Woman, savior of the Navajo—and the bastard who killed all the Mesopotamian gods back in the massacre of 823 CE.*

I said, *He spent his summers in Canyon de Chelly. Climbing cliffs is a habit.*

He's still unnatural. Mercury crossed his arms and scowled. *Don't be messing around with any other gods, ya hear me?*

I let it go. The only gods Mercury feared were the North Americans. Apparently, when the Old World gods were beaten by Christianity and the Dark Ages descended upon the land, they crossed the Atlantic to convert the indigenous tribes. Instead, they got their asses kicked by the local deities. There's still bad blood.

Or I'm hopelessly insane.

Never have figured that out.

Miguel asked Zack Ames if he would behave himself and Zack nodded with vigor. The tape came off.

"You two are interfering with a government employee in the execution of his duties, which is a felony by—"

Miguel yanked the man's pants to his ankles, a schoolyard prank that shut him up. It also revealed a tattoo on his butt. It was a square cross on an interlocking circle, the cross filled in solid. It was vaguely Celtic. And decidedly not CIA.

Miguel said, "Next step is stress positions, Zack. All I want is for you to tell my man here what you're getting him into."

Zack nodded and pulled his pants back up as best he could with duct-taped wrists.

I said, "Start with why you're involved. The undercover agent was FBI."

Ames said, "The FBI surveilled several guys from Indianapolis heading to the Kraków meeting I told you about. About fifty guys met up in Atlanta and went from there to Poland. The FBI managed to get a man on the trip. But they didn't have the clandestine resources to support him properly outside the country. That's our department. Once Brady got here, he couldn't shake loose. They had someone sitting on him in the EU. They moved around a lot."

"You lost him."

"That's all history. It doesn't matter anymore."

"Not to you," I said. I thumbed at Miguel. "Guess why he's here? He tends NOT to lose people. You know why? Because he gives a damn. He doesn't go home at six o'clock and hope to figure it out in the morning."

"We didn't know, OK?" Ames struggled against his bound wrists. He was dying to take a swing at me. "They don't usually kill their own. They couldn't have known he was undercover. He never communicated. Listen. We did our best under the circumstances."

"I'm sure Brady appreciates your effort." I looked skyward. "Wherever he may be."

"Not funny, Stearne."

"Do you know why Miguel brought you here, Zack?"

"You want to know the plan."

"Tell us about that, Zack."

"There'll be a bunch of groups in Úbeda for the Identity Defense Conference. I'll recap for you. Kraków was their international meeting. They were supposed to come together and form a united front politically and socially. Instead, they split into three big, well-financed factions, Birth Right, Fair Heritage, and Free Origins.

"There'll be hundreds of unassociated 'floaters' going to the conference. The associations will compete for new members during the events. As I told you before, one of those groups is planning something big and violent. Rumors are it's something bigger than Christchurch. We don't know what or when or where. Whatever it is, we can't let it happen."

Zack took a breath and squinted at me. I think he was trying to intimidate me, but with his hands taped, it wasn't working for him.

"Your mission is to go there as an attendee," he said. "Don't ask questions—that'll give you away. I want you to keep your eyes and ears open. Each night, I'll meet you at a café in town. We need to discover three things: which group is planning it, who's in charge, and who or what Ross Gio is. When we've it figured out, we'll arrange an extraction for you. Hugo and I will take it from there. There's just one thing you must be clear on."

"Oh?" I asked.

Zack lifted his nose. "I call the shots."

I looked at Miguel. He shrugged. We each took one of Zack's arms and legs, turned him upside down and dangled him over the balcony railing. I said, "Or?"

Zack got busy calculating the distance to the ground—and our willingness to drop him. He writhed in our grip, which didn't help our hold. "Or. Um. We can listen to any alternative ideas you might offer."

I said, "Or?"

"Or we can do whatever you want."

"Or?"

"OK. OK. I'll clear out. I'll stay out of Úbeda."

"Stay out of where?"

"Spain. I'll stay out of Spain. I'll wait until you send word. Put me the fuck down!"

We pulled him back and set him on the balcony.

When he landed, his eyes bulged and the veins on his neck pulsed. "You two might think you're pretty clever, but Brady was cocky too. He didn't want me around either." Zack pushed his face up to mine. "They slit his throat with a razor and left his body where it fell."

Mercury tilted his head. *Yeah, homie, why not trust this guy? He knows the players, the terrain, the GIGN guys.*

I said, *Because I've been to war with one of these two guys. I don't know Ames. But I know Miguel would take a bullet for me. Ames might, but not on his coffee break.*

Mercury said, *Miguel and racists don't mix. Too easy to spot.*

I said, *True that. But he'll figure something out.*

On that sobering thought, I put my faith in Miguel.

He told me they would take Sabel Three but send it back to Paris before dawn.

Miguel hoisted the short guy on his big shoulder and crawled over the railing. Ames complained he wanted to use the elevator. Not happening. I had a guest and didn't want to get caught up in awkward explanations.

After Googling cross tattoos and finding thousands, I gave up. I crashed for two hours before hearing Nema wandering around. I popped up, told her to order room service, and hopped in the shower.

I reverted to my jeans and jacket look. Even grabbed one of my better t-shirts. It read, "War: It's not fun until someone loses an eye."

Nema had not ordered breakfast. She still had her evening dress on. She looked quite embarrassed and wouldn't face me. She said, "About last night."

It was a definitive statement. I felt compelled to respond. "Nothing happened. You didn't do anything … and I didn't do anything …"

"No. Not that. Um." She turned from the window. "I appreciate that you bought me the dress and all, but I can't go out in the morning …"

When she didn't finish her sentence, Mercury stroked his chin. *Aw, dude. I think she's old fashioned. There was a time when women didn't want to be seen slinking out of hotel rooms in last night's party dress. Now it's a badge of honor. Of course, she might not be worried about the shame of hotel-slinking.*

I said, *What would she be worried about then?*

Mercury grinned. *The shame of being seen with you, dawg.*

Walked right into that one. While he howled with laughter, I looked in the dressing room and found the package of our old clothes from *Kooples*. When the sales lady offered to have them incinerated, I'd told her to have them couriered back to the hotel instead. Turned out to be a good idea. The sight of her old things gave Nema comfort. After some coaxing and a hundred assurances about being on my best behavior, she took a shower and changed.

The café had its umbrellas out, which helped with the drizzle that nearly qualified as rain.

Waiting under one was Lugh. While we were still a few yards out, he hailed us with a sneer. "I see you two hit it off well."

Walking straight to his chair, I stretched out my hand. He instinctively took it. I yanked him to standing. "Show the lady some respect, Lugh."

"Are you threatening me?"

"Threats are idle."

He sniffed and retook his seat. He held out an envelope that I shoved in my back pocket. Lugh said, "Two thousand now. It's all we could raise overnight. Another three this evening. The remainder upon completion."

I didn't move.

"We're good for it." A few beads of sweat broke out on his forehead when I stayed silent. "Nema will vouch for us. We always pay our debts. Don't we, sweetie?"

Nema faced the table. She sank another inch closer to it as Lugh leaned to her with a hard look in his gaze.

"Tell him, you stupid bitch." Lugh's voice struck a tone I didn't care for. "He needs to hear it from you."

"Free Origins always pays its bills." She sounded like a first grader forced to recite a poem.

My gaze never left Lugh. He felt it and glanced my way. My angry glare caused him pain. He flinched.

"What'd I tell you about disrespect?" I asked.

"I, uh …" His shoulders turned inward. He looked away.

Mercury said, *Don't be wasting time on this fool, bro. You need to get to work on this Paladin fellow. And find out about Ross Gio. Trouble's brewing in Úbeda and you're in Paris. If you want to win Jenny back, you're gonna need a Caesar Parade in New York City when you get home.*

I almost asked what a Caesar Parade was, but I figured he meant ticker tape. I don't know if they even do those anymore. He might have a point, though. Surely Jenny would accept my invitation to ride next to me in the convertible and wave at adoring fans.

Mercury said, *Ah, you see it now, dontcha? This is why people want to be Caesar—babes dig guys with crowns. Let's stop this atrocity and grab some headlines.*

I sent for an Uber without saying another word to Lugh. Nor did I say anything to him when it pulled to the curb.

I opened the door for Nema and swept her in with a gesture. She got in and scooted over, leaving room for one more in the back.

Lugh stepped toward the open door. I stopped him. He looked up. I said, "You'll need a separate Uber."

"What on Earth for?"

"You need to go to a hospital."

"No, I don't." He frowned as if I were stupid.

My left hand grabbed his wrist and pulled it forward while twisting it hard. My right hand smacked inside the crook of his elbow. My knee came up with blinding speed and slammed into his radius and ulna. A doctor had once told me you couldn't break a bone by hitting it straight on or from the side. There must always be a bit of a twist involved. It turns out he was right. Both Lugh's bones snapped like matchsticks.

"I told you to treat her with respect."

Lugh's open mouth could only inhale in shock; he couldn't even scream.

I slid in the car and told the driver to go. I turned to Nema. "Lugh decided to make a quick stop along the way. He'll meet us there."

CHAPTER 14

ANDALUSIA ROLLED OUT FROM THE town of Úbeda as a heaving sea of olive trees and arid farmland. IDC's organizers had taken every room in the eleventh century city. My assigned room was in a sixteenth century palace turned into a hotel. The entrance opened onto a tourist plaza with an ancient stone church on the otherside. The lobby was a large open space with an ornate skylight two stories above us. Nema told me she had other accommodations but came with me to make sure everything went smoothly.

While I stumbled through my rudimentary Spanish with the clerk, a notable woman entered the building. I could tell because the clerk looked over my shoulder and let his mouth fall open. Nema's attention also turned to the front door with a shudder of excitement or fear or both. I followed their lead and craned around.

Waves of dark curls rolled over the woman's shoulders. She walked like a samba. A rhythmic, fluid motion of eyes and hair and body and legs and arms. With her eyes fixed on mine, she strode toward me at a leisurely pace, each foot dramatically swinging around the other like a model on a catwalk.

Tall and lean, her fashion statement was breathtaking and simple. A smooth green dress that looked like it had been shrink-wrapped on her. The neckline formed a V deep enough to make a man look but not enough to show cleavage. Her lipstick was red; neither bright and sexy nor dark and smoky. It was serious red. Her eyes were naturally dark and equally serious.

She stopped half an arm's length from me, close enough for me to catch the scent of her perfume. It was the same kind Ms. Sabel wears, something expensive. She said, "When the crowds found out about it, they followed him; and he welcomed them, and spoke to them about the kingdom of God, and healed those who needed to be cured. Luke 9:48."

Bible-thumpers always catch me off guard. I never know what they're talking about, much less how to respond. So, I didn't say anything.

She held out her hand. "Arrianne, but you can call me Gospeler like everyone else."

Mercury leaned an elbow on the clerk's desk. *Whooee, dawg. Don't she think a lot of herself? Gospelers were the ones who sang the Gospel after the Christians trashed Rome and took illiteracy to new heights. Nobody knew how to read, so gospelers sang it to help the people remember the words.*

I said, *Is a gospeler a good thing?*

Mercury said, *Not in my book. My worshippers were educated.*

"Stearne." I swallowed hard.

"I know. Your reputation precedes you. You're quite the hero. I like heroes." Arrianne glanced at Nema. "Thank you, Nema."

Nema also hadn't taken her eyes off Arrianne since the grand entrance. She swallowed hard, then scurried to the exit.

I broke the spell with Arrianne and watched Nema. "I was just beginning to like her."

"Why?"

I faced Arrianne. "Because no one else does."

The woman snapped her fingers, and Nema stopped in front of twin ironwork doors. She didn't turn around.

"Shepherd of the meek, are we?" Arrianne asked me.

"Why would people refer to you as a singer of the Gospels?"

"I find people who live in fear, like Nema, to be tedious. I prefer those who take charge of their lives." She drew a fingertip down my shoulder. "Men of action."

I gave her a slow once-over. "You don't look like a church-goer."

"You're here as an employee of my conference. I'm here to explain your position. Once you accept, I'll show you to the training grounds."

"Are you going to explain where the rest of my money is?"

"We put you in the best hotel, but you'll be paying all your expenses from your exorbitant fee."

"Sounds like an excuse for 'I can't afford you.'"

A smile creased her serious lipstick. "That's not a problem."

"Then prove it."

Arrianne's eyes indicated she didn't like my impertinence. She took a long, slow inhale through her nose as if practicing some form of anger management. I didn't move. She craned over her shoulder. "Nema, find Paladin, and get this man his chump change."

Nema fled, her shoes clattering down the ancient stone entry steps to the plaza outside.

Arrianne faced me with a scowl. "That girl pleases you? Really?"

"Your seduction-schtick must make men swoon. A month ago, I would've fallen for it. But right now, I'm not interested in you—or Nema. I'm here because someone said your program needed a dose of reality. That's it. So, drop the act."

I turned to the clerk, whose mouth was still open. I grabbed the key out of his hand. "You heard the lady call ten thousand euros 'chump change,' so charge the room and incidentals to her. She can afford it."

I paced through the large lobby, heading to my room.

Halfway across the space, Arrianne said, "She must've been someone special."

I froze mid-stride. My fists involuntarily clenched. Then I moved on.

Mercury floated up the wide stone staircase on his wings while I climbed. *You're supposed to fit in as one of them, dude. Pia-Caesar-Sabel wants you to get inside this operation and figure out their scheme. How are you gonna do that when you be acting like a jerk?*

I said, *When a grunt asks questions, it raises suspicions. But they offer intel to a trusted advisor to get his opinion. If I just rolled over and took her shit, they'd never trust me with their secrets.*

Mercury frowned. *That actually makes sense, homie. I musta taught you that.*

I opened my room. *Uh-huh.*

Mercury said, *Still, it would be a lot easier if you did what you usually do and fall for her.*

I dumped my bag on a four-poster bed and faced my mythological god. *Jenny left me yesterday. YESTERDAY. And no, I'm not over it.*

Mercury said, *That's because you didn't take up Nema. And now you're passing on Arrianne. If you keep turning these opportunities down, you'll never get Jenny back.*

I said, *Is that what you did in Rome? Screw your way back into a relationship?*

Mercury looked at me like I was missing the obvious. *Ever hear of Roman orgies, dawg? Oh, those were good times, let me tell you. You start making it with someone else, and the ex gets totally jeally! Then you get the I-want-you-back sex that leaves you sore for a week.*

I put my hands over my ears. *La la la ...*

Mercury shook his head as he floated off my balcony. I looked out at the narrow alley below. Inspired by Miguel's midnight climb, I shimmied down a drainpipe to the cobblestones. The newest brick in the lane was three hundred years old. I jogged around to the hotel's entrance and stuck my head in the front door.

I snapped my fingers to get Arrianne's attention. "You said you were going to show me the training grounds."

She glanced at the stairs, then back at me. She shrugged and followed me outside.

Her ride was an Audi convertible parked out front. We drove out of town, up a one-lane road and into the hills.

"We got off to a bad start," she said. "Despite what the French police are saying, I think you're the hero of Paris. As I said, I like heroes. We want to learn what you look for when you take down a terrorist. I look forward to learning new things. But Lugh recommended you, which makes me suspicious."

I twisted in my seat to observe her. The twisty road kept her focused, though she managed to steal a glance at me now and then.

"There are many bureaucrats from Washington to Bucharest who dislike us." She stole one of those glances. "They've done things that we find offensive. This conference is about defensive skills. Yet they act like we're committing crimes. They've hassled us and taken some of us in for questioning. Our people are uneasy. There are many among us who feel a certain paranoia about newcomers."

She didn't ask a question, so I waited her out.

"We need your expertise. But we are not willing to give you any control. We need you to understand who you work for and what we need from you."

I stayed still.

"My organization is called Birth Right. This is our conference. I am in charge. Some of the other groups, like Paladin's, are putting up with me for the week. We have something of a truce going on. You might call it cooperation for the common good. But some of these people have violent tendencies." She tried another dark-eyed glance. "It's important that you respect the hierarchy. If you do, you'll fit in. If you don't, well ... some of the dogs around here tend to eat the other dogs."

We crested a hill. Before us lay an open valley with a small village of sixteen houses off to the right. All the roofs had been removed.

On the left was a large shooting range where two dozen men practiced their aim. She turned down a dirt track to the left.

We got out and approached the firing lanes. The rangemaster saw us and shouted at the shooters. They secured their weapons and stood. They took off their hats and lowered their eyes.

I checked Arrianne in my peripheral vision. She wasn't surprised by their deference to her. A smirk of privilege lurked on her face.

The rangemaster greeted her as Gospeler. The other men introduced themselves. Half were Americans, the other half came from all over Europe. They showed off rifles of varied types and quality. Hunting rifles and civilian assault rifles were the most popular. A few had scopes. None looked fully automatic. Downrange the paper targets were prints of famous Arabs from Yasser Arafat to Saudi Crown Prince Mohammed bin Salman. Others had Martin Luther King, Ralph Abernathy, and Nelson Mandela.

Mercury walked just behind my left shoulder. *We knew this was gonna be one ugly assignment, brutha. But this is uglier than I thought. Can you do this?*

I said, *It's starting to get real, but yes, I've got this.*

Mercury said, *Something huge is lurking in these shooting lanes, bro. You have to find out who or what Ross Gio is and which group is involved. Do you really got this?*

He wasn't helping my confidence any. But the men I'd just met weren't Christchurch types. They were more like warrior wannabes, the kind who spend their weekends at paintball fields.

Arrianne sent the men back to shooting their targets. I watched them from behind the rangemaster. They were neither impressive nor hopeless.

"What do you think?" Arrianne asked. "Can you make heroes out of these men?"

"Heroes aren't made. They rise up out of the dust when needed and return to it when the danger passes."

We got back in her car and crossed the valley to the small town. As we came nearer, I could see the buildings had been riddled with bullets. One house stood apart, a quarter-mile from the others. It retained its roof and windows. Bullet-proof plexiglass walls shielded it from the town. The observation deck.

She drove up to the house. Outside was ancient block and stone, like every place in Úbeda. Inside were four simple rooms. Overstuffed leather furniture filled the living room. An expensive table and chairs left little space in the dining room. An open arch led to a recently remodeled kitchen. The bedroom had no door but did have a four-poster bed just like the one in my hotel room. We walked out on the veranda overlooking the shot-up village.

Two sets of binoculars hung on the wall. She took one and handed me the other.

"This is our urban warfare zone or UWZ." She swept an arm across the view. "We call it the Ooze for fun."

"Quite a big place here. You rented this for the conference?"

"Spain still has 3.4 million unsold houses left over from the 2008 recession. I bought it cheap." She winked at me.

I checked the landscape.

She nudged her shoulder against mine. I followed her inside. She said, "The conference starts in two days. It lasts five. We have sixty-four heroes we need you to raise up out of the dust."

CHAPTER 15

ARRIANNE UNZIPPED HER DRESS, DROPPED it to the floor, and kicked it into the bedroom. With a slow turn, she lifted her dark locks from her bra. "Would you help me?"

Her flesh was smooth and inviting, her curves as round as a pinup model from the '40s. Somewhere between Rita Hayworth and Sophia Loren. I should've drooled. Instead, my eyes turned away. A vision of Jenny's slow unveiling on our first night in Paris came to mind. Half of me wanted to get the image of Jenny out of my head and unhook Arrianne. The other half wanted to dump the mission and fly back to DC to beg Jenny for a second chance.

I said, "No thanks."

She said, "'But I say to you that everyone who looks at a woman with lust has already committed adultery with her in his heart.' Matthew 5:28."

I opened the front door. "I need to study your Ooze … uhm."

Without a glance back, I walked downhill to the bullet-riddled village.

Mercury walked with me. *Y'know, most people get dumped, and there's a billboard everyone-but-you can see that says, AVOID THIS PERSON LIKE A FREAKIN' STD. They can't buy a date. Months later, when they finally get a date, the billboard changes to, ASK THIS PERSON OUT NOW BEFORE IT'S TOO LATE! They have nothing but dating offers. Not you, though, homie. You get dumped like Ebola-infected feces, and you've got two women stalking you—the next day!*

I said, *Means nothing. I miss Jenny.*

Mercury said, *A week from now, you're gonna slap your forehead and say, 'I coulda had Arrianne AND Nema. What was I thinkin'?'*

I ignored him and walked through the narrow lanes of the UWZ. Weeds sprouted between the cobblestones. Walls of crude stone and mortar, worn and weathered, stood against time. If they'd ever been plastered and whitewashed, the coatings had disintegrated decades ago. Some walls had openings cut in them shored up by new, unfinished planks. Most of the buildings were two stories. Some had open decks instead of upper levels. Spent shell casings littered the ground in places. The largest piles lay below the better shooting positions.

Three lanes met in an oddly shaped plaza of sorts. A large piece of iron capped an old well. Curious arrows spray-painted on the ground gave measurements with abbreviations. Not many of them made sense without a key. I followed the clues and tried to inventory them. A few houses away, one stood out. An arrow pointing out of town read, "St. Paul's 500 ft."

Mercury appeared next to me. *What do they got against Paul, brutha? My boy Nero beheaded the dude, wasn't that enough?*

I said, *Saint Paul's could mean a lot of things. Got any useful ideas?*

Mercury said, *Saint Paul was a busy boy, almost as busy as Mother Mary. He's got a city in Minnesota, a cathedral in London, a college in Virginia. There are fifty-seven places in France named after him. Minerva-only-knows how many places are named 'San Pablo' in Spain.*

I kept wandering the town. I ducked in and out of houses. I found more of the curious markings. There were quite a few with distances measured in feet. They varied from ten to thirty, but few went beyond that. Then I found two quite different from the others. They had double-line arrows as if for emphasis. One read, "Amen" and the other "Warwick." On a wall in a small room, another read, "Queens Head" and the last one I could find, "Rose."

Warwick sounded English, but Queens Head could be something out of the French Revolution for all I knew. Were they re-enacting a scenario? Planning something? If it was a plan, they hadn't left any handy clues about when. I needed Miguel to see these markings. Raising my fist in the air for black power was the signal for danger, so that wasn't appropriate.

I looked around. Arrianne's crib had a good view of the whole town. She stood on the veranda in tight leggings and an athletic top. She waved.

I took stairs to the second level of a house. A wall had been removed on the upper level, improving the view from Arrianne's veranda. I checked the sightlines to the street and neighboring houses. It was a perfect sniper position. On the floor lay a pile of spent casings. There were more arrows with initials. A small grappling hook attached to thirty feet of nylon rope lay in the corner.

Directly below my position was a hole cut into an old wall. Scratches left by the hooks indicated someone had rappelled to the floor below. Looking at the spot where I'd seen the distance to Saint Paul's, there was no sightline. As if they wanted to rappel without being seen by Saint Paul.

I made my way to the lower level and checked the entry point. Small piles of brass lay on either side of the opening. From their positions, it looked like someone had conducted a standard room-clearing procedure for SWAT teams and regular army. Across the street was an empty house. There were no boot prints in the dust, no ejected casings. Rangers, SEALS, and other special ops teams would've cleared the room from across the street. A sniper in a distant position would take the first shots, confusing and scattering the enemy's response. Then they would send in the bullet-chewers.

That told me these guys were not elite killers. But they were good enough to do serious damage to regular police and first responders. In the average big city, they could wreak havoc. In an unsuspecting medium city, with less training for law enforcement, they would be devastating.

I went back to the arrow pointing to Saint Paul's and paced out 500 feet. When I reached that point, I turned around and checked the town. None of the places where I'd found ejected casings were visible. Making Saint Paul's something they were going out of their way to avoid.

A bush near a wall outside the village whispered to me as I strode by. "We don't know what the markings mean either."

CHAPTER 16

IT WAS TANIA'S VOICE. A former sniper, she knew how to become invisible like the best of them. Even so, being this close to Arrianne's house in the daylight was a big risk.

"You saw the Saint Paul reference?" I kept my face down as I spoke in case the lady of the house had her binoculars trained on me.

"No idea. We're checking all the Saint Pauls in London, Rome, New York, Tokyo; you name it."

A large SUV crossed the hillside and parked outside Arrianne's house. Four men got out and appeared on the veranda with Arrianne a few seconds later. A man's voice called out to me. I couldn't make out the words at that distance, but they wanted me back there.

I climbed the hill at my own pace.

As I stepped onto the front porch, Lugh opened the door. His arm was in a cast held in a sling. Behind him, two men held Arrianne's arms. I didn't see the fourth man until his tactical baton crashed into my stomach. I doubled over.

The big man wielding the weapon knew what he was doing. He had driven it in with an upward arc and pulled it back without a split second of hesitation. It was effective. He'd managed to compress all my innards upward into my diaphragm at the bottom of my lungs, expelling all my breathable air. The quick removal made sure the sting was instant and long-lasting. He pulled back for a second swing.

"Stop!" Arrianne screamed. "Don't hurt him."

The man held the baton over his head, ready to render another blow. It was a Euro Security Products collapsible baton with a weighted end, an anodized steel shaft, and a non-slip, rubberized grip. Good for breaking bones. Baton-man looked to Lugh. Lugh shook him off. The man took a parade rest posture, hands behind his back, feet apart. He kept the baton extended.

"Do I have your attention now, soldier?" Lugh asked.

My lungs struggled to reflate. I stood, fighting against the pain searing through my core.

I analyzed him in my peripheral vision. Baton-man evoked a Russian Spetsnaz background. At parade rest, they hold their chins a little higher and cocked to one side, a form meant to convey superiority. Americans go for straight forward confidence with a level jaw and gaze. The men holding Arrianne let go of her and formed the same posture. These guys had not been at the shooting range. They were on a whole different level. My level. But there were more of them than there was of me.

Not good.

Lugh held up a passport. "This is yours. I'll hold it until you've completed your duties here."

"That's ... illegal." I found it hard to be a smart-ass when my internal organs were in desperate need of medical attention.

"Aleksei will help you find your way around the grounds." Lugh pointed at baton-man. "And we will keep your phone until you're ready to leave."

One of his goons grabbed my Sabel phone—my only link to safety—and handed it to Lugh.

"This is my conference." Arrianne stepped out from behind the two Neanderthals. "Birth Right is paying him. He goes where I say."

"None of that changes." Lugh glanced at his goons to intimidate her. "Everyone's worried about your safety, given this man's propensity toward violence. Aleksei is here to ensure he doesn't hurt you."

"All you had to do ..." Talking increased the pain in my core. "Treat the ladies with respect."

I turned my back on Aleksei while addressing Lugh. A tactical mistake. I heard the whoosh an instant before my kidneys screamed out in pain. My world went silent while my brain worked to bring the systems back online. I was on my knees. Arrianne was shouting at Lugh.

Gentle hands tugged at my arm.

It was Nema. She helped me to a standing position. My gut wrenched and convulsed. It took all my strength not to get sick. There was no way I was going to puke in front of these guys.

Holy Saturn, dude. Mercury stood on the other side of her shaking his head. *Without me, you get blindsided by a freakin' Russian? I can't leave you alone for a minute, homeboy.*

I said, *I got this.*

Nema's got this, Mercury said. *You can't even stand up on your own. This is SO embarrassing. Don't you dare tell the other gods about this.*

I said, *Tell them what?*

Mercury crossed his arms. *The man I'm trying to make into a Caesar had to be rescued by a girl.*

"Get your testosterone out of here." Arrianne grabbed a book off the coffee table and threw it at Lugh. "You deserved that broken arm."

"You were supposed to tell him who's in charge." Lugh caught the book and tossed it back.

"I did. He gets it. We didn't need you. Now get out of here."

Nema turned to Arrianne. "He needs a doctor."

"So what?" Lugh asked.

"How's he supposed to teach your Free Origins' people his tactics from a hospital bed?"

Lugh faced me. "Who's in charge?"

Mercury said, *Punch him, homie. Or—better yet—kick him in the balls.*

I said, *What's the first of Sun Tzu's Five Essential Elements of Victory? The victor knows when to fight and when not to.*

Mercury scrunched up his face. *You talking about 'Art of War' Sun Tzu? Dude, he was nothing but a mercenary when Tarquinius Superbus brought him in as an intern. That was when the Romans whupped the Volsci. That little Chinaman learned it all from Tarinius then went home and acted all big.*

I said, *Riiiight.*

"Right?" Lugh looked at me funny. "Who then?"

"You are, Lugh."

"Take him back to the hotel." Lugh looked at Nema. "Aleksei will collect him in the morning. He'll work through his pain."

Lugh lifted his cast before ushering his men out. Aleksei gave me a sick grin. I winked at him. Even that hurt.

The women eased me into the car and drove me back to town in the heat of the late afternoon. It was all I could do to keep my insides from coming up and out. Every bump and turn made something hurt. Nema had come to deliver the rest of my money. She wasn't happy about the scene she'd found. She sat in the back, arms crossed, scowling at the countryside. Arrianne ignored her and stroked my leg while she drove.

Climbing the stone steps was a chore. I kept getting dizzy and almost fainted. They helped me to my bed. Nema wiped my forehead with a damp washcloth while Arrianne watched from the foot of the bed.

Nema lifted my shirt. My belly was purple, and my six-pack abs looked like a swollen pillow. She looked at Arrianne. "He needs a doctor. He must have internal bleeding."

"Get him a bag of ice. Let's see if that works."

Nema handed off washcloth duties and ran downstairs. Arrianne smiled and wiped my face with a luxurious stroke. She did her best to brush her tight yellow racerback top across my skin. Any other time, it would've gotten my attention. At that moment, it was all I could do not to dump my lunch on her. She examined the cloth and determined it was too dry.

While Arrianne rewet the washcloth, Mercury sat on the edge of my bed with a golden goblet. *Drink this, homie.*

I said, *Oh, no. I'm not falling for that one again.*

Mercury said, *What? This is the tonic of the gods. It will stop all your internal bleeding, put your spleen back where it belongs and sew the two halves of your intestines back together again. You need this.*

I said, *It's Bellona's menstrual flow. You pulled this one on me once.*

Yeah! Remember how it cured you quicker than Ethan Hunt can come back from certain death? Mercury pushed the goblet to my lips. *You've drunk worse than this at a frat party, brutha. C'mon now, drink up. Vejovis got it straight from the goddess of war and conquest herself.*

I pushed it away.

"Too cold?" Arrianne held the washcloth over my face. "Or is Nema the only one allowed to touch you?"

"I'm fine for now. Thanks."

She looked away like a woman rejected.

"You and Lugh aren't on the same page," I said. "Competing for control of the IDC? Isn't he in a different organization?"

"We had a falling out about a year ago." She looked to the ceiling. "I'd had enough of his misogyny. Paladin wouldn't do anything about him. That's why I started Birth Right. Nema helped me get started, but they lured her back several months ago." Her soft, dark eyes came back to me. "I must say, you were a bit heavy-handed breaking his arm. But I can think of several times I considered doing the same thing. I like a man who takes action when it's needed."

"Bullies usually need someone to ..." Pain cut through my thinking. I writhed and breathed and beat it back.

"You're right about him." She wiped my face again. "He's a bully. I'm so sick of the macho crap coming out of those Free Origins guys. Paladin seems nicer, but that's because he has Lugh do all his dirty work. The Fair Heritage people are just like them." A dreamy gaze came over her and drifted to the ceiling. "You know, I'm getting out of this business soon. A couple more deals and I'm gone. I've got a little mill house in Vermont. Needs some work but it's paid for. I plan to go back there and leave all them behind. It has a little brook, a mill wheel, and trees. Peaceful and quiet. You could come with me."

"Vermont?"

"Yes. It's 92 percent white."

Mercury said, *You've got her talking, dawg. Now's the time to ask her what's up with that Ooze. Get her to take her clothes off, and you can ask her anything.*

I said, *I don't think that's how it works. If she gets undressed, I'd be the one telling her anything.*

Mercury changed position as if he were about to watch a movie. *Never know til you try. Go for it.*

I said, *I think we're still at the indirect stage for questions.*

"What is Free Origins all about? And don't tell me self-defense, I heard that. There's something deeper going on. Something that binds your organizations when you obviously hate each other. What are the origins? Why connect 'free' to that word?"

"They're about freedom based on scientific research." Arrianne tossed the washcloth in her hand absently and stared at a far corner of the room. "Experts from Stanford and Berkeley researched why certain races are worse than others at getting screened for preventable diseases like heart disease, hypertension, and diabetes. They found that people respond better if their doctor is of the same race. There's a *Hidden Brain* podcast about it called *People Like Us*. Another study found similar results in education. At-risk black youths are twenty percent more likely to graduate high school and go to college if their teachers are also black. Free Origins thinks people shy away too much from the fact that people need to seek out their origins."

I felt distant. I was fading fast. I heard my voice say, "Sounds like segregation."

"Freedom to choose. If you went to a party and you saw three black people, three Asians, and three people from your hometown, which group would you approach?"

CHAPTER 17

ARRIANNE AND NEMA TOOK SHIFTS through the night. I blacked out a few times. The pain of my internal injuries kept me from sleeping. I would black out, wake up, black out again. They were concerned I might die on them. But not concerned enough to call a doctor. Which raised more than a few questions about their sincerity. Not that I could do anything about it.

Arrianne went home well after midnight. Nema fell asleep in a chair. I finally dozed off for good early in the morning.

Sunshine knifing between my curtains woke me. An empty golden goblet lay in the bed next to me. I picked it up and stared at it.

Nema stretched and yawned and said, "Where'd that come from?"

Mercury said, *Don't thank me. I know you'd rather die than drink the divine fluids of the goddess of war, but I had to do something. Your kidneys were shutting down.*

If he were real, I'd have beaten him with the goblet. I hate being healed by miracles.

I stared at him. *I cannot believe you took advantage of me like that.*

"Oh, no," Nema said. "I didn't do anything. I just took off your shirt. You kept tugging at it in your sleep. I thought that's what you wanted."

I tossed the sheets back and stood before thinking. I looked down. At least she left my boxers in place.

"What the hell?" She jumped to her feet and pointed at me.

"I'm fine."

"I can see that." She looked completely freaked. "I mean, how ... what happened to the bruising?"

"Who took my pants off?" I asked.

"Who do you think?" She stole an angry glance at the door. "But what happened?"

"Did you guys give me some kind of drug?"

"No. Of course not." She walked around to the side of me, looking me up and down.

I spied my jeans on a balcony chair. My t-shirt lay on the chair next to it. Both had been handwashed. I picked them up and came back in. "Thank you."

The door opened without a knock. Arrianne strode in like she owned the place. Since I'd charged the room to her, I guess she did. A familiar-looking bodybuilder came in behind her. The two of them stopped in the doorway, their eyes bouncing back and forth from Nema to me.

"Sorry," Arrianne said. "We'll leave you two alone."

In Arrianne's hand was a Spanish tabloid featuring a picture of Jenny and me taken the day before she left. A graphic lightning bolt separated us.

Those razor-sharp spears sliced through my ribs and into my heart all over again. I missed Jenny so much it hurt. How do we get so wrapped up in someone that life and death revolve around their smile? Why is it we don't sense how precious those moments are until we lose them?

"Don't go!" Nema scowled. "He just woke up. It's not what you think."

My shirt was still wadded in one hand my trousers in the other. I pointed at the guy. "You're the guy from the street fight. Thanks again for the help."

His movie-star chin allowed his Hollywood smile to beam at me. "Dude, you're looking fine. The girls made it sound like you were on death's door. I was worried something happened to the hero of Saint Germain. That's not what they're calling you back in Paris. They still think you're a terrorist. But you're a hero to everyone at Free Origins."

He gave me a handclasp as if we were arm wrestling and pulled me in for a bro hug. I leaned into it for politeness sake, patted his back, then put my pants on.

All three stared at my abs while I lowered the t-shirt over them. When my head popped up, they kept staring at my tummy as if they'd seen something miraculous. I said, "Where can I get a cup of American coffee?"

"What's that about?" The guy pointed to my t-shirt.

It had a rendering of a soldier blasting a .50 cal BMG, spent casings flying out and piling at his feet. Below him were the words, "Slaughter is the best medicine."

Not the kind of thing you'd wear to pick up your niece from ballet. Or to impress people paying twenty times the going rate for your services.

"Uh. Yeah. Something from my Ranger days." I crossed my arms over it. "Coffee?"

The other two looked at Nema. She hung her head and slouched.

Arrianne touched Nema's arm and faced her. "Please?"

Nema lit up. "I know a place. Be right back."

"You got a name?" I asked the movie star.

"They call me Paladin."

"Lugh says you walk on water. He works for you?"

"Whoa!" Paladin waved me off. "What he did yesterday was not sanctioned. I came here to apologize."

"Nice organizational command structure. What did you do about it?"

Paladin winced. Arrianne tossed him a sympathetic glance. He wisely took a moment to gather his thoughts, then said, "We're not a big group like the Army. We don't have a bench full of qualified leaders to step up if we relieve a man of his command."

"Four key words in your statement: we, not, don't, and if. Are you a passive leader barely hanging onto the reins at the whim of your staff? Or a commander obscuring your order executed by your lieutenant?"

Mercury stood behind Paladin with a disapproving look. *Very Caesar-like, homie. Maybe there's hope for you yet. Did you check the reaction of your biggest fan?*

Arrianne's eyes had gone soft and glowed admiration my way. I said, *How come Jenny doesn't see this side of me?*

Mercury said, *Who cares? The raven-haired beauty would make a fine substitute.*

I said, *There are no substitutes.*

Paladin bit the inside of his cheek while he ran through a hundred possible replies. In the end, he decided on honesty. He grinned that magnetic Tom Cruise smile and shook a finger my way. "Oh, you're good. I see why Lugh wanted you here. Yes, the order to teach you a lesson came from me. I did not order a beating quite so violent, though."

"You're telling me you don't know how to give commands?" I stepped close and checked him out. "Or that your people don't follow them?"

The tension in his face flexed his cheek as he fought an internal battle over whether to escalate or lighten the situation. I could take him in an instant, overbuilt muscles and all. But he had a Russian named Aleksei—who I suspected to be loitering in the hallway outside—who could take me down for trying.

He slapped my shoulder and gave me another Oscar-winning grin. "That's why we need you, Jacob, to help me get my act together. I see the injuries didn't slow you down. So, what do you say, no harm, no foul?"

"Sure." I play-punched his shoulder hard enough to make him take a step back. "You'll return my passport?"

The smile disappeared, and Paladin-the-tough-guy took its place. "When we get our money's worth."

I pointed to the balcony. "How about we sit down for a bit. You can tell me your expectations for the training sessions. Maybe I can conjure up a lesson plan."

We took chairs in the early sunshine. Nema arrived just in time with coffee and a folder. She gave out drinks and handed the folder to Paladin.

Mercury leaned against the railing and raised his face to the sun. *These people get along fine for a bunch of warring factions. Was Zack Ames wrong about them?*

I said, *Lemme guess. You're going to make me figure it out on my own?*

Mercury said, *The only thing better than watching a mortal die from a pox they could've prevented with a simple vaccination is watching you guys think about things you're not quite smart enough to figure out—but think you are.*

Paladin opened the folder and handed me a few crude maps of the

Ooze. He said, "Lots of guys wish they were you. They'd like to stop a terrorist attack but lack the skills or the courage. Every now and then, a guy like you comes along. We want to know how to tell the difference. Which guy is capable of rising to the occasion?"

"Why would you want to know that?" I asked. If Zack Ames was right about these guys, knowing which people in a crowd were threats and which weren't would be a primary strategy in a mass-shooter's plans. "Aren't your guys trying to become the ones rising up?"

Paladin looked stunned for a second then pulled himself together. "We're all about defense. We're hoping to find more guys like you to join our team. I don't want to spend our time and effort on daydreamers."

I didn't believe him for a second. "OK."

He pointed to his maps. A couple were blanks; a couple had X's and O's. "This one's a scenario we'd like to start with in the morning. It's a hostage situation. The O's are victims. The X's are the terrorists. We want to know how to kill all the terrorists and free the hostages."

A noble endeavor except for one frightening detail: the X's were in the wrong places. They were guarding the entrances, not the exits or the hostages. This wasn't a rescue. This was a blueprint for an attack.

CHAPTER 18

AFTER CHOKING DOWN MY REACTIONS to the scenarios Paladin showed me, I had a decision to make, run away or keep playing the game. A guy named Brady tried what I was doing, and it didn't end well. Undercover work is not my specialty. I've had zero hours of training. My expertise is breach and kill. That's when it crossed my mind to kill them all and be done with it.

Mercury said, *Killing a thousand people would be considered a terrorist attack all by itself, young blood. And the French already set you up for it.*

I thought IDC was a couple hundred, I said. *You're saying it's that big? A thousand people?*

"They won't all show up," Arrianne said. "So far, we've had fifty cancellations."

"Still, that's impressive." I glanced around, uncertain how much of my sacred dialogue had spilled out.

"Don't let that bother you." Paladin slapped my shoulder. "You only have to worry about the top guys. We call them the 'Sixty-Four.'"

Paladin declared we should visit the Ooze before Arrianne's people served an American-style breakfast. The early-arriving conference attendees would be there.

While the big Spanish cities have gone more mainstream, rural towns still cling to the old ways. Their business day starts after nine AM, has a siesta in the middle and goes until nine PM. Spaniards eat breakfast when I expect lunch and so on. Arrianne had arranged IDC's schedule on the American timing to accommodate the majority of the attendees. Which was fine with me. I was starving with nothing but a large, weak coffee in me. Not to mention some holy fluids I'd rather forget about.

Aleksei met us in the lobby. He frowned when he looked me over.

"I'm hard to damage," I said. "I'm even harder to kill."

A smirk of amusement flittered across the Russian's face. I hadn't won him over, only challenged him to try harder. He waved a hand at my core and said, "This not possible."

Only it sounded like "theees" and "poz-bul."

Arrianne scowled at him. She said, "Jesus looked at them and said, 'For mortals it is impossible, but for God all things are possible.' Matthew 19:26."

Mercury leaned an elbow on Arrianne's shoulder. *She sure is trying to earn that Gospeler nickname, huh homie. She gets who helps you out. She might read the wrong book, but she's closer to the divine truth than you.*

I said, *OK, so you healed me. Thank you. Are you happy now?*

That's what I like, an attitude of gratitude. Mercury straightened up with a grin. *Even if you didn't mean it, it's a step. Say, you gonna win these people over before they kill you like they did Brady?*

I said, *Thanks for the confidence builder.*

Arrianne and Nema left to organize the meal.

"The first batch of the Sixty-Four arrived this morning," Paladin said.

We got in an SUV. Aleksei drove us to the shooting range.

Twenty men between the ages of twenty and forty waited for us. For most of them, this appeared to be their first trip past the edge of the trailer park where they were raised. From the look of them, what those trailer parks lacked in worldliness they made up for in meanness.

They introduced themselves to me, first names only, no points of origin. Half were Americans, the rest from all over judging by their accents. This group was better equipped than the men I met the day before. They had clean, fairly new assault rifles.

One man twirled something between his fingers. I grabbed his wrist and pulled his hand up between us. It was a piece of twisted coat hanger with a unique but identifiable Y-ending. I said, "You made a DIAS out of a coat hanger?"

"Yeah." He grinned with all three front teeth. "Works great."

"Show me."

Several of the others scoffed as if a Drop In Auto Sear (DIAS) that wasn't made of carefully machined steel was beneath them. What concerned me was the casual manner in which they all regarded the illegal modifier that converted a semi-automatic into a machine gun. In the US a DIAS could get you ten years. Saturn only knows what the Spanish authorities, with their much tighter gun laws, would do.

The man strode confidently to one of the tables, inserted his DIAS, and checked with the rangemaster. When he got the nod, he pulled the trigger once. Thirty rounds spewed in smooth, automatic succession.

Another man thumped my shoulder and showed me his rifle. His DIAS was machined metal. He took a position at a shooting lane, got the rangemaster's nod, and unloaded his magazine. His aim was above average. He left a tight grouping of holes dead center in the target.

I did a double-take on the bull's eye. Where yesterday's crew had been firing at famous Muslims, today's targets were pictures of me. All the posts had the screengrab of me from the Saint-Sulpice video. It wasn't flattering. I was in the act of killing a man.

Aleksei shoved my shoulder as soon as I got the joke. They crowded around me and started laughing. I did my best to laugh with them. There's a fine line between making fun of the trainer and telegraphing a death threat.

Someone clanged pots together at the back of the mob. We turned to find Arrianne with a breakfast buffet set up. Nema helped her dish out scrambled eggs and bacon. We grabbed our chow and sat in a circle, paper plates in our laps.

Mercury sat next to me. *You better win these guys over before they use your face—and not a facsimile of it—for target practice. Find some common ground with these guys. Get the leaders to respect you.*

I pointed at one grizzly looking guy's shoulder. "Is that an Airborne patch?"

He glanced at his shirt before scowling at me. "173rd Airborne, Operation Northern Delay at Bashur. You ever jump?"

"A few times." I ate a bite to delay the punchline. "My first was Objective Serpent."

Eggs fell from his open mouth. The few veterans in the group went quiet at the mention of the legendary night raid conducted under heavy fire. He pointed his fork at me. "How many tours?"

"Eight."

"Lotsa night jumps?"

"Beats making yourself an easy target."

"Any HALO?"

Mercury turned to me. *Izzat some kind of Christian code? You're not converting on me, are you, bro?*

I said, *He's talking about High Altitude Low Opening jumps. Different kind of halo.*

Yeah. I knew that, Mercury said. *Just checking.*

"My favorite is a nighttime, wingsuit HALO," I told Grizzly. "I can jump from 40,000 feet, fly straight to your 'hood, and land on your outhouse roof."

The others laughed and shoved Grizzly. It took him a minute, but he laughed too.

Paladin, sitting across the group, said, "I've done a lot of skydiving, have a B license. I'd love to do a HALO."

"You? HALO?" Grizzly laughed at him. "You gotta have balls of steel for that shit."

"You have the balls, right?" I asked Paladin. "Because, I can arrange a HALO jump."

After a glance around at everyone watching him, he nodded.

I turned to Aleksei. "You've jumped for the Spetsnaz, right?"

The Russian smacked his chest with his fist. "Dozen night jumps."

"Are you ready for HALO?"

"Sure." He ate some eggs. "Whenever you ready. You crap pants before HALO."

The group laughed.

Paladin said, "I'm in. When can we do this?"

"How about three hours from now?" I asked.

"Sure." The Russian kept eating. He suddenly jerked his head up. "Today? Three hours?"

"Yep. I have eight rigs and a jet, ready to rock and roll. We can get over the Pyrenees, jump from 35,000 feet, and be back here before the siesta is over. What do you say?" I paused a beat. "You have the balls for it?"

Every man in the circle turned to Paladin.

"Uh." He swallowed hard. "Sounds great. I'm in."

I turned to Aleksei and waited.

He finished his eggs and wiped his mouth. "You jump, I jump next. You get scared; I push you."

The group hooted and laughed.

I stood. "That's three. It's the most dangerous jump you will ever attempt. I can't guarantee you won't die of a heart attack in the air— which has happened more than you might expect. And I can't guarantee the strain of falling that far and fast won't cause you to black out and forget to pull your chute—which has happened even more than heart attacks. I've got five more rigs. Anyone man enough to join us?"

A few hands went into the air.

Mercury said, *Headsup, homie. Remember the crew that jumped you outside of that bar in Paris?*

I said, *Yes, I do. And I see him.*

One of the raised hands had a tattoo the size of a watch. It was round and made of a thick circle with an equally thick triangle in the middle of it. Identical to the man who tried to beat me up outside the Junkyard.

I picked him first.

CHAPTER 19

WE DROVE TO THE AIRPORT where Sabel Three waited for me in a private hangar. Miguel and Tania wore coveralls from the local executive jet service company. I was impressed they put together such a great cover story on short notice. Tania met everyone outside the small side door and called out something in Spanish.

Paladin looked at me. "She wants the guy who's paying. We're to wait here."

I started in. He grabbed my arm and said, "A lot of these guys don't trust you. Maybe I should go with you to translate."

"If they don't trust me, tell them not to get on the jet." I looked over at Tania. "Someone in there probably speaks English. If not, I'll give you a holler."

I jogged over to Tania. The main doors for aircraft were closed. We entered through a human-size side door with a small window in it. Paladin pressed his face to the glass to watch me. Inside, Tania showed me a table with all the harnesses, suits, and rigs laid out. Miguel stood behind it. He went through the motions of showing me the equipment, as if I were inspecting it.

"You counted on us to hear your HALO challenge on our directional mics?" Tania asked. "Pretty risky."

"I believe in you."

"We picked up a few side conversations," Miguel said. "They talked about Ross Gio. They're low-key about him. Whatever's going down, he might be the leader or mastermind. We think he's coming in soon."

"They keep pushing Paladin as the big dog," I said.

"He's in a three-way power struggle with Arrianne and someone else.

We think it's this Ross Gio."

"What do we know about any of them?" I asked.

"Nothing." Tania was disgusted. "They've been careful with social media, passports, and any facial recognition. We can't get past those codenames."

Miguel added, "Not just Paladin and Arrianne. Most of these guys have been off the grid for years. Arrianne and a couple of her guys have been off the grid since they were kids. No fingerprints, no arrest records, nothing. Or—and we're not sure about this—some agency or another has suppressed them. Like they do for witness protection."

"Any news on the Moulin Rouge bomb?"

"Inconclusive," Miguel said. "Virtually every government requires explosive manufacturers to add special chemical markers in C4 and dynamite, anything that goes boom. This had nothing. And you know what that means."

"Professional assassins." Tania gave me a grave look. "Free Origins and Birth Right are both well financed. This means they're better connected and more dangerous than we thought. We don't know about Fair Heritage, but the safe play is to assume the same."

"What about the rosary?" I asked.

"No solid leads," Tania said. "Anglican, Lutheran, Episcopal, any number of churches sell that brand. However, an Anglican outpost in Málaga sells it in their bookstore. When I showed them a picture of Diego, they clammed up. It could be they know him, or maybe they saw his picture from Saint-Sulpice. We're still working that angle."

"And the markings at the UWZ?"

"Street names in London's financial district." Miguel lifted an oxygen bottle and face mask as if he were showing me the finer points. "Saint Paul's Cathedral fits for distance, but they seem focused on a set of office buildings. It doesn't make sense for any kind of terrorism. The buildings are only half-occupied and mostly by business consultants. No cash, no valuables, white English males, not a high-value target. Can you ask about that?"

"I can try. Too many questions will invite suspicion."

"OK, let's get these guys suited up." Tania turned to the entrance and shouted in Spanish again.

The seven handpicked jumpers filed in and crossed the big space. In addition to Paladin and Aleksei, I brought Grizzly and the tattooed guy plus three others who seemed influential and had at least a skydiver's B license. The B license certified at least 30 minutes of free fall. A C license means sixty minutes. Miguel and I were way over the D license requirement of three hours. I suspected Aleksei was near our level, but the Russians don't fund a lot of expensive HALO jumps.

Tania shouted directions in Spanish. Paladin translated to English. Several of the men treated her with disdain. No one said anything about Miguel. When a man meets someone big enough to crush his skull with one hand, he tends not to say anything rude.

Grizzly grabbed my shoulder. "I want a rig that wasn't packed by a monkey."

Tania looked back and forth at us, pretending not to understand English and waiting for an explanation of the problem in Spanish. Paladin provided what he considered a pleasant version. She said something rude to him, pulled enough chute out of the pack to require a re-pack, tossed it roughly at Grizzly, and pointed to the folding table.

Aleksei laughed and gave him a push.

Grizzly walked to the table, scowling at us. "Fuck you, Aleksei. You're going to die because you let a monkey pack your chute. You'll see."

"Work fast," Paladin called out. "We're not waiting for you." Then he turned to me. "What were you thinking, Jacob? You didn't ask for qualified specialists?"

Mercury leaned between us. *Yeah, brutha, wazzup with that? Just cuz she's been packin' her own chute since she was a teenager doesn't mean she knows what she's doing. Holy Neptune, dude. I didn't know people like this still existed. Cut his suspension lines, see if he lands on his feet like a cat.*

I said, *Need to know who Ross Gio is first.*

Refolding your chute isn't unheard of in the military, but never because of race.

I pointed Paladin at the folding table. Paladin picked up his rig and indicated he was satisfied.

We strapped in. Miguel checked the harnesses and slapped their helmets. Grizzly was the last one ready. They may have laughed at me in the morning, but they listened intently to my instructions in the early afternoon. The only difference between HALO and regular skydiving is the sheer terror, the temperature at 60 degrees below zero Fahrenheit that can stop your heart if your suit doesn't fit right, the added stress on your chute and harness, hypoxia, and twenty other deadly problems. But they were men and they weren't going to back out now.

CHAPTER 20

WE TOOK OFF FOR NORTHERN Spain and the Pyrenees mountain range. I sat facing Paladin. Across the aisle from us were Aleksei and Grizzly. Neither had been in a private jet and amused themselves with the folding tables and the pop-up TV screens. Paladin tried to act like he flew private all the time.

"You must be a big shot at Sabel Security," Paladin said. He waved his hands at the jet's interior.

"I saved Ms. Sabel's life a couple times. She lets me use her old jet when it's not busy on corporate trips."

"How did they know to have the HALO gear ready?"

"I called from the hotel."

"You Sabel guys work with the police all the time."

"Ninety percent of our business is corporate security. The company does work with law enforcement here and there, I've heard. But that's not my thing. I'm on Ms. Sabel's personal security. I fetch sunglasses, pull her out of burning cars, jump in front of bullets, that kind of thing."

"Did you call the cops from the hotel?" he asked.

I squinted. "About what?"

He tossed a subtle glance at Aleksei. I laughed him off.

I said, "I heard Free Origins and Birth Right had a nasty divorce, but you and Arrianne seem to get along fine."

"Free Origins are apologists," Grizzly barked across the aisle at me. He glared at Paladin. "I'm with Birth Right. We give a damn."

"We have a truce for the conference." Paladin held a hand to the man and spoke to me. "An uneasy one."

Aleksei and Grizzly started arguing about their respective gangs. The finer points were lost on me, but the gist was clear. Each thought the other was bent on destroying the human race.

The man with the heavy circle tattoo walked toward the cockpit. He stopped next to me. "Is there a bathroom this way?"

He was definitely the guy who jumped me in Paris. He had the confidence of a man who'd gotten away with it. While he'd worn a ski mask, he forgot I could identify his mark.

"What's your name?" I asked.

"Earl." No codename.

"Second door." I pointed then tapped his wrist. "What does the symbol stand for?"

He leaned in close to my face. "It's the symbol of Fair Heritage, the defenders of roots and ancestry. We gonna put a stop to ethnic fracture and the failure of coexistence." He glanced at Paladin, Aleksei, and Grizzly. "We ain't weak children."

He went to the bathroom.

Mercury stood in the aisle and watched the man. *What in the name of Mars is ethnic fracture?*

I said, *I was going to ask you the same thing. What's the failure of coexistence?*

Mercury said, *Sounds like something you'd say while banging a war drum.*

I said, *Or an excuse for flunking out of high school.*

I turned to Paladin. "More than two organizations at the conference?"

"There are a lot of splinter groups." Paladin looked me over with growing suspicion.

"Fair Heritage is the oldest and largest," Grizzly said. "And the most violent."

Aleksei kicked Grizzly. "Violent. *Mu-dak.* You crazy people to follow woman."

The two started yelling at each other. Paladin shouted at them. "This is a time to come together. A common cause. Mind your manners when you're Jacob Stearne's guest."

Aleksei calmed himself. Grizzly lowered his voice, not his glare.

I turned to Paladin. "You know my real name. What's yours?"

All three of them faced me with serious looks. One question too many.

The pilot gave me the signal. It was time to prepare everyone. A business jet is not a jump plane by any stretch of the imagination. It should only be done if the jet is going down. Which means no one suspects it for covert missions. Which is why we'd mastered the HALO technique. It's come in handy for many special occasions.

When I decided we were prepped and ready, and the cabin depressurized, and the co-pilot told us we had two minutes left before the jump, Paladin huddled his people together in the cargo bay. They put their fists together in the middle. Paladin bellowed, "For Ross Gio!"

The rest answered, "Ross Gio."

And then they were ready.

The copilot checked the first man's oxygen mask, altimeter, and other essential gear, then gave the man the signal. He dove out of the cargo bay door. Then the second. And third.

I asked Paladin, "Who is Ross Gio?"

Grizzly stepped between us and faced me. "You ask a lot of questions for an instructor."

Paladin jumped with a hearty "yahoo!" that disappeared with him. Aleksei went out silently, like a pro. Grizzly followed. I counted the dots falling through the sky, then jumped.

Shortly after stabilizing my fall, I saw Grizzly in a nosedive heading straight for Aleksei. They tangled and fought in the air. Not a smart thing to do at 35,000 feet when you're falling at over 130 miles per hour. I tucked my arms in and turned myself into a missile heading straight for them.

As I neared, Grizzly produced a knife and sliced Aleksei's air hose. The Russian tried to grab the knife. Grizzly tried stabbing the man. I arrived falling ten miles an hour faster than the pair of fighters. As I reached them, I slid my right hand to Grizzly's ripcord and yanked it.

Instantly, the American was hundreds of feet above us with no way to catch up. His descent would take a lot longer than ours. The wind would carry him miles from the landing zone. Where he would wind up was anyone's guess. That didn't bother me in the least.

Aleksei fought to reattach his oxygen hose. What he couldn't see, because it was directly below his chin, was that Grizzly had severed it in the middle. When we take our first breath at extremely high-altitude, which Aleksei would've done before he knew his hose was severed, our bodies immediately react to the lowered pressure and oxygen levels by breathing more rapidly. We hyperventilate. Which burns more oxygen, reduces strength in the muscles, and draws needed energy from the brain. In other words, everything goes downhill fast. Exponentially fast.

Aleksei was a Spetsnaz pro, but with the elevated heart rate that goes with any jump, plus the sliced hose, even the strongest man would black out. He needed another ninety seconds of oxygen.

I maneuvered close to him and pointed to my hose and the break. He understood his problem. Using hand-gestures, I told him my plan. It would involve a lot of turbulence for which he would need to compensate. He nodded.

Then his eyes fluttered. He was beginning to lose consciousness.

I moved quickly to get underneath him and turned around so I could see the hose. I was free-falling backward. Aleksei was struggling to stay with me. The wind buffeted us together, which bounced us apart. Three times, I got in close before I could grab his rig. I held on with one hand and pulled the two pieces of hose together with my other hand. Wrapping my palm around the sliced hose, I bumped foreheads to let him know he could breathe.

Aleksei didn't respond to the first bump. Or the second. Three times worked. He gasped air. It took another minute to get his brain functioning again. When his gaze finally connected with me in a meaningful way, I showed him my altimeter. We were nearing 10,000 feet. The implication being that he could pull his chute and make it the rest of the way without the need for oxygen. He shook his head.

If I was going down to the deck, he was going to the deck. Tough guys don't let proximity to death change their plans.

We stayed connected until we got below five thousand feet. At that point, the oxygen was nice, but not necessary. I let him go.

We gave each other some room. He waved a challenge to be the last man to pull his chute. I waved back that the death race was on.

Mercury nosed between us. *WAAA-HOOOO! Whaddya think, yo? We're gonna win this one. Remember that jump back at the castle in Germany?*

I said, *You mean the one where I almost landed on a gargoyle before opening my chute?*

Mercury said, *I saved your butt that time, you ingrate. Just keep your ear open, and I'll tell you when to release.*

Letting a forgotten immortal guide my modern parachute would be insane.

Base jumpers often open at 100 feet but aren't traveling at the high rate of speed we were. In the military, we stuck with 2,500 feet but often trained as low as 250 feet. Given the stresses already on our rigs, my comfort level was around 2,000 feet.

I pulled my chute at 1,500. Aleksei went sailing down another five hundred.

Mercury said, *I hate that you let him win, man. Sucks.*

I said, *Trying to win friends and influence people. Remember?*

I flared to a perfect stop. The rest floated down hooting and hollering. Paladin was the first guy to catch up to me. He dropped his gear and ran toward me. "HOLY SHIT! That was the most exciting thing I've ever done! You ROCK!"

CHAPTER 21

I RAISED MY SHOT GLASS full of Pacharán, a local form of brandy that can be habit-forming. "To Aleksei, who opened his chute a thousand feet below me!"

Cheers from my guests at the dinner table went up. The guys next to him slapped his back. He grinned from ear to ear. We downed our drinks. Laughter filled the banquet room at Oriza in Seville at sunset. The staff swept away the remnants of my tuna loin dinner.

Aleksei staggered to his feet and rambled through a toast for me in Russian. When he said, *"Za zhenshchin!"* A common Russian toast, *to the women!* He downed a shot of vodka. The rest of us followed with Pacharán. Aleksei started another toast when the man next to him pulled his arm down and got him back in his chair.

Earl—a Fair Heritage member and the guy who attacked me outside the Junkyard—teased Aleksei and the Free Origins men for getting drunk. His banter sounded less threatening than Grizzly's attack.

Mercury appeared in his formal toga with red edging. *You gotta nice big bromance going down tonight, homie. Spending money like a Caesar and drinking like a hound-dawg. Now it's time to ask them questions. Get us some intel.*

I said, *Think they're drunk enough? They were suspicious last time.*

Mercury said, *You ask too many questions, they kill you. No big deal. Zack Ames can find a third informant.*

A waiter brought a chair and squeezed it into the corner of the table between Paladin and me. We looked up as Arrianne entered with that supermodel walk of hers. Her dark curls formed the perfect backdrop for sparkly diamond earrings and equally glittery necklace. Her backless dress must have been sewn on. It clung in all the right places and stretched in all the others. Or was it the other way around? Teasing wafts of lilacs scented the air around her.

The table noise dropped into the background while my brain conjured up Chris Isaak singing "Wicked Game." It was indeed a wicked game she was playing. I didn't want to fall in love—and I wasn't going to. I took a deep breath, rose, and took the hand she offered. Paladin held her chair. She seated herself like a princess.

"You would not believe the rush," Paladin started in.

He explained the afternoon's adventure in excruciating detail and boundless enthusiasm. Arrianne laughed at the appropriate places but never took her eyes off me.

"It was mean of you—" Arrianne interrupted Paladin "—to leave Caleb in the Pyrenees."

"He tried to kill Aleksei," I said after recalling Grizzly's real name. "Attempted murder tends to wear out your welcome on my expeditions."

"For if you forgive others for their trespasses, your heavenly Father will also forgive you." She watched my eyes. "Matthew 6:14. While you're still my hero, Jacob, Caleb is an important part of the Birth Right movement. He's important to me."

I nodded slowly and held her gaze. "Then he can ride with you."

"You left him at the other end of the country."

"And not by accident." I tried not to lose my temper. "I should've turned him over to the police."

She leaned back and considered me.

Paladin sensed the tension and turned his attention elsewhere. Another toast went up.

Arrianne and I remained locked in our staring contest. I said, "Why are you so keen to have a murderer on your team?"

"Why did you date a murderer?" She leaned forward and squeezed her breasts between her arms, presenting some impressive cleavage. "That tabloid didn't paint a flattering picture of your girl."

I leaned back and poured two glasses of Pacharán. I handed one to Arrianne. "The man who raped Jenny got off on a technicality and came back for a second round. She shot him through the eye. Tell me something, Arrianne, in the same situation, would you have done what Jesus commanded you to do—forgive your rapist?"

She lost the staring contest to avoid answering. We sipped our drinks and breathed. Already squeezed awkwardly at the corner of the table between Paladin and me, she scooted in a notch. In the tight positioning of chairs, her knees went between mine. She let her left leg brush the inside of my knee. Jenny's memory began to fade. I took a deep breath.

Mercury leaned between us with a towel draped over one arm and carrying a silver tray full of dog shit on toast. *She's giving you the whole show, dawg. Can you keep your eyes on hers? Or will you sneak a peek at the goods?*

I said, *I won't fall for it.*

Mercury said, *If you show her a good time tonight, you can reap the rewards of pillow talk.*

I said, *She's trying to get something out of me. She's not foolish enough to climb in bed for it.*

Mercury said, *Desire makes people foolish. She desires you—that foolish girl.*

I said, *And I desire Jenny. No one gets what they want.*

Jenny's words floated through my brain like a torch song. *Don't wait for me, Jacob. I'm not playing a game here. I don't want to be pursued.*

Arrianne took a long time composing her next topic. When she was ready, she ran a fingernail down my forearm. "Birth Right is not made up of the kind of people who ride around in private jets. My parents raised us in the gig economy. Dad was an accountant. He was replaced. Now he drives for Uber and cleans offices. Mom's job went to Shanghai, and she went to the pills. Overdosed." Arrianne grabbed my wrist. "We're being invaded. We're being replaced. I won't stand by and let my people be slaughtered. I have a plan, and Caleb is part of it. I need you to find him and bring him back."

"Caleb tried to stab a man in the back at 35,000 feet. If he shows up for training tomorrow, Aleksei will gut him." I took her hand off my wrist. "I'll side with Aleksei."

"Caleb won't be there. His team has been training for the last three days so they could get ahead of schedule. We're leaving tomorrow afternoon for a business trip."

That took me by surprise as much as it did Mercury. My personal god said, *That means they were the ones who made all the markings about London. If they leave early tomorrow, where will they be going, bro? Betcha a thousand aurei they be going to what Londoners call the Square Mile.*

I said, *I'm not taking that bet. How can I find out?*

Mercury said, *You have a way.*

I said, *I'm not sleeping with her.*

Mercury rolled his eyes. *I get it, bro, you're saving yourself for the return of Saint Jenny—or the next Ice Age. You have other ways that will suit your Victorian morals and get the info you need.*

I said, *You're right. I need to get word to Miguel and Tania. Their directional mics won't pick up this conversation. How the hell am I going to call them?*

Mercury tapped my forehead with one finger. *Think. I know that's hard for you, homie, but you can do it if you try.*

"Where are you going?" I asked Arrianne.

She smiled and leaned in close enough for a kiss. Almost. "I have a business trip. I have to pay for my fashion habit, you know. I need my people—especially Caleb—with me." Her warm breath smelled fresh despite the booze. "We'll be back in two days. You must help me get Caleb back here before our flight out of Seville leaves. It's not a big airport. They don't have flights every day. You took him north; don't you feel responsible for bringing him back?"

She stroked my cheek with her fingertips. Several of the guys at the table stopped talking. They watched us. Aleksei said something in Russian then translated it, "Get a room!"

Everyone laughed. Paladin looked at us, saw everyone staring, then proposed a toast to distract the others.

"You really are my hero, you know." She ran her fingertips down my neck. "You were so brave in Saint-Sulpice. I've never met a man with the courage to take on two heavily armed men—and defeat them. That kind of selfless valor makes me ..."

She closed her eyes and inhaled.

"I had the impression those men in Paris were connected to Birth

Right." I watched her shock and gauged her reaction. "Weren't they friends of yours?"

"Not mine." She shook her head too much. Her eyes darted around while she thought up what to say next. "If they were members of Free Origins or Fair Heritage, I would be surprised. That's why we brought you in. We need someone who can help us get rid of the worst elements."

Satisfied with her answer, she gave me the big eyes again. "How am I going to get my team together for our trip?"

I raised her chin with my knuckle. "Well. You know. I guess I could help you. Do you know where Caleb is now?"

"A town called Manresa."

"Rent him a car, have him meet us in Seville."

She pulled back a little. "That would take all day. He'd miss our flight. Our reservations are for two PM. How does that help?"

I stroked her cheek with my fingertips and ran them down her shoulder. She smiled and purred. I said, "You're too beautiful to fly commercial. We'll fly straight there, no security lines, no need to change planes. After tomorrow's training session, I'll take you anywhere you want. Within reason."

Arrianne's eyes perked up when I called her beautiful. Then her shoulders sank.

"Uhm." She looked out the window at the traffic passing in the night while she composed her reply. "That would be too much to ask."

"No problem. The company jet's at my disposal for another day. May as well put it to good use. One-way, though. They told me they have to ferry some company execs around the next couple days."

"Oh, that's so nice of you." Her voice didn't match her words. She sounded worried. "Does your company have ties to any government agencies?"

"Very little. Most governments are hardly fans of Sabel Security. They think we're vigilantes." I whispered, "We show them up too often."

"You are indeed a man of action, in so many ways. I wish there were a way I could express my gratitude."

She let her hand trail down my chest and leg. I felt my nerve endings rise to attention at her touch. I winked at her. Jenny started to recede into the mist.

CHAPTER 22

A HUMAN PRESENCE AT THE side of my bed woke me. My eyes focused on an intense face staring down at me. I ran my fingers through my hair. "What's up, Nema?"

"You protected me from Lugh. I appreciate that." She looked at her hands, folded in front of her. "You were too harsh. He didn't do anything to deserve that."

"Not at that moment, and not because of how he treated you, but bullies like that will go much further in the future until they encounter resistance. My sister had a boyfriend who ... What are you doing here?"

"I need help." She turned away. "There are 942 people arriving for the conference this morning. Eight hundred twelve of them are men. Like you, a good number of them think the wrong thing about me. They assume I'm gay if I don't flirt with them. If I don't wear sexy dresses or makeup. And they don't like homosexuals."

I tossed back the covers, sat up, and checked out her plaid flannel shirt over jeans and Doc Martens. If she was going with the I'm-not-gay story, her fashion choices weren't helping. But, not my problem. There was a deep bitterness in her voice, one that had a bigger story behind it. Maybe I did have her all wrong. I asked, "Your brother protected you in the past?"

"How do you know I had a brother?"

It dawned on me that I'd learned her family story from Miguel. "You mentioned him at the Moulin Rouge."

"Oh." A skeptical expression squished her eyes together. "He hasn't been around lately."

She turned away while I pulled on a pair of jeans and a t-shirt that read, "All you need is love—All I need is ammo."

I said, "You came here because you want something. What is it?"

"Well, I shouldn't. I don't want to come between you and Gospeler."

"Arrianne and I aren't a thing."

She spun to scowl at me. "She left here pretty late last night."

Mercury leaned over her shoulder. *You finally seduced Arrianne, bro? Dayam. You were getting downright salty after going a whole four days without getting any. And now you've got our little pixie Nema stalking you? Dawg! Are you gonna double dip?*

I said, *Even together, they don't add up to Jenny.*

Facing Nema, I said, "I don't know when she left the hotel, but she didn't come to my room. To be honest, she's pretty damn persuasive. It was all I could do to use my big brain, but I'm still not in the market for a new girlfriend. And I don't like being stalked. Nor do I like having a creepy woman staring at me while I sleep. Whatever's going on between you two, don't put me in the middle of it."

She started for the door.

It took me a minute to realize what she was asking.

"Wait," I said. "You want me to be your guy so the others won't harass you? What do they call that, the beard?"

"You'll do it? Thank you." She ran to me, folded her hands under her chin, tucked her elbows to her ribs, and laid her cheek on my chest. The perfect package for wrapping my arms around. Which I did slowly. She said, "You understand me."

As much as I loathed hugging a racist, she was warm and smelled good. And she had a tremble of fear that vibrated in her skin. The girl had some scars. We'd been through a bombing together. I couldn't turn down her request. I held her for a long time. Something about the hug felt right. She'd made an effective appeal for my natural drive to protect others.

At the same time, it felt terribly wrong. She radiated hate. It came off her in endless waves like lava from a volcano.

While holding her, I noticed the hotel's room phone had been removed. Paladin didn't want me calling ahead to my flight crew anymore.

DEATH AND CONSPIRACY

She told me Paladin had sent her to collect me. We drove out to the Ooze.

A crowd waited for me at the training grounds. When we stepped out of the car, Nema put on an act that could've won her an Oscar. She threw her arms around my neck, puckered up, and planted one square on my lips.

She whispered into my ear, "Be sure to teach them all that stuff about how to identify terrorists. That's the most important part. We want to know what you look for."

Mercury said, *You have an alternate list of terrorist-identifiers ready, homie?*

I said, *I'm only telling them irrelevant stuff. The terrorists you see in movies with the mean eyes and facial scars.*

Then Nema smiled like she'd won the Spanish lottery, glanced over her shoulder at my would-be students, the Sixty-Four, and skipped up to Arrianne's house, adding a couple spins with cutesy waves to me as she went.

Mercury watched her dance up the hill. *Dude, have you ever considered dating someone who isn't a total psycho? I mean, let's examine the evidence here starting two girlfriends back. Sylvia's in jail for a multimillion-euro art fraud; Jenny's a murderess who thinks you're not good enough for her; Arrianne would do you in the street—and who do you hook up with? A gay girl. My divine opinion? It's not them—it's you. You're a whack-job-magnet.*

I said, *Can we work on your motivational speeches? I'm thinking there's room for improvement.*

I faced the assembled men waiting for me to offer my tips on how to kill people. The Sixty-Four were sixty-three, being short one Caleb, aka Grizzly. When I walked over, Aleksei slapped my back hard enough to knock me into the coffee buffet. I grabbed a large coffee urn to keep it from falling over. He said something in Russian that included Arrianne and Nema's names. Before I could right myself, he slapped my back again. Everyone laughed.

Lugh stood at the edge of the group, a scowl on his face and a coffee mug extended from his sling. Paladin stood next to him, shining his

131

megawatt smile my way. He gave me a wink and thumbs up.

Nema won that round.

On the hill above us, Arrianne watched with binoculars. Nema appeared at her side. It was hard to tell at that distance, but it did not look like they spoke to each other. Something about their casual attitude tugged at the back of my brain.

Mercury said, *Exactly what I was thinking, homeboy. You're not the kinda guy women fight over—unless it's which one has to dump you on the curb for trash-day—but shouldn't those two be sniping at each other right now? Whazzup with that?*

CHAPTER 23

THE MEN WAITED FOR MY words of wisdom at the edge of the Ooze. I started by explaining the training scenarios. I broke them into four main groups containing three teams each. Each team was designated hostage, terrorist, or rescue. They would alternate positions through the sessions so they could see what a rescue scenario looked like from each point of view. I then laid out how we would conduct each raid and rescue. Each terrorist team would be allowed to arrange their defensive positions and hostages as they saw fit.

They moaned when I told them to grab the low-velocity paintball guns.

They wanted live ammo. In a training session.

We started with the first set of Paladin's sketches. I placed teams in Paladin's scenario, then walked everyone through a hostage-rescue in slow motion. I moved each player into position, showed them how to cover each other, how to cause a diversion, and the importance of synchronized movements. They weren't attentive. They kept moving out of position as if the hostages were the targets and not the terrorists guarding them. Actions that confirmed Zack Ames's theories about the conference.

The town had space to run three scenarios simultaneously. I assigned Lugh, Aleksei, and Paladin to each group as observers. I would observe them all. Everyone wore butcher-paper ponchos for the paint. Observers wore white sashes for easy identification. The penalty for painting one of the observers was sitting out the round. We sent them to take positions. I let Paladin have the honor of sounding the air horn to begin.

As soon as the blast set things in motion, their offensive intent was obvious. Instead of doing what I'd told them, they surprised the guards from behind, forcing those guards to shoot over the heads of the hostages. The morning progressed like this until the participants were pretty good at forcing the guards to kill each other and the hostages. Their mistakes were purposeful. They intended to maximize fear and confusion.

Mercury walked among the bodies covered in paint. *Life is strange, right brutha? One day you're in the US Army, getting medals for defending your country. The next, you're teaching a bunch of terrorists how to kill people with new and innovative ideas. Your mom will be proud.*

I said, *How in the name of Minerva am I supposed to figure out what they're planning from these scenarios?*

Mercury pointed to the lane that led out of the village. *Have you checked out Saint Paul's lately?*

I crossed to where the graffiti had been a couple days before. It had been painted over in tan and bore a new designation in red lettering. Now it read, "Temple Sholom." A synagogue name as ubiquitous as Saint Paul's. The arrow previously pointing out of town now pointed into town, directly at one of the hostage sites. I walked in the direction of the arrow and found another label painted at the base of a wall. It read, "Masjid Abu Bakar." Its arrow pointed in the direction of the second hostage site.

I said, *Masjid, sounds familiar. Seems like I've seen that in Singapore or Indonesia.*

Mercury looked at it. *Means Burning Ash Mosque in Malay. You gotta get word to Miguel and Tania about this. They came in the night to check this stuff out, but this was painted fresh this morning.*

I said, *I'll see them when we take the jet to wherever Arrianne is going.*

Mercury said, *Paladin and Lugh don't seem to care that you can see this stuff. Yet Arrianne said they don't trust you. How does that square up?*

I said, *And they aren't paying attention to what I tell them. They aren't interested in my help as an instructor.*

Mercury said, *You know what that means, homie? They plan to keep you off the streets and kill you as soon as eight hundred witnesses have left IDC.*

I said, *About those motivational speeches ...*

The men laughed and fired like they'd rediscovered childhood. The training session broke down into chaos. I strolled through the town. I came across another graffiti marking. It read, "Duomo di Milano" with an arrow pointing to the right. Below it, "Synagoga Centrale" with an arrow pointing left. Another arrow pointed straight ahead and read, "COREIS."

The sites listed were in different languages, indicating different cities. Were they working out which site was the easiest to hit? Or ranking them for body-count? The most likely scenario seemed to be they were picking the target with the most impact and keeping track of alternates. If Zack Ames was right about these guys, they were evil in every regard.

Without warning, the men poured out of the buildings into the streets and plastered me with paintballs. It was hilarious. For them.

When we broke for lunch, Nema had fresh clothes ready for me. She played the dutiful girlfriend and bitched out the Sixty-Four in English and French. They laughed at her. She took it well, then retreated to the observation deck.

While we ate, Paladin and Lugh disappeared. I followed them down the cobblestone lanes and watched them spray painting over the old graffiti and laying down new directions.

I went to one of the higher points in the village to get a better look at their work. At the top, in a spot not used in any of our previous scenarios was a freshly painted circle with one word in it, "ROSGEO."

Mercury stood next to me. *Dude, Ross Gio is ROSGEO, it's not a name. What is it, a location? A place? An abbreviation?*

I said, *They're looking at a lot of places. Zack Ames said they were planning something like Christchurch or Sri Lanka. I'm thinking this is bigger. Duomo is Italian for cathedral. We saw Malay and English. It could be anywhere in the world.*

Mercury said, *Maybe you were a little hasty treating the CIA agent so badly.*

We looked at each other and cracked up.

I said, *Seriously though. They're suspicious when I ask questions. At least we know how ROSGEO is spelled, but how am I going to figure out what it means? Is ROSGEO a person, place or thing? Which group is involved, Free Origins, Birth Right, or Fair Heritage? And who's in charge?*

I scratched my head. Arrianne planned to leave town this evening. She would be gone a couple days. Nema had stepped in this morning, playing on my instinct to protect her. They tag-teamed me. They made sure I couldn't contact anyone.

I said, *Does that mean they know I'm working with Hugo and Ames?*

Mercury said, *I can't read their minds, but they aren't paying attention to your lesson plans. Which means, you're already an ex-disciple. A disciple who has gone on to his great reward. You will soon be deceased, passed on, resting in peace, pushing up daisies, shuffling off your mortal coil—*

Yeah. I patted his shoulder. *Thanks.*

I had a stroke of genius for the afternoon session. I limited the participants to three paintballs each. That slowed the mayhem and prevented them from reverting to sixth-grade boys. It also allowed me to walk the streets to inventory the markings.

At day's end, I walked up the hill to Arrianne's with Paladin, Aleksei, and Lugh. Nema met me at the door and gave me a peck on the cheek.

I delivered a report I hoped would keep me alive for another day or two. "Your Sixty-Four suck at pretty much everything. If they ever find themselves in a life-and-death situation, they'll fail miserably. If they're going to free hostages from real terrorists, they'll die in short order. I doubt they could save anyone."

"You were unarmed," Nema said. "Yet you took down two men with automatic weapons. What makes you so different from them?"

For a moment, I considered telling them that the real problem was Paladin. He only gave praise, never criticism. While it's pleasant, a real leader knows no one is perfect. Nor does anyone under his command expect to be perfect. Without constructive criticism, people are inherently distrustful of the leader. They have a subconscious fear he's not telling them everything. But I didn't want them to improve their management. I wanted to deliver as little help as possible in case I died before they launched their evil plan.

"First, I take it seriously. Second, watch him." I pointed to Aleksei with one hand. With the other, I pulled a table knife stolen at lunch from my pocket. While they were misdirected, I pressed the knife hard against Paladin's jugular. It took a couple seconds before they figured out they were looking in the wrong direction. Everyone except Aleksei jumped and gasped.

"Difference is knowing danger in the heart." Aleksei grinned and fisted his chest. "I not flinch because he not danger to Paladin. Butter knife. Not sharp. Can see this in instant. Quick eyes learned behavior from many live-fire situations. Jacob is right. Men think is game."

"They're your people," I said. "Talk to them tonight. Get them serious about it."

I turned to Arrianne. "Are you ready to go?"

Nema's eyes bounced between us. She screeched, "You two are going together?"

CHAPTER 24

"WE GOT UNDER NEMA'S SKIN, didn't we?" Arrianne shoulder-nudged me as we crossed to Sabel Three in the hangar at the Seville airport. She wore a business dress made from a uniquely stretchy material. While it covered everything from her shoulders to just above her knees, the geometric lines strained around her curves. When I didn't answer, she said, "Don't you want to plant your seed in fertile soil?"

I kept my gaze on the concrete. "'Let us live honorably as in the day, not in reveling and drunkenness, not in debauchery and licentiousness, not in quarreling and jealousy.' Romans 13:13."

She shot a dark glance my way, then raised her chin.

Mercury said, *Dude, keep it up, and you're gonna be seeing the fury of a woman scorned.*

I said, *Most women will bat their eyelashes a couple times, and if that doesn't work, they'll announce sour grapes and trash your rep. Yet she keeps coming back for more.*

Mercury said, *If you're right and they're planning to kill you, she's either gonna be an ally or an enemy. You need to figure that shit out.*

At the far end of the hangar, Miguel pretended to work on something. Tania kept a low profile on the other side. A real executive jet service representative from the Seville operations center greeted me. Two others put the luggage in the cargo hold.

Grizzly-Caleb had rented a car and driven across Spain in time to join us. I was dying to get a few words with my team. Arrianne had confirmed her destination as London, but with her right-hand man now tagging along a step behind Arrianne, I couldn't risk it. He had seen them both on the last outing when they appeared to be skydiving outfitters.

I signed off on the services performed while Caleb watched over one shoulder and Arrianne over the other. I stopped just before signing and looked at one, then the other. They weren't intimidated. I signed.

Arrianne went aboard first. I followed. Caleb crowded behind me. I leaned into the cockpit to say hello to the crew. With any luck, I could relay instructions to get London cops to meet us on landing.

Arrianne craned around me to get a look at the pilots while her team of eleven filed into the back.

In the tight confines, I elbowed her. "Oh, sorry. I didn't see you there."

"Can I have a look?"

"Sure, but don't cross the threshold. You shouldn't crowd the pilots."

I squeezed past her. She had effectively silenced my communications. Were they on to me for something specific? Was it the general paranoia Arrianne told me about when we first met? Whatever it was, it soured my mood.

Grizzly-Caleb sat in the forward chair. I said, "That's my chair. Out."

"I like it." He smirked and pushed the button and tilted back.

I grabbed a fistful of his shirt and yanked him to standing. "My seat. If the pilots have a question or need information, I don't want them searching for me in your crabs-in-a-barrel crowd."

He yanked free of my hand and nosed up to me. "You think you're real tough, don't you, Stearne?"

"All modesty aside, yes I do." I punched him in the gut, spun him around and gripped him in a headlock. "When I flex my forearm, your windpipe gets cut off like this." I flexed. He choked. "When I unflex it, you can breathe. Like this, see?" I unflexed. He gasped for air. "Before you ask a stupid question, ask yourself if you need to piss off a guy whose picture hangs in the Ranger Hall of Fame."

I kneed him in the butt and shoved him face down in the aisle at the feet of his men.

He pushed up, blood rushing to his face, ready for a fight. Then he thought better of it. "I'll get you, motherfucker. I'll get you from behind like you did Diego."

"Hey, now." Arrianne tugged my arm. "Was that necessary?"

140

I resisted her pull. "Yes, it was."

Zack Ames figured only one of the three groups pursued a violent solution to their perceived problems. That group had to be Arrianne's Birth Right people. They were the ones going to London. So why were Lugh and Paladin spray painting what had to be targets on the walls and curbs of the town? Maybe they were fantasizing. Maybe they were competing. There had to be more going on than London.

To keep my eye on Paladin, I would drop her off, contact the local authorities, explain things without getting caught in a bureaucratic interrogation, and get back to Úbeda before dawn. No problem. Especially the part about walking into the offices of the London Counter Terrorism Command to say, "I just popped in to drop off twelve terrorists, but I must run. Good luck stopping them. Cheers!"

If I didn't get back to Úbeda and the British caught Arrianne, it would hit the news. As soon as they saw it, Lugh and company would know it was me who turned in their friends. Even if they disagreed on fundamental approaches, they wouldn't take kindly to a snitch in their midst.

I needed a lot more information.

I turned to Arrianne, who'd taken the seat across the aisle. "You said a couple things I didn't understand last night. What did you mean your dad was replaced?"

"He was an accountant." She narrowed her eyes and dropped her voice. "They hired a Jew to replace him."

Mercury leaned over her head. *The fact that her dad drank a bottle of gin every night had nothing to do with it. His mistakes were just rounding errors of ten to twenty percent.*

"I'm sorry to hear that. And your mother, what did you say about her?"

"Her company brought in a new VP who outsourced their production to China. She was depressed and fell down a flight of stairs. A Pakistani doctor got her hooked on Hydrocodone. He kept telling her to take more and more. But the Negro pharmacist wouldn't fill her prescriptions. Claimed they were forged. She had to go to the street to find pain medications."

Mercury started to say something. I cut him off. *Yeah. I figured that one out without a heavenly message.*

"And that's why you feel your people are being slaughtered?" I asked.

"Damn straight." Flames in her dark eyes. "Don't you see it? Our kind are endangered. There's an invasion going on. You can't stop them. Our people are shoved to the back of the bus. Our people are the ones being fed opioids. They're trying to make us look like the problem so they can replace us."

Mercury said, *I haven't heard that logic since the Spanish Inquisition. The Spanish claimed the Moors and the Jews were taking everything away from Christians, so they tortured them for heresy and next thing you know, the Christians owned all the land. Wasn't that convenient?*

That was all I could take for one sitting. But Arrianne kept going. My eyes glazed over and my mind wandered while I listened for any reference to ROSGEO or some of the other places like Duomo di Milano or Masjid Abu Bakar. She wasn't giving those up. She was on a long, pointless rant about who forced her mom to become a junkie. I felt sorry for her on a human level but still wondered what she had planned in London.

When we landed, we dropped Arrianne and the Birth Right crowd at the main terminal. I went to the cargo hold and tossed their bags down to them. I double-checked my estimate of their weight and scent. I'm not a bomb-sniffing dog, but no obvious signs of weapons stood out. I waved goodbye. Arrianne thanked me for the ride and blew me a kiss. I watched them walk across the apron in the gathering gloom of a drizzling sunset.

Mercury helped me close the cargo door. *You know what you gotta do, homie. It's time to suck it up and make that call.*

I said, *I can't call the cops without my phone. Besides, which one of the fifty police divisions in the UK would take me seriously?*

Mercury said, *Use the pilot's phone. You're changing flight crews here in London anyway. And, don't play dumb—you know who you have to call.*

I said, *I'm not calling him.*

Mercury said, *You got to, bro. Put all your issues aside and call him.*

I plodded forward like a condemned man. The pilot handed me his phone. I dialed.

The man I didn't want to call answered.

"Jacob, is that you?" Zack Ames asked. "We've been waiting for this call. Do not get out of the jet. Have your pilots taxi to hangar 7A. Hugo is there with a team from SO15. Your people kept us informed about the targets. We've been waiting an hour for you. You better have a damn good idea of what they're going to attack."

"Actually, I don't have a handle on what—"

"After all the shit you put me through, you're telling me you just popped in to drop off twelve terrorists?"

CHAPTER 25

THREE TRUCKS FILLED WITH HEAVILY armed SWAT team members waited for me in the designated hangar. It turned out, SO15 is shorthand for London's Counter Terrorism Command. They were assigned by the National Counter Terrorism Policing Network after Miguel and Tania first made the connection between the markings in the Ooze and the streets in the Financial District. My people kept SO15 informed right up to the minute my jet left Seville. Lots of people got involved. MI6 and MI5, not to mention Lieutenant Colonel Hugo and his sidekick, Zack Ames. They all waited to take credit for my undercover work.

We traveled in support vehicles to the City of London, sometimes called the Square Mile. It's the historic town, well inside the metropolitan area, originally settled by the Romans. SO15 set up the command center for the brass near the remnants of an ancient Roman fort. Hugo, Zack, and I observed from a separate "guest" van with audio and video feeds from the SWAT teams.

Mercury wandered around outside, beside himself that the local Christians couldn't be bothered to maintain a perfectly good military position for a few thousand years. *It was made out of brick when the Angles were still living in mud huts. They could've replaced the bricks, shored up the walls. See, young blood? This is why Christianity is hopeless. Lazy-ass mofos.*

The team leader informed us over the video link that Arrianne had procured three rental cars for her team. MI5 used a six-car surveillance team, which was an impressive expenditure of personnel and resources. They weren't messing around. A helicopter took over at certain points to make sure the tail went undetected. They augmented with CCTV in places. They followed Arrianne straight to the financial district. They were confident she had no idea they were watching her.

The London Stock Exchange takes up a city block between Rose Street and Queens Head Passage, two of the markings back at the Ooze. Arrianne took the next street over, Warwick Lane. Saint Paul's Cathedral, and its round-the-clock security, was three hundred feet away, but around a corner and out of visual range. The markings from the Ooze began to add up.

It was night, after hours for stockbrokers, the place was deserted. Arrianne's crew passed Amen Court and parked illegally next to a chrome sculpture. A large truck met them there. Three men got out, handed off bags heavy enough to make them stagger when they walked. Arrianne and her crew, having changed into black ninja-outfits, hoisted the bags and jogged across the street. The men who'd met them took their rental cars and left the scene. MI5's surveillance team dispatched a car to tail the rapidly disappearing rental cars.

Mercury banged on the window of my van. *You need to get back to Spain, homie.*

I said, *I want to see this through. Whatever's going down will take an hour. I've got plenty of time.*

Mercury said, *No you don't. What you think is happening is not really happening. Something else is going on.*

I said, *What do you mean? What's going on?*

Mercury said, *I don't know.*

I said, *What kind of messenger brings a message saying, 'I dunno?'*

Mercury said, *Hey, it's not easy being a divinity. You want to try it sometime? All you get are complaints. People go to temples and churches and get down on their knees—to whine. Do they give thanks for the cancer we let them beat? No. They whine about the weather. They whine about their son's car accident. They whine ...*

Movement on the monitor grabbed my attention. The surveillance team had lost Arrianne and the Birth Righters when they entered an office building. It appeared to be a standard office building with a few international consulting firms. No obvious targets. The cameraman reacquired Arrianne's crew on the roof. The Birth Righters were laying out rappelling lines and setting up jump points.

They wasted no time. Right after they tested the anchors, they walked down the glass face of the office building. Two people stayed on the roof. The rest dropped down three stories, leveling out at the fourth floor. They pulled out glass-breaking hammers and smashed their way through the five-foot-tall, hurricane-proof glass. After clearing four windows, they went inside.

A helicopter splashed daylight on Arrianne and another man on the roof. Two SWAT teams ran from the street into the building. Two more teams rappelled from choppers hovering overhead. Arrianne was easily identifiable by the dark curls pouring out from under her balaclava. When the SWAT team reached them, they pulled the mask off the man next to her. No surprise, Grizzly-Caleb.

The MI5 commander started barking orders over the comms. "Stand down. Do not breach. Again. Stand down."

The SO15 commander responded. "Too late, suspects in custody."

"Bloody hell," the MI5 man said. "This has gone pear-shaped."

A series of cars flew by outside the van. I slid the door open and caught the flash of blue emergency lights as the last one screamed past. It had a crown on it and the initials NCA.

I closed the door and turned to Hugo. "Who are they?"

"National Chaos Agency." He rolled his eyes. "*Anglais typique.*"

From the other side of him, Ames said, "Crime. National Crime Agency. What the hell did you get us into, Stearne?"

On the monitors, the NCA cars pulled to a stop in front of the building. The SWAT people emerged from the building with Arrianne and her crew. The two factions of officials faced off. The sound stopped.

Hugo fiddled with the volume knobs. "They cut the comm."

Ames leaned around the Frenchman. "You know what that means, Stearne?"

"They're talking about us."

I turned to Mercury. *What in Avernus is going on here?*

"That." Ames pointed at the monitor. "What's Avernus?"

"A volcano believed to be the mouth of hell."

Arrianne's balaclava was off, her pretty face in full view. A man stood behind her, removing her handcuffs. When he had them off, he shoved her and Grizzly-Caleb toward the NCA people. They were escorted to a minibus and got in back. The minibus drove up the street toward us.

I reached for the door handle, ready to slide it open and jump the bastards when they drove by. Hugo grabbed my arm with an iron grip. I looked at him, surprised.

"You are the friend of France, oui?" he asked.

"Uh, yeah."

"Then, with the British, we must be friends. Difficult as they make it."

I relaxed my reach and watched the screen for clues.

MI-6, MI-5, and SO15 were being sidelined by the NCA. How could that happen? I didn't know much about British internal politics, but that had to mean Arrianne meant something to them that I hadn't figured out. Worse, she hadn't been on a terrorist mission. Did she break into an office on behalf of the NCA? Not while heavily armed in a country that banned personal weapons. She couldn't be working undercover at IDC because the MI divisions would've known about it. And they were not aware of Arrianne's value to the NCA.

Whatever happened, I had orchestrated a very large, expensive, and high-profile operation. One that would be a stain on many careers throughout the UK. Not to mention a big embarrassment for Hugo and Ames.

The sound came back on. The MI5 commander shouted, "Bring me that bloody American tosser!"

CHAPTER 26

I DIDN'T GET BACK TO the hotel in Úbeda until five in the morning. Twenty-two hours without sleep, and my brain still churned through my expulsion from London.

They'd dragged me into their mobile command center where the ranking officer from MI-6 was yelling at the ranking officer from MI-5. Who then yelled at the ranking officer of SO15, who yelled at the MI-6 guy. It devolved into a shouting match joined by the junior officers. Hugo held up a hand. They all got quiet. Hugo lowered his hand. Then he pointed at me. Their collective gazes followed. Hugo said, *"Américain stupide,"* which needed no translation. They had their scape goat.

SO15's commander yanked me by the collar, tossed me out of the trailer, and told me to walk home.

Ames followed me for five yards while giving me his estimation of my critical thinking skills. A statement excessively punctuated with f-bombs.

The conference filled the town with rednecks from all over the world. They got drunk every night and slept late. On my return, everything had changed. In the predawn darkness, the streets teamed with attendees, sober, armed, and focused.

Stumbling out of the Uber, I climbed the hotel steps and nodded at the bellman as I crossed the lobby.

Mercury kept pace with me. *How they expect you to know Arrianne was working for the NCA? It looked like a mass shooting, it walked like a mass shooting, it smelled like a mass shooting—it coulda been a mass shooting. Holy Apollo, they don't deserve you.*

I said, *You're getting better on the inspirational stuff. Thanks.*

Mercury said, *Course, if you were Roman, you would've had the decency to fall on your sword for the screwup.*

I said, *Do you and the Dii Consentes ever wonder why Christianity spread through Rome like wildfire?*

Mercury said, *Miguel told you Arrianne and her people had no digital past. Not even from childhood.*

I said, *As if they were government informants. But what kind of informant does the NCA have? And how could they pull rank on counterterrorism? Birth Righters smashed windows in an office building.*

Mercury said, *Your first two points are good ones, but the last bit about broken windows, that doesn't sound like terrorism. Maybe they were doing something else.*

I said, *Like what?*

The Roman god of eloquence shrugged.

I opened the door to my room and flipped on the lights. Something in my bed wriggled under the covers.

Nema sat up wearing one of my t-shirts. "Where've you been?"

"You're in my bed."

"The guys were talking. Saying things." She hid her face in her shoulder. "Where have you been all this time? Arrianne was arrested an hour after you dropped her in London."

I tossed my jacket on the chair. "Arrested? What for?"

"Where were you?"

"Waiting for a hydraulic pressure sensor replacement on the apron. Not a stocked item at Heathrow. Had to send a pilot to Biggin Hill Airport."

She squinted at me. Confusion. Perfect.

"Why are you in my bed?" I asked.

"I wasn't going to sleep in the chair again." Her eyes got big and wet. "And some of those creeps followed me around. I couldn't go to my room alone. I got scared."

I sat on the edge of the bed and pulled off my boots. "What did Arrianne do that got her arrested?"

"She didn't say. Paladin wired her money for a lawyer. She didn't have time to explain it."

I was beat. I needed to rack out. I wasn't going to sleep in my jeans. But Nema wasn't getting out. The bed was a queen with plenty of room. I kept my boxers on. She could deal with it or go home.

She pulled the covers up to her neck and watched me. The tattoo on her neck peeked out from under her hair again. Crossed keys.

"What's the tattoo about?" I asked.

"Ancestors. The town my grandfather came from. We used to be tight." She turned away to make me drop the topic.

She started texting someone on her phone using her index finger like my grandmother. She caught me watching her and fumbled the phone into the covers. She reached for it like a lightning strike. Sensing me watching her, she snapped, "I'm not good with tech. Chuck does that stuff."

"Who's Chuck?"

"A guy back in the States. Never mind." She blanked her phone screen and hugged her knees again.

I turned out the light and faced away from her.

Without reason, my mind recalled an image of Jenny from a week ago. We'd just had a two-hour sex romp. She stared out the window and whispered to herself, "There should be more." A warning sign missed. As I lay there thinking about that, another memory surfaced. Jenny looked at her phone as it rang. She sent it to voicemail. When I asked who she was ignoring, she said, "I feel so isolated sometimes." On top of that, she flinched every time I touched her unexpectedly. Not a normal flinch of surprise, but a defensive flinch. She flipped out at loud noises. Sometimes, friends of mine would duck under the counter if you slapped a plate on the table too hard, but those guys had just gotten back from days-long firefights.

I craned over my shoulder to check on my uninvited guest. Nema remained sitting up, with the covers still pulled tight. I had the sense she was staring at me. I wasn't going to respond to unspoken communication. If she wanted something, she knew where the door was.

Jenny once told me she didn't want to talk to her family after her release from prison. When I asked if I could meet her childhood friends, to better understand her, she said she wasn't into emotional attachments.

Mercury sat at the foot of the bed. *Told you this long time ago, homie. RTS. Rape Trauma Syndrome.*

I said, *And I ignored all the signs?*

Mercury said, *She only wanted the sex. When sex was over, reality set in and she looked at any possible relationship as her next broken heart. You were falling in love—she wasn't going there. She wasn't ready.*

I recalled her post-orgasm expression. She looked like she'd scored the winning goal in the World Cup. She would walk out of the bedroom as if she were marching in a victory parade. She would come back morose.

Whenever I suggested it, she scoffed at the idea of counseling. She would say, "Are you saying there's something wrong with me?"

"Jacob?" Nema's voice was soft and tentative. "Will you hold me? Um. Just … hold me, nothing else."

Her silhouette turned away from me. Regular-Jacob couldn't stand the thought of holding a racist who might be part of a terrorist plot. Undercover-Jacob didn't see a way out. I wrapped my arms around her from behind. She relaxed into my hug. We slowly lowered ourselves to the sheets and spooned. While we embraced, she made sure it was a non-sexual encounter. Which is quite a trick.

Holding Jenny had been a warm, loving experience. I felt an odd form of energy flowing out of Nema. Mercury was right. Hate radiates out of some people.

She laughed a little. "Your smile reminds me of wine and roses."

"Thanks." It sounded vaguely romantic but I didn't want to find out.

Mercury said, *Hate to break up your orgy, dawg, but I need to point out that everyone in the intelligence business thinks you're an idiot for fingering Arrianne as the queen of terrorism. The only way you're gonna redeem yourself is by figuring out what ROSGEO means.*

I said, *I gave them the targets. They can figure it out without me.*

Mercury said, *That is so not you, brutha. Leave the evil mastermind out there to come up with secondary targets? Make alternate plans when you're not looking? How many sites were they working on besides London? You need to know what's going down or you're going down with it.*

My unemployed deity had a point. If one of the other groups had contingency plans, I'd be responsible for having left them uncovered. With or without Hugo or Ames or anyone else, I had to stop ROSGEO or go down in history as a conspirator to mass murder.

I squeezed Nema gently. "Tell me something. Who runs Free Origins?"

"Paladin. Lugh told you that already."

"He's the pretty face. He's the big smile when outsiders come around. That guy couldn't lead men into a movie theater if he gave out free popcorn."

She twisted to look back at me. "What makes you say that?"

"I've been in lots of battles. I've seen officers who aced West Point flip out when the firefight starts. I've seen corporals rise up to lead when their officers died. I've seen officers shit their pants, then pull it together to lead the charge. I can tell by looking a man in the eye what he'll do when he faces death."

She nodded in the dark and put her hand on top of mine. "What did you find out about that rosary? Did you ever turn it over to the police?"

"Lugh sure as hell can't lead the group. He wants to, but he has the wrong instincts. Having me beaten was pointless."

"What could you possibly learn from a string of beads?"

"Who was the guy who tried to kill you at the Moulin Rouge?" I asked.

She pulled away and faced me. "It was a terrorist attack."

"The kind meant for you and anyone near you. And you knew it."

"What makes you say that?"

"Most people would run when someone screams 'bomb.' Everyone else would run after the bomb goes off. But you kept looking for the guy. You recognized him through the disguise. After you figured he wasn't coming back, you went to help the survivors. It was a betrayal, and it shocked you."

She dropped back to the bed and pulled my arms around her. "You're wrong. I'll explain." She sighed long and slow. "But you have to answer something first. Why do you think I'm gay?"

"You don't like fashion, you don't wear makeup, short hair—all that stuff."

"Why do women go for fashions and glamor?" She stroked my arm. "Why does Arrianne dress like that? Why does she spend an hour on her hair and makeup?"

"She wants to look attractive."

"Right. She wants people to adore her. What's the downside to being beautiful and sexy?"

"Too many admirers?"

"She wants someone to love her. She wants to attract as many men as possible so she can choose the best suitor. But she attracts both good men and bad men. She attracts men who are looking for a wife. She also attracts men who have no respect. Men who will seduce her and if that doesn't work, force the issue."

I lay still.

"What if we took a different approach in life?" she asked. "What if we realized we don't really want mass adoration? What if we realized we aren't really looking for someone who loves us? What if we realized what we really need, more than anything else, is someone we can love?"

I stayed quiet.

Mercury popped up on the other side of her. *She's right, dawg. You need someone you can pour your love over. Like a daughter you can read to at bedtime. A son you can teach to fish. A wife you can buy flowers for. You've been looking at it all wrong.*

I said to Nema, "You make yourself less attractive so you can hang back from the singles scene and observe people before they come at you leering and drooling?"

"I…" She hesitated. "I was raped at fifteen."

CHAPTER 27

"YOU'VE GOT TO BE FUCKING kidding me." Arrianne stood over me, sunshine on her face. "You told me it was just for show."

I was on the hallway side of the bed, facing the room's door. Arrianne fixed her gaze over my shoulder. I assumed she was staring at Nema. I dared not look. I'd fallen asleep so hard the Pope could've hopped in bed with us.

Nema poked me in the back. After she dropped her bombshell, she'd asked me to protect her. I had wrestled with that one long enough to piss her off. A racist training people to kill didn't seem worthy of my professional shield, no matter how low in the org chart she ranked. But I couldn't say no to a woman who fits snuggly in my arms. And she knew it.

But that wasn't what bothered me the most.

I turned to Mercury. *How the hell did Arrianne get out of London? No matter what kind of relationship she had with the NCA, she broke into an office building. That should warrant an interrogation at least.*

Mercury said, *She must have dirt on someone big. MI6, SO15, and MI5 never heard of her. NCA does crime, like drugs and gangs.*

I said, *There's only one way they'd let her go like that. If she was an informant.*

Mercury said, *Racists do like their meth. And, if the story about her folks is true, you gotta wonder where she got the money to put on this conference.*

"Heard you got arrested," I said. I rose and forced Arrianne back a couple steps.

A pair of panties flew over my shoulder and landed on Arrianne's face. Nema shouted, "Check if you want! They're clean. We didn't do anything."

Arrianne tossed the panties aside. She flashed her dark eyes at me. "You have no idea what's going on around here. NONE!"

"I have an idea about that *Hidden Brain* podcast you told me about. Listened to it on the flight back. You must not have listened to the whole thing."

Turning on her heel, she strode out in some snug and colorful yoga pants with an equally snug and colorful top. The heavy oak door slammed hard.

I turned to find Nema boiling over. I couldn't tell if her anger was aimed at me or Arrianne. Why was she ticked off?

I said, "You never answered my question. Who runs Free Origins?"

"None of your business. You're a hired hand." She put her clothes on so fast the tattoo on her left hip almost escaped my attention. Then it came to me. It was very much like the one on Zack Ames's butt. A vaguely Celtic square cross on an interlocking circle. Where his had been filled in, hers read, "14 / 88."

She stormed out the door before I found my toothbrush.

Mercury appeared in the mirror. *Stearne, the whack-job-magnet. Everyone from Jupiter to Vesta is laughing about your new girlfriend, dawg. They think you love the criminal element. Art forgers, murderers, and ... I dunno, what's this one gonna be convicted of?*

I said, *She was a victim. Don't the gods have any sympathy?*

Mercury said, *Get focused on the present. You need to find out those three things about ROSGEO: which group is planning it; who's in charge; and what is it?*

He was right about that. My personal problems had to wait. I cleaned up and went to Arrianne's command center on the hill. Along the way, I saw more of the IDC attendees than ever scouring the hillsides like they were looking for something.

Paladin and Lugh stood in the kitchen, making lewd jokes about Arrianne. She jotted notes in a notebook while ignoring them. I helped myself to the coffee and joined the boys. Tapping on Lugh's sling, I said, "Didn't get the message the first time, Lugh? Treat women with respect."

He growled at me.

Paladin stepped between us. "We weeded out several men. They weren't up to the task."

"Who?"

He showed me the master list of the Sixty-Four. Twelve names had a line through them.

"Why them?" I asked. "They were no better or worse than the others."

"You don't need to know," Lugh hissed.

"You hired me to help you. If I understand your standards, I'll be in a better position to do that."

Lugh growled again and turned his back. Which left him facing the wall. Not a strategic planner. He was definitely not the real leader of Free Origins.

Paladin beamed his electric smile my way. "We appreciate your help, Jacob. This is an internal issue. A gut feeling about interactions between the men. Some fit in. Some don't."

"They quit." Arrianne looked up from her notebook.

Mercury stood next to Lugh. *Is this dude growling at your main squeeze now? What is this guy, a werewolf?*

I said, *Tensions are mounting in the management ranks around here. Whatever's going down—it must be soon.*

Paladin headed for the door. Lugh took after him. I started to follow when Arrianne grabbed my trailing arm.

"Want some?" She held out a packet of Orbit gum with a Spanish label. Sticking out of it was a sliver of white paper. Her gaze drew mine to it. I took the paper and a piece of gum.

"Did she just give you something?" Lugh breathed over my left shoulder.

I slipped my left toe behind his ankle and spun around, acting surprised. My elbow flew into his midsection. He landed on his ass.

"Sorry, Lugh." I offered a hand up. "You were close enough to sodomize me. Quite a shock. I didn't think you guys were the type. Not that I care. A few guys in the Forward Operating Bases got into that kind of thing just to pass the time. Never appealed to me, though."

"Shut up, asshole!" He scrambled to his feet and got in my face. "She gave you something."

Paladin appeared, put an open hand on Lugh's chest, and pushed him back.

"Gum." I flashed the Orbit at him. "Ask if you want some. You don't need to blow a gasket."

Arrianne leaned the box Lugh's way. He looked inside it, then slapped it to the floor.

"We already had one talk about your manners, Lugh." I grabbed his good forearm. "Do you need another lesson?"

Paladin pushed Lugh toward the door. "We're good. We'll see you down at the Ooze."

He pushed his lieutenant outside. The two walked down the hill.

Arrianne had a finger across her lips when I turned back. With her hands in between us, she pointed in three directions. Video cameras. Then she put her hands on my shoulders and looked at me as if we were going to kiss. She didn't complete the act.

It took me a second, but I got it. I pulled the paper out, using her as a shield against prying eyes and cameras. It read, "Sex = privacy. Since you turned me down, this note. Hoped you could save me from them. You need to leave ASAP. They figured you out. They know."

Paladin stuck his head in the front door. "Hey, Jacob, are you going to join us?"

I ate the note.

"Yeah, just ..." I said over my shoulder. I turned around and kissed Arrianne's forehead. "I'll be back. Keep the home fires burning, babe."

Mercury walked on the far side of Paladin as we walked downhill. *Did I tell you to forget about Jenny and do the dark-haired raven?*

I said, *Yes.*

And did you listen to your heavenly messenger?

I said, *No.*

Mercury said, *Next time your chosen god gives you permission to whoop it up with one sexy-as-Venus babe, are you gonna say no?*

Yes.

And so it went all the way down the hill. Mercury knew how to pound life-lessons into my head with a jackhammer—after the fact. In my defense, how in Diana's name am I supposed to know the difference between his messages about killing everyone who defies me (bad idea) and sleeping with a relative stranger (turns out to have been a good idea)?

We reached the town, but Mercury hadn't finished. *Now you need an exfiltration. Only problem is Tania was kidnapped off the street about three and a half minutes ago.*

I said, *What? No way. Who took her?*

Mercury said, *I'll give you three guesses, and the first two don't count.*

We kicked off the morning training session with new graffiti all over the Ooze. I looked for a way to give the ex-fil sign, the black-power fist—which would look odd in a white supremacy conference. I should've insisted on a different signal from the beginning, but it sounded kinda cool at the time.

Aleksei and his two fellow Spetsnaz goons stayed with me everywhere I went. They carried collapsible batons on their belts.

All morning, the group went about their training without regard to anything I said or advised. A bad sign. I wandered and watched.

The iron cover on the ancient town well lay on the ground next to it. Many of the paintball sets and other things we used in training were packed up in boxes.

More bad signs.

It meant they didn't need me anymore. From the beginning, I'd expected them to kill me to save themselves the final payment. The open well would be a good place to stash my corpse.

My trip to London and Arrianne's arrest confirmed their suspicions that I was in league with the authorities. Nema had asked about my travels, and I did my best to cover the gap. They didn't buy it. But they wouldn't do anything while the larger group was still here. Since the Sixty-Four, now down to fifty-two, were scheduled to stay a day after the conference ended, they would make their move soon. That meant I still had time to figure out what they had planned and who was planning it.

Then I had a terrifying thought. I checked the boxes again. All their training gear was packed for shipping today, a full day before the scheduled end of IDC. They were bugging out tonight. My exploits in London forced them to move up their timetable.

Lunch was served for both the target-practice guys and Paladin's men at the top of the hill. I wandered through the crowd looking for Earl, the guy with the Fair Heritage tattoo. He'd been one of the original Sixty-Four. Paladin had a line drawn through his name. I pulled up a piece of dirt next to him. Aleksei and his buddies joked in Russian five yards away.

"Why did you guys leave the program?" I asked.

He looked me over as if I stank. "I beat up a few Mexicans and niggers now and then, but I ain't in on ROSGEO. That shit ain't right. 'Back to Africa' maybe, but multiple mass-shootings on the same weekend? Ain't going there."

His phrase hit me like a bulldozer. I choked.

They hadn't been working out which was the softest target, they were working out how to hit them all at once. The running tally I kept of named sites was forty-seven. Some of those had to be alternate sites, but even if the final number was a quarter of that, they were planning the most horrific terrorist attack since 9/11. Worse, there were more men than locations. They weren't planning a series of lone-wolf attacks, they were planning to attack many locations with whole squads carrying automatic weapons. Where one man in Christchurch killed fifty, five men could take out ten times that.

I needed to get my intel out to the authorities right away.

But at this stage, it was all guesswork. I needed confirmation.

I nodded at Earl as if I understood. "I'm conflicted about it myself."

"Then get the fuck outta here." He chewed and swallowed, then whispered. "I'm leaving tonight. Don't wanna be anywhere near these guys when it goes down. They'll get us all thrown in jail for life."

I pointed at my minders. "They paid for my services, and they're determined to get their money's worth."

"Aleksei works for Paladin. Don't you work for the woman?" The last word spilled out with a derogatory emphasis.

His question made me think about the next piece of the puzzle, which group was planning it? I'd ruled out Birth Right—the hard way—in London. And Fair Heritage had been a non-entity from the start. Free Origins was the group planning the attack. Had to be. So who was their leader?

It wasn't Paladin or Lugh. Arrianne ran a conference for a thousand people yet never lifted a little finger. Most organizers ran around events pulling twenty-hour days to deal with everything from stopped-up toilets to vegan menus. Someone else was running the show. Arrianne was a captive at her own conference.

Earl and I ate in silence for a few more bites.

"Back in Paris," I said. "You and your pals jumped me. But when Paladin came along, you said, 'We're doing this for you.' What did you mean?"

"Somabitch asked us to rough you up. He called us to tell us where you were. Then he comes out throwing punches like the hero. All an act. It's been the same thing ever since I got here, one big act after another. Fuck Paladin. Fuck Free Origins. Fuck ROSGEO." He glared at me. "And fuck you for helping them."

He got up and walked away.

The scene in Paris when Paladin came to my rescue replayed in my head. Earl was right, it was an act. Everything was an act. Arrianne acted like a lover. Paladin acted like a boss. Lugh wasn't acting. He was naturally stupid. What was Nema's act? And what about Aleksei? I began piecing together a picture of who was running what and how they pulled it off. It was still a cloudy picture, but it started coming to me like a dark figure in a mist. And it wasn't pretty.

A couple more scenes of great acting played in my head. They coalesced into a recognizable shape. A shocking and identifiable shape. It couldn't be.

I stood.

Pieces of a Bible verse came to mind. I hadn't been to Sunday School since I was a kid, but it sticks with you. The Gospeler had dragged some of it back out of the recesses of my mind. The verse was something about leaders and servants, the humbled and the exalted.

Then it came to me. I did know who was in charge. I'd known it all along.

The cleverness of it was diabolical. Anyone planning the most horrific, global terrorist attack in history would want to keep a low profile. Stay out of the limelight. Osama bin Laden had lived in a cave half a world away from the Twin Towers. Cowards never stand on the front line.

Now all I needed were the specifics about ROSGEO. And I knew who could tell me.

CHAPTER 28

I MARCHED OVER TO ALEKSEI. "C'mon, time to go. I want to check on Arrianne before we restart the session."

As I hoped, his companions were too lazy to make the extra loop to Arrianne's house. They headed straight for the Ooze. Aleksei kept up stride-for-stride despite the long walk.

"You not careful with woman, Jacob." Aleksei slapped my back. "Nobody get Nema's panties off. Now you move on Arrianne, same day? Make troubles for yourself."

"I can make it work. Somehow."

We neared the house where Paladin's SUV was parked. Aleksei always drove.

"You pour gasoline on fire to be stud muffin? Bad idea for military strategy. But." He stopped at the bottom of the steps and held up a forearm for a bump. "Respect."

I smiled and started to bump. Instead, I smacked him hard under the jaw with my forearm. Shocked, he spun away. I whipped his baton out of its holster, released it, locked it, and slammed it into his lower back. He let out an anguished shout and arched backward. The second blow was a full-swing into his exposed gut. At that point, we were even. That never works for me. I like being ahead. I smacked his skull hard enough for a class three concussion, just short of crushing bone. He landed on his face, twitching. I took the car keys out of his pocket.

Arrianne appeared in the open door. "Jacob! What are you doing?" Her eyes were wide, her lips trembling beneath the fingertips covering them.

"Leaving," I said. "You've got three seconds to choose: stay or leave."

Blood drained from her face. "I, I, can't. Everything I have is invested ..."

I counted on her coming with me. Only she could confirm my theories about ROSGEO and who was running Free Origins.

She took a deep breath. She closed her eyes. She leaned forward and ran to me.

She wanted me to wrap her up in a hug, but there wasn't time. I pushed her toward the SUV. She jumped into the passenger seat. I fired it up, dropped it in gear, reversed in a half-circle and fled. We went up and over the hill with no one behind us.

"Why did you get arrested in London?" I asked.

She looked like a spanked child. "I used to be a drug dealer for the Estonian Cartel."

"And the NCA caught you. You offered up your bosses on a platter. You're a witness."

"I'm a survivor. I had to."

"I'm not taking the Estonian's side here. You did the right thing. But what were you doing in London?"

"Free Origins ... They're planning something terrible. I have to get away from them. But they have all my money locked up in their project. And the Brits have my passport. The Estonians keep tons of cash in that office. I was going to steal it and get the hell out of Europe."

"What is ROSGEO?" I asked.

"Paladin has people all over town. They'll shoot us."

"You have to know about ROSGEO. It's why you started Birth Right and why you split from Free Origins, isn't it?"

She looked around the car. She tore through the glove compartment and the center console.

"You don't have any weapons. Oh god. I never should've given you that note." She covered her face with her hands.

Mercury leaned between the front seats. *Wahoo! This is what it's all about, right brutha? Living on the edge. Fleeing a superior force with odds of 942 to one. Heart rate skyrocketing into call-the-cardiologist territory. I've got a thousand aurei on you dying in a hail of gunfire.*

DEATH AND CONSPIRACY

Cliché way to go—but money in the bank. Yeah BABAY!

I said, *You bet against me?*

Mercury said, *Don't worry. I have to even the odds out some or the other gods will think I rigged the game. You have a 70/30 chance. Probably. Rip through that olive grove on the left.*

No cars in the rearview mirror. No tail yet. A dust cloud rising behind us would telegraph our route. It sounded like one of his bad ideas. But I decided to take the word of god anyway, even though he was betting against me. I couldn't believe he'd do that. What kind of god bets against his worshippers? OK. I'm not exactly a worshipper, more like a victim. But still.

"Why did you warn me?" I asked Arrianne.

"I counted on Caleb to be my champion. I thought he might get me out of this nightmare. But when I saw the Saint-Sulpice video, I knew it had to be you. They hated you, Paladin and the rest. You killed their heroes. That's how I knew I could count on you. I need help, Jacob."

"The terrorists at Saint-Sulpice—they were your people?"

"That's why they invited you here. From the beginning, they had a plan for you. Like burning you at the stake or something. Like a closing ceremony. Paladin loves his ceremonies." She grabbed my arm and pulled herself close to me. "I had nothing to do with that. I'm not with them."

"You're in deep. There's no getting out unless you go to the authorities and tell them everything you know."

"Where are you going?" She held the dashboard as we banged over the old track. "Do you know where this road leads? It could be a dead end."

"I get messages. They usually work out." I reached over to grab her hand. "What is ROSGEO?"

"Oh. My. God. They're going to kill me."

I raised my voice. "What is ROSGEO?"

"It was all a setup. They forced me to seduce you. They wanted me to lead you like a lamb to the slaughter. I tried because I hoped to reason with you. I hoped you could save me from Free Origins. I thought you'd see the light. I should've known you'd be hopeless. You were

165

brainwashed by the government into believing in coexistence."

Half a mile into the grove, I slammed on the brakes. When we stopped, I reached across and opened her door. Dust swirled in. "On my second tour, my lieutenant was a rich Jew from Newport Beach. His dad was a doctor. David was going to be a doctor too. He didn't need the Army. He chose to put his life on the line for his country between college and med school. He crossed that line outside of Fallujah. People like you—who never got so much as a papercut protecting someone else—make me sick. David Cohen didn't replace your father; he died so your alcoholic dad could keep drinking cheap booze and making excuses for why he got fired. Now get out."

I gave her a push.

"Wait." She clung to her seatbelt. "ROSGEO ... it's an attack. Mass shootings. Lots of them. All over the world, coordinated within hours of each other. Thirteen sites, six different religions, five-man teams, each with a goal of killing over 100 people. They want a minimum of 1,300 dead."

Arrianne burst into tears.

Confirmed. They were planning Armageddon. I needed a phone. I needed to get an army out here to round up these monsters.

A dust cloud appeared in the mirror. They were on to us. I put it in drive and stepped on the gas.

Mercury pointed to a gate. *Crash through there but don't use the bridge over the stream. Drive to the left about thirty yards. You'll see it.*

I followed his instructions. The diversion was rough ground, slowing my progress. Thirty yards from the bridge were two tracks of rocks for crossing when the water was low enough. Judging by the approaching cloud, the car behind us was quickly closing the gap. I splashed through the stream and rejoined the dirt road before our pursuers rounded the last bend. I floored it. The big SUV bounced and cratered on the rough road. I could barely hang onto the steering wheel.

Arrianne twisted around the headrest to see out the back. "How the hell did you know that bridge would give out?"

In the mirror, I saw the chase vehicle nose-down in the stream, its back wheels spinning in the air.

"I told you, I get messages." I glanced at her. "Tell me about ROSGEO."

"It's an acronym, sort of. It stands for Return of Saint George, R-O-S-GEO."

"George? The dragon-slayer?"

"Where are you going?" she screamed.

I dodged a pothole big enough to bury three bodies. "Talk."

"They'll radio the guards in the town. You can't go through Úbeda."

Mercury said, *You don't have to go through Úbeda, homie. The back roads all lead there. But I'll get you on connecting roads that get you around the city.*

"Why Saint George?" I asked. "He's the patron saint of military campaigns."

"And the patron saint of the Crusades against Islam."

I thought about the markings. Synagogues, cathedrals, and mosques. A crusade against all religion? That didn't make sense given their vaguely Christian references.

"If you guys are going to restart the Crusades, why attack a Catholic church?" As soon as I asked her, I knew the answer. Diego tried shouting the call of an Islamic terrorist. And he'd held prayer beads before the attack. I said, "You're trying to spark an all-out religious war."

"I'm not. I'm not involved in their plot."

"The hell you're not." I gave her the side-eye. "You know about it and haven't reported it. See something, say something. You're an accessory if not a coconspirator."

She choked back tears and looked out the window.

"What's the endgame?" I asked. "What do they think will happen after a war that pits religions against each other?"

"Ethnopluralism. Like I told you, people prefer working with their own kind. Colored patients prefer colored doctors, non-white students do better with non-white teachers, and so on. After the war, people will go back to their own neighborhoods and stay there. It's natural."

"Charlie Manson thought he was going to start a race war. The Tree of Life synagogue and the Emanuel AME church shootings were supposed to spark race wars. They never do; they just kill a lot of innocent people. What makes ROSGEO different?"

"Lone-wolf attacks don't work because they're isolated incidents. The world reacts with thoughts and prayers but figures it won't happen to them. That's why politicians never speak out against racism. There's a war on drugs, there's a war on terrorism, but there's no war on racism. ROSGEO is a plan to shoot up a whole bunch of places at once. An attack so big, everyone will be terrorized. Not just Jews but Christians, Muslims, Hindus, everyone. Like a global Sri Lanka on steroids."

Mercury said, *All those places they mapped out in their little shoot-em-up village are gonna be hit at the same time. Chicago, Milan, Lyon, Budapest, Istanbul, Hanoi, the rest. That'd take massive coordination.*

I said, *And communications. The Sixty-Four packed up this morning. It must be soon.*

Mercury said, *You gotta find out when. If you put people on high alert, they lose focus after a week. You GOTTA find out when this goes down.*

"When is this ROSGEO?" I asked.

"They wouldn't tell me if I asked them. And I know better than to ask them."

"Ask Mary Surratt if claiming ignorance will save you from the death penalty."

And if I didn't say something to someone soon, I was going to end up in the same boat as Arrianne. Since my cover was blown, I needed to contact my squad. I said, "Arrianne, I need you to make a call for me."

"There's no cell service out here. Only in the middle of town."

I turned on the next road, heading for the city.

"You're crazy!" Arrianne shrieked. "I told you Paladin has people there. They found surveillance gear out by the Ooze and sent a bunch of wannabees out to find the people behind them. By now, they've radioed those same yahoos, and everyone's looking for us."

"We have to get word out. Even if that means getting captured."

"They're not going to capture you; they're going kill you. And me." She grabbed my shoulder, tears falling down her cheeks. "I don't want to die, Jacob."

"I saw the well cap on the ground. They'll toss us down the hole, and dump a yard of concrete on top, put the cap back on. I'll do my best to get us out of this. Just figure we're already dead. Anything less will be good news. Our top priority is to get the word out. We have to save the innocent."

She didn't like my pep talk.

We came up on Úbeda from the south. Our dirt road connected to an almost-paved road. I followed it in. Mercury gave me turn-by-turn instructions. Better than Google Maps. I should've used lube to squeeze into the narrow lanes but managed to get through two before losing a mirror.

Arrianne got a bar of signal and dialed the Sabel Security helpdesk number I fed her. Someone picked up, but her call dropped. She redialed.

Suddenly, the truck slowed. I pushed the gas pedal. Nothing happened.

"What are you doing?" Arrianne sounded as stressed out as I felt.

I pumped the gas. We continued to slow, rolling to a quiet stop in the middle of an ancient and slim cobblestone lane.

Mercury said, *Say, bro, did you know rental cars have a remote-disable switch? OnStar works everywhere, even here in the middle of Andalusia. Surprised the Orcus outta me. Huh. What will they think of next?*

Our doors wouldn't open in the narrow street. Men with rifles appeared, two in front and one in back. The guy in back lifted the hatch.

CHAPTER 29

THEY DUMPED US IN A dungeon. I'm not sure if there was a castle involved, but it was a deep, dark cellar with a shaft of light coming through a small, barred window on one side. Stone arches filled the room. It smelled dank and musty and old. They ignored the five stone steps below the door and shoved me in. I landed on my side. Arrianne landed on top of me. Our wrists and ankles were bound. We wriggled free of each other.

"Izzat you, Jacob?" The voice came from the darkest corner of the room.

"Tania?" I recognized the voice of my friend from the army.

She hopped toward me. I made it to my feet and hopped to meet her. We stopped with the beam of sunlight between us. She wore a blood-stained tank-top and running shorts. Under normal circumstances, she would hide the burn scars on her legs under long pants. She must have gone out in a hurry to fix the video feeds.

They'd given her a black eye and a bruised shoulder.

"Is that your girlfriend?" Tania nosed at Arrianne.

"One of many."

"Trust her?"

"Not for a second."

She nodded, then looked to the window and shook her head. She looked to the door and nodded. Message received: The window was too small to get out. We'd have to rely on a frontal assault through the door.

The light beaming through the window was high on the opposite wall, meaning the sun outside was low. They'd driven us around for a long time with hoods on our heads to disorient us. We'd lost most of the afternoon.

"Let me guess," I said. "You checked on the surveillance gear, and they jumped you?"

"They were smart. They didn't wreck it; they knocked a couple cameras sideways to make it look like a goat had done it. I went out before dawn. They'd been waiting for me all night."

The roving mobs of conference attendees had been looking to ambush my team. I should've seen that and warned them.

"Miguel knows you're here?" I asked.

"You know him. He'll rescue us. He's a one-man wrecking crew."

"You have someone on the outside?" Arrianne asked with the first hint of hope in her voice since we left her place. "He can save us?"

The door clanked open. A hulking shadow filled the frame. They gave the shadow a shove.

Miguel landed in a heap on the floor next to Arrianne. His wrists and ankles were bound just like ours.

Tania and I hopped over to our friend and squatted next to him. He'd taken a blow to the head. His unfocused eyes wandered over us. We pulled him up to sitting, which isn't easy given his size.

"This is your savior?" Arrianne burst into tears. "Oh, God, we're dead."

"Don't count him out," I said. "He's got skills. Mad skills."

Arrianne scooted back, not wanting to sit next to two non-white people.

Tania gave her a once-over. "You know what? I served with men and women from all walks of life. All of them signed up to die for you. If you can't hang with people who volunteered to pay the ultimate price to save your sorry ass from all threats foreign and domestic—you can just drop fucking dead."

Arrianne's mouth fell open.

I pulled the small, razor-sharp knife hidden in my belt buckle and carefully sawed through almost all of Tania's bindings. She did the same for me. We left enough rope intact to keep the guards from noticing while being able to break free with a good tug. Miguel was waking from the bump on his head, but he grasped the plan.

The door clanked again. It opened slowly. In the opening stood the pixie-silhouette of Nema holding a silver tea service in her hands.

A guard with a Beretta AR70/90 stepped in front of her. He came down the steps brandishing his weapon. We understood and moved back. Behind him, covering from the top of the stairs was our jailer's twin, also aiming a Beretta at our heads.

Mercury said, *The Hungarian brothers have itchy trigger fingers, brutha. No sudden moves.*

I said, *I'd hoped to reason with them. Do they speak English?*

Not a lick. Mercury smiled. *Good news is, no one around here can communicate with them. They're not even sure what Nema's doing here. I told you I'd level the playing field. A little.*

"Are you all right?" Nema tread cautiously down the steps with her tray. "I came as soon as I heard."

"Don't pretend to care," I said. "I know it's you."

"What's me?" She batted her eyes like a '50s starlet.

"You run Free Origins. You masterminded ROSGEO."

"What are you talking about?"

"Ethnopluralism," I said. "You planned mass shootings thinking the result will be a race and religious war that will redraw geopolitical maps."

The look Nema gave Arrianne telegraphed a death sentence.

Her gaze softened considerably when she turned back to me. "Did they beat you?"

"When do you plan to start your little nightmare?"

"You don't look hurt." She stepped closer and lifted the tray to me. "Tea? Take the cup nearest you."

Tania, Miguel and I hopped forward. I moved straight toward her. The other two used the opportunity to get closer to the guard while widening the separation from each other. The guard wasn't a professional, but he instinctively knew their flanking maneuver wasn't going to work out well for him. When he pointed his muzzle at Miguel to intimidate him, Tania moved closer.

He realized his problem. He could only get one before the other tackled him. He nodded to his brother on the landing above. They adjusted their aim to cover both my friends.

"I smell bitter almonds, Nema." I gave her my soldier stare while she worked out what I was saying. "Army training includes a lot of how-not-to-get-killed-by-the-enemy seminars. I learned how to smell cyanide."

Arrianne gasped. "Oh my God, Nema. How could you?"

"Shut up." Nema threw the tea service at me. I batted it aside. She glared at Arrianne. "Your treachery sealed your fate. Paladin has decided how to deal with you."

"I'll do everything I can to stop you," Arrianne shrieked.

"We found Tyler." Nema's voice turned hard and cold. "Poor little Tyler is safe now."

Arrianne froze, then sobbed and turned away.

"When is ROSGEO?" I asked.

"They're on their way here for you." Nema gave me her big eyes. "Paladin has plans for you."

"Why not have them shoot me?" I nodded at the Hungarians.

"We don't trust them. They might talk." She threw daggers at Arrianne with her gaze. "Some people have no loyalty."

"Why ethnopluralism?"

"Come with me, Jacob." Nema stepped close. "Paladin has a plan for you. A glorious plan. We'll keep your friends here in case you don't put your back into it."

I said, "I'd rather die in the company of honorable people than help you."

"We aren't going to kill you. It's the colored people and the Muslims who are killing us all. I'm offering you a chance to do something about it."

"That's your excuse for killing thousands of innocent people?" I asked.

"I don't need an excuse." She jutted out her jaw. "I'm sick of people judging me. I hate walking in the street where people judge my body. I hate the rich ladies who judge my clothes. I hate my family for judging what kind of girl I am. Paladin's going to fix this broken world. He's going to set it all straight."

Her outburst about judging didn't fit in the conversation. It had to have been about her rape. That was driving her hatred. How it fit together wasn't clear.

She prowled around me like a predator. "People like you are pathetic. White people can't stand still and let an invasion of animals with violence in their DNA interbreed with our kind. You don't see eagles breeding with owls or coyotes breeding with hyenas, do you?"

"For your analogy to be relevant," I said, "you'd need to correlate Western Coyotes breeding with Central Coyotes, and yes, that happens all the time. But what are you talking about, violence in DNA?"

"Black people are more violent. Proven by criminal statistics." Nema pointed at Tania. "She's more violent than our kind."

"Name three black serial killers."

Nema stared and frowned and stammered.

"I'll spot you the first one, Wayne Williams, Atlanta. On the white side, there's Ted Bundy, John Wayne Gacy, Jeffrey Dahmer, and a long, long list. Then there're the mass shootings like Las Vegas, El Paso, Sandy Hook, which are dominated by American men. But after ROSGEO, you'll be the worst."

"I'm not a serial killer."

"Not yet," I said. "Only because Ace and Diego failed."

"I didn't have anything to do with them. Those guys were acting alone when—"

"How did you know who I'm talking about? The press didn't release their codenames. I got them from a CIA agent who's been tracking you guys for a year."

Nema staggered back a step with her hand over her mouth.

Tania piped up. "We found Diego's family. His real name was Sergio Navas. He had a little shrine to Nema in his room. He was in love with her."

Nema's eyes registered recognition at Diego's real name.

"Did he know she didn't care about him?" I asked Tania.

"Hell no."

"Shut up!" Nema yelled. "I hate the world and everyone in it. You're all falling for the plot to replace us. The Jews and the Muslims and the Mexicans are replacing the white people in every country. They're like a plague of locusts. You can't stop them with walls or laws. Paladin has a plan to make them all go back where they came from. I'm with him a hundred percent. My family blamed me for what happened. To hell with them. To hell with everyone else too. It's time for Paladin to turn the world black. Everything. Turn it all black. Black out the sun, blot out the sky. Turn the streets black with drying blood. You can't talk me out of it. He promised me a year ago not to let another Pentecost pass without acting."

Mercury looked over her shoulder. *Tell me you heard that about blame, homie.*

I said, *I heard it. I don't know what it means, but I'm counting on you to tell me later.*

Like everyone else, I only know the world I see from inside my head. Once in a great while, I feel how others might feel in a certain situation. Empathy. I feel connected to that person afterward. The hate Nema just spewed gave me one of those windows into how she felt. I didn't feel connected to her at all. While the anger she ejected was the result of a rape, she had intentionally cultivated and nurtured that hatred. At some point, she actively chose to become evil.

I said, "Don't blame Paladin. You run the show. You call the shots. And you alone can stop it."

"You're still wrong about me," she snarled. "You don't know shit."

"You know what gave it away? You blew it the morning Arrianne caught us in bed together. You wanted me to cozy up to you, tell you about the rosary. Tell you what we look for when we're hunting terrorists. I never answered those questions because I never intended to help you. That frustrated you. That's why you wanted me to hold you all night long. You figured if I wouldn't fall for Arrianne, maybe I'd fall for you. It didn't work. And you lost your cool in the morning. You called me a hired hand. Peers don't see each other that way. Bosses do. No one believes Paladin is running anything. We know it's you, Nema. You're the only one who can stop ROSGEO."

"I won't stop anything."

Nema would never change her mind. I had all the information I needed to stop the tragedy from unfolding. I knew what ROSGEO was, and when it would happen. It was time to go. I gave Tania the nod. She broke her shackles and threw Nema into the Hungarian. His head banged off the pillar behind him with a sickening thud.

At the same time, Miguel bolted up the stairs. The second Hungarian looked shocked at the turn of events and raised his rifle. He fumbled the safety and mode selector, which saved Miguel's life. That extra second was all Miguel needed to tackle the man.

I grabbed Arrianne's hand and tugged before realizing I hadn't sliced her ropes. Tania was bounding up the steps. I pulled my knife out and started cutting. In the corner, Nema started pulling herself together. She grabbed the rifle out of the Hungarian's hands. I freed Arrianne's wrists.

"I'll shoot." Nema leveled the rifle at me.

From the top of the steps, Miguel aimed the other rifle at her but wisely held his fire. In our stone dungeon, a ricochet could kill any one of us.

I kept working on the bindings around Arrianne's ankles.

Nema fired a bullet. As predicted, shooting inside a stone chamber turned out to be a terrible idea. The round flew past my ear and ricocheted six times in a thousandth of a second. Everyone ducked. Nema didn't look up until the danger was over.

"Run," Arrianne said. "Leave me."

The Hungarian pulled a sidearm. He was still too woozy to shoot but coming around fast. If I stuck around long enough to kill Nema, he'd kill me.

I finished Arrianne's ankle ropes, grabbed her wrist, and headed for the steps.

Mercury stepped in front of me with a deformed bullet in the palm of his hand. He said, *You're welcome.*

His eyes moved from mine to the bullet and back.

Oh for crying out loud, I said. *Luck. You catch a random break, and then you want me to believe it was divine intervention?*

CHAPTER 30

I BOUNDED UP THE STEPS with Arrianne right behind me. Miguel aimed his weapon at Nema to cover us.

Nema screamed her anger. It rattled the stones and echoed through the house. Miguel slammed the door and bolted it from the outside.

We were in the hallway of an empty wine cellar. Ancient wooden racks stood empty as if they'd been robbed. The second Hungarian lay on the floor. His pockets had been turned inside out.

"Shoot her," I said and pointed Miguel at Nema.

He showed me the rifle he'd taken from the man. The charging handle was bent into the upper receiver. I glanced at the Hungarian and saw a matching dent in his forehead. Miguel had taken the weapon from him and knocked him unconscious with it. And damaged our only weapon in the process. He shrugged.

Stranger things have happened during life-and-death struggles. Not many, though.

Half a magazine of bullets flew through the wood next to us. Splinters flew around us. Nema must've realized we were just beyond the door and that her bullets wouldn't ricochet if she fired through the wood.

"Let's go." Tania disappeared around the corner. Arrianne followed her.

We found ourselves in a large and aging hacienda. Red-tile floors stretched across a large dining room. We ran through it to the living room. It opened onto a courtyard full of flowers glowing in the warm light of dusk. Walkways crisscrossed between flowerbeds. The house enclosed the entire courtyard.

"Where's the exit?" I asked.

"Ask that good-for-nothing god of yours," Tania sneered. "If he exists."

Miguel faced Arrianne, turning the question to her.

"How would I know?" Arrianne answered. "I've never been here before, I only heard about it. This is where Paladin and his crew stayed."

She turned to Tania. "What god are you talking about?" Then me. "Jacob, you're a Christian man, aren't you?"

I said, "It's possible."

We ran from doorway to doorway, looking in each room for a foyer or a front door.

"This is a nice place," I said. "You didn't rent this for the conference."

"A donor let them use it. The guy who owns this orchard loves Free Origins. He's in Madrid for the month."

Miguel found the exit. From the house only. It led us to a much larger farmyard. It was a cobblestone space the size of a football field surrounded by machine sheds and barns. Behind them, surrounding the entire compound, stood a wall fifteen feet high topped with razor wire. At the far end of the farmyard, a large gate made of solid iron sat on steel wheels. Its upper support frame was the only place on the wall devoid of deadly wire. In the middle of the yard, a black VW Tiguan waited for us.

We ran to it and got in. Tania landed in the driver's seat. She checked the console and the visor and under the mats. "How come in the movies, the convenient car always has keys in the ignition?" She looked at us. "Someone have the keys?"

"The guy I tackled didn't have any," Miguel said. "I didn't see any on the counters near him either."

We all leaned to the middle. In unison, we said, "Nema."

Mercury howled with laughter. *Ah, homie. When you guys run for it, you really know how to roll. Leave the keys in the pocket of the only person around who has a loaded—and working—machine gun.*

I said, *Now would be a good time for divine intervention. Can you help me out?*

He said, *I already leveled the playing field for you and gave you a couple good chances. The other gods are satisfied this is an honest game now. So, you gotta get out on your own. Good luck, brutha.*

I said, *Good luck? You bet against me.*

Mercury laughed as he rose into the sky on his little flappy wings. Bastard.

Just when the gods restore your faith in their benevolent powers, they remind you that your life is just a game to them.

We got out and scattered in different directions as Nema and one of the Hungarians came out of the hacienda. Miguel leveled his rifle at them, keeping the damaged charging handle from view, which forced them to duck.

Somewhere beyond the compound, the sun painted the western sky in oranges and yellows. Dark approached but not quickly enough to use it against our pursuers.

A machine shed with a half-open door looked like a good spot to me. I ran in with Arrianne hot on my heels. To my disappointment, I learned the Spanish weren't big on back doors to their sheds. We ducked behind a giant tractor with a strange device on the front. It had what looked like cloth scoops that would fan out to either side. An olive harvester.

When I peered around the five-foot tire, I found a big, black man standing in front of me. He wore a bronze breastplate, a cape, and a skirt. A manly skirt, but still.

I said, *Let me guess. You're Mars, god of war.*

The giant smiled.

I closed my eyes. *I gotta take my meds. Gotta take my meds. Gotta take my meds ...*

He tapped me on the shoulder, caught my gaze, then nosed at the tractor. The keys were in it. Which didn't matter because a twelve-year-old could outrun a tractor. Then he nosed at the wall. A spool of baling twine hung on a peg among a bunch of tools. Different from the kind most people keep in the kitchen junk drawer, baling twine holds thousand-pound bales of hay together. It would work fine.

I looked back at Mars. *Thanks.*

I grabbed the twine and a pair of sheers off the wall. I climbed up to the tractor and fired it up. Arrianne followed me into the enclosed cab and sat on a toolbox next to me. I pushed the throttle forward and knocked the meager barn door off the entrance.

We crossed the farmyard to the barn where I'd last seen Miguel. He and Tania ran out and climbed onboard.

Bullets pinged off the back. I didn't mind. Tractors are made to weigh a lot. It keeps them grounded when they're hauling heavy loads in mud or rain-slicked fields. The back ends are always big chunks of steel. You can accessorize with additional steel plates. This one had three steel plates on the back and five on the front. Nema whittled down her ammo figuring that out.

"Hang on!" I yelled.

Everyone on my rig grabbed anything they could hang on to. I aimed for the center of the big, iron gate in the outer wall. It was far too thick to break, but when we hit it, I got the desired result. It bent in a triangular pattern around the front of the tractor. It would never slide open again.

Miguel aimed his useless rifle at Nema. She ducked back. The Hungarian ducked as well.

I looped my twine through a metal fitting on the tractor and tossed the spool over the wall. I climbed to the tractor's roof and gave Tania a hand up. With a boost, she grabbed the twine and scampered up the wall. Once over the top, she would use the twine to rappel down.

Arrianne stuck her head out of the cab as Tania disappeared over the top. "Nema's going to shoot me. I'll stay here. Maybe I can talk her down."

"You have ten seconds to get over this wall. Don't make me carry you."

"I appreciate you saving me," she said. "You're truly my hero, but things have gotten more complicated."

"Shut up and get over that wall."

Nema stuck her head out and fired at us. It was beginning to dawn on her why Miguel wasn't shooting back.

Arrianne reached up a hand. I grabbed it below her wrist and yanked her up to the roof with me. I picked her up by the waist and tossed her to the top.

She landed bent in half and took her time getting over her fears. I could hear Tania talking to her on the other side. I couldn't hear the words, but I knew she was giving Arrianne encouragement and instructions. Arrianne's dark mane disappeared a second later.

I grabbed the twine and followed her up and over to the other side. Beyond us, olive orchards filled every inch of the gently rolling terrain. Here and there, vineyards took up a field or two.

Miguel came over the top as bullets pinged off the iron gate. When he reached the ground, I snipped the twine and pulled the remainder through the loop on the tractor. Five seconds later, Nema couldn't follow us without a fifteen-foot jump. Not impossible, but a high probability of injury.

We looked at the long driveway. Dirt for a quarter mile before it met with another dirt road.

Arrianne pointed into the distance.

We couldn't see the vehicle approaching at an aggressive speed, but we could see the rooster tail of dirt it kicked up in the gathering darkness.

CHAPTER 31

"DOES ANYONE HAVE A PHONE?" I asked.

"They put a hood over my head," Tania said, "took all my stuff, drove around in circles for a long time. They didn't take the hood off until they dumped me in the basement."

"Same," the rest of us said.

Miguel led us across stones set in the dirt at the base of the wall. They prevented mud from splashing up on the whitewashed wall. They also kept our footprints out of the dust. Arrianne was not happy. Something about her white walking shoes.

We made it to the opposite side of the compound by the time the new arrivals discovered their gate problem. Voices shouted to each other over the wall. We ran for the olive grove, running down the rows between trees single file. It was getting dark when we split into separate rows to confuse our tracks until we reached a road. We crossed it and continued down the rows another fifty yards until we reached another dirt track. Then we backed up, stepping in our footprints to further obscure our path.

The subterfuge chewed up a lot of our head start. We could see flashlights and hear voices not far away.

A farmhouse in the distance caught our eye. We walked single file to the dark structure, hoping for a phone. Once we alerted the authorities, they could swoop in and clean up the Free Origins people. The closer we got to our destination, the more we understood that wasn't going to happen. The front door was missing. None of the windows had glass. Some had plywood.

After a quick check, we determined it had been abandoned for years.

A small pickup drove by, shining a spotlight on the house. We managed to keep low and out of sight. I ventured a peek and saw the silhouettes of two men in the truck bed. Voices called from the back to the cab before it sped up and away.

We climbed out a back window and made our way up the gently sloping hill behind the house. We zigzagged and back-tracked and single-filed until we reached the summit. Tania climbed on Miguel's shoulders to see over the olive trees.

"They found our tracks," she said. "Nearest house is on the other side of them. Too dangerous."

She went silent for a moment.

"What is it?" Arrianne asked.

"Either the back roads are busy this evening, or there's a bunch of them looking for us." Tania jumped down. "We can't use the roads anymore. But there's another house half a mile that way."

She started jogging in the opposite direction from the searchers.

"Wait," Arrianne said. "I can't keep up with you. I'm tired and thirsty and hungry."

"I thought y'all were supposed to be the Master Race," Tania said. "If I can do this—you can do this."

"Yeah, but …"

"And didn't you say there's a thousand of them trying to kill us?"

"Yes."

"Get moving, sister."

We jogged down a ravine and crossed a marshy area. Our feet sank into mud. We turned downstream for a few hundred yards. The wetland turned into a retaining pond. We skirted it and came out by a road. Headlights preceded a small Toyota Hilux, the preferred cheap-and-redneck rental for conference attendees, coming down a crossroad. We ducked back to the marsh and hid in the reeds. The compact pickup turned onto the lane. Its headlights flashed across us.

We could only hope there were enough reeds between them and us to keep us concealed.

There weren't.

The truck skidded to a stop a hundred yards up the road. Two guys in the back jumped down. As they came down the road, the little pickup backed up, illuminating the two men on foot. One was Earl, the tattooed man who'd advised me to run. He held an AK-47 at the ready. His companion held a shotgun.

The truck stopped just short of lighting us up. They'd misjudged our position by a few critical feet. The peripheral glow from the lights illuminated us like daylight. But our eyes were used to the dark. The hunters had been staring into the bright cone in front of them. They couldn't see us.

The driver leaned out and pointed just north of us. "They're in there somewhere."

Using our fingers, we mapped out a plan. I held tight to Arrianne's wrist and gave her a serious look about staying silent. She was doing well so far, shaking like she had palsy, but contained. One gasp or surprised shriek from the schoolgirl bottled up inside her, and we were toast. Tania gave her an equally serious glare.

Earl said, "Fuck this."

He opened up with an automatic burst. The spray came near our crouching heads.

I slipped my hand over Arrianne's mouth just in time to catch a yelp of fear and muffled it. She twisted, which made a splash.

Earl cocked an ear in our direction. He raised his rifle and squeezed off another burst. This time five bullets flew over our heads with half an inch to spare.

Arrianne couldn't take it. She exploded out of my grip, splashed across the water, pushing reeds left and right and screaming.

Her commotion drew our enemies' attention. Earl saw the movement, aimed and fired.

Tania reached out of the grass, yanked Arrianne's wrist and dragged her to the ground.

Miguel flew out of the reeds into Earl's left side. He wrapped up the shooter and drove him to the ground. The guy with the shotgun aimed at the writhing bodies. Miguel rolled over, holding Earl between the shotgun and himself. He kept Earl's arms pinned to his side.

Which confused the guy with the shotgun long enough for me to tackle him from behind.

The shotgun went off when we hit the ground. The man wielding it was so surprised by the violence of my actions that he hesitated. Which cost him dearly. I jerked the weapon from his hands and slammed the butt into his temple. He twitched.

Miguel's adversary wasn't going as gently into that same good night. They were struggling and squirming and throwing elbows.

Behind me, the driver's door opened. I wheeled on the interloper and fired a blast. Shotguns are deadly short-range weapons. At twenty-five yards, they'll kill anything in front of the barrel. It was the driver's lucky night. He was a good fifty yards away. Buckshot spreads out in an ever-widening pattern after leaving the barrel. And I fired a touch too early during my turn. Pellets pinged off the glass and hood.

He jumped back in and floored the truck in a bid to run me down.

I stood my ground and pumped a second shell and aimed and fired.

The windshield spider-cracked into a thousand square shards. It was held together by the plastic sandwiched in the middle that qualified it as safety glass. I pumped again.

He slammed on the brakes and lost control, sliding sideways. Dirt and gravel flew into my eyes. He found the gas pedal, his tires spun then caught, his truck careened into the olive grove.

I gave him another taste of buckshot despite the distance. I pumped again. Empty.

The shotgun owner popped to his feet and raised a fist. I slammed the rifle butt into his forehead. He went down again. You might think a redneck would learn his lesson the first time.

A voice squawked over a radio. "Mikey, you copy? We found 'em. Out here. We're at ... Hold on."

The radio was on Earl's belt. He was doing a great job of wrestling Miguel despite the weight differential. I pushed the shotgun barrel in his face.

He stopped squirming.

Miguel took Earl's rifle, stood, and hauled Earl to his feet.

Mercury floated down from the sky in his formal toga. *Tell me the truth, homie. Did Mars render assistance in that awesome—but very expensive to me—escape from the compound?*

I said, *Not now. Go away.*

Mercury said, *I'm serious, dude.*

I said, *Does that mean Mars bet on me surviving? Can you send him over here? I need some help.*

Mercury grew uncharacteristically stern. *Did you see Mars?*

I said, *I saw him. But he never said a word.*

Mercury's suspicious gaze scanned me head to toe. *OK, Ima take your word for it. And hey, nice to see you made it through the first quarter of the game. Don't keep it up. I need that thousand aurei.*

Sure, I said. *Anything to help you out.*

Mercury smiled and patted my back and rose into the night sky. Flipping gods are going to drive me crazy.

When my gaze returned to Earth, it landed on Miguel, who was squinting at me. He said, "You OK?"

"When we get home, remind me to refill my prescription."

The truck came back crashing across the hillside through the olive trees. He hit the road two hundred yards uphill and smashed down the gas pedal. His headlights lit us up.

"You?" Earl looked me over. "They told us sand niggers was gonna blow up the conference, kill us all."

"They lied." I shrugged. "Shocker."

Earl stepped into the headlight beams and flagged down the truck. Miguel backed him up with the AK-47, just in case the driver didn't take directions well.

The truck slowed to a stop. Earl said, "Stand down, Tommy. Turns out, just more bullshit from Paladin. This here's a good guy and—" he looked over his shoulder at a big man holding an assault rifle and wisely decided to refrain from racial epithets "—a friend of his."

"You guys have a phone?" I asked.

"Grabbed our guns and a radio. Don't even have an extra magazine." Earl scratched his chin. "Make you a deal. We radio in the wrong location, give you a head start. You let us go."

"Great idea." I patted him on the back. "For you. But you see, we're taking your truck, your rifle, your ammo, and your radios. Consider it the penalty for attempted murder."

The former owner of the shotgun moaned and rose to his knees. He threw up. Tommy got out of the truck. We frisked them all, pocketing three knives plus the pistol in Tommy's boot.

Tania and Arrianne staggered toward us out of the marsh. Arrianne's face glowed white in the darkness. A bullet had grazed her back, leaving a long, ugly scratch. Her stretchy top barely stayed on her shoulders. We helped Arrianne into the truck bed. Tania climbed in, whipped off her shirt, leaving her in a sports bra, and used it to bandage Arrianne.

Miguel rode shotgun. Or AK-47, in this case. I brushed the last crumbs of glass out of the windshield frame and took off.

Headlights crested the hill behind us.

CHAPTER 32

I PUT THE HAMMER DOWN, and the little rental whined its way down the road.

Tania pounded on the back glass, screaming about a box of #00 shells in back. Miguel passed her the shotgun through the sliding back window. She loaded as our pursuers gained on us.

Miguel opened his door, stood on the seat leaning out, wrapped his seatbelt around his forearm for safety, and took a couple shots at the oncoming headlights.

The radio in the console squawked. "Tommy, that you? Don't shoot at us."

I picked it up. "Who is this? Paladin?"

"Hell no. Those Free Origins assholes left an hour ago. Went on their mission."

The news made me ill. ROSGEO was underway.

And we were flying around olive orchards being pursued by a bunch of well-armed morons.

Not to mention the fact that my personal deity had bet against me.

"Paladin lied to you," I said. "There aren't any Arabs. I'm Jacob Stearne."

A different voice crackled on the radio. "Holy shit. Where are you?"

There was a certain amount of glee in the newcomer's voice. An amount that spoke volumes about how big a bounty Paladin had put on our heads.

Another pair of headlights appeared. This time, five hundred yards in front of me.

A third voice jumped on the radio. "I see 'em. They got Tommy's pickup."

Arrianne leaned in the back window. "There's a back road on the left. It goes through a thicker grove. Maybe they won't see us."

"Hang on!" I warned my passengers a split-second before sliding sideways onto Arrianne's track. Gravel and dirt spewed from the tires. I drove up a hill, praying there was no one coming up the other side because we caught air at the top. When we crashed back to earth, something broke. I wasn't sure what, but you can't hit the ground that hard without breaking something.

As soon as I stepped on the gas, I knew what had broken. The tailpipe. If they couldn't see us, they could hear us.

"You can't be serious." Tania's voice assaulted my ears through the slider window. She was talking to Arrianne. "Jacob?"

There was a pout in Arrianne's answer. "A hero like Jacob would make the perfect provider for his family and a great defender of the white race."

"If that's your theory, what about me? I'm the one who saved your cracker ass and dressed your wound."

"Well, that's your job, isn't it?"

Tania stuck her face in the window. "Stop the car. I'm shoving this bitch out on the road."

I twisted to glance at her. "Just ignore her."

"I'm done 'ignoring' dumbass white people. I've been patient. I've forgiven them their trespasses. Where does it get me? Nowhere. Why don't you white people stop being assholes for a change, huh? I just saved some screaming idiot from getting shot in the back, and she treats me like hired help. I don't need to be patient."

Miguel gave her a fist bump. They both looked at me.

I felt their stares. I glanced back and forth at them. "Hey! Who pulled you out of a burning Humvee during the war?"

Tania said, "Some of y'all aren't so bad."

She pulled out of the window and said to Arrianne, "One more racist word out of you and you're going over the side."

"For what it's worth, Arrianne—" I called through the sliding window "—there's a reason I never slept with you. I could never love a racist.

With that much hate in your heart, where will it turn next?"

A pair of headlights flew over the ridge and gained on us with aggressive speed.

Miguel leaned out the window again and offered them the disincentive of a couple rounds. One bullet took out a headlight.

They answered with half a magazine.

I drove serpentine, swerving left and right without a pattern. We rounded a long, sweeping turn.

Miguel leaned in the cab. "They're hunting us."

His point was crystal clear, one truck chased us while the other got in position to shoot. I killed the headlights, sped up, jammed the brakes, threw the steering wheel into a hard left, pounded the accelerator, and did three doughnuts in the road. A choking cloud of dust arose. I backed in between rows of olive trees and waited for the happy hunters to drive through my dirt-smoke screen.

They approached at a high rate of speed. Miguel blew out the front tire with an award-winning shot. The compact SUV's nose plowed into the road, flipping the vehicle in the air.

Miguel and Tania hit the ground running. They got to the crash site before I could find Tommy's 9-mil. I arrived after they'd picked through the wreckage. Lights above the trees told me a second truck was coming.

I said, "Anything?"

"What's wrong with these people?" Tania yelled. "Can't bring a freaking phone on a car chase? None of them?"

"Rifle's nosed into the dirt," Miguel said. He tossed the useless weapon aside.

I said, "OK, give it up. Back to the truck."

As we turned to run, I found a phone. It had bounced ten yards from the wreck. It was bent like an elbow, the glass shattered. It couldn't possibly work.

We made it twenty yards into the trees as the second truck came through. A more cautious driver, he sensed something wrong and slowed before running into his pals. They found the wreckage and rendered aid.

Tania reached our truck first. "Where's Arrianne?"

Our plan to drive away in the opposite direction disappeared.

We stood still, straining our ears to hear her running or thrashing through olive branches. Nothing.

She knew the area well enough to know about the thin road we were on, yet she'd done nothing to help us find a house or a phone earlier. I wondered what she was doing.

Down at the wreckage, someone let out a primal scream in anger. We couldn't hear their words, but the intent was clear. They were pissed that we'd taken their friends out and were ratcheting up the stakes. They wanted us before. Now they wanted us even more. A burst of automatic gunfire punctuated their feelings. From the muzzle flashes, they appeared to be firing into the olive trees randomly.

"We have to find Arrianne," I said.

"Screw her," Tania said.

Miguel shrugged. He never took sides between Tania and me.

"We need Arrianne to tell Ames and Hugo about Free Origins. We don't know enough of the details and they'll need independent confirmation."

Random gunfire flew through the leaves and branches closer than the last burst. They were setting up a grid to find us by firing a pattern.

"We don't have time for your lovers, Jacob." Tania clenched a fist. "We tell them what we know, which is plenty. We'll be the confirmation."

"She's not my ..."

I stopped talking as another spray of bullets slapped leaves in the next row over. This crew had a lot more ammunition at their disposal than Earl left us. Tania was right. We were out of time.

I jumped in the driver's seat. Tania and Miguel braced themselves in the bed and readied their weapons.

We drove down the row. Tania blasted a few rounds of buckshot as we went. The effect was meaningless, but the noise told our enemies not to come too close.

One of them ignored the message. The figure of a man stepped into the beam of our headlights. Miguel fired over the cab in an attempt to brush him back. The stranger stood his ground and let loose a barrage that had us ducking. I aimed to run him over before I bent below the firewall, hoping to use the engine block as body armor. Nothing else on a car is bulletproof.

He managed a three-round burst before I hit him. His body went flying into the air. If he landed with any life left, the gods were on his side. Knowing them, I doubted it.

But the man's retribution rose from the engine compartment in the form of steam and oil. All the dashboard lights came on. A loud mechanical thumping sound came from under the hood. I lost power. Then something extra-loud clanked, and the pickup skidded into a fence post.

We took off on foot through a vineyard that led to an olive grove. We ran to the top of a ridge.

Leading our way, Miguel came to a disappointed stop. "Damn."

We came alongside him and saw where he was looking.

Below us sprawled the hacienda from which we'd recently escaped.

CHAPTER 33

WE ENTERED THE COMPOUND CAUTIOUSLY. The bent gate lay on the ground; the tractor I'd bent it with had been backed into the courtyard. The hacienda door stood open. Some lights were on. The hunters had said Paladin and company skipped town, but there could be stragglers. We checked carefully. There weren't. They'd left in a hurry. Tania and Miguel cleared the extended parts of the house. The only thing I cared about was the phone.

It had a dial tone when I found it. I dialed Zack Ames. Voicemail.

Mercury appeared next to me. *Thanks a lot, brother.*

A harsh emphasis on the last word. He dropped onto the dark leather sofa next to me.

Mercury said, *The other gods called it. Game over. They say you lived. I lost a thousand aurei. A thousand! Can't you die like most mortals? How come that tattooed guy can fire twenty-three rounds and only one of them singes your hair?*

I ran my fingers through my hair. Definitely a singed part on the left. Huh.

I dialed the Sabel Security helpdesk. After identifying myself, I asked them to track Zack Ames or his boss, the CIA's Paris Chief of Station. I'd take Lieutenant Colonel Hugo in a pinch. They promised to call me back at the hacienda as soon as they had one of them on the line.

I sat down next to Mercury. *Change your bet to me winning. Double down, help me out, and you can turn your loss into a win for both of us.*

Mercury said, *You're the biggest screw-up I've ever seen on a battlefield, homeboy. Without my help, you'd have died at the ripe old age of eighteen. Nah, for you to win, I'd have to help you every step of the way. The other gods would never let me do that. And that means I'd have to rely on you to win every battle without divine intervention.*

I said, *Pep talks. Remember? They're supposed to invigorate me. Make me feel invincible.*

Mercury looked me over as if something had just occurred to him. *Y'know what, dude? You're right. You are invincible. As a matter of fact, you should run out front and greet those guys coming in the gate.* He stood and spread his arms wide. *Your winning smile will make them change their minds about killing you. You've got this, brutha. You're golden.*

It took me a moment to figure out what he was doing. I got to my feet. *You son of a ... the game's still on and you're trying to get me killed. Thanks. With gods like you, who needs ... Ugh.*

"Miguel, Tania, we got company!" I yelled as I ran through the house looking for my squad. They called back from opposite ends.

From then on, we were silent. Each of us found a darkened room with a view of the courtyard. To get anywhere in the ancient house, visitors had to go through it. We had a decent crossfire set up. We were ready.

The only problem with our plan: They didn't come through the courtyard.

A pan clattered to the red tile floor in the kitchen. They'd come through a servant's entrance. Having been in several rich people's houses, I should've known this place had one of those. The uber-wealthy don't like to see the help staggering in from the car with the daily groceries. It makes them feel guilty about not helping.

A silhouette crouched through the garden. If Mercury had been right, there were two sneaking in the back.

Miguel and Tania were on the far side of the courtyard from the kitchen. I was closer but not by much. I backed away from my vantage point and crept through a drawing room to the edge of the dining room. Backlit by the kitchen, two silhouettes entered the dining room with Beretta AR70/90s leading their vision.

Behind me, the phone rang. In fact, four phones and a loud outside bell rang at the same time.

I was expecting the call, so it didn't throw me as much as it did our interlopers. Most people are used to hearing a cell phone ring in their pocket. But farms, ranches, and orchards don't have mobile coverage. They rely on land lines and really loud ringers you can hear anywhere on the property. The noise made our assassins jump.

A muffled bang from the garden broke the silence between rings. I didn't see the man go down, but I heard his head hit the paved walkway. Since I didn't hear Tania swearing, the dead man had to be our intruder. Miguel would've taken the shot, and if anything bad happened to him as a result, she would've come in like Hippolyta of the Greek Amazons and cut her enemy's head off. All was quiet in the garden. Meaning Miguel and Tania won their battle.

The startled players in the kitchen backed up into known territory to assess the noise. A smart defensive move.

I used the confusion to reposition myself next to the archway between the two rooms. The lights in the kitchen cast their shadows toward me, telegraphing their position.

The phone rang again.

In the dead silence between rings, I bumped a chair at the dining table. Shit happens. The wood-on-tile scuff alerted my enemies to my presence. In the back of my mind, it occurred to me that Mercury might've pushed me into that chair. The result was, I had lost the element of surprise.

The phone rang again.

My assassins used the standard operating procedure. One flew into the room, aiming forward, then left, and right. The second man covered him from the archway. Before the first man finished his sweep, I calculated his wingman's position based on his shadow and reached my pistol around the corner. I jammed it beneath his jaw and pushed his head upward. He had a decision to make, surrender, or jump to one side and take his chances.

Aleksei chose the latter. It was the last decision he ever made. My 9-mil fired at the same time his finger squeezed his trigger, but before he could bring the barrel around. Instead of killing me, he killed his teammate.

I flipped the lights on. "Clear."

Miguel answered the phone, being closest. "It's for you. Helpdesk."

I answered, and the voice started right away. "This is Lieutenant Colonel Hugo speaking. Is this Jacob Stearne?"

"I have bad news about the plans for the group out here at the Identity Defense Conference. They're planning multiple—"

"You went back to the conference, IDC? After London?"

"Uh." It took me a minute to figure out the disconnect. "Didn't Zack Ames update you? The job wasn't done. He wanted me to keep working it."

"And this you did?"

"Yes."

"Have you no shame?" he asked with a nasty twinge in his voice.

I looked around for Mercury. I wondered if my forgotten deity could be pulling the Frenchman's strings. It sounded like a god trying to demoralize me.

"Listen to me, Hugo." I reverted to my master sergeant voice. Delivered right, even generals will follow my orders. "I've uncovered their real plan. It's not pretty."

I laid it out for him briefly. From the time we landed until the London fiasco, Miguel and Tania had kept Zack Ames updated on the locations as we discovered them. I filled Hugo in on when ROSGEO would go down. What we didn't know was their command center's location. When I finished, Hugo went silent for a moment.

"This is a plan most horrible," he said. "You must come to my office, *tout de suite*. Ehm. Quickly. Bring your physical evidence"

We clicked off.

Miguel and Tania spent the call rifling through the dead Russians' effects. They collected two pistols, three Italian automatic rifles, and three phones. The phones were locked. The facial recognition software was unimpressed with the faces of their late owners. We used the emergency call function to call a special number at Sabel Technologies. Our experts would automatically download the contents of the phones, make a million software images of them, then try every possible password combination until they were unlocked. It would take a few hours and a bazillion computing horsepower, but eventually, they'd get some answers.

Tania held up car keys taken from a dead man's pocket. We drove to Seville and climbed aboard Sabel Three.

CHAPTER 34

THE HEADQUARTERS OF *Groupe d'intervention de la Gendarmerie nationale*, GIGN, is on a military-industrial park not far from the Palace of Versailles. We were ushered from guardhouse to division building to Hugo's waiting area. Several soldiers in fatigues came and went from the office while the three of us picked through a stack of French magazines.

Like my dentist's office, the magazines were six months old. The date was all I could read since I didn't read French. Miguel did and read with great interest from one called *Charlie Hebdo*. From time to time, he burst out laughing.

Hugo's aide-de-camp asked me for background information. I retold the story I'd told Hugo over the phone. The aide asked for proof of anything. Which pissed me off because I didn't have any. It's not like terrorists draw up project management Gantt charts and Pert diagrams for their evil plans. I told him to check with the Spanish authorities who must've found several dead and injured people lying around Úbeda. He agreed to have them check Arrianne's house and the Ooze for any remaining evidence. The man took extensive notes and asked the right questions. Then he left. I felt good about Hugo's operation.

Mercury sat next to me with a scowl and crossed arms. *Thanks a lot, homie. The game is officially over now. I'm out two thousand aurei. You happy? Do you have any idea how hard it is to get your hands on one aureus much less two thousand? Nobody's made any for fifteen hundred years.*

I said, *I thought you bet a thousand.*

Mercury said, *When Aleksei showed up with three Berettas, I doubled down. What were you thinking? You said, and I quote, "Sure. Anything to help you out." But did you do anything to help me? No. I can NOT believe I trusted a mortal. I should have my head examined.*

I said, *That makes two of us.*

A different young lieutenant standing in front of me frowned. "*Excusez-moi*, but Lieutenant Colonel Hugo said most clearly, just you. Not two. Not three. Only one, the Jacob Stearne."

I looked at Miguel and Tania. She muttered, "Sick of being patient with white people."

They sighed and went back to their magazines.

Hugo greeted me from behind his desk with an extended handshake. When the door closed, he turned to his window. He had a second-story view of rather drab training grounds. Tank tracks led through a wooded area dotted with sheds and walls and obstacles of all sorts.

"You have connected with Monsieur Ames?" he asked.

"I keep getting his voicemail. Do you know where he is?"

"Vacation." He craned over his shoulder. "So I am told by his superior. Your boyfriend visits many times to extol your heroism at Moulin Rouge. He argues against Pavard's findings at Saint-Sulpice. With you, he is quite, how do you say, enamored."

He curled a lip while handing me Benoît's card.

"We have to act quickly," I said, ignoring his comment. "Pentecost is this coming Sunday. Why did you leave us hanging in your outer office so long?"

He faced me with a scowl. "Your word is quite diminished in the community intelligence. Ehm, London, you know."

"We have to get the word out to all the cities involved." I tossed up my hands. "Did you start that process?"

"Verification is of utmost importance to this case. Yet it is most difficult to prove your story."

"Locations, dates, codenames. What did you miss, Hugo?"

"Contradictions have reached me from persons outside your—" he waved his hand toward the waiting area "—special group."

Outside his door, a commotion sprang up featuring Tania's outraged voice. I couldn't make out any words. Then the office door opened. Arrianne strode in wearing a floral print dress of the kind seen at royal tennis matches. Her shoes and purse matched the dress.

"Ah, the lovely Arrianne," Hugo waved her to a chair. "I understand you two are knowing each other. She came to us and offered the accounts most informative of your actions."

"Is that right?" I gave her my soldier stare.

She flinched and sat and adjusted her skirt and kept her gaze on Hugo.

"Ms. Arrianne, have you witnessed the training of persons to engage in a program called ROSGEO?" Hugo asked.

"Never," she said with the hint of a southern drawl. "After I refused Jacob's advances, he called you about my London trip. From then on, he blamed me for ruining his reputation. I do believe just yesterday he announced he would stop at nothing to regain his status in the world."

"You see the problem?" Hugo asked. "I have a decorated veteran with the dramatic story on one hand, and the respected confidential informant of the British NCA on the other. You have not the shred of evidence. Also, you have involved several military intelligence officers of Britain in a career-ending operation based on information most unreliable."

He turned to the window and clasped his hands behind his back.

I was speechless. "Career-ending" is the most dreaded phrase in military bureaucracies around the world. Arrianne must've run straight from the truck in Spain to Hugo just to derail me. Her loyalty had flipped over once again. Which pissed me off. On top of that, she managed to shower and dress for success. While I rushed in without even shaving. I probably smelled bad too.

Arrianne kept her gaze fixed on Hugo.

Hugo broke the silence. Quietly, he said, "We will investigate your claims, monsieur. But to be honest, you are sounding like your not-trustworthy friend, Zack Ames."

Mercury stood on the far side of her. *Dawg, I told you to show her a good time. Give her a romp in the hay. Did you? No, you scorned her. You told her, 'I could never love a racist.' And now you see the adage proved. Hell hath no fury like this witch.*

I said, *What did he mean about Zack?*

Mercury said, *Find me two thousand aurei, and I'll tell you. Home.*

Boy.

I patted Arrianne's shoulder hard where the bullet had grazed her. She winced in pain and gave me dagger looks.

"Do you like her name, Hugo?" I asked.

"Arrianne? Very European."

"Arrianne or … Aryan? C'mon Hugo, you're smarter than that."

His face flew through a few moods in a second, hurt and embarrassed before settling on outraged. At me. For making him look dumb. Which was a mistake on my part. Sun Tzu advised leaving a golden bridge for your opponent's retreat. Instead, I built it out of balsa and set it alight.

"If you won't do anything about it," I snarled at Hugo, "we will. There are other counterterrorism forces in the sea. I'll go to Pavard."

It was the only name I knew in France. He politely stifled his laugh.

I turned and walked to his door.

He said, "If you threaten any persons in the EU, it is you who will be the terrorist, Monsieur Stearne. Pavard believes firmly that you did this once already. We will not tolerate anymore the cow-boy."

I slammed the door.

CHAPTER 35

WE SET UP A MEETING with the CIA's Paris Chief of Station—COS—
and were headed there when he called to reroute us to the United
Kingdom's Embassy. The back door. Secrecy and all that. A
representative of MI6 would be joining us. It was two buildings away
from the US Embassy, so we couldn't complain.

"I don't have a good feeling about that," Tania said.

"At least they're going to see all three of us this time," Miguel said.

We arrived on Avenue Gabriel and found the unmarked, solid-steel
gate. A British officer met us curbside. He used facial recognition
software on his phone to identify us since we hadn't replaced our
passports and phones yet. All we had was a phone we borrowed from one
of our pilots. The guard waited until our Uber left before opening the
gate and letting us through. Inside was a park lined with trees. Stone
benches overlooked a long flower garden with a bowling lawn. It was
another fine day in Paris, and everything was in bloom.

We strolled down a paved walkway toward the main building.
Alcoves on the right and left featured groupings of wooden park benches.
Two men in suits waited in one alcove. The man with his back to us
turned and waved. We veered toward them and took seats. Each of us
took a separate bench. I sat next to waving-man. Tania sat alone.

"I'm COS," waving-man said. "We'll dispense with names since this
will be a short meeting. I'm not a fan of yours, Mr. Stearne. The killing
of civilians in Saint-Sulpice is a crime and should be prosecuted. Don't
let the fact that your boss's connections let you skate on that one make
your head too big. Half of Paris still wants you dead."

"Nice to meet you, too," I said. I turned to the Brit. "Did you serve in the military?"

"Indeed," he said.

"Did you see the video from the church?"

"I did." He sniffed for punctuation. "I dare say, I find myself at odds with the official narrative, if that's where you're going with this."

"Thank you."

"But I was in the City of London for your last fiasco as well." He scowled. "Dan Bonham-Carter was a friend of mine. He was demoted just this morning."

The name sounded familiar. I think he was the MI-6 guy.

Mercury sat between the Brit and Miguel. *You don't play well with others. You ever notice that, homie? Maybe if you made a burnt offering to your own personal god once in a while, things would get better. Maybe if you appreciated all I do for you, the insults would go away. Just thinking out loud here.*

I said, *Does this mean you're going to help me this time?*

Mercury said, *There any money in it for me?*

I said, *Thinking like that is why Christianity got the jump on you guys. It's not about money with them.*

Mercury said, *Oh really, homes? Really? Been to the Vatican lately?*

The COS was looking at me funny.

I said, "Your man Ames asked me to go undercover and then went on vacation. Don't you guys hand off these missions?"

"Zack Ames didn't tell me anything about engaging you."

"What kind of station are you running?"

"Not one that uses vigilantes for undercover work."

"And yet here I am." I stood and waved my arms.

"There are no operations in Paris that I don't know about and I'm telling you, there are no ops involving alt-right groups." He got to his feet and faced off with me.

"Are you forgetting the one aiding an FBI agent named Brady?" I snarled.

"We don't get involved with FBI agents. When they cross the pond, they work with local law enforcement."

"Are you saying you abandoned an American on a dangerous

assignment?"

"See here," the Brit said, "You've no right to cast aspersions on Mr. … On the COS here. He's a good man. I've worked with him for years. He would never leave an op uncovered."

I faced the Brit. "Then where is Nuristan Zack?"

"You've heard of him before, I see." The COS tapped my shoulder. "When did Ames talk to you about this operation?"

"Right after Saint-Sulpice and again after the bombing at the Moulin Rouge. He was in London with me."

"He's been on vacation for two weeks." The COS pinched his nose. "What did he look like?"

I held my hand out flat below eye level. "About five-eight, one-fifty, bald."

The COS and the Brit exchanged glances. The COS played with his phone and pulled up a picture. He showed it to me. "Did he look like this?"

A thick guy with a full head of hair stood in a photo above a departmental ID. It listed him as six-two, one-ninety, no tattoos. Zack W. Ames.

The COS shook his head at me. "Guy walks into a bar in Mexico City, tells everyone there he's with the CIA. The smart people ask for some ID. Other people take his word for it, that's not my problem. You believed he's one of mine—and you didn't ask for ID. That's your problem."

He and the Brit turned to leave.

"Wait, I didn't ask him for ID because he was with Lieutenant Colonel Hugo of the GIGN."

The COS and the Brit exchanged another worried glance. The COS said, "Did you verify Hugo's ID?"

"Thin, middle-aged, acts like the King of France and has a hundred people at GIGN headquarters acting like he's their lieutenant colonel."

The spy chiefs nodded at each other. "That's him. He introduced you to this other Zack Ames?"

I nodded.

They conferred in silence. People who work together for a long time work out a type of telepathy. They came to a decision.

"Check with the Spanish. They must've found the operation by now—"

The COS put a hand on my shoulder. "We'll take it from here."

"Like hell." I pushed his hand off. "We watched terrorists train for multiple mass-shootings. A man posing as a CIA agent working with the GIGN co-opted us. We're not taking your word for it that it's handled. We want in. We want to be part of the solution."

"It's not up to you," the Brit said. He put two fingers in his mouth and gave a loud whistle.

"You have to sound the alarm," I said. "This could be going down in the next few days. You have to warn all the countries targeted about these people. If you don't, and something bad happens, we go to the press."

The Brit scoffed. The American said, "You do that. They've been having a field day with you all week."

The sound of boots on gravel marched down from the main building. Twelve British soldiers arrived to help us find the way out.

CHAPTER 36

THE MOTORIZED GATE SLID CLOSED behind us, leaving us on the street.

A man in a car cruising slowly down the lane rolled his window down. "Tania! It is Florian!"

Tania stooped to look in the window. She waved us into the car in a hurry. Once we strapped in, the driver took off. He was the manager of Sabel Security Paris. He looked like he hadn't slept in a week. His shirt was rumpled, his eyes sagged. He had been trying to reach us for hours. He had set up a meeting with the FBI's man at the embassy. The same embassy the COS wouldn't let us enter because of "secrecy". It was around the corner half a block. Florian drove because he said we were Americans and he knew we didn't walk anywhere.

Florian provided sidearms along with a warning about how they're illegal to carry in public in most EU countries despite our special licenses. And he gave us new phones. He also handed out packets of handheld Sabel Darts, small injectors containing a non-lethal dose of inland Taipan snake venom that causes instant flaccid paralysis. The venom's backed with a high dosage of sleep medication. The victim of a dart would be paralyzed long enough to fall asleep for four hours.

I felt human again with my phone replacement. Sabel Satellites remotely updated it. Mine showed 352 missed messages. One from Jenny.

Mercury leaned over my shoulder. *And you were this close to forgetting about her.*

I said, *I'll never forget Jenny.*

Mercury said, *Two weeks, bro. You hardly knew her.*

I said, *She was special. Meeting her was destiny.*

I put my finger over the button to playback Jenny's message. I wavered. She might've reconsidered and left a message begging me to take her back. It might be one of those and-the-horse-you-rode-in-on messages. Most likely it was more of the it's-not-you-it's-me stuff. No matter what kind of message it was, it would distract me from stopping ROSGEO. I'd have to listen to it later.

An embassy aide left Florian in the lobby and led us upstairs. The aide took us on a long walk through meandering hallways before we found the guy. He introduced himself as Mark. He explained that the FBI has jurisdiction in the USA but maintains sixty-three legal attaché offices, called legats, in foreign countries to exchange information on criminal activities ranging from drug running to terrorism. Mark was the legat for Paris.

"First, let me clue you in on one key factor." Mark pursed his lips and chose his words. "The last administration was a nightmare. The president went through cabinet secretaries like shirts. He gutted the State Department and the intelligence services. And I—" he bowed his head and extended his arms "—arrived in Paris the day after your heroic act in Saint-Sulpice."

"You're not buying the local narrative?" I asked.

"Not for a minute. I came here straight from Afghanistan, the country with the most deaths by terrorism last year. I know terrorists. So do a lot of people in the GIGN."

"Except Hugo."

"Tell me your story." He pulled a yellow pad out of his desk and began to take notes.

We sat in his office and explained everything. Miguel and Tania recounted the observations they'd made via video and directional microphones. They gave him access to the recordings kept on the Sabel cloud. I went over my experiences at the Ooze. I skipped a few details about the ladies. Mark took copious notes. He was interested.

Which was a tremendous relief.

"Now, tell me why you think this Arrianne is a drug dealer?" he asked.

"The UK's NCA broke her out of Counter Terrorism's grip," I said.

"That's an exceptional trick. The NCA handles drugs and crime. The office she and her team broke into was an international services company with no clients. Yet the three-year-old company had offices next door to the London Stock Exchange."

"Lots of money but no known sources." Mark scratched his chin. "Money laundering for a drug business is one possible explanation. Why would she break in and why would NCA free her?"

"We couldn't find anything on her," Tania said. "Her passport, social media, visas, everything had been quashed."

"That's what the US Marshals do before they relocate a witness." Mark nodded. "They'd relocate her to a different city to prevent witness tampering and move her permanently after the trial. You think the NCA had her as a witness?"

I said, "Her group dealt crystal meth in the EU's alt-right circles. They nailed her and offered her witness protection in exchange for testifying against the kingpin."

"I'm with you on all that," Mark said. "It makes sense. So why would she break into the kingpin's offices?"

"Cash. She told me she'd dealt drugs for the Estonian Cartel." I let that one sit there a few seconds. "She was going to the cartel's office to steal money. She needed a lot. Once she discovered what ROSGEO was all about, she wanted out in the worst way. In their deal, the NCA had told her not to leave the EU, but she needed an alibi for ROSGEO. A continental alibi. She knew where to find a ton of cash—the kingpin's office where it waits to be laundered. She planned to grab the cash and buy her way out of Europe. She wants to be in Argentina or Greenland when ROSGEO goes down."

"Arrianne's the one running the conference," Mark said. "She must have cash on hand."

"When I made a run for it, I offered Arrianne a ride. She hesitated because everything she had was tied up in the conference. Then she got in the car and was ready to leave it all behind. Not even say goodbye to her lieutenant. The only reason a young businesswoman would leave like that is if she's no longer in control of her accounts.

"Nema claimed to be an artist. I figured out her art. Acting. After last year's meeting in Kraków, when Arrianne started her own, less-violent group, Nema joined her. Nema offers to help people. She makes you feel like she's your servant. It's all part of her act. She made herself invaluable to Arrianne as an assistant. Once Arrianne trusted Nema, Nema took control of the bookkeeping, then the accounts. Nema's even better with men. She makes them desire her by underplaying her role. I almost fell for it. The first clue I had that she wasn't who she appeared to be happened on my first day in Úbeda. Lugh had my phone and passport the day I arrived, yet he'd never come near me after I broke his arm. Who stole them? Nema."

Mark tapped his pen on his notepad. "So Nema robbed Arrianne, transferred all the accounts to her control. Why?"

"Nema wants ROSGEO to be untraceable. She needed someone else's bank accounts to buy the Beretta machine guns, airplane tickets, whatever they needed."

"That's a logical explanation, but what makes you think Nema controlled the accounts?"

"When I arrived, I demanded my fee. Arrianne sent Nema to get it. Birth Right is not a big organization. Arrianne should be the only one who signs checks. Yet Paladin signed mine."

"Doesn't that make Paladin the leader?" Mark asked.

"I liked the guy right off. Everyone presented him as the man in charge. But as I got to know him, it became clear his only gift is a smile. He's nothing but an oxygen thief. Nema pulls his strings. Desire makes people do strange things, and Nema is great at making people desire her. And she's smart. She never completes the deal. She has him signing checks, thinking he's in charge. All the fingerprints are his, not hers. When it all goes down, she expects him to die. He signed the checks for her. The nightmare will appear to be his alone."

"From what I've read in the reports, this Free Origins group is misogynist as well as racist. Why would they follow a woman?"

"That's what tripped me up for a long time." I shook my head. "Nema's good. Real good. I doubt anyone besides Paladin and Arrianne know she's calling the shots. There were many confusing signs. Like the fact that Birth Right and Free Origins hated each other yet worked together. Then, the Russian, Aleksei, made a condescending remark to Arrianne's lieutenant about working for a woman. That made me look elsewhere for leadership. But I couldn't find any. Zero suspects.

"They call Arrianne the Gospeler because she spouts Bible passages from time to time. That got me thinking back to my own Sunday School lessons. One passage came to mind. 'The greatest among you will be your servant. All who exalt themselves will be humbled, and all who humble themselves will be exalted. – Matthew, 23:11-12.' Nema was everyone's servant and the humblest person there. Unassuming, blending in with the woodwork, barely noticeable. Unless she wanted you to desire her, then she would make full-body contact. It's hard for a man to hold a woman in his arms, to feel her flesh and smell her scent—and not desire her."

"Diego, Paladin, Aleksei," Tania said. "And god knows who else. Men are such idiots."

The three of us looked at her but said nothing.

"Sometimes," she said.

"Nema is truly an evil genius." Mark scribbled more notes.

Mercury stood behind Mark. *I think you won this guy over. Maybe I can double down again. Only this time, Ima bet on you to live through it.*

I said, *That would be a welcome change.*

"She's on the verge of making this happen," I told Mark. "She said it would happen before Pentecost. I'm not up on the church calendar, but I think that's in the next few days. We have to stop her."

At that moment, all three of our Sabel phones chirped an important message.

Miguel updated us, "Our people decoded the phones from the Free Origins guys. Everything they did was over E2EE apps."

"E2EE?" I asked.

Everyone in the room cocked their heads in my direction. Guess I missed the latest developments on the technology front.

Mark said, "End-to-end encryption. No traces left on a server, autodeleted on both ends, nothing left for law enforcement to subpoena. Perfect for criminals and terrorists."

I said, "Oh."

I checked my phone for Protestant church calendars.

Miguel continued. "What they did find were itineraries. One guy was going to Luxembourg, another to Antwerp, and Aleksei was headed to Cologne."

Mark flipped back a few pages. "The target locations you gave me don't match those destinations. Where are they going?"

"Pentecost is Sunday." I ran my fingers through my hair. "They should be at their destinations for recon by tomorrow at the latest."

"Unless," Miguel said, "they're going to the command center for a big pep-talk to make sure they're committed to the cause. Terrorists often use a rally to build up their resolve."

"A send-off would be right up Paladin's alley," Tania said. "He made more toasts at their dinners than a frat boy running for chapter president."

"Then why are they going in three directions?" Mark asked. "Near each other, a hundred-mile triangle give or take, but not all in the same spot. Are they obscuring their tracks? Maybe they plan to take a train to a central location?"

I snapped my fingers and pointed at him. "That's it, Mark. Genius. Now, can you get your people mobilized to round them up?"

Miguel, Tania and I turned our expectant faces to Mark, FBI legal attaché for Paris.

Mercury said, *You had to ask about that, homie? Weren't you listening to him earlier?*

I said, *He's FBI. They have thirteen thousand people. They have international connections Sabel Security can only dream about.*

Mercury said, *I'm losing confidence you can stop ROSGEO.*

Mark looked as if I'd made a dirty joke about his mother. "Uh. Remember the part about the previous administration destroying American institutions around the world?"

"Yeesss," we said in unison.

"A lot of good people left the State Department and the FBI and the intelligence services, and hell, most overseas postings. President Charles Williams has only been in office for three weeks. He'll get things sorted out eventually." He swallowed hard. "You're onto something huge and villainous and evil here but … I don't have any 'people.' None of the legat offices have any 'people' left. I'll make some calls. I met a guy named Pavard in the Paris police department. He's a nice guy. I'll talk to him."

"Don't bother," I said. "He's the one who started the story about me killing two innocent tourists."

"Oh. Well, then." He made a note on his yellow pad about Pavard. "Dennis is out in front of us on this, and god only knows what he'll do— if anything. I'll confront him about it." Mark sighed and wiped his face with his hands. "He'll do what he did last time, tell me to keep in my lane. Hell. This is bad."

Miguel stood.

"But, I'm getting right on it." Mark looked up at the giant Navajo. "You guys shouldn't do anything. You don't have a great rep in France. Or Western Europe for that matter. Eastern Europe either. Rest assured, I will make things happen. I will sound the alarm."

Tania stood.

"Who's Dennis?" I asked. I rose as well.

"Station chief, the drama queen who played James Bond with you in the garden next door." Mark rolled his eyes.

Nice to know we had the same opinion of the CIA's man in France.

"Thanks for your help. We're going to pop smoke." I extended a hand.

He shook it. "Pop smoke?"

"Call for extraction. When you're outnumbered and call for evac, you pop a smoke bomb so the bird can find you."

He nodded. "My duties in Kabul were with the police there. I didn't hear many military terms. Look, you must leave this in our hands now. We can't afford any more ambiguous incidents like Saint-Sulpice. We'll make things happen, Jacob. You can count on me."

CHAPTER 37

"WE CAN'T COUNT ON HIM," Tania said as we waited for Florian outside the embassy. "The Bureau is good, but they never get it done quicker'n six weeks."

"At least he listened to us." Miguel, the optimist.

I looked around for directional mics that might feed our conversation to Dennis-of-the-CIA. The building appeared devoid of cameras and microphones. That meant they were well hidden.

"Oh, isn't that nice?" Tania snarked. "Face it, he's a self-licking ice cream cone. The only people he knows in Europe are standing outside his embassy."

Mercury hopped out of a cab and walked up to me. *Yo. Is Sunday getting closer or further away? Get moving. I just doubled down on you getting this worked out.*

You bet on me to succeed? I asked. *I thought you were joking. As usual. Thank you for having a little faith in me for once. Where should we look?*

Mercury slapped his hand over my mouth and looked both ways, plus up. *I can't be telling you that shit, bro. You know that. Especially when you know where three of them were headed. Think about it. On second thought, have Miguel and Tania think about it. When it comes to thinking, they outclass you.*

"We know where they're going." I pulled my phone and brought up a map. "We could split up and search all three cities."

"What is this, a horror movie?" Miguel asked. "Split up so we can die in different cities together?"

"Better ideas?"

"We gotta think about this," Tania said. "Fake-Zack said these guys were experts at going off the grid. There's no way they were going to Cologne or Antwerp. Luxembourg maybe. They have the highest incidence of racial violence in Europe after Finland. Maybe they feel safe there."

"Finland?" I asked. "I thought they were the Canadians of Europe."

"That's Netherlands." She noticed me wondering how she knew stuff like that. "When you're a person of color who travels a lot, you keep an eye on certain statistics. And a Glock. You keep a Glock handy in case the stats are wrong. Anyway, the answer's right in front of us. I can feel it."

Florian pulled to the curb. We piled in.

I tapped our driver. "How many Sabel people can we get to help us? We need to search three cities."

"Is this all?" He craned around to scowl at me. "Ms. Sabel exposes money laundering by the previous American administration, and suddenly we become the most popular security company in the world. Everyone is deployed, working extra shifts, eighty-hour weeks. Over a hundred job openings are availble in the Paris office alone. This is my thirty-sixth consecutive hour on the clock. This is SO not French."

He drove us to the Sabel offices while we explained our three-city problem. He had little to offer other than the approximate populations. Cologne is the largest at roughly a million; Antwerp has half that; and the entire country of Luxembourg rounds up to six hundred thousand. Then he went back to work, leaving us in a meeting room.

We borrowed laptops to bring up a wall map of the region. In the triangle between the cities, we found little to stand out as a central meeting place. Liège, Aachen, Eindhoven, Hasselt, and Maastricht were too small for the anonymity they would need. We looked for private estates like the one they used in Spain. Nothing popped out at us. If they had a benefactor in the region, like the owner of the hacienda in Spain, they were in the wind.

Tania tired of speculation and stared out the window.

"What about Fake-Zack?" I asked Miguel. "What do we know about him?"

DEATH AND CONSPIRACY

"He's heavier than he looks." Miguel stared at the map. "His French was fair, his English fully American, so I doubt he was one of Hugo's men pretending to be American."

"Pretending!" Tania came back to the table. She picked up her phone. "Seville is not Paris when it comes to European aviation. If you fly from Seville to some rando town, you have to change planes."

She dialed a number and walked away from us.

Miguel and I weren't following her logic and she didn't explain, so we turned back to our maps. We searched for shooting ranges and large spaces like the one in Andalusia. The region has a much higher population density than Spain, making obvious locations harder to spot. Satellite maps didn't help.

Where would terrorists party before flying around the world for an attack? Anywhere. An office building, an estate, a farm, an abandoned warehouse.

When the project felt overwhelming, my thoughts returned to Jenny. I toyed with the idea of listening to her voicemail. Her dumping sounded damn final. If she wanted me to bring a pastry back from Paris, that would be painful. If she wanted to tell me to buzz off again, that would be even more painful. If she regretted dumping me and wanted to get back together again, that would lead me to abandon the search for Nema and go back like a dog with my tail between my legs. Which would lead to me feeling guilty the rest of my life for letting ROSGEO happen. Even more painful.

The Sabel Security helpdesk texted me. They found contact information for Dennis Trapp, CIA Chief of Station, Paris. I called him.

As soon as he picked up, I said, "Dennis, have you found them yet?"

"Who is this?"

"Jacob Stearne. If I'm right, and ROSGEO goes down without you lifting a little finger, how will you sleep?"

"I've lifted a finger. Do you know what I found under it? A confidential informant for the British Crown who claims you made the whole thing up when she refused your advances."

"Did she offer you video proof of that? Because I'm sending you a clip I think you'll find works against her story." I texted him the video

221

Miguel took when we boarded the jet to London. Arrianne, being her sexy-self, smiled and chatted and bumped against me as we crossed the hangar. I looked and walked straight ahead before saying something to her that left her crestfallen. I said, "More importantly, did Hugo tell you why he introduced me to Zack Ames?"

"Our server won't allow videos. Too much spyware." His voice didn't move an inch from hardass. "Hugo claims he presented Zack as our agricultural attaché to you at Saint-Sulpice and any assumptions from there were your own."

That much was true. I screwed that one up because of my hatred for Nuristan Zack. I asked, "Why did Fake-Zack pick the name of a hated agent?"

"Not my problem." He clicked off.

Tania strode back to the table, put her hands on it, and leaned over. She had a smug look on her face. "Amsterdam."

Miguel and I looked at each other, then back at her.

"Idiots." She rolled her eyes. "All three of those guys flew from Seville to Amsterdam. They were then supposed to change planes to reach their final destinations. If you want to drop off the grid—skip your connecting flight. They're gonna drop off the grid in Amsterdam."

"Passports?" I asked. "Never mind, they're inside the Schengen Area. No passports required. You're right, walk straight out the door and onto the street. That makes a lot of sense."

Miguel nodded. "It makes sense, but it's a guess. A good one, but we can't bet everything on a guess. What if they're meeting in Cologne or Luxembourg? We could wander the streets of Amsterdam for days and never find them."

"We have to split up." I stared at the map. Something in my memory banks itched. "Cover our bases."

"Remember, Nema's real name is Joan Vanrijn," Miguel said. "Why does that feel important?"

I Googled it. It came up as the surname of Rembrandt. We looked at each other and shrugged. Highly unlikely Nema was a descendant of Rembrandt. We resumed thinking in silence for a few minutes.

Florian came in to see if we needed anything. He waited hoping we didn't with the expression of a very tired person.

"She has a tattoo on her neck," I said. "Crossed keys, like this."

I drew two antique keys with the handles at the bottom, and the teeth turned outward.

I'm no artist. Never said I was. My compatriots looked like art patrons asked to explain a Rothko painting. I said, "Keys. They're keys."

"It looks like a drunken X," Miguel said.

Florian looked over my shoulder.

I said, "She said they had something to do with her grandfather. It was a memento, or something."

"Ah, the keys of Leiden," Florian said. He pointed at the map on the wall screen.

To the left and a bit down from Amsterdam was a town called Leiden. Wikipedia showed a flag with crossed keys in the middle.

Florian continued, "Leiden's like a miniature version of Amsterdam with canals and guild houses. It is home to the University of Leiden, Airbus headquarters, and it was Rembrandt's hometown. They've been successful attracting companies that would normally go to Amsterdam, Paris, or London but want lower rent. Lots of commercial renovation."

"Holy shit," we said in unison.

"Rembrandt's hometown. Maybe she's a descendant," I said. "She introduced herself as an artist."

Miguel said, "Renovated office buildings would make the perfect cover for Free Origins' command center."

"It makes sense," I said, "but you're right, we're still drawing conclusions from threads of clues. We don't have anything concrete to go on but a tattoo and a surname. And we have to find that command center. It's our only chance to stop all the attacks at once."

"Damn. We do have to split up." Miguel nodded as he came to his conclusion. "Tania goes to Antwerp; I go to Cologne; you go to Leiden."

"Why do I get Leiden?"

Tania looked as if the answer were obvious. "It has the best chance of being filled with forty-nine terrorists having a rah-rah party, and that means whoever goes there is most likely to die."

"Yeah." Miguel nodded with her, then shrugged. "Better you than me."

CHAPTER 38

EVERYONE RIDES BICYCLES IN LEIDEN. The machines lean against every building in every street. Not the fancy bikes Americans ride dressed in all their spandex splendor, but sensible utility vehicles. Most were designed in 1939. Some of them looked like they were built then too. Two-wheeled tech hasn't changed much over the last eighty years. They came with mudguards and a rack for small items. The fancy ones had hand brakes. The one I rented was basic, which was fine by me. I hadn't spent much time on a bike since I got my driver's license.

I was the only customer sitting inside the Café Barrera. Everyone in their right mind enjoyed the warm, sunny day at the sidewalk tables scattered around the intersection of Rapenburg and Nonnenbrug. The former meaning "turnip town" and the latter meaning "nun's bridge," if my translation app was any good.

My favorite deity insisted I watch the university on the other side of the canal from inside so no Free Origins people would see me. As bougie cafés go, Barrera ranked up there with the best. Plenty of avocado toast for a smidgen under €10. I often wished I'd been the guy who thought of smashing fifty cents worth of avocado on a piece of leftover toast.

Mercury sat next to me, nursing a strange-looking coffee. *Quit messing with your ankle, brutha. Keep your eyes on the university across the canal.*

I said, *I tweaked it on the landing. I need some Motrin.*

Mercury said, *I thought you were an expert HALO jumper.*

I said, *You can't see every gopher hole.*

Mercury said, *Tania and Miguel making you jump was mean.*

I said, *Who keeps reminding me Sunday is coming? They didn't have time for a drop-off at an airport. That doesn't matter. What I want to know is why would Free Origins need a university? Most of those guys struggled in eighth grade.*

Mercury said, *Leiden has a celebrated language department. They need more religious phrases than "Allahu Akbar".*

I said, *And they want to stay off the grid, so they're not going to use Google. Got it.*

Right then, a man with his arm in a sling crossed the Nonnenbrug heading straight for me.

Lugh.

When he turned up Kloksteeg, I bolted for the door. My bike was down the canal in the other direction. I decided to follow on foot. He paced quickly up the cobblestone lane between the sidewalk cafés.

Lugh would recognize the guy who broke his arm from a hundred yards. I kept a respectable distance. I didn't need to. He didn't pay attention to anything around him. His mind was on something else. He crossed an open plaza and ripped open the bright red door to an ancient church.

I kept to the south side of the plaza and checked my phone. The maps called it Pieterskerk, a twelfth century church converted into an event hall. The perfect place to host a send-off for forty-nine terrorists intent on attacking religious sites. Their website offered parties as large as 500 in the nave and seventy in the café. There were meeting rooms, short-stay facilities, wedding capabilities, and all kinds of other things.

It would make a good location for a pre-game party with Paladin making toasts. It was a guess, but it was unlikely Lugh strolled Leiden for any good reason. The organization wouldn't send their second-in-command as a decoy. A look inside could tell me more.

They wouldn't have rented it for the command center. I'd have to find that later.

The most likely scenario was that phase one of ROSGEO was underway. There might be two or three phases. One to pump up the terrorists, the next to spark the war. The third would be alternate attacks to ensure the success of the first two. If I was right, the first attack would happen in the morning. Time was short.

DEATH AND CONSPIRACY

I texted Miguel and Tania to turn the jet around and HALO into Leiden.

Standing out in the open was dangerous. Lugh walking around in daylight would be countered by a precautionary protocol on the part of Free Origins.

I stood across a small plaza from Lugh's big red door surrounded by ancient red brick buildings with signs in Dutch that I didn't understand. I opened the nearest door.

I found myself in a school office. A woman behind the desk looked up and asked me something in Dutch. I shrugged and made myself thin behind the door frame to escape notice from outside.

Across the plaza, the Hungarians from the hacienda strolled out of Pieterskerk's red door. They scanned every direction before turning left and walking away.

The lady at the desk asked in English, "Are you here for a reason?"

My welcome was wearing thin.

I kept watching and was rewarded for my patience. At the end of the plaza, one of the Hungarians abruptly turned around and walked in my direction. Great way to expose and confront a tail. The reflected light on the outside of the door helped shield me for a moment.

I turned to the lady at the desk. "Could you help me? I was following my sister's ex-husband, and I think he saw me. He has a terrible temper and is quite violent. Do you have a back door?"

She shook her head. "We are a pre-school for faculty only."

Like American schools, security had risen to alarming levels for Dutch children. Doors remain locked. Only known parents, teachers, and students are allowed in. Her gaze went to the window where the Hungarian, who looked like Central Casting had sent him to play thug #3, stood in the plaza searching for any sign of trouble.

"Maybe you could go through the playground to the Kerkhof, turn right and go outside." She pressed a button under her desk. The door to my left clacked.

I went through it to a tiny courtyard filled with toddler-sized toys. At the other end was a red door like the one on Pieterskerk. On the other side of the red door I found a graveyard. I wondered if the four-year-olds on the playground knew their great-grandmothers were so near.

On the far end of the graveyard was a gate that led to a street. I peeked my way around each corner, hoping the Hungarian hadn't figured out my ruse. I assessed the situation. Lugh had probably been going out and coming back all morning. Walking purposeful routes like that could expose anyone following him. The Hungarians backtracking was part of that plan. It came down to one of two options: either Lugh saw me, or it was standard procedure. If it's the former, I'd have to mount a frontal assault on forty-nine terrorists. If it's the latter, I could observe, check their defenses, and wait for Tania and Miguel to even the odds.

Mercury spoke from behind me. *You could always give yourself up, homie. If they don't kill you, you'll learn a lot more from the inside than the outside.*

After nearly jumping out of my skin, I said, *Do NOT sneak up on me like that in a cemetery. Holy crap. So. What do you think they're going to do, serve me a tea and stroopwafel?*

Mercury said, *Oh, they'll kill you, bro, but not until they move you to a more private place. There's a lot of non-Free Origins staff manning Pieterskerk, caterers, cleaning people, managers. Think about it. While you're inside, you can sow seeds of doubt and confusion. Maybe distract them long enough for Tania or Miguel to stop them. That way, you could at least die a hero. I mean, let's face it, you're just not ruthless enough to be a Caesar.*

I said, *I thought you bet on me to win.*

Mercury said, *Not exactly. I bet on your team to prevail. If you die in the process and Tania carries it over the line for a win, I come out ahead.*

I said, *Isn't that nice.*

My very-important-deity wasn't helping. Typical. I'd have to figure it out myself. We could never stop forty-nine of them, but if we could find the command center, we could issue a stand-down order or discover where and when each attack was taking place and have local authorities intercede.

I checked my maps and the layout of the local streets. The church was in a U-shaped area, surrounded by renovated commercial buildings that retained the town's sixteenth century feel. There were few video cameras on the street. I kept my head down and circled the block.

Once I was satisfied there were no Hungarians on the east side of the church, I scaled a wall using the tiny toe and finger holds in the mortar for purchase. Once on the slick metal roof, I made my way to a narrow place where the church's windows rose above the modern neighbors. It took a little more scaling to get a secure spot next to the glass.

The light frosting, meant to keep out direct sunlight, obscured the nave like greasy sunglasses. I could make out shapes and movement but couldn't quite get a fix on more detail. There were a good number of people milling about inside. A party had been set up. I moved to another window, looking for less frosting. Farther over, I found a vent pane the size of a pizza box open a crack at the bottom. I couldn't get it open any wider.

Pressing my nose to one side, then the other, I made out a couple familiar people from the training sessions at the Ooze. After adjusting a fourth time, I saw what I never expected, Lieutenant Colonel Hugo and Arrianne. She gestured at various people and things around the room while he nodded. Either he was part of this evil plan, or he was a sad old man falling for the attentions of a beautiful young woman.

I slid down the nearest metal roof to a climbable corner and lowered myself to the ground. Walking quickly away, I pulled out my phone to text Miguel and Tania the news. Before my thumbs could press send, I felt the distinctive pinch of two Taser probes hit my back and, an instant later, felt the horrific shock.

CHAPTER 39

THE LUMP ON MY HEAD hurt. The drugs coursing through my veins made me sick. Whatever they gave me clouded the events from when I was tased in the alley to the darkness surrounding me.

I wasn't shackled. I wasn't cuffed. I wasn't dead. No doubt due to the number of witnesses milling around the area.

Party noise came from somewhere nearby. A DJ mixing club music. It made my head thump worse.

I sat up and inventoried my surroundings in the faint light. I had been lying on a stone slab. It had words carved into it. Dutch words, so they didn't mean much to me. But the numbers made its purpose clear: 1510-1568. Someone's sarcophagus. I scanned the chamber. A crypt.

I appeared to be in the basement of Pieterskerk. Every old church has a crypt, so it came as no surprise this ancient place would. Architects of the Dark Ages would fill a foundation's useable space with the denizens least likely to complain about the damp. What surprised me was the locked iron bars on the entrance. After thinking about it, the lock made sense. They'd turned a church into a venue for events serving booze. At some point, they had been forced to protect certain portions of the building from drunks with hilarious ideas.

Mercury stood outside the bars in his formal toga. *You done with your nap, homeboy?*

I said, *If you want me to win this thing, why not give me some warning about being followed?*

Mercury said, *I did. I distinctly remember telling you there was more to learn inside than out.*

I said, *But in that scenario, I die. I want to win and stay alive at the same time. Is that too much to ask from an all-powerful being?*

Mercury said, *All-powerful? Sheeyit, dawg. You should talk to my wife. Only thing she thinks my powers are good for is doing the dishes.*

I said, *Could you help me out here? How do I get out of this crypt— alive?*

Mercury said, *What is with you mortals? Always whining about wanting to win without dying. Saving humanity isn't good enough for you, you wanna live through it too. Well then, do it your way. You never listen to me, you never tell anyone the good news about the Dii Consentes, and you never make offerings to the gods who save your ass every day. All you do is complain.*

I said, *Does that mean there's a way out of here? And if I promise to do all those things, you'll tell me what it is?*

Mercury gripped the bars and looked up at the ceiling. *Trying my patience, yo. You know what people do when they're in trouble? They pray and pray and promise and promise. Then we bestow blessings upon them, and they are redeemed. What happens to all those promises they made us? Nothing. They forget all about us. Liars, the whole stinking bunch of you.*

I said, *I did that purification ceremony once. I think.*

Mercury said, *Rite of Parilia, and you did it backward.*

I said, *I'll do it again—just as soon as I can find some sheep.*

Mercury said, *That was such a terrible display of cultural misappropriation that we would rather you not.*

I said, *Just tell me what to do, I'll do it. I swear. Will you help me?*

Mercury said, *Igne natura renovatur integra, brutha.*

I said, *Huh?*

Mercury closed his eyes and inhaled slowly. Then he said, *Through fire, nature is reborn whole. You don't need my help. You need to understand yourself.*

Something like a hammer struck my soul. Ideas started bubbling up inside my head. I said, *What do you mean? That I always use you so that I can end up being the hero? That I'm always on a quest for glory, expecting you to save me every time? That everything I do, I do so that others will think I'm the greatest and adore me?*

Mercury smiled. *Now you're getting it, homie.*

More concepts popped into my head. *I don't need your help to become a hero. I don't need Sabel Security or Miguel or Tania. I only need to do what no one else wants to do—die trying. It's not about the glory or the parade at the end. It's about saving the world even if that means doing the ugly stuff no one else wants to do. Death is a risk one must ignore.*

All that thinking led me to the dark side. *That means I miss out on all the joys in life. I'll be giving up Jenny for good. I'll never have Thanksgiving with my parents again. I'll never taste chocolate again. I'll never have children and enjoy the thrill of parenting.*

Mercury said, *Now that you mention it, you could make a lot of people happy by sacrificing yourself.*

I ignored his comment. *I'd be giving up my future for the greater good because it's the honorable thing to do.*

Mercury pressed his hands to his chest. *When you finally figure stuff out, it almost makes me wanna cry. Almost. Now, all you have to do to get out of there is click your heels three times and say, "There's no place like home."*

I said, *No fucking way.*

Mercury nodded, grinned, then evaporated into the dark.

I rattled the iron bars. Locked solid. Barely enough wiggle to make a noise. There were a lot of things I was willing to do in the name of freedom. There were many indignations I'd suffered to get out of tight spots in the past. But there was no way in Avernus I was going to click my heels three times. I mean, come on.

Mercury's voice echoed in the stone chamber. *Then crawl in the tomb with the dead guy. When the party ends, they gonna drag you out and shoot you in the marsh. And if that happens, ROSGEO is going to happen. Hundreds of people will die—because you're too important to do a scene from Wizard of Oz.*

The only guilt trip worse than my mother's is Mercury's. What really torqued me was knowing he could help me if he wanted. He had a sick sense of humor and insisted on making me do stupid stuff for the amusement of the gods. They're bored. But. Who am I to argue with god?

I closed my eyes, held my nose, clicked my boot heels together three times and said, "There's no place like home."

"Is that you, Jacob?" A voice in the darkness.

"Who's there?"

"Zack Ames." The short, wiry bald guy slid around a corner. "Who were you talking to?"

CHAPTER 40

"YOU'RE NOT ZACK AMES," I said.

"Close enough for government work. Shut up and stand back." He placed a small charge on the lock.

I jumped back just as it blew. The iron gate swung open.

I stared at Fake-Zack for a moment. He held up a phone, a packet of handheld Sabel Darts and a pistol. Mine. I took them, shoved the phone in my pocket, and clipped the holster and Glock to my belt at the back. I flopped my shirttail over it.

"What's going on?" I asked.

"I'm springing you." He turned and flattened himself against the wall. "There's a loud party upstairs. It's just winding down. We need to get out of here before the music stops."

"Who are you really?" I asked.

"Later." He led the way up a stone stair to a kitchen area.

Five people packed plates and pots into containers and rolled them out a back door. The dinner was long over, and they were wrapping up. If the party was over, that meant ROSGEO would soon be underway.

Through an open arch inside the old church, I caught a glimpse of the party. Paladin stood at the front with a microphone in one hand and a stein of beer in the other. He made a joke I couldn't hear. It got laughs and hoots.

Fake-Zack grabbed my arm and yanked. We hoofed it to the caterer's van and peeked around the corner. One of the Hungarians stood outside, watching the cobblestones in the moonlight. I took out one of my darts and looked for a place I could poke the guy. The injection is automatic, the system simple. The only drawback is that the short needle doesn't penetrate more than a single layer of cloth. Oh. And a rare allergic reaction kills one out of 743 people on average. If the Hungarian turned out to be allergic, I wasn't going to lose sleep over it. I took three quick steps and swung my dart at his neck.

As it turns out, Hungarians are tough street fighters. They don't go down easy. He must have heard my rushed steps because he turned with an arm moving fast in a sweeping arc. He caught my forearm extended, batted it out of the way then landed a right in my abdomen. My dart went flying. I recovered and threw an uppercut. He responded with a combination into my breadbasket. I tried two more blows to his face. He raised his defenses and brushed back my punches.

We eyed each other, squaring off for a real boxing match. He was no slouch. He had moves. I train several times a week with Ms. Sabel. She uses speed and feints to make up for the smaller muscle mass in women. Sparring with her has taken my game to the next level.

I tried one of Ms. Sabel's favorite moves. I pulled back my right for a well-telegraphed jab and waited for his gaze to follow my fist. The instant his eyes moved, my left cross landed the heel of my hand on his temple. Another trick Ms. Sabel taught me: Don't use a clenched fist without a boxing glove. If you hit bone, you'll break your knuckles. Use the heel of your hand, the elbow, or the crown of your head instead. Unfortunately he sensed my ruse and slipped to his left. My punch only glanced off his skull. The move left me in a terrible position with my left shoulder twisting away from him. I was completely exposed. His eyes bulged at the opportunity. With a heavy push off his back foot, he threw a right cross straight at my head.

It landed softly. The Hungarian had a funny look in his eyes before he fell on his face.

Fake-Zack stood behind him, examining the Sabel Dart in his hand. "Say, that worked well. What is it?"

"You're supposed to leave it in him for ten seconds. Now he's going to come around in minutes. Where's your car?"

"You can't get a car down these streets."

"You came to rescue me on a bike?"

With a grumpy frown, he asked, "Where's your car?"

236

"Yeah." I pointed down Kloksteeg. "My bike's that way."

As I pointed, two Free Origins guys came up the lane. They hadn't seen us yet. They were more likely to drown me in the canal since the number of witnesses in the area had waned. We snuck back around the caterer's van and trotted down a side street.

Two blocks later, we found the canal that could lead us around the bend to our bikes. We calculated the time it would take Nema's people to discover my escape and search the area. We decided to keep going away from the enemy instead of doubling back to get our bikes.

I texted Miguel and Tania. Neither made an immediate reply. Not unusual in a tight operation where they could be observing from a dark alley, and the screen light would give them away.

To blend in with the people on the street, we strolled through a small park to a lane filled with shops.

"Thanks for the rescue," I said. "Who are you?"

"Why confuse things? Just call me Zack."

"The tattoo on your butt. That's Free Origins?"

"No." He sighed. "It doesn't represent any particular group. The racist hate-site Stormfront popularized it. It's their version of the Celtic Cross and represents my past."

"Which is?"

"Was. I was a CIA officer. I was a racist. I was an attendee at the Kraków conference. I was in a meeting where Paladin described starting Armageddon. I was sickened to my core. I was the guy who went to the Slovaks."

He'd lied to me before, but for some strange reason I believed him this time. It felt honest. "You weren't there to support Brady?"

"I was stationed in Paris until sixteen months ago. I'd always been a racist. It ran in the family, from my uncle who blamed his business failure on the Jewish conspiracy to replace us to my mother who thought Mexicans were invading the country. Even after attending culture and gender sensitivity training at the Company, I clung to the myths. When they rotated me back to Langley, I fell in with some Free Origins people. I made some statements on Facebook. Those statements cost me my job. Free Origins scooped me up like a family. They had deep pockets. They sponsored my trip to Kraków.

"That's where I ran into Brady. I spotted him as a Feeb right off and confronted him. He asked me not to blow his cover before I checked out Paladin. Brady led me to Paladin's meeting. Brady turned me around. He exposed the true path I was on. It was a descent into the hell of hatred and loathing. I chose to pull up and follow the Golden Rule. I owe the guy."

"What about the FBI? Don't they owe Brady?" I asked. We strolled through a neighborhood of small shops and neatly kept homes. Both Fake-Zack and I kept our gazes roving over potential ambush spots while doing our best to look casual.

"You may have noticed that over the last few years, our cherished institutions fell into disarray. Most cabinet-level positions are filled by partisans with 'acting' in front of their titles. Trickle that down to ground level and the turnover is killing us. Did you know they don't have a legat in Paris?"

"New guy just arrived," I said. "Why should I believe you after you lied to me?"

"I was desperate then. This is my redemption mission. Now that you've seen what they can do, I know you're looking to stop them with the same vigor I am. That's why I saved you."

We stared into each other's eyes for a moment. He didn't flinch. I decided to trust him for another thirty seconds.

I asked, "Was Nema at the Kraków meeting?"

"You figured her out?" he asked. "She was in the corner, pulling Paladin's strings. You know, six months ago, she killed her brother. He caught me following them in Paris. I told him about Paladin's meeting and how they were planning something cataclysmic. He didn't believe me. He told me he would go to the police if it were true. But I tweaked his curiosity. I had a bug in her apartment. I heard him confront her. Things escalated. He brought up things she did as a teenager. He wasn't nice about it. He called her names a brother should never call his sister. She slashed his throat with a kitchen knife and never reported him missing. As luck would have it, my recorder stopped working before the killing. I had no proof."

"Nice girl." We walked along the canal banks. "Did Paladin know about the brother?"

"Who do you think dumped the body?" Fake-Zack shook his head. "Anyway, after Kraków, I went to the Slovaks. They took my statement but didn't know what to believe. It's not a big country; they don't have a sophisticated intel operation. I hung around a while, then went to Paris. I tried to get people to listen, but I had nothing. No recordings, no evidence, nothing actionable they could use for a warrant. All the players dropped off the grid after the Kraków conclave. I got depressed. Hundreds of people were going to die, and no one would listen to me.

"Not long ago, I hit the idea of reactivating myself in the CIA. I visited old friends at the Paris embassy. While I was there, I snagged a couple business cards off the new guy's desk. Went to see Hugo as a CIA man instead of an unemployed loser. We'd met when I was stationed there. He knew I was an official, but he didn't know me well enough to know my name. It worked. I got a meeting with him. I reeled him in as best I could."

One by one, the shops around us closed. The ranks of bikes and pedestrians thinned.

"But it didn't work." I held up a hand to stop his story. "Does that mean Hugo's part of it?"

"No. He's a hardcore anti-terrorist from the old school. The school that believes all terrorists are Saudi Muslims."

"He doesn't count mass-shootings like the seventy-seven killed in Norway or the fifty in Christchurch?"

"The cynical side of me says he's a closet racist who secretly cheers those attacks. The realist in me says he's blind to horrific acts perpetrated by people who look like him. But then, aren't we all guilty of that bias? Most Americans paid more attention to the Pulse Nightclub attack than the Tree of Life synagogue. Whatever the case, Free Origins doesn't fit in his world view. When I saw the video from Saint-Sulpice, I realized you were the answer I'd been looking for."

I checked my phone for updates from Miguel and Tania. Nothing.

"What's Arrianne's story?" I asked.

"She's a chameleon now. Nema owns her, and she doesn't see a way out."

We discussed theories about Arrianne and agreed the most likely scenario was that Nema had some kind of leverage over her. Zack had witnessed her split from Paladin and Free Origins. He's also tracked Nema's takeover of Arrianne's operation. He summed her up. "Arrianne is a master manipulator who met her match in little Nema. Not that it's any excuse. Nema might be the mastermind, but Paladin, Lugh, all of them are active participants in one of the ugliest conspiracies of the century."

"What about you?" I asked. "Where are you drawing the line between right and wrong?"

"I saw where the road paved with hate leads. Right off the cliff of annihilation." He sighed and shoved his hands in his pockets. "I'm doing my best to reform. The Quakers have a twelve-step program for racists. I've found it healing. My anger is subsiding more and more every day."

My phone buzzed. Miguel said, "We followed your GPS signal. It led us to Hugo's car. We staked it out. You weren't there. Then it was offline again. Hugo held a mini-press conference. He said some mean things about you, then left. We just found your new location. Why were you hanging with Hugo?"

CHAPTER 41

"MY PHONE WAS CONFISCATED," I told Miguel. "It's a long embarrassing story, and I'd rather not talk about it."

"You got caught by Nema's people?" Miguel asked. "I'd rather not talk about it, either. I like to think of you as mildly competent, and that would blow the whole fantasy. Stay in that shopping district. We'll be right over."

I pulled up Hugo's impromptu press conference on my phone. It was in French with Dutch subtitles. Fake-Zack translated for me. Hugo went the long way around to tell everyone there had been accusations that Free Origins might be a threat to public safety. He had personally spoken to the members and found them intelligent, capable, hardworking members of society. He then went out of his way to reiterate his opinion that Jacob Stearne and a man posing as an American CIA agent were planning a terrorist attack of some kind. Working with Interpol, Europol, and several other "pol" organizations, he would bring the two maniacs to justice. He closed by distributing photographs of Fake-Zack and me.

Mine was that very nice screengrab from the video the instant before I killed Ace of Free Origins.

"Sorry," Fake-Zack said, "I've dragged your reputation down. Hugo might've believed you if I hadn't pulled the CIA-stunt in Paris."

I couldn't disagree with him, but we were past the point for recriminations. We were now wanted men. Around us, the narrow lanes were nearly deserted. We weren't worried about someone calling the cops on us.

Mercury pedaled by on a wobbly bike. He crashed into the stone railing at the canal. *Who invented these damn things, dude? Couldn't have been a man, cuz there's no place to put your jewels. And they're no match for a chariot. Now, you ride your ass through town on a four-horse chariot and people get out of your way in a big ol' hurry.*

I said, *Are you bringing me a message?*

Mercury said, *Never have been one for small talk, huh? OK then, here it is. Notice how Fake-Zack is ready to give his life for the cause?*

I said, *No.*

Mercury threw his hands up. *The man got your phone out of Hugo's car before they could decrypt it, he snuck into your dungeon and blew the door open, he risked his life getting you out.*

I said, *So?*

Mercury picked up the bike and looked it over. *What's it take for you to realize what this guy thinks is at stake?*

I said, *Do you know his name?*

Mercury straddled the bike. *Dude, he's ex-CIA. None of the gods know his name. But I know this, he's willing to kill people. What you want to know is who.*

I wasn't sure what in the Orcus he was talking about. But I watched my unemployed god wobble down the lane, curse, throw the bike down, then fly off on his impossibly tiny wings.

"Did you see something?" Fake-Zack followed my gaze down the lane.

"Checking the shadows." I started walking again. "So, you talked Hugo into sending me undercover because you couldn't. Everyone at Free Origins knew you. You were willing to risk my life to stop them."

He shrugged. "I'm perfectly willing to risk mine instead. It just wouldn't have been effective. We do what we need to do. You're a soldier. You've made that choice before, who lives and who dies. It's not easy. You make the best decision you know how then blow up ten people to save five hundred. Even if one of the ten is you."

That one stopped me in my tracks. That was what Mercury was talking about. I slapped his shoulder. "It was you. The Moulin Rouge. You planted the bomb. Nema recognized you, that's why she was so shocked."

He faced me. "I did what had to be done."

The backpack had been a shaped charge. It was meant to destroy everything directly in front of it. When I turned over the table, it landed upside down and blew out structural beams in the ceiling. Fake-Zack was willing to kill me if it meant killing Nema and stopping ROSGEO.

He read my face. "I asked you to help. You turned me down. Then you started falling for Nema. I didn't see any downside."

What a thoughtful guy. Although, had the roles been reversed, I would've done the same.

"What do you want out of this?" I asked. "Why did you rescue me from Pieterskerk?"

"I have to stop them. I can't do it alone. I don't expect you to do any more than you already have. But, I hope you're still in."

I understood his sentiment. Once you know what these people are up to, you can't walk away. If you see something, do something. Zack did something. He sent me into harm's way on his behalf. But he didn't leave it at that. He'd been following Nema ever since, looking for an opportunity to wreck her day.

I resumed walking. "Tell me something I can use to bring down Nema and Paladin. You can start with where they built their command center."

"If I knew that, I would have destroyed it by now." Something spooked him. He glanced around.

I heard it too. People talking is one thing. People talking about you is another. There's something sinister in the attempt to disguise meaning that gives whispered words an evil cadence.

Two old ladies approached under the cone of a streetlamp. They gave us the side-eye.

Fake-Zack tipped a fake hat in their direction and said, "*Bonsoir.*"

They picked up their pace and passed by.

"They recognize us from Hugo's pictures," I said.

"To blend in, don't act guilty. Few people can identify you from a photo." We picked up our pace. "Where are those friends of yours?"

Tania and Miguel waited in a rental car parked on a tiny bridge three hundred yards ahead. Tania stood on the passenger seat, her head out the sunroof, aiming binoculars in my general direction. On her second pass, she saw me. Fake-Zack and I headed toward her.

A bullet buzzed in front of our noses. We instinctively hit the cobblestones.

Nema's voice called across the canal. "Jacob Stearne, we need to talk."

CHAPTER 42

I CRAWLED ACROSS THE LANE toward the canal and peered over the stone balustrade. A suppressed round fired away from us. I snuck a glance down the canal.

Nema's people were shooting at Tania and Miguel. Which was a mistake on their part. Shooting at a guy like Miguel makes him forget his manners and shoot back. While charging forward at a dead run.

Miguel's boots slapped down the cobblestones. Tania, the former sniper, took up a position at the bridge's parapet to cover him.

Squeezing a look between the balustrade's newel posts, I saw a man with an M20 rocket launcher, commonly known as a bazooka. While it was an outdated weapon on the modern battlefield, it could still blow up a small rental car. Which it did.

The flash from the explosion illuminated Tania for a second. She was already running from the blast. The car flew into the air, over the railing, and splashed into the canal.

"Tell your friend to stop," Nema called out, "or he gets the next one."

I didn't need to relay that to Miguel. He saw the flash.

"What do you want?" I called back.

In the distance, sirens cranked up from several points. I checked our surroundings to assess the potential collateral damage. Most of the lower levels of our surroundings were brick or stone. Several storefronts were glass, the lights were out. Hopefully, no one worked in the back rooms.

I moved laterally, keeping the origin point of her voice triangulated in my head. Fake-Zack was twenty yards away, doing the same thing. I popped up and aimed and fired. So did my new friend. A perfect crossfire in daylight. This late at night, it was hard to tell if the shadow I pinged was Nema or a potted plant.

Mercury crouched next to me. *Why are you shooting that poor ficus, brutha?*

I said, *Can you give me a hint where she is?*

Mercury said, *She was behind it. Fake-Zack has the angle.*

I ran to Fake-Zack's position.

"What are you doing?" he asked. "We had her in a kill-zone."

Two bullets pinged off the stone railing an inch from our heads. I figured the origin to be another block over. I said, "Either they're moving, or she has helpers."

He nodded. "Where did they get a bazooka?"

"Same place they bought a cache of AR70/90s. They have someone in the arms business, helping them out."

"Jacob." Nema's voice crossed the canal from a different point of origin. "I'm going to send you a phone. You need to take it."

Fake-Zack popped up and fired two rounds.

"Stop shooting, you idiot," she said. "We need to talk."

"All we need to talk about is how you're going to stop ROSGEO."

"You have it backward. We need to talk about how you're going to lead ROSGEO."

Fake-Zack looked at me. I could feel Miguel and Tania looking my way from their position three hundred yards down the canal. For a moment, the approaching sirens fell into the background.

"We registered that bazooka in your name," Nema called out. "We sent videos of you training my liberation fighters to all the major media outlets. You need to come with me, Jacob. It's time you took your place at the head of ROSGEO."

"Holy … She had you from the beginning." Fake-Zack slumped to the ground behind the balustrade. "This is my fault. Oh my god. I am so sorry, Jacob."

Mercury slid up against the stone next to me. *What's he mean, homie?*

I said, *He means Nema took me to Spain knowing I was undercover and planning to use it against me all along.*

Wowza, she really knows how to get things done, Mercury said. *This*

might be a bad time to mention it, but she might make a decent Caesar.
Think you can bring her into the fold?

I saw movement across the canal. The shadow was small and quick.
Peering through the newels, I calculated her movements. I rose and
aimed but found only her shadow. She slipped behind a wall.

"Stop shooting." Her voice echoed over the stones. "We need to talk."

A noisy drone started up and floated above the cobblestones. It
crossed the canal with a small bag attached to the underside. It came
down our lane, veered a little before correcting and approached us. Fake-
Zack aimed at it. I grabbed his arm and lowered his weapon.

"It's the phone she mentioned."

"Or a bomb," he said. "You don't know that woman like I know that
woman."

I looked at him, unsure if he was referring to the biblical sense.

He read my mind. He said, "No one's had sex with her. She doesn't
have sex. She hates everyone."

"She mentioned that."

The drone approached within a few feet. It settled a foot above the
ground, dropped its package, then flew up and away.

Fake-Zack shot it down. When I glared at him, he said, "One less
asset for them."

"Take the phone, Jacob." Nema's voice remained calm despite the
approaching sirens. "I'll call you in five minutes."

I jumped to my feet and looked down the alleys, aiming with my 9-
mil. I found a target squatting a block to my left. As I tried to determine
friend or foe, a bright flash erupted from his shoulder. The bazooka. The
rockets fired by the M20 travel at 180 miles per hour. Which is fast, but
much slower than a bullet. They're so slow in terms of lethal weapons
that a soldier has time to react. He can jump out of the way. That's why
they're never used against people. They're used against tanks and other
large vehicles that don't react quickly.

I did not react quickly. I was stunned. It didn't make sense. Why
would Nema give me a phone, then have me killed?

Fake-Zack did react quickly. In one lightning-fast step, he mounted
the railing and jumped into the path of the incoming rocket. His

momentum took them both into the canal wall where the explosion blew him into two pieces.

I looked up to see if they were going to fire again. Miguel's large shadow rounded the corner next to the squatting bazooka man. Miguel stabbed the man with a dart and left him there with his warm bazooka.

Miguel started trotting my way. On my side of the canal, Tania headed for me.

I was still staring at Fake-Zack's body in the canal. He was slowly sinking beneath the water.

Mercury put an arm on my shoulder. *Typical CIA, right homie?*

I said, *What do you mean?*

He died for you, and you'll never know his name.

My friends converged on me at the same time the phone started ringing.

I picked it up and clicked on. "Hello."

"Sorry about Caleb, Jacob," Nema said. "He's still pissed at you for that HALO incident."

"I thought he was sitting this out with Arrianne."

"After someone cut my ranks by significant numbers, I needed auxiliary forces. So I made her an offer she couldn't refuse."

"You have some dirt on her?"

"I have dirt on everyone, Jacob. But 'dirt' isn't the right term. I think leverage is better." She paused with what sounded like a repressed giggle. "I have leverage on you too."

"Like what?"

"Would you like to see Jenny?"

CHAPTER 43

NEMA SENT A PRERECORDED VIDEO clip. The camera focused on close-ups showing Jenny bound to a chair with her hands behind her back, her mouth gagged, and her feet tied to the chair's legs. The worst part was strapped tight to her chest. A suicide vest thick with explosives. A radio activated device on her breast had a light that blinked green. She struggled and fought against her bindings. The video stopped.

Miguel, Tania, and I jogged away from the incoming police cars. We made it to an alley just as the police set up barriers behind us.

"You owe me," Nema said. "You took Ace and Diego off the board. They were the tip of our spear. Everyone in Free Origins looked up to them as our heroes. They were ROSGEO's first wave. You stopped them cold. My people hate you with a passion. Do you know how hard it was to keep you alive in Úbeda?"

Mercury pressed his ear to mine as if he could hear the phone straight through my head. *She's crafty, gotta give her that. But you can stop playing Mr. Nice and kill her. I'm sick of her shit.*

I said, *Where. Is. Jenny?*

Mercury said, *Kill Nema first, we'll find your ex later. Or a new girl.*

I said, *If Nema's crafty, someone else holds the vest's trigger. I'm sure her instructions were to press the button if anything happens to her.*

Mercury scratched his chin. *That would be extra-crafty. I'll bet you're right. Ima go check.*

"You set me up from the beginning. You're one hell of an actress, Nema."

"I tried being an actress. Can you believe they only gave me bit parts? All the speaking roles went to 'people of color.' People who don't even speak English."

"Your hatred won't work on me," I said. "It won't start a race war either. You'll kill a bunch of people; then they'll catch you. They always catch the masterminds."

"You haven't been paying attention." She laughed. "What happened after Christchurch? Sri Lanka. Around the world, people are tired of mixing with other races and religions. Call it populism, call it nationalism, it doesn't matter. It's nature's law. Keep to your kind. When thirteen houses of worship go up in flames, the call for retribution will go out. People will flock to their kind to protect themselves. They'll realize what they've always felt inside but never summoned the courage to do. They'll throw off the shackles of political correctness."

"Political correctness? That used to be called the Golden Rule until someone made hate fashionable."

"You should listen to your messages," Nema said. "You would've heard Jenny pleading for help."

I put the phone on mute when I said, "SHIT!"

"Do you want Jenny back or not?" Nema snarled.

"Don't worry. I'll get her back—over your dead body."

"Nice threat for a guy who has no idea where she is." Nema snickered. "I have a job for you, Jacob. You turn yourself over to me, no tricks, no phones, no tracking. You'll take over the mission from Ace and Diego. The kickoff to ROSGEO, the first attack. We're going to live stream it. Do it right, and little Jenny walks away. Do it any less than right and ... BOOM!"

Nema laughed out loud.

Mercury appeared in front of me. *Worse than we thought, bro. She has a dead man's switch in the hands of one of her henchmen. He's in the room with Jenny. His finger is on the trigger. If he lets go, like if you shoot him, the whole room explodes.*

I said, *I know what a dead man's switch is.*

Mercury said, *Oh. You don't need my help then?*

I said, *I'm sorry. Thank you for the information. You're a good and loving god.*

Mercury said, *That's better. Now you guys have to decide if you're up for doing what needs to be done. Go ahead, talk amongst yourselves.*

I glanced up at Tania and Miguel. After so many years together, we knew where this ordeal would lead. We knew what we would do next. We knew each of our roles in making our unspoken plan work. The three of us could overwhelm Nema. It would take some doing, and some courage, and some luck. But killing her along with the first few people who tried to stop us, would cause the rest of them to melt away. We nodded at each other. We were ready to go, no matter what.

"One more video for you, Jacob." Nema sent a new clip. "It's not just Jenny's life at stake. No one cares about a murderous billionaire."

In the second video, the camera panned across the same stone basement. A shaft of daylight streamed in a small window. In the shadows surrounding Jenny were seventeen small children. Kindergartners. All tied together. All crying. The video stopped.

"Meet me in Plantsoen Park in two minutes." Nema cackled. "You'll need to run."

"Wait!" I looked at my companions.

The children forced a change in plans. No longer a shoot-em-all-and-sort-it-out-later plan; we had a tougher commitment to make.

Nema's evil genius had us in a vice. This whole time I thought she kept me alive because she was afraid of witnesses, but that wasn't the case at all. From the moment I tackled Diego in Saint-Sulpice, she planned to force me into leading the first terrorist attack. By putting me in the starring role, she destroyed what was left of my credibility with the authorities. With the lives of children at stake, Miguel and Tania were neutralized as well. Even the extensive resources of Sabel Security were sidelined until the kids were safe.

There was no choice. We had to make a complex plan work with zero planning and no time for discussion. Tania whispered, "Attu Island."

The operation on Attu had been successful. Each of us had played a dangerous role that relied on a deadly choreography. She was right—it was the only way out.

We each took a deep breath and silently nodded our agreement. A pact with each other. I knew they would do their parts. They would count on me to do mine. If anyone failed, we all died. And so would Jenny and the children.

Tania reached in her fanny pack and slid me a thumb-sized pill, a GPS locator. I took it and hoped for water. My friends shrugged. I swallowed it dry. I hate those things.

Miguel put his hand between us, flat. He said, "For the children."

Tania and I put our hands on his and repeated the vow.

I pulled the phone back up. "Nema, my friends will trade places with the kids. You can have Miguel and Tania as hostages."

"No deal. We're going to kill them anyway."

"OK then, they're coming for you."

Tania and Miguel ran to the canal bank, rifles slung over their shoulders. They jumped up on the stone railing and dove into the water to hunt her down.

"Good luck, Nema. They've spent years killing people like you. They'll have five bullets in your body before any of your Hungarian goons see them coming."

"I have fifteen men in the alley," she said. "And I've already left. Get to the park, Jacob. If anything happens to me, the timer goes off, and Jenny escorts those kids to hell."

CHAPTER 44

THEY DIDN'T TAKE THE HOOD off until we were on the plane. The drugs had worn off an hour earlier, but the hangover was still pounding away. I sat in a four-engine turboprop with an interior that looked a lot like a C-130. I would know—Rangers jump out of them all the time.

The Free Origins people wore HALO gear. Paladin stepped in front of me with everything I needed to join them.

"You know she expects you to die," I said.

"All you need to do is show these guys how it's done." Paladin gestured at four others behind him.

"You'll go down as one of the most hated people of the twenty-first century."

"You were kind enough to give them lessons on HALO jumps. We sent those videos to the media already."

"Your own mother will deny your existence," I said.

"Put on your rig, we're about to depressurize."

"Nema has it set up so she walks away without so much as a fingerprint on the whole evil plan. People will come from miles around to spit on your grave, and none of them will know she was the brains of the outfit." It was my best gambit. But Paladin remained unmoved.

"The guys will be happy to knock you unconscious and put it on you. If you want."

I grabbed the rig and noticed it was light. No chute. I stepped into it. "Were you with her when she called me? She laughed about your leadership. She thinks you're a joke. The fool who tossed her brother in the Seine."

Paladin stepped back. His head tilted.

"How did I know about that?" I asked. I could only hope Fake-Zack told me the truth. "She has pictures of you dumping his body in the river. She's so far ahead of you, you'll never get out of it. You're in worse than Arrianne."

"Shut up and button up. Get your oxygen mask on." He craned over his shoulder at the others to determine if they'd heard me. He raised his voice with his movie star chin. "These guys are looking to you for leadership, Jacob. You're the best killer the USA ever produced. It's an honor to serve with you on this mission. You're going down there to lead an assault on Muslims, the scourge of the human race."

The other men hooted their approval. Caleb stood among them. He had a Go-Pro on his helmet recording Paladin's speech for posterity.

I faced the camera. "You're nothing but a bunch of murderers. You took children hostage to make me go on this jump. You think that's clever. But I promise you. Only one of you will be alive by nightfall, and he'll regret it. I'll kill one of you on the way down. Another on the way in. The rest as soon as the opportunity arises."

They laughed. Caleb said, "Don't worry, we'll edit that part out before we send it off."

The loadmaster depressurized the cargo bay. Then he lowered the loading ramp.

Paladin grabbed my shoulder. "You're going to stick the landing, Jacob."

The others grabbed my arms and legs. They carried me to the back and out to the end of the ramp. We were a little less than 30,000 feet over an arid coastline. It was midday on a Friday, almost time for Jumu'ah, the weekly service for Muslims. The locals would be gathering in great numbers.

They heaved me back and forth three times, then tossed me out.

They made a fatal mistake with my lightened pack. While they took out the main and backup chutes, they wanted the appearance of a functioning rig, so they left the drogue chute attached.

As I fell, I carefully pulled the drogue out without letting it open. I hadn't used a wingsuit in three years, but the aerodynamic principles behind them hadn't changed. Besides, I didn't need to fly to an exact spot. I only needed to fly to one of the Free Origins guys.

Mercury flew alongside me. *This is the life, right bro? Face first from high altitude, only an oxygen mask to land on. But you got this. You know Caleb is the one with the dweeb-looking camera on his helmet.*

I said, *I'm taking the first one I come to. If it's Caleb, all the better.*

I managed to get a good grip on both ends of the material. I spread it out under me and pushed my arms out wide. At 120 miles per hour, a great deal of strength is required. It didn't work well. But it worked well enough. I flew in a circle that cut my descent by a good margin. The Free Origins men fell toward me.

The material began to slip from my fingers. I had to hold on a little longer. My fingers ached. My arms grew weak from the strain. The circle began to spiral. I was going into the equivalent of a tailspin. Only I was both the tail and the spin. The g-forces were making me dizzy.

A surprised Caleb came at me going twenty miles an hour faster. I dove into his path.

We collided. I dug my arms into the straps of his gear and hugged him chest to chest.

I released my drogue. It disappeared into the sky. I headbutted Caleb. He tried to push me off. I headbutted him a second time. I ripped his oxygen mask off, tossed it, then got hold of his chinstrap. His helmet, GoPro and all, flew off into the air.

Caleb's eyes nearly poked me in the face when they bulged out of his head. He couldn't believe what was happening. The cold air forced him to hyperventilate. He panicked a lot more and a lot faster than Aleksei.

"I promised to take one of you on the way down, Caleb." I stuck my hand in his pockets as we hurtled toward Earth. "This is an honor for you, remember?"

I found what I was looking for, his map. I stuffed it in my pocket. Then I found his knife.

I gutted him.

He screamed and shouted. The worst thing about being gutted is knowing you're going to die and there's nothing you can do about it. But it doesn't kill you right away. You have several minutes of life left.

"Save your breath, Caleb. Use your remaining time to reflect on your sins."

As we fell at terminal velocity, I unhooked him from his rig and pushed him away. His arms worked furiously to stuff his entrails back in his body. I'd seen men do that on the battlefield. The image sticks with you for a long time.

I tried climbing into the straps. It was a difficult dance just to get one leg in. I was exhausted from the effort.

Mercury said, *Get that other leg in. You're nearing twenty-five hundred feet and don't even have your chest buckled or your arms in.*

I said, *Leave me alone. I need to concentrate.*

Mercury said, *Then concentrate on his altimeter. He has his AAD set to deploy at five hundred feet.*

That kind of message is why I count on the messenger of the gods. I turned off the Automatic Activation Device and finished climbing into the rig. I cinched the straps and checked the altitude. 400 feet.

I needed to deploy my chute before the ground rendered it unnecessary.

I looked around. The other men were a quarter-mile north of me. They'd deployed at two thousand feet and used the altitude to carry them to their destination.

When I deployed the drogue chute, it fluttered in the wind. It didn't open, which meant it wasn't going to pull the main chute out. Jostling a pack inflight can severely disrupt the folds. I held my breath as I fell below 250 feet. There was no time left to cut it loose and try the backup.

The instant I was about to say my final prayers, I heard Mercury's voice. *Who's your favorite god?*

I said with more impatience than gratitude, *You are. Now pull the damn chute!*

CHAPTER 45

I MANAGED TO LAND ON a soccer field. Empty for Jumu'ah. My map said I was in Rabat, the capital of Morocco. The mosque in question appeared to be a good-sized one. It was a long way away, and the other guys landed a lot closer. The clock was ticking.

A lone cab drove by, the driver leaning to the passenger side, watching me untangle my gear. I flagged him down.

Being fluent in Arabic saved me several times in the war. Most of those times were on the eastern end of the Arabic-speaking world, Iraq, Syria, and Kuwait. I was on the western end. The farther west you go, the more the languages diverge from the core spoken in Saudi Arabia. The Moroccans had taken things a step further with a good mix of Berber and Spanish Latin mixed in. We could communicate, but not without some confusion.

The cab driver thought I was reporting an attack on the King of Morocco. I showed him the map I took from Caleb. He scratched his beard and shook his head. Finally, he did what I asked and called the police. They didn't believe him. The mosque in question was an official state mosque with guards. They called. There was no attack in progress. The translation had fallen short.

I offered the cab driver the parachute rig in exchange for a ride. He decided I was a decent guy despite not having a wallet, passport, or any cash. And he didn't like that the cops dissed him for believing an American parachuted out of nowhere. A significant factor in his decision to drive me was the fact that the HALO rig was worth more than his car.

I asked if he had any weapons. Which was not a good question for an American to be asking after he'd just reported a mass-shooting in progress. Half a mile later, I saw one of the Free Origins guys jogging down a hot, dusty street with an AR70/90 slung on his shoulder.

I asked the cabbie if he liked *Fast and Furious* movies. He did. At my request, he drove close to the armed American. I threw the door open, slamming him in the back. I leapt from the cab, landed on his shoulders, rode him to the ground, and smashed his face into the tiled sidewalk. I put my boot on his head.

One of these guys needed to live so he could explain the plan to the authorities. But I couldn't leave him in a state that would allow him to commit another act of terrorism in his lifetime. Taking his rifle, I pressed the barrel to his spine. "What's your name?"

"Thompson." His words mushed into the dirty sidewalk with his drool.

"Want to know the sad truth about your future, Thompson?"

"What?"

"I'm going to put a bullet through your thoracic spinal cord. That's the part between your neck and belt. I'm going to angle it so it won't kill you. I'll be sure the bullet exits through your lungs. Allah gave you extra lung capacity so you could survive this type of injury. But, you'll never walk or screw again. And that sad part I was telling you about? It's that you're going to lie here begging Africans to save your life."

I sent the round as promised. I failed to warn him it was an excruciatingly painful injury. Probably the worst this side of childbirth. But he discovered that on his own quickly enough.

I left Thompson howling like a werewolf.

The cabbie waited for me. Not because he was a loyal cab driver, but because he was in such a state of shock, he couldn't move. I asked him if I should take a different cab. He shook his head, looked at my new rifle with big eyes, then put it in gear. In English, he said, "We go, fast and furious."

When we arrived at the mosque, the first thing we saw was a uniformed man lying on the sidewalk, bleeding out. I pointed to the injured man and told the cabbie to call an ambulance and the cops who didn't believe him.

I went inside.

DEATH AND CONSPIRACY

The last two Free Origins guys huddled in the center of a crowd of old men and young boys. They held a rifle and pistol in each hand, aimed at the heads of the men. On the left, a street cop held a 9-mil aimed at the Americans, but he was shaking too much to be effective. On the right, a civilian, also shaking, held a revolver aimed in the general direction of the Americans.

On the floor were three dead bodies and four wounded men.

The Free Origins men had lost their nerve when the reality of blood and guts slapped them in the face.

Mercury strolled around the Americans. *Classic, homie. A standoff. You can work this out in Arabic.*

I said, *My Arabic is the wrong dialect. I've been having trouble getting a handle on past tense and present tense. That could make a mess out of any plans.*

Mercury spread his arms wide and grinned. *Those Christian posers weren't the only ones who can speak in tongues, brutha. Trust in your god in your hour of need.*

I said, *Promise me the end result will be two dead Americans and no one else.*

I so promise, Mercury said. *Probably. I can't control everything.*

In Arabic, I said, "I'm going to kill those two terrorists. I'm going to need everyone's help."

"Hey, motherfucker," the more eloquent terrorist said, "what are you saying to them?"

He aimed his pistol at me, then put it back to the head of an old man.

"I told them I'm going to kill you," I said. "They seem to like that idea."

Mercury said, *There's only one way to get out of this alive. But you can't miss. You hurt one of the locals, and you'll spend eternity with Dante in that inferno he cooked up.*

I looked down the iron sights on my rifle. The margin of error was close. I could do it, but I couldn't hit two small targets in rapid succession. One of the victims could move into the line of fire for the second shot. Or the second man might pull his trigger on full auto. Too many innocent people could die. The only thing that would work would be a complicated dance move.

In Arabic, I said to the group, "When I give the word, everyone must do the *Sujud* faster than you've ever done it before."

All the Moroccans gave me odd looks.

Outside, distant sirens fired up. Music that was fast becoming the soundtrack to my life.

I repeated the instruction. I was asking the faithful to do something they considered culturally insensitive. Continuing in Arabic, I said, "Allah wants you to live, and this is what you need to do."

The Imam observed me for a moment, then understood my idea and agreed in Arabic.

"What are you doing, Stearne?" one of the terrorists said. "You try anything, and I'm going to kill you first."

I said, "Go for it. It'll be the last move you ever make."

While the Americans' attention was on me, I gave the word in Arabic. All the Moroccans dropped to their knees and put their foreheads on the floor.

The two American terrorists died half a second apart.

The people rose in shock and stared at the bodies. I handed my rifle to the policeman. In Arabic, I said, "Tell everyone to say you did it. I was never here."

Outside, cop cars screeched to a stop. Loudspeakers barked orders. Men marshaled to their commander's instructions.

I ran through the building, looking for the back door.

CHAPTER 46

OUTSIDE, THE CABBIE WAS FLEEING in my direction. He picked me up. It turned out he wasn't a licensed cabbie. King Mohammed VI frowns on that kind of behavior for thirty days at a time. Promising to keep his secret, I borrowed his phone to call the Sabel helpdesk.

They transferred me to Ms. Sabel directly. She said, "Thank god, you made it out. We've been tracking your movements through the GPS tracker. We have an exfil team waiting for you."

"What about Jenny?" I asked.

"We have a team working on that right now." She paused. "You got out quicker than we imagined possible. We hope that buys us time without triggering Nema's wrath."

She gave me instructions about where to meet the exfiltration team. I told the cabbie.

He gave me a skeptical glance, then put the hammer down and said, "We go, fast and furious."

When we arrived, I understood his skepticism. We drove down the bluff on which the city was built to an old unfinished dock on an alluvial floodplain. The pier had been started back when men still went to the moon. Nearby a series of large pylons rose out of the water at regular intervals crossing the river. It was an unfinished bridge as old as the dock.

"What happened here?" I asked the cabbie in Arabic.

"The plans of the old king. He died."

Ah, the joys of monarchies.

About then, a beautiful cigarette boat pulled up to the dock. I hopped out and thanked the cabbie. Thirty feet above us, on the main road, cop cars flew by. They were looking for me. Whether they wanted to thank me, shoot me, or ask me questions didn't matter. I needed to save Jenny and the kids.

The dock was twenty feet wide, but they never finished the dock by putting a deck on the structural members. All I had to do was cross a sixty-foot-long pier on four-inch-wide girders spaced four feet apart. The distance was longer than a stride, shorter than a jump.

Two cop cars followed my cabbie as he made a quick exit from the river's edge.

It was a wide and shallow riverbed. The old king had laid the foundations for a riverside resort. A wide stretch of concrete covered much of the floodplain, affording my cab driver a good deal of room to run.

One of the cop cars peeled off, turned around, and came back for me. I didn't look local in my jeans and t-shirt.

With only one option left, I ran across the girders. My days as a high school track star were long gone, but with my life hanging in the balance, not to mention the potential for breaking a leg, I scampered across and jumped into the boat.

Until I crashed into the cushions, I hadn't realized who piloted the thing. Mercury and Miguel. It was unclear which had the helm. Whoever it was, he threw the throttle back. I landed on my butt, squashed up against the engine compartment.

Mercury said, *Welcome aboard, homie!*

I said, *Is Jenny safe? The kids?*

Mercury said, *Was I alone in thinking that video came from the dungeon in Úbeda? Tania thought so. Miguel thought the stones looked lighter in color. Pia-Caesar-Sabel sent a team from Sabel Security to liberate the hacienda. All they found was an old man ranting about the tenants who wrecked his gate and shot up his wine cellar.*

I said, *Damn. Where's Jenny then? And how come there wasn't any wine in his wine cellar?*

Mercury said, *The old man joined AA a few years back. The wimp. Bianca's team is working on accessing the cellphone Nema used. They covered the GPS and IP addresses from the video, but she thinks she can isolate the transmission and follow it back to the source. Not easy, I'm told. Everything you clowns do with electricity these days is too much for my brain. All I know about this high-tech stuff is that without power, it's useless. How do I know that? The number-one prayer all gods get is for another ten minutes of battery life for those stupid phones.*

Miguel kept his eyes forward. He didn't speak. I looked behind us. Our wake spread out wide, obscuring the view, swamping local fishermen and generally causing a nuisance. Which explained the police boat a quarter mile back with sirens blaring.

We had a significant speed advantage.

Miguel swished the boat back and forth, chopping a huge wake. The police bounced over it and almost capsized. They backed off and receded into the distance.

The river narrowed. Miguel kept the speed up. We neared a marina. He threw the boat sideways.

The Navajo tribe is not known for their watercraft skills, most likely due to their reservation being in the high Arizona desert. I'd never seen Miguel in a boat much less at the helm. He made a valiant effort at the high-speed maneuver. The boat began turning, but the arc was going wide. We would clip the seawall. We came close enough to see the irises on the seagull's eyes widen. Crabs scattered out of the way. Miguel looked at me for ideas.

Mercury slapped his palm to his face. *Reverse, homie. Reverse!*

I reached for the throttle and pulled it straight back to reverse it. The big engines churned and clanked and were as unhappy as inanimate objects can be. But we slowed. The arc improved.

"How did you know to do that?" Miguel asked.

"I get—"

He finished for me, "—messages. Yeah. OK. And he knows all about powerboats."

I shrugged.

Miguel put it in forward again. Slower this time. We zoomed into the little harbor and bounced off a wharf.

A local man tied it up. Miguel said thanks to him and kept striding up the gangway towards land. Miguel and I are flatlanders, landlubbers, whatever you want to call us. That ride scared the hell out of us both—only we weren't going to let it show.

"Are you going to pay the man for renting that thing?" I asked.

"Rent? I bought it." Miguel whipped out my wallet and handed it back to me. "Or, more accurately, you bought it. You're right, that black card gets attention."

Nice that everyone spends Ms. Sabel's money like it was water out of the ocean, but I'm the guy Accounting calls to ask, WTF? In this case, they would be asking WT-actual-F? And I couldn't blame them.

But then, it's hard to argue with results. Sirens circled the neighborhood on the wrong side of the river. We could make a clean getaway.

Tania waited in a Toyota Quest. I asked if I'd bought the car too. They swore it was a rental. I'm never sure if I should trust these two or not.

We arrived at the Rabat-Salé airport's executive terminal a short time later. Seconds after wheels-up the bad news hit.

The pilot announced on the intercom, "There's a Royal Moroccan Air Force F-16 telling us we must return to the airport.".

I ran forward and opened the cockpit. "Can you stall them long enough to get into international airspace?"

Pilots have restrictions on how much time they can spend at the controls. That's how they fight off fatigue. It also requires Sabel Industries to keep contractors on retainer around the world. Most of the time we have no idea who's flying the jet. Occasionally, we'll see a familiar face. The guy in the pilot's seat craned over his shoulder. He knew me.

"Stearne, right?" He rolled his eyes. "This is just like Oman. They'll shoot us down."

"No, they won't. And the Omanis didn't shoot us down."

"I'm not prepared to take that risk. And the reason we lived that time is because the Omani's missile failed."

I didn't see any reason to tell him we were protected by god then and now. That kind of stuff usually derails the conversation. They call me a nut case. God knows why.

"Yes, you are ready to take that risk. We're on our way to save seventeen kids and one adult who are strapped to a bomb."

The copilot tapped his pilot. "Remember when I told you never accept a gig from Sabel? It's always something sketchy."

He looked me over. Then he looked over my shoulder at Tania. "Is he for real?"

"Yes." Of course, she would've said the same thing with equal conviction if I'd lied. No better backup than Tania.

Miguel squeezed in behind us. "Just got the word from Bianca. They figured it out. Basel, Switzerland. There's an empty castle there called Angenstein. She believes the kids are in the basement."

"I'm gonna lose my license over this." The pilot turned back to his controls. He clicked his mic. "Sorry, control tower has not given me a vector."

He sparred with the Royal Moroccans for several minutes. At 500 miles per hour, it didn't take long to leave the coastal capital and Morocco's airspace. Unfortunately, it took us west. We had to skirt the country and fly over Spain. Air traffic controllers demanded we explain ourselves and our flight path. We promised to land in Paris and asked to be met at the airport by Lieutenant Colonel Hugo of the GIGN.

That bought us enough time to head northeast over Geneva.

Miguel had wisely repacked our HALO gear and stored it on Sabel Three after the jump in the Netherlands. We suited up. The pilot could only get down to 40,000 feet and could only slow to 200 miles per hour. Both would make the jump extremely difficult for us.

We dove out into bright sunshine. The Alps scratched at the sky far below us. Way far below us. We fell for close to three minutes before pulling our chutes. When we did, we floated to a steep hillside above the sixteenth century castle.

"What's with Nema and her thing for the late Renaissance?" Tania asked.

I said, "Segregated times."

CHAPTER 47

WE HIKED DOWN THE HILLSIDE through the forest having landed far enough uphill that a farmer wouldn't see us floating out of the sky. And also so that a Free Origins guard wouldn't spot us coming in for the big Hollywood rescue. The downside was the walk. It took an excruciating amount of time. The lives of seventeen children and my ex-girlfriend were on the line.

At some point, Nema would not see the news flashes she wanted to see coming out of Morocco. We'd already seen some reporting of an incident, but King Mohammed VI keeps a tight lid on his press. No rumors or sensationalized reporting came out of Rabat, only limited reports of a shooting with fatalities. She expected her people to die. She didn't expect them to call in a full report. How much time that bought us was anyone's guess.

Halfway through the forest, we heard my theme song playing. Police sirens. They sped down the highway in front of the castle. Not good.

We arrived at the edge of the forest in time to see the police arrive in Teslas and cordon off the area and enter the building.

I discovered we'd gotten a text from Ms. Sabel while falling forty thousand feet. It read, "After updating FBI Director Shikowitz, he determined the local authorities should be made aware of the situation."

Mercury stepped out of the trees. *They're aware all right, homeboy. The local authorities have arrived and are ready to save the day. That'd be a problem for you, though. These cops are good, but they don't know the full extent of Nema's evil mind. You need to go down there and act all Caesar-like.*

I said, *What's wrong with letting them handle it? They have professional hostage negotiators.*

Mercury said, *Who wanna appeal to the terrorist's humanity to make them see the light. Only problem is, Nema put the trigger in the hands of an unwilling participant. Standard negotiating tactics will only add to the feeling of hopelessness. The more they work on him, the more despondent he'll feel. Only you can do something.*

I said, *Am I still a wanted man in France?*

Mercury said, *That's not your biggest problem.*

I said, *What does that mean?*

Mercury said, *The authorities in Morocco consider you one of the terrorists and have asked EU countries to arrest you on sight. But don't go getting depressed, yo. The Swiss aren't in the EU.*

We stopped at the tree line. The scene wasn't what I'd imagined. As castles go, this one was small. It had no outer wall, no crenelated parapets, no watchtowers. It did have thick stone walls with a few scattered windows and one big front door that looked like it could stop anything smaller than a tank. Five stories up was a modern roof.

Mercury stood in the castle's driveway, looking up at the roof. *What a view from there, huh, homie? Especially with those funny looking metal thingys. Highly suspicious objects if you ask me.*

He's not always wrong.

On the roof were three Yagi antennas pointing in three different directions. Yagi antennas are directional. They're also an old technology dating to the 1920s. Naturally, the military uses them. They come in handy as a backup system in battlefield scenarios should the satellites go down. They can be adapted for high-speed internet access if you want to mask your physical location. Yagi antenna A sits on the castle, beaming a signal in a straight line of sight to Yagi antenna B. The B antenna could be miles away. They must have been the reason Bianca had so much trouble finding the location.

They would also make it harder to find Nema's command center once we disarmed Jenny's suicide vest. I texted Bianca a heads-up about the antennas.

Among the police was a tall, middle-aged woman who had raised children through their teenage years. Mothers who survived teens are easy to spot; they have that permanent your-bullshit-won't-fly-with-me look on their faces. I figured she must be in charge. We approached and introduced ourselves.

Before I finished talking, I was facedown on the asphalt and cuffed. Someone grabbed me by the hair and yanked me to standing. I faced the serious woman. Someone introduced her as Kommandant of Police for the Canton of Basel-Stadt. No name was given.

In crisp German-tinted English, Kommandant said, "You are responsible for this heinous crime?"

"That sounded past tense," I said. "Tell me they haven't triggered the bomb."

"You know this bomb? That man is one of your people?"

"The victim is my girlfriend. I don't know who else might be involved. But I can neutralize this situation. Please, don't send anyone in there. Let me go."

"And let you kill all these children? No."

"I worked undercover. I infiltrated the terrorists who put all this together. I can stop it."

"We have assessed the situation. You will not be involved."

Two of her officers began dragging me away.

Mercury leaned over her shoulder. *Tell Kommandant you talk to the gods, homie. She'll understand. She's the kind of woman who respects power. I can get Juno in here for a consultation. Go ahead now. Tell her you have a direct line to Mercury, winged messenger of the Roman gods.*

I said, *I'm going to pass on that one. But thanks for the tip.*

I called out, "Call FBI Director Shikowitz. He knows me. He'll tell you I can resolve this situation."

"You are FBI agent?" She peered at me with more suspicion than I wanted.

"Not exactly. But I know Shikowitz. I swear. Call him."

Tania handed her my phone with Shikowitz's cell number teed up and ready to dial.

She gave Tania a withering glance. She took out her own phone and handed it to an aide. In German, she told him to call the FBI headquarters and ask for the director. Not that I speak German, but the cross-over words combined with the side-eye she gave me translated it all for me. The two men holding me pushed us farther away from the action.

Kommandant turned to a man who'd just emerged from the castle. While I couldn't hear him, his body language spoke volumes. These people had been to training. They had mastered horrific scenarios on paper. But a nice sleepy little canton like Basel-Stadt didn't see a lot of violent crime. I could tell by the mixture of determination and fear on their faces. The man giving the report was explaining a hopeless situation.

Miguel and Tania scanned the police personnel holding us back. I followed suit, taking stock of the mostly male force, including the two guarding the three of us. Then my team members turned their gazes to me with a barely perceptible nod. The glance told me they were ready to take down the cops if it came to that. Like a pitcher communicating with his catcher, I shook them off. We would win the battle, but cops on edge have a tendency to pull their triggers a little too quickly. Someone could get hurt, and that would make me the terrorist that Kommandant—and everyone else in Europe—thought I was.

Kommandant questioned her man, he answered, and then she looked across the patrol cars at me. The officer she'd tasked with reaching the FBI Director handed over her phone. She spoke into it. Her gaze stayed locked on me while she spoke. Her your-bullshit-won't-fly-with-me face hardened.

Mercury stepped into my line of sight. *You know what that guy said? He said the situation is hopeless; we should let the American take the blame.*

I said, *You could hear them?*

Mercury said, *No. But I know how commanders think when defeat and destruction are inevitable.*

Kommandant told her men to bring me forward. When they deposited me in front of her, they took my cuffs off.

"Director Shikowitz thinks well of you." Kommandant observed me like she was going to pull my spleen out with her fingernails. "You know the situation?"

"Not the details." I gave her my soldier stare. "I know the people who put it together, and I can stop them. Guaranteed."

She took a moment to observe me with a hint of respect. She turned to three men waiting for instructions. They argued in German. Their voices rose, their faces turned red. All four of them were angry. Then, all at once, they stopped talking.

She turned to me. "Guaranteed?"

"Absolutely."

Kommandant gave me a second, longer visual assessment. I stood stock-still, my eyes never leaving hers. She pointed to the huge front door. "Through the foyer, stairs on the left going down. Do not come back without the children."

"As soon as I go in, give Tania a sniper rifle and let her disable all three Yagi antennas."

She looked up, saw them, and grasped their role immediately. She snapped her fingers and barked in German. Men scrambled around the Teslas. One came back with a rifle. Tania took it and gave me a nod.

Miguel patted me on the back. "Good luck."

"You can take this one if you'd like."

"Better if you do it. If it goes bad, the world will only be short one white man."

"Thanks." I marched to the door and my doom.

The only man who'd been inside gave me a grim look with a hint of thank-god-it's-you-and-not-me in it. Behind me, the Kommandant's men exhaled in muted protest.

Mercury marched alongside me. *That was powerful, bro. You told her in no uncertain terms. Now that's the way to go Caesar. Keep doing that, and we might have a future. So. What's your plan?*

My plan? I stopped in my tracks. *Don't you have a plan?*

Mercury looked puzzled. *Why would I have a plan? You were all over this.*

I said, *What's the bomb look like? What's going on down there?*

Mercury said, *How in the name of Minerva would I know?*

I said, *Because you're a god. Wait. What are you telling me? Oh no. You really are a figment of my imagination? You don't really exist? All those doctors were right?*

Mercury said, *No. I'm Mercury, messenger of the Roman—*

I said, *Then how come you can't see anything I can't see? If you do exist, you could tell me what's going on in there.*

"Are you all right?" Kommandant called out to me.

"Just having a word with god." I stood still, contemplating whether I wanted to go in there now that I knew we are alone in the universe. But there was no turning back. Jenny and seventeen kids depended on me.

Just in case my existential moment was off by a god or two, I said, *You have thirty seconds to think of something, or I go back on my meds for the rest of my life. However short that might be.*

CHAPTER 48

AT THE BOTTOM OF THE stairs, two of the Kommandant's bravest men stood next to a thick wooden door. They were sweating. There was a bomb inside, and they stood in the blast radius. Worse, there was a good chance they knew the children inside. I gave them a smile and patted their shoulders and displayed confidence as best I could. They weren't buying it. One of them reached for the door's handle with a hand shaking so badly I caught his arm and pushed it back. I opened the door myself.

Inside was dark. It stank of fear and urine. Children cried and sniffled softly in the dark.

My vision began to adjust slowly. Back in Iowa, we would call a room like this a root cellar. The place where you stored your potatoes, carrots, melons, and other supplies that didn't need a refrigerator but did need a cool space. Stone steps led down to a granite floor far below. The ceiling was arched and high. In the center, a wooden chair hung from a pulley. It was high enough off the floor to break bones if the occupant tried to jump down. The ropes holding it in place ran through the pulley and down to a tie-off point at the bottom of the steps.

In the chair was Lugh, his broken arm still in a sling. In his good hand, he held an electronic device with a big red button on top. The dead man's switch. His thumb had turned white from holding it down for hours.

As my eyes adjusted, the darker corner of the room became visible. My heart stopped beating. Clawed animals tried to scratch their way out of my stomach. Jenny was tied to the chair I'd seen in Nema's video, her mouth taped. Behind her cowered seventeen trembling children. Everyone's face was streaked with tears. Jenny and Lugh as well as the kids.

I inched down steps built long before any building codes. There were no handrails. The treads were slick and damp and narrow. Lugh watched every movement with a look of sheer terror. When I reached the bottom, I gently felt the rope that held him in the air.

"Don't touch that!" Lugh shouted.

I held both my hands up in surrender. Then I strolled casually to Jenny. I pulled the tape off her mouth. While doing that, I checked the bomb in my peripheral vision. I didn't want to remind her of the danger and trigger a spasm of fear.

It was ugly. Big packages of C-4 were sewn into the vest. Military blasting caps had been pushed deep into each one. The wires ran to a device the size of a cigarette pack on her breast. The light on it still blinked green. Two wires ran from it to one of those extended batteries built for heavy phone users.

Nema wanted to make sure there was enough power for me to finish the mission before having a chance to watch them die.

"Jacob, run." Jenny shook her head free of the last bit of tape. "Get out of here. He explained it. It's only a matter of time."

I wiped the tears off her face with my thumb. "Good to see you again."

I turned around to face Lugh only to find Mercury standing in my path. Mercury said, *You should listen to her. This is hopeless. Run for it.*

I said, *Keep thinking. You'll come up with something. If you don't, your last believer will end up in a million pieces.*

I looked up at Lugh. The rig was ingenious. If he leaned forward, or dropped his trigger, or got shot, or fell asleep, everyone in the room died. Including Lugh.

"Don't worry," I said to him, "I'll get you down safe and sound."

"He's a terrorist!" Jenny cried. "He's going to kill us all. What are you doing?"

"What I should've done with you," I said while maintaining eye contact with Lugh. "Engaging in conversation."

"It was never about you," she said. "It's me. I don't know how to deal with …"

DEATH AND CONSPIRACY

She started crying again.

"We'll get through it," I said, turning to her. "You'll go to counseling. We'll restart our relationship from the beginning. Take it slower, easier. One step at a time. Maybe you'll want to date me, maybe not. We'll see after counseling."

She looked up with red eyes. "I wanted to go somewhere no one had ever heard of me."

"You came here? Basel?" I asked. "I thought you went home."

"I found a job online at a daycare facility." She looked at the kids and started crying again. "A place where no one knows about the killer heiress."

"What the hell are you doing?" Lugh snarled.

"Chill, dude." I gave him a frown. Then I noticed the pool of liquid on the stones directly below him. "I'll get everyone out of here safe and sound. Tell me the truth, are the kids wired to any kind of trigger?"

"No." Lugh sounded as if he were going to cry. "This button ... I can't ..."

I glanced at Mercury. *Figured it out yet? I need something here.*

Mercury said, *Don't look at me. Not even Mars knows anything about all this new-fangled bomb shit. Sorry, brutha, I don't know electronics.*

Something Mercury had said in Rabat ticked in my brain. It took a second for the gears to fall into place, but they did. I said, *Yes, actually, you do know something about electronics. Only one thing, but it's a life-saving thing. Thanks, Mercury.*

He hooked his thumbs in his toga and grinned like a proud papa. *Anytime, homie. You can count on the Dii Consentes to save your wretched soul. Uh, what exactly is it that I know?*

I faced Jenny and leaned down. I looked over the bombs. I checked a couple wires to make sure they were secure. I tugged two of them a little harder than the rest. They didn't come loose, but I could tell how much tension would be required to disconnect them. If they were the right ones to disconnect. I looked at all the other wires. Did I have this right? Were these two the ones I needed to pull? It was a matter of faith. Was Mercury right about electronics?

I looked at the little faces next to me. Big expectant eyes met my

SEELEY JAMES

gaze.

"Were you on the bomb squad?" Jenny asked. "Tell me you were on the bomb squad."

"Nope," I confessed. "But I did go to science class in the sixth grade once. It was worth it."

I turned back to Lugh. "We're going to let the children go. Then I'm going to do something that I'm pretty sure will get us out of here alive. But it might not."

"No way," Lugh said. He looked at a corner of the room. "She has a remote switch."

I followed his gaze and saw the video camera. He thought Nema was still watching us. With her Yagi antennas disabled she'd lost her live feed. Probably.

In case Lugh still had some misplaced sense of loyalty to the woman who set him up to die, I thought it best to lie. I said, "Lugh, she knows I'm here. She can see me. She knows what I'm doing. She doesn't want to be the one who kills a bunch of kids."

"She hates children!" His voice shook with fear.

"Trust me on this."

I faced Jenny. "You must speak German if you got the job. Shout to the guards outside to come get the kids."

She did. Seconds later, two scared cops came in and rushed the kids up the stairs.

I leaned to Jenny. "Do you trust me?"

She looked up at me. Tears filled her eyes. Even her skin shook. Her body trembled. She nodded. "Kiss me first?"

In the movies, bombs have ten wires in every imaginable hue. Those are complicated circuits with backup systems and failsafes and remote detonators. They're hard to make. Plenty of terrorist bombmakers had gone to their reward trying to overcomplicate a basic on-off device. My gamble was based on what Mercury had told me was the extent of his electronics prowess, that without power, our gizmos were useless. The device on Jenny's breast didn't look all that complicated.

I gave her a gentle, confident kiss.

And pulled the wires from the battery.

276

With any luck, the battery was the only power source. If there was a battery inside the controller, we would soon be three dead people. I looked at the blinking light. It stopped blinking. We weren't out of the woods yet.

Lugh screamed his anguish and, in the process, dropped the switch. It clattered to the floor. The red button had been released. We stared at it.

Nothing exploded.

I unwrapped Jenny's wrists and gently removed the vest. I set it on the floor. The tape on her ankles came off next. The instant her feet were free, she leapt from the chair into my arms. She wrapped me in a hug and squeezed so tight I wondered if I would ever breathe again. She held me, and I her, without moving for a long time. Then she kissed me. A long, ravenous kiss.

I broke it off. "We need to clear the area."

She backed up a couple steps to give me room. I went to the ropes and untethered the chair. I lowered Lugh to the floor. He rose and faced me with an awkward expression. He hated me—yet I'd saved his life. He wasn't sure about the proper etiquette.

Jenny took a few quick steps and kicked Lugh in the nuts. "You son of a bitch! How could you do that."

Her voice shook the stone chamber. She kicked him in the shin. He fell to his knees.

"It was supposed to be just the two of us, you and me." Lugh looked up with pathetic eyes. "You saw it. She brought the kids in after she tied me to the ceiling. I never should've trusted that bitch."

"You tried to kill me!" Jenny kicked him in the face. He fell to the floor. She took a big step and kicked him in the stomach. He doubled up in pain. She kicked him in the face again. And again. And again.

"He's going to jail." I pulled her off. "I don't want you to go with him."

CHAPTER 49

KOMMANDANT WAS A DIFFERENT WOMAN when we emerged. She wrapped me up in a big motherly hug. An expected reaction since I saved her career along with the children. The parents were on their way. The press strained at the police barriers. Onlookers cheered me in the Swiss dusk.

Jenny wanted to talk. I wanted to talk. But. We had no privacy.

Tania pushed me to get my attention. "Bianca has a fix on what she thinks is the command center for Free Origins. She said spotting the Yagi antennas was a big help. There's a lot of encrypted messages coming and going from a farmhouse in northern Denmark, near Skagen. It's a two-hour flight. We've got to get moving."

Miguel shoulder-punched me. "Nice work, friend. You saved the day for them, but there are still a thousand lives at stake if we don't get moving."

I faced Jenny and started to say something. She put her finger to my lips to stop me. She said, "I know. Before this, well … I thought you were just a guy. I know, 'just a guy' who saved my mother's life and helped me get a pardon, but it wasn't just Mom you saved, was it? I get it now. This is what you do. And while I may be safe, there are others. Go. Do what you do. We can talk later."

I kissed her, hugged her one more time, and followed Tania and Miguel to a place where a big Eurocopter waited. It took us to our jet at the airport. The jet took us to Skagen. The whole time we traveled, people talked to me, said things, showed me stuff. All I could see was that last tear rolling down Jenny's cheek.

I came out of my stupor when the rental car Miguel was driving stopped at a roadblock. It was dark, and we were near the top of the Jutland peninsula. The Skagen website showed pictures of people in bathing suits on sunny, sandy beaches. My eyes stretched across weedy dunes hugged by a gray sky, and a grayer sea made even grayer by the darkening night.

Mercury tapped my shoulder. *That Shikowitz likes to steal your thunder. He called the Danish police before you left Switzerland.*

I said, *That's what FBI directors do. Warning foreign governments about American-grown terrorists is his responsibility.*

Mercury said, *But you can still go in there and get all the glory.*

I said, *That could be a suicide mission.*

Mercury said, *Exactly! Then everyone would know how serious you are about doing what the Roman gods tell you.*

And that's when I reached for my meds. My hand went to the empty front pocket of my jeans. I ran out ages ago. While Miguel spoke through the window to an officer, I made a mental note to refill my prescription. One of these days, I might fall for one of his self-immolating ideas.

The cop waved us through. Miguel drove over a ridge where a large police operation was underway. We drove up to a mobile command center with *Politiets Efterretningstjenestes* emblazoned on it.

A young man in full battle rattle opened my door. "Mr. Stearne, Afdelingschef Dalsgaard requests your presence. We have heard a great deal about you, and he has many questions."

"What are we, chopped liver?" Tania asked.

The young man looked up and saw my squad for the first time.

I said, "They're with me. We're the holy trinity—as far as you know. What's that Aff-word you used? Since it ended in 'chief' does that mean he's the head of whatever that says on the van there?"

The young man looked back and forth. His English was perfect, no accent. But so was his Danish. Which doesn't sound as much like German as I expected. He said, "Denmark's Security and Intelligence Service. We're the counter terrorism division, and yes, he is the chief. I am Jannik, your translator for now."

He took us to a stout, older man with thin gray hair brushed straight back. The chief had a trimmed beard and sharp eyes that stabbed at all our critical points. Jannik warned us Dalsgaard was of the older generation who did not learn English in school and did not think it was cool to speak it. He was a traditionalist who insisted his people speak Danish in the office. Everyone else spoke English when he wasn't around.

"Chief Dalsgaard has many concerns about you." Jannik shifted his weight from one foot to the other. "Ehm. Major Pavard of the—"

"Fuck Major Pavard." I gave young Jannik my soldier stare. When he flinched, I continued. "Does Dalsgaard want to stop a tragedy or be the guy who watched it happen? Don't just stand there flapping your lips, ask him."

Jannik turned barn-red and prefaced his translation as a direct translation.

Dalsgaard responded at length in a cool voice.

Jannik faced me. "It is not just Pavard, whom Chief Dalsgaard does not know. There are also the videos of you training American terrorists in Úbeda, and Lieutenant Hugo's report from Leiden, that give him grave concern."

"That's Lieutenant Colonel to you, Jannik. And for the record, fuck Lieutenant Colonel Hugo too."

Mercury came running around the corner. *Dude, they have a robot checking out the farmhouse on the other side of that rise. They've got snipers in position and a bunch of guys primed and ready to rock. Guess what's on top of the farmhouse. Yagi antennas. It's them. C'mon, don't stand there yakking it up with these fobbits. Get out there. Caesars are always out front.*

I said, *They'd shoot me in the back.*

Mercury said, *So? There's work to be done. Glory to be seized! Carthago delenda est, damn it.*

I said, *What?*

Mercury said, *Carthago delenda est. Carthage must be seized. Do you ever read those books I make you buy, or do you just stick 'em on your bookshelf to impress the ladies?*

I said, *I read them. Some of them. A couple.*

Jannik said, "Are you all right, sir?"

"No. I'm not all right." I faced Dalsgaard. "Thirteen religious communities are about to be attacked. Hundreds could die in a matter of hours. What did your robot find?"

"He insists on answers to his concerns, or he will have you escorted back to your jet." He shifted his weight and fidgeted. "One other question, if you don't mind. I lived in America for six years. I studied English and thought I knew it very well. But this one word I don't understand. What is a *fobbit*?"

My heart stopped.

Mercury's mouth fell open. He slapped my shoulder. *Brutha, you didn't say fobbit, I did. Does this mean Jannik can hear me?*

I said, *Impossible. You're not real.*

Mercury said, *Not real? Holy Jupiter. Who told you how to save Jenny and the kids? Who said, and I quote, 'All I know about this high-tech stuff is that without power, it's useless.' Who saves your ass every time you're about to die?*

I said, *I wish I knew.*

"Obscure term," I said to Jannik. "Most army bases near the warzone were called a Forward Operating Base or FOB. A fobbit is a guy who never left the FOB. Never heard the hornets. Never dropped to the dirt, wondering if he was still alive. We called those guys fobbits in a not-nice way."

"Heard the hornets?" Jannik mumbled. He turned a light shade of green the way people do when they hear casual references to warzones and realize how unprepared they are for the trial by fire ahead of them.

"When bullets fly within an inch of your ear, they sound like angry hornets."

Jannik's green darkened a shade. He turned to Dalsgaard and translated. Dalsgaard responded at length.

"He said the robot found blocks of C-4 spaced six inches apart all the way around the house. That's 380 blocks visible." Jannik took a deep breath. "Everything is wired to a central location inside. Video cameras surround the building. The robot is equipped to breach the front door. We have two snipers and an assault team standing by. We are ready to commit, but we are concerned about blowing the building."

That much C-4 could blow a tunnel to Gothenburg, Sweden, a mere fifty miles across the Baltic from here.

"Do you have another sniper rifle you could loan my sister-in-arms?"

Jannik smiled. "Do you have a plan, sir?"

I looked at Mercury. "Maybe."

CHAPTER 50

AS I SUSPECTED, DALSGAARD HAD also spoken to Basel-Stadt's Kommandant. Like hers, his men wanted the glory of taking down the terrorists while he wanted the option of having someone to blame should it all go to Acheron in a handbasket. As a bonus for him, all the news feeds coming out of Basel featured Kommandant. Only a few insiders knew it was Sabel Security. We'd left the glory for her.

Miguel and I went to the mobile command center and checked out the video of the bombs while Tania donned sniper gear and went to meet the other snipers.

The Danes's robot had recorded the bombs in detail. Each bomb sat in a U-shaped metal container bolted to the side of the house at waist level. Each container had been coated with nuts and bolts as anti-personnel shrapnel.

One power line ran to the building from the street. Our hopes of shutting down ROSGEO by pulling the plug were dashed when another video showed a new generator installation. We had to figure they had battery backup inside as well.

No one knew how many people were inside or who they were. The Danes tried using a thermal sensor that could identify people by heat signatures through walls, but the farmhouse had too much insulation. Only one car sat outside. It was a rental issued to Paladin. It was paid for by a credit card issued to Birth Right Christians, LLC.

Once again, no trace of Nema to be found.

"We believe they will blow the building if they feel threatened." Jannik translated Dalsgaard's concerns. "What we don't understand is what they're doing."

"We don't want them blowing the building," I said. "We need to hijack their communications system so we can send a stand-down order to the terrorists on the ground. It has to come from their leadership, and it will have to contain special code words. We need that building and it's gear intact."

Miguel filled them in while I continued flipping back and forth through videos. Miguel said, "They plan to attack thirteen holy places as close to simultaneously as possible. Since different religions worship at different times, we believe they're coordinating primary and alternate sites and services from here."

"But different religions have services on different days."

"Most religious communities keep their grounds busy with Bible studies, charity programs, community meetings, things like that. Combined with the time differences, they expect to have ample targets for their plan."

"Why alternate sites?" Jannik asked.

"They're trying to find the optimal number of people on the grounds with the least amount of security," Miguel said. "They attacked a mosque in Morocco this morning. They expected that attack to raise the alarms at other sites. But the Moroccans kept a lid on it, which led to their delay. If the primary site is heavily defended or the service is cancelled, they'll switch to an alternate site. What they don't want to do is show up ready to kill and find an empty temple or cathedral.

"They intended to build the impression of a growing rush of Muslims seeking reprisals against Christians. Then they'll stage Jewish attacks on Muslims, Christians on Hindus, and so on. They expect that everyone will attack someone else. Armageddon worldwide. And for all that to work, they need news feeds, fast internet, and a central point of control."

Jannik discussed the scenario with Dalsgaard before returning with another question. "They only need one person to coordinate? And that person could be in a bomb-proof shelter inside the house?"

While they speculated, Mercury squeezed in next to me. *Think there's something wrong with those bombs, homie?*

I said, *They look like they're anti-personnel, and they'll hurt people near them, but that's not their primary purpose. They're rigged to blow inwards, not outwards. Why would they do that?*

Mercury said, *Good question.*

Bianca called from Sabel Technologies. "We still haven't figured out how they're communicating with their suicide squads. They're relaying internet traffic to a spectrum of hijacked servers and computers around the world, but in the end, they need to tell their teams go or no-go. How are they doing that? You need to get inside."

I replied, "You haven't seen the explosives rigged to the house."

"Something is missing. They have one last trick, like the Yagi antennas, that's making it impossible to trace. Get inside and see what they're doing."

"No problem." I clicked off.

Mercury wasn't the only one who wanted me to commit suicide.

Nice to know.

A monitor above me showed a shiny new Eurocopter approaching. It flew the French flag and the letters, GIGN on its side. Which could only mean my old friend Lieutenant Colonel Hugo had arrived.

Tania gave me her signal. Her newly formed sniper team was ready.

I said to Jannik and Dalsgaard, "Tell me about the robot. Does it have two-way video communications onboard?"

"Yes. We can talk to hostages and criminals over it. You want to send it inside?"

When I told him that was my plan, he had to discuss it with Dalsgaard. They argued before saying no. I explained that we need to know the communications system. They said it was an expensive machine, and then they looked at me as if to imply I should go in.

Mercury laughed. *See, homie? Your real name is Jacob 'Expendable' Stearne. You're not as valuable as a robot. Even Jenny sent you on your way hoping you'll die saving the world.*

I said, *And we're back to that not-motivational thing you do.*

I tuned him out.

Hugo strode into the room, acting like a king. Again. Two aides followed him. The aides backed to the wall in the cramped space. Hugo rattled off French to no one in particular. Dalsgaard replied in French. Knowing people are talking about you in a foreign language tends to raise your paranoia level.

Mercury said, *Remember my old pal, Oscar Wilde? He said the only thing in life worse than being talked about is not. Get on with what you're doing, brutha.*

I glanced at Miguel, who spoke French. He didn't seem alarmed by their conversation, so I took my used god's advice and focused on the job at hand.

I turned to Jannik. "We need to send the robot in. I need to see what's inside."

He and Dalsgaard spoke to Hugo. Something he said got the Danes nodding. They agreed to send in the robot.

Hugo removed himself a step from the situation. He gave me a polite nod. I couldn't tell if he meant to arrest me after the operation or what. I decided to ignore him.

The robot operator sent the machine to the front door. It was a compact thing that looked like a miniature tank with funny arms reaching up from its knee-high body. One arm had an articulating hand with six fingers. The second arm had a bright light and pepper spray. The third arm had a camera and video screen. The operator put a tablet in front of me. If we encountered anyone, I would do the talking.

I sent Bianca a text about the robot going in. She replied that her people had hacked the robot's feed and would be watching along with me. She'd text me if she wanted to see anything in greater detail. She noted that she had shared the feed with the FBI and CIA. I considered telling my Danish hosts about her hack then decided, what they didn't know might not hurt them. After all, they would've preferred I commit suicide to save them the cost of a replacement robot.

The operator used the fingery-thing to open the door, which was unlocked. When the door opened, nothing greeted it but a dark and empty foyer with a staircase going up on the right. The robot went in, going slowly while scanning for tripwires or boobytraps. It wandered through a dining room and kitchen before finding a downstairs den.

The room glowed with video screens and green dots on computers and devices. I counted twelve screens and seven computers. A lone figure sat in a chair watching the screens, his back to us. Several news sites and video feeds were open in multiple windows on each screen. Some were blocked by his chair, and others were visible. The *Chicago Tribune* site and the *Atlanta Journal* were identifiable. Many of the others were in foreign languages.

The figure in the chair turned to face the robot. He wasn't surprised to see my face on the screen.

"Jacob, how are you doing?" Paladin asked.

"Well, I killed Caleb in mid-air and shot the others in Morocco. I left one of them alive but paralyzed so he could squeal on you. In Basel, I kicked Lugh half to death and left him for the authorities. So, overall, I'm doing pretty damn good, thanks for asking. How about you?"

Behind me, I heard Miguel chatting with Hugo in French. I resisted the urge to shut them up because my paranoia was cranking up another notch. Instead, I focused on Paladin.

Bianca texted me. "On the desk behind him are several phones. They're plugged into something. I need a closer look at the phones."

I slid my phone to the robot operator sitting next to me. He read it. He scowled, then tapped her earlier text about hacking the robot's video. He looked at me as if I'd betrayed him.

I rolled my hand for him to get on with it.

Reluctantly, he went back to his controls.

The video camera rose to Paladin's eye level and peeked over his shoulder.

"I'm doing better than you." Paladin gave me his movie-star smile. "I'm about to change the world. We're minutes away. Would you like to watch me issue the final command?"

"You're not waiting for the outrage to surge through Islam about the attack in Morocco?"

"It would appear they killed only six. The towelheads kill each other in bigger numbers than that every week, so that won't go far."

"But you're waiting for something."

His grin turned wistful. "You know how it is. Timing's got to be just right."

Mercury leaned over my shoulder. *He's waiting for Nema to give him the signal.*

SEELEY JAMES

I said, *Is she in the house with him?*

Mercury said, *How would I know? But I'd bet five thousand aurei she's not the type to even enter a house wired to blow.*

I said, *Are the Yagis the only internet connection he has?*

Mercury said, *If you're thinking she's gonna email it in, then you should do something about that.*

The camera rose another notch above Paladin to get a better angle. The operator moved the camera off the handsome face to follow the wires. USB cords connected the cheap phones to one of the computers.

Bianca texted us. "I need that computer or at least one of those phones. You have to retrieve it."

The operator nodded when I slid the instruction to him.

Paladin's eyes followed the camera. He asked, "You know the difference between a human and a robot, Jacob?"

"Yes, but I'm interested in your answer."

"When you shoot a human, he may or may not die right away. He might stay alive long enough to shoot back. But when you shoot a robot—pretty much anywhere—it dies."

I turned to the operator. "Is that thing armored?"

He shrugged. "It is a prototype."

Paladin pulled a big revolver off his desk and shot the robot. The screens went blank.

CHAPTER 51

"SHIT!" THE OPERATOR AND I said in unison.

Tania repeated that her snipers were ready and frosty. Which also implied that if they didn't act soon, they might lose their edge.

It was a gamble that the building would not implode when Tania did her thing. I flipped a coin in my head and told Tania to go when she was ready.

A minute later, she reported that her team had blown away all three Yagi antennas.

We waited. The building did not blow up.

I started for the door. Dalsgaard, Hugo, and Jannik started talking at once in three languages.

"I'm going in. We need one of those phones." I grabbed Jannik's pistol and walked out into the dark heading for the farmhouse. Miguel matched my stride with a Danish rifle on his shoulder.

I got six paces before Hugo caught up with me. He didn't say anything. He held out his phone with a video playing. I took it and watched. The mosque in Morocco. The old men and boys shook and trembled as the Americans held 9-mils and rifles to their heads. After words were exchanged, the Moroccans dropped to their knees, heads down. The terrorists died a split second later.

Mercury stuck his head over my shoulder. *Y'know who took that video, homie?*

I said, *Who? The cop and the civilian are in the frame. I'm in front of the camera. I didn't notice someone standing behind me. Wait. You're not going to tell me it was you.*

Mercury looked offended. *Dude. Please. We got people who record the acts of mortals for us. We never watch 'em though. Boring AF the first time around. Anyway, it was the cab driver. They caught him after you left in the boat. He had the video. That's why they didn't shoot you down.*

Hugo said, "I owe you the apology. My aide confirmed your story with the Spaniards. They confirmed many things you said. Ms. Arrianne lied to me. You have been the true hero while I, well ... I have been an old man."

"Thanks, Hugo." I looked him over as we walked. "Apology accepted. I understand. Arrianne is persuasive where men are concerned. I came close to falling for her myself. Now, you should go back with Dalsgaard."

"Apologies are meaningless without the actions." He kept looking and walking straight ahead at the farmhouse. "I go where you go."

I glanced at Miguel.

My best friend shrugged. "We could use the help."

The front door stood open. Miguel cleared the kitchen and dining room while Hugo bounded up the stairs. I went to the den.

In the center, with his chair pushed back, stood Paladin. A dead man's switch in his hand. His thumb pressed it hard. He didn't look like a handsome and famous celebrity anymore.

He looked like a scared boy. All his bravado during our video chat evaporated when three armed men invaded his space. Terrorists always dream of everything going according to some dreamed up plan, but when reality lands like a punch in the nose and their dream burns off, they begin to fall apart. Many terrorists chicken out at the last minute. That's why Nema wanted squads—they kept each other on point. She never expected us to find her boy Paladin. And he never expected to end up holding a deadman's switch as his world crumbled around him.

"This was her plan for you all along, you know," I said.

"She had nothing to do with this. I'm in charge. I call the shots." He waved at his equipment like he was showing off a new car. "I'm the visionary who came up with this plan."

Mercury said, *If you can get one hand on his bomb-switch, you can grab it out of his hands.*

I said, *You really don't get these newfangled electronic gizmos, do you.*

"Too late. She already admitted to her pulling all the strings. We can get you out of this. We know she used you, Paladin."

"If she used me—" his lip trembled "—she did it well."

"Yeah," I slid to his left side. "She's good at it, all right. Hey. Tell me again what makes it all worthwhile. I'm not getting it. Maybe I'll convert."

"Free Origins stands for everyone's right to return to where they came from. People prefer people of their kind. Nature's law. You don't see birds—"

"I heard that bullshit from Nema." I moved within reach of a couple phones.

Behind me, Miguel filled the doorframe. "I'm good with you going back where you came from."

Paladin squinted.

"He's Native American," I said. "We're all illegal aliens to them."

Paladin nodded. "Figures."

"Where will you go, Paladin?" I asked. "Where are you from?"

"Don't worry about me. I have a nice little farm with trees, water—and all-white neighbors."

He was still clinging to the dream that he'd walk out of there and live in a segregated world with his arm around little evil Nema. I almost felt sorry for him.

"Young man—" Hugo pushed past Miguel "—you have no need for doing this. Let me hold the trigger for you."

Hugo stuck his shoulder in front of mine.

I understood what Hugo was trying to do. I didn't like it at all.

Mercury said, *It's now or never, homie.*

I said, *I'm not going to leave Hugo here.*

Mercury said, *Two options: two people die here, or four people die here. You know Miguel won't leave without you. So. What's it gonna be?*

I said, *There has to be a way to defuse the bombs.*

Mercury said, *The robot guys went over the house with a fine-tooth comb. There are no options. Tania disconnected the internet. Then she shot out the electric lines. And then, without your permission, she shot out the generator. Nema had a lot more time to build a complex system for her command center. Everything is running on a battery system now. It has a couple minutes of juice left. There are no movie-magical endings here. When the battery runs out—BANG!*

I jumped.

Everyone looked at me. "We need to go. C'mon, Paladin. You can come with us. We'll tape it down and walk away."

Paladin shook his head slowly. He lifted his shirt. A small box with a blinking green light was taped to his body. "Proximity backup with biometrics. I can't take it off and I can't cross the threshold."

Mercury said, *Holy Bellona, your little Nema has more evil in her head than Caligula ever dreamed possible.*

"What happened to your little place with trees and springs?"

"You waste time," Hugo snapped.

Miguel tapped my shoulder and nosed toward the exit. We'd seen it in battle. The Joe who knows he can save the squad by throwing himself on the IED. He dies, his friends live. A terrible and heroic bargain.

Hugo knew he was going to die. His hard eyes never left Paladin's. His regal bearing never wavered. "You must go now."

I grabbed two phones and yanked them from their cables.

"Hey!" Paladin shouted.

While his eyes followed my actions, Hugo grabbed his wrist with one hand and clamped his other hand down on top of Paladin's trigger thumb. The two started wrestling for control of the button.

Miguel grabbed my shoulders and pushed me out of the room. We took off in a dead run. Through the front door. Up the rise and over the sand dune and through the beach weeds where I tripped and somersaulted down a ten-foot hill.

The explosion blew five feet off the top of the rise. The shock wave pounded every square inch of my body. The fireball lit up the peninsula. Heat singed my feet. Smoke filled my lungs. Pieces of clapboard and shingles and structural beams and plumbing flew over my head. Miguel grabbed my arms, hauled me to standing. We took off running again as the bigger objects began falling from the sky and landing around us like mortar shells.

CHAPTER 52

TANIA, CAMOUFLAGED TO BLEND IN with the beach weeds, appeared out of thin air, running for all she was worth. I patted her back, the only way I could say thanks for taking out all the critical points on the house. If she could've seen Paladin through the window, she would've blown the trigger out of his hand. It might've worked.

Weighing on our hearts was the final analysis: we won the war because of Hugo's sacrifice. The man died with honor.

The three of us reached Dalsgaard's mobile unit and ripped the door open.

Everyone cheered when we staggered in.

We wanted shelter. They wanted heroes.

I uploaded the two phones stolen from Paladin to Bianca's people.

She called. I put her on speakerphone. "Nice work, Jacob. We'll get these broken down and send messages to the terrorist groups. We'll tell them to stand down. When they read their messages, we'll have a fix on them. The CIA, FBI, and every international law enforcement group is standing by, ready to take them down."

Ms. Sabel broke into the conversation. She said, "The French gave us a bodycam feed from Hugo. We are deeply saddened by his loss and thankful for his sacrifice. What he did was the most heroic act of selflessness I've ever witnessed. What the three of you did is equally heroic. You've made us proud. More importantly, you've saved hundreds of lives."

President Charles Williams broke into Ms. Sabel's praise and offered some of his own. Then it was Director Shikowitz's turn. I put the phone down.

Hugo's two aides stood silently in the corner. I approached and started to speak. One guy shook his head. "We know."

"He was a brave man." It was all I could think of.

"He believes in duty above all else," the other one said. He paused. "Believed."

Dalsgaard produced a bottle of akvavit, the Danish version of schnapps, while Jannik passed out shot glasses. No mobile command center is complete without shot glasses. Dalsgaard poured for the French aides first, then the rest of us. He said something long in Danish, then French. A tear formed in everyone's eye. Except Tania and me. We spoke neither language. But we could tell it was a good eulogy.

The Frenchmen appreciated his gesture. They drank, hugged everyone, turned, and walked out. A minute later, the French bird fired up its engines and roared into the night sky. They didn't wait around because they knew there wouldn't be enough pieces of Hugo to bring home.

Dalsgaard was happy and sad. He would smile for a minute, then shed a tear. We wondered where the mastermind, Nema, had gone. And her victim-accomplice Arrianne, for that matter. In the end, we decided they were a problem best left to the FBI or Interpol. They would soon be rounded up with their killers.

We ran out of things to say or do. The press began piling up outside. Someone needed to make a statement. We figured we should be gone before that statement came out. We said our goodbyes.

I grabbed my phone. Someone was still talking. They were congratulating us on a job well done. I mouthed to Tania, "Who is that?"

"Secretary of the Interior, I think."

"Homeland," Miguel said.

"You sure?" she asked.

"No, but every Indian knows that Interior jerk. He still owes us a mess of blankets from 1873. They all say the same thing, 'soon.' Anyway. That's not him."

I pulled up the phone. "Uh, hey, excuse me. They need our statements here. We have to go. Probably. Thanks. And everything." I clicked off.

Miguel and Tania stared their disappointment at me.

I said, "What?"

"Ain't that god of yours supposed to be eloquent or something?" Tania asked.

Mercury stood behind her. *If you'd asked me, I would've told you to say, "Who alone suffers, suffers most i'the mind, Leaving free things and happy shows behind. But then the mind much sufferance doth o'erskip, When grief hath mates and bearing fellowship." But you were winging it. Which is an eloquence of its own kind. In a way. For you.*

I said, *I don't even know what all that means.*

Mercury sighed and tossed up his hands. *I give up.*

"Let's go." I walked out, and they followed.

Miguel drove us to the jet, and the jet flew into the night sky, heading toward home. I stretched out on one of the sofas. Miguel took the other one. Tania lowered two facing seats to form the third bed. We were dead tired. I closed my eyes as we crossed north of Scotland, south of Iceland, and then the tip of Greenland heading toward Newfoundland and Labrador.

The whole trip, I tried to visualize Jenny. Instead, I kept seeing Nema laughing her little pixie head off.

Finally, it dawned on me. I jumped to my feet. *Holy shit! She has a backup site. There are still a thousand lives at stake.*

Mercury said, *Why do you say that, homeboy?*

I said, *The house was wired to blow. She didn't care about Paladin— she was going to kill him the minute he sent the orders to attack. But just in case something went wrong, she still wants her darkness to descend on the world.*

Mercury said, *That bothered me, too. How could anyone with her cleverness not have a redundant system?*

I said, *I keep going over the numbers in my head. The original plan called for five guys for each of thirteen sites. She had forty-nine terrorists when I bailed, but she picked up five, including Caleb. Holding out Lugh and Paladin left her with four per site, smaller crews than she wanted.*

Mercury said, *What're you saying, brutha? If she wanted a backup system to Paladin, she would have to do it herself?*

I said, *But she's not technical at all.*

Mercury said, *Which leaves you?*

I said, *Arrianne.*

Mercury touched his nose. *Whad'ya know? Some of y'all white boys aren't so dumb after all.*

I let it go. Arguing with god never works out for me.

I said, *Where did they go?*

Mercury said, *Remember what she told you?*

He looked at the video display on the bulkhead. If you don't put on a movie, the screen shows a map of your flight path. We were going home to Washington DC. The map showed us 700 miles away. Over an hour out. I looked back at my forgotten god and shrugged. He waved his arms in the air, then aimed his hands at the display again, like Vanna White turning letters on that show, *Wheel of* ... something.

He was giving me a clue. I hate that deities never tell you stuff. If they did, having faith wouldn't be a question. We would all believe. But they like to confuse us to the point we never know for sure. Even the people who say they believe without a doubt, have doubts. The gods love to watch us suffer. Sadistic bastards.

I got up and looked at the map. Quebec City, Montreal, Albany, Philadelphia, then home. We flew at 41,000 feet because private jets like to keep out of the lanes for commercial flights.

The screens held my attention for some reason I couldn't place. Something about the big cities on the left and right of our flight path caught my eye. I zeroed in on Quebec City, Montreal, Albany. I checked the map. Maine, New Hampshire, Vermont, New York.

Then it hit me like Arrianne's perfume. *Vermont because it's 92% white.*

Mercury was right. She had told me.

I called Bianca. She had been asleep. She was not happy with me. I said, "When you sent out the stand-down message, did one of them go to Vermont?"

"I think so. I can check."

"We also need to check for a signature. They would have a system of proof that the text came from Paladin and not someone pretending to be him."

"We thought of that. They were all signed with the single letter P. We did the same when we sent our note."

"A while back, you told me you guys in management sent emojis in texts that were programmed to respond when us regular people read a text."

"That's not public information, Jacob," she said. "But it's true. Why?"

"Were they sending a letter P—or one of those emoji-things that looked like a P?"

"Holy shit. We didn't check for that. I can't believe I didn't think of it. It has to be an emoji because an app could check the code on it to make sure ... Damn." I heard her tossing the covers back and jumping to her feet.

I said, "Then we have to find out if the cops found anyone at any of the phone locations. If the Free Origins terrorists knew it was a fake message, they would've abandoned the location."

Mercury waved his hand to get my attention. *Because they would've been waiting for the order to attack in a safe house, but they'd also have a backup safe house. When they get the fake message, they abandon the first spot for the second and leave the phone behind. All except one person. Who would that be, homie?*

I said, *Nema is using Arrianne's mill house for the backup command center. She can't leave, so she runs out and puts the phone in a passing car. Holy crap. We're hours behind them now.*

Mercury said, *Lucky for you, blowing up Paladin set their timetable back a day. You have until sunrise to find little Nema and wreck her party.*

I said, "Bianca, there's going to be a phone in Vermont. I'm sure of it. Can you find its location at the time it received your stand-down message? Not where it is now, but where it was then?"

"Yes."

"Get me those coordinates. And get the international police on alert. This isn't over."

"I'm on it." She clicked off.

I ran to the cockpit. "Can you veer a bit west of our flight path and drop to 30,000 feet?"

"We can check with traffic control. Why?"

"I need to do a HALO jump."

I ran back to wake up Tania and Miguel. They huffed and complained and swore at me, then got up. They followed me to the baggage compartment.

Tania, bless her still-cursing soul, had repacked all the HALO suits and readied the wingsuits as part of our ready-for-anything plan. I would've kissed her were it not for the likelihood she'd deck me.

We donned the suits, checked our oxygen, and grabbed pistols and rifles from the armory chest.

Bianca sent the coordinates for the Vermont phone via text. She also noted the State Police sent a SWAT team out of Burlington, but the destination was rural. Very rural. Their ETA was forty-five minutes.

I texted Bianca back, "We're five minutes away. We'll get there first. Tell them not to shoot us. Please."

The co-pilot came aft to close the door behind us. When we reached the right place, the pilot dove, leveled out, then gave us the signal. We opened the cargo door and jumped into the darkness.

Our wingsuits worked great. Falling five miles down at 100 miles per hour doesn't take long. We zeroed in on the target in two minutes.

We landed at the end of an old grass airfield at 0319 hours. We ditched our gear, put on our Sabel Visors for night vision and thermal sensing. We saw our surroundings as bright as day, with a touch of video-game feel. Earbud communications fed an open channel between the three of us and sent livestreamed video back to Bianca's team in Maryland. We snuck up on an aging and dilapidated mill house. A big wheel creaked slowly as the stream flowed beneath it.

All the lights were on.

CHAPTER 53

TANIA TOOK THE BACK. MIGUEL took the side. I went for the front porch. We peered in windows, measured rooms, checked corners, counted doors. We met back behind a stand of poplar trees.

"Yagi antennas on the shed roof," Tania said. "Kitchen's a mess. One guy wandered in for a Diet Coke. He wasn't with them in Spain. He seems like an IT loser, not Arrianne's kind of guy."

"Nema has a boyfriend?" I asked. Tania shrugged.

"Saw Arrianne working on computers," Miguel added. "From what I saw on her screens, she was working on alternate sites. Nema was pacing behind her with a dead man's trigger. She hadn't pressed the switch yet."

"I saw that room from the other angle." There was something wrong with the scenario. Something I couldn't put my finger on. "Did anyone see any explosives?"

They shook their heads.

Miguel said, "She's not the type to die for her cause. But she's fond of bombs. Has to be something different this time."

"So where is the bomb that goes with her trigger?" Tania asked. "Only places we haven't seen are the attic and basement. Let's start with the basement."

We snuck silently back to the mill house and found a door to the lower level near the stream. There were no windows.

Bianca texted us, "They're active on the internet researching targets. We need to disconnect the Yagi antenna and take them offline."

Miguel, Tania, and I exchanged glances. We wouldn't take them offline until we had the bomb disabled. If Nema knew we were here, they might choose to blow us all up. Tania went to the shed where she'd

SEELEY JAMES

seen the antenna. She would deactivate it on my command and not before. Miguel went to the window where he had a good view of the command center. I went through the basement door.

There wasn't enough light in the pitch-black space for night vision to work. I flipped on the infrared we use in these situations. It wasn't a basement. It was the working room of the mill. The shaft from the wheel had long ago rusted out, but stone wheels, six feet across, stood ready to grind.

Mercury stood in the dark, looking around. *Shame about that door.*

I said, *What do you mean?*

Mercury said, *What did they call these places back in the day? Drafty. Opening that door sucked air from upstairs. Unless she's clueless, she'll be down here in a minute.*

I said, *Couldn't be helped. Had to get in somehow.*

My visor caught a heat signature in the corner, obscured by something.

Moving cautiously, I pulled back a plastic shower curtain. The spitting image of Arrianne, only male and maybe two years younger, faced me. He wore a suicide vest with a lot more wires sticking out of it than Jenny's. His eyes were wide with terror. He trembled so hard he could barely keep standing.

Nema wasn't big on family. She killed her brother and broke off contact with her parents. Using Arrianne's little brother was as evil as the rest of Nema's plan. All part of her darkness. Then it came to me. I understood why Nema hated so many people.

A bright light came on. It lit up the mill room.

"Don't move, Jacob." Nema's voice.

I stepped away from the bomb and faced her. She stood at the top of a long wooden staircase with a rifle aimed at me. "Or what?"

"Don't think I won't shoot you."

"I don't doubt you'll try." I tugged at my body armor. "But you'll have to hit my face because the rest of me is covered. I don't think you're that good a shot. You'll be lucky to pull the trigger before I respond. From this angle, I can hit your thalamus and medulla with one bullet. The thalamus controls your sensory information, sending data off

302

to different parts of the brain for processing. The medulla tells your heart to beat and your lungs to breathe. Doing it that way, you won't feel a thing."

She gulped and regrouped. "Why didn't you, then?"

"Because this poor bastard might end up dead." I thumbed over my shoulder at her victim. "I've not figured out how to disable the vest."

"Pulling the battery won't work this time. We figured it out. The only way you could've freed those kids was to unplug it. We built in a secondary."

"We?"

Nema realized she gave something away.

Bianca's voice slipped into my earbud. "Jacob, can you get a close up look at the wiring on the vest?"

I said to Nema, "You mean that guy upstairs? The one you're saving yourself for? Or so he thinks."

"Shut up, Jacob. Get up here."

"And leave Arrianne's innocent little brother to die? I don't think so. Make you a deal here. Let me take the vest and give him the body armor."

"How about I take the body armor?" she asked.

"Won't fit, but you're welcome to try. Before I shed it, I have a question for you." I turned to her victim and let the camera take in the wiring. "Is it going to blow when I take it off him?"

"No." Her voice betrayed her indignation that I would question her honesty in a deal like this.

"Y'know, I don't trust you. I'm going to keep my armor on while I take the vest off him."

I unclipped three clasps in the front. I turned him around and checked the back, all the while sending a video stream to Bianca. Nothing appeared to have body sensors. It was a simple device. With an extra battery. And more wires. Nema wasn't bluffing about the advanced triggering options.

"Got a name?" I asked the guy.

"Tyler."

A memory flashed in my brain. Back in the Andalusian wine cellar that had no wine, Nema reminded Arrianne of Tyler. A threat against her family. No wonder Arrianne turned against us after that. She was trying to save her little brother instead of the world. Tough choice.

Mercury looked the vest over. *Don't take the vest, homie. There's no way out of this one.*

I said, *I have a way out, guaranteed.*

Mercury said, *I'm an immortal god, and I'm telling you, putting this thing on is a death sentence—and this time you won't die a hero. You'll just die.*

I said, *But you're the one who taught me about mortals. I'm basing my plan on your teachings.*

I took the vest off Tyler and handed him my rifle. Quietly, I said, "When I get this vest on, you give me the rifle back, then run out that door and don't look back. She isn't exactly good with stationary targets, so there's little chance she's going to hit you if you keep moving. Run outside and down the road until you see cops. I'll get your sister out of this."

He nodded.

"What are you two whispering about?" Nema shouted.

"Standard guy-debate. Is Nema hot or not?" I took the vest in my hand and slipped an arm in. I took the rifle back and slipped the other arm in. "Sorry, the consensus is unanimous: not."

I raised my brows at Tyler.

He stared at me blankly.

"Now is good," I said. He didn't move. "NOW."

His face lit up. His eyes darted to Nema. He bolted for the door.

Nema raised her rifle.

I put a bullet in the wood next to her nose. The suppressor on my rifle kept the noise down to what sounded like a soda being opened.

Tyler was out the door, up the riverbank, and gone.

Nema froze mid-breath.

"Intentional miss," I said. "Want to try your luck by not dropping your weapon?"

"You said I'd get the armor."

"Yeah, about that." I paused for dramatic effect. "I lied."

She tilted her head and furrowed her brow. She was shocked. No one had lied to her before. Which meant it was true—she'd never dated.

"Heel," I said and put a bullet through the heel of her shoe. "I like to call my shots."

After a repressed scream of shock and fear, Nema laid the rifle down gently. I checked her out. No sign of the deadman switch.

"Hands in the air, face the wall."

She complied.

Bianca cut into my comms again. "We don't see a way out this time, Jacob. The wiring looks solid. Someone presses the button, and you're, uh …"

She choked up.

I said, "Don't worry about it."

Nema looked over her shoulder at my non sequitur. She hadn't seen my earbud in the dark.

I climbed the stairs and put the muzzle in her back. "I'm just dying to meet your boyfriend. Lead the way."

"He's not my boyfriend."

"Diego thought he was your boyfriend. Paladin thought he was your boyfriend. A hundred bucks says this guy thinks he is too."

She stopped to glare over her shoulder at me.

"A bullet right here—" I pushed the muzzle between two vertebrae, "—and you're paralyzed for life."

She started climbing the remaining steps. "We can blow that vest any time."

"That's why I'm staying close, Nema. I'm counting on you to save my life. See, there's one thing I've noticed about suicide bombers over the years. The boss-lady who talks them into dying for the cause is never willing to go that far herself."

We walked down a hall and into the den being used for a computer room. I gave Nema a rough shove that sent her to the floor.

Arrianne looked up and immediately drained of all color. The guy next to her had glasses that were thicker up close than I'd noticed from outside. But not thick enough to mask his shock at seeing me standing there with twenty-eight pounds of C-4 strapped to my chest.

He reached for his trigger. I put a round under his hand. He pulled his paw back and looked at his fingers; amazed everything was still attached.

He looked up, angry and powerless.

"Got a name?" I asked him.

"Chuck, uh … Humbert."

"Chuck-uh-Humbert, did Nema tell you she slept with me?"

He snapped around to face Nema, his face reddened by pain and fury.

Nema turned on her back and sat up on her elbows. "Not true."

"Oh yes, it is." I put the barrel under Chuck-uh-Humbert's chin and turned him to face me. "Arrianne can verify."

"Whoa, don't drag me … I, um, well …" Arrianne swallowed hard.

"Your brother's running down the road," I told her.

I watched the calculations going through her head. Whose side should she take this time? After realizing her brother wasn't the guy wearing the suicide vest and I was telling the truth, she made the right decision. She tossed Nema a look that could kill.

"It's true." Arrianne looked at Chuck-uh-Humbert. "I woke them up. They spent the night in the same bed."

The poor guy started to collapse before my eyes. Just as he melted into a puddle, he appeared to change his mind about who was at fault. He scowled at Nema. "You lied to me?"

"Thank you, Arrianne," I said to her. "Now go find your brother."

Arrianne said, "Shoot her. She was going to kill Tyler. Kill her now."

"We need her to stop ROSGEO."

"Shoot her anyway."

"I'm not your biggest fan." I gave her my soldier stare. "Get out while you still can."

Arrianne's gaze dropped to my vest. She fled like a cockroach when the lights come on.

I faced Chuck-uh-Humbert. "Not only me. Diego had a shrine to her back at his house in Málaga. So, whatever your girlfriend promised you in exchange for all this—" I waved the rifle around at the computers before sticking it back under his chin "—was not exclusive."

He had trouble swallowing with his chin pushed up by the muzzle.

"You're going to send a command to all the operatives out there. Tell them plans have been delayed. They're to await further instructions."

Bianca broke into the comm again. "No! Don't let him touch anything."

Mercury grabbed my shoulder. *Bad idea, homes. Never let a nerd near a computer.*

I said, *Why not? We have to get the terrorists to stand down. The cops will swoop in moments later.*

Chuck-uh-Humbert started typing.

A green light on my chest began blinking. A large box appeared on one of the computer screens. It read 120, then 119, 118 …

Mercury said, *Because he just remotely armed your vest.*

CHAPTER 54

EVERYONE STARTED TALKING AT ONCE. Bianca and Tania talked over each other on the comm link.

Miguel came in and stood in the den's doorway, blocking the exit.

Chuck-uh-Humbert and I stared at each other, both resolute.

"I'm not going anywhere," I said. "You'll die with me."

"I thought she was real." He threw an ice-cold glance at Nema. "Turns out, she's just like every other woman. All they do is manipulate you for their own validation." He snarled at her, "Fuck you."

He had a point where Nema was concerned, but the broad generalization wasn't true. Nonetheless, it spoke to something uglier inside him.

Bianca's voice came through the comm. "They've changed the system since Denmark. We need her password to open their app. It's eighteen characters, too long for us to break in time. You have to get her password."

The counter on the computer read 106.

Mercury said, *Whatever you think I taught you about mortals, bro, I'm not seeing how that's gonna help us.*

I said, *You think I'm not paying attention, but I am. I heard you talking about mortals loud and clear. They're rarely willing to risk their lives for the cause. I'm counting on Nema to be the coward here.*

Nema scrambled to her feet. She looked at Miguel, who filled the door frame. "Hey, Geronimo, get out of my way. These two are going to die over some kind of toxic masculinity."

He pushed her back. "Geronimo was Bedonkohe. I'm Diné."

"So?" she said. "We're going to die. Get out of my way."

"That's like calling you a Canadian when you're a Mexican. Not the same thing."

"Did you hear what I said? That vest is going to kill us all."

"OK."

She pounded on him. He didn't move.

"She meant everything to me," Chuck-uh-Humbert said in a lonesome, resigned voice to no one in particular. "But she even lied about being a virgin. If I don't get her, nobody does."

His attempt to sound suicidal sounded more like bluster to my ear. But plenty of blusters turn real all too quickly. I shrugged and relaxed, at peace with the world, in the hopes my fatalistic attitude would make him rethink his.

Chuck's gaze broke. It slid to the screen.

The counter read 97.

After watching a couple more seconds tick off, Chuck-uh-Humbert turned to Nema, "You lied. You filthy slut."

"Have a little sensitivity here." I pushed the muzzle into his throat to get him focused. "She doesn't just hate you, Chuck-uh-Humbert, she hates everybody. All this racist crap is part of her bullshit."

"You don't know anything about me." Nema fisted her hips and stuck out her jaw.

"Sure, I do," I said. "I know there's a decent woman inside you who wants to call off ROSGEO. I'm counting on you to do that as soon as you work through your personal problems."

"You're going to die," Chuck-uh-Humbert yelled at Nema. "I'm going to make you pay for your lies."

Nema and I turned to him and said in unison, "Shut up!"

Nema spun back to me. "I don't have any personal problems."

"Rape is not about sex. It's about power." I watched her gaze dart around the floor. "Someone violated you, held that power over you. Forced you to do something you didn't want to do. Terrible thing. The guy deserves life in prison if not the death penalty."

"Rape?" Chuck-uh-Humbert asked. "What are you talking about?"

Nema's gaze wandered around in a circle before swinging back to the computer screen.

The counter read 85.

"She didn't tell you she was raped at fifteen?" I said.

Nema flushed and turned away. She hugged herself. "I never told anyone about that before. Just Mom. I trusted you. Thanks for blabbing it to everyone."

The poor sod's gaze swung back and forth between Nema and me.

"Your mom blamed you," I said. "Told you it was your fault for dressing the way teens do. She shamed you. She told you not to tell anyone, not to report it, not to get counseling. Is that about right?"

Nema nodded her back still to me.

"Oh, God," Chuck-uh-Humbert yelled. "You got yourself raped."

I pushed him backward with the muzzle. He nearly fell out of his chair. Which he would have deserved for such an idiotic remark.

Bianca cut back into my comm. "I found this guy's online postings. He's a regular on Reddit's Incel forum. Involuntarily Celibates. Guys whose blatant sexism and terrible attitudes make them repulsive. They blame women instead of themselves. One of his forum mates killed ten people in Toronto."

That explained a lot about this guy. But I needed to focus on Nema.

I said to her, "It was a relative, wasn't it? An uncle?"

She didn't answer.

"And you've been blaming yourself and hating everyone around you—including Chuck-uh-Humbert—ever since."

"You don't know anything!" She shouted and faced me.

"You're not alone, Nema. I know a woman who shot her rapist in the head. But he was guilty. You're taking it out on innocent women and children."

She didn't react. Something would get through to her. I needed to figure out what.

"You grew up working to get power over others," I said. "You figured out how a smaller, weaker woman can control people. You tried all kinds of methods. And finally discovered the servant can lead through invisible means."

She gave me a dirty look. It told me I'd hit the target dead center.

I kept going. "You've been exercising your power over a whole class of people who imagine they've been victimized: the racists. You knew they weren't really victims of any conspiracy to hold them back, to dilute their culture. You understand real victimization, not just from your rapist but from your family as well. And that led you to have nothing but contempt for people like Paladin and Arrianne and Lugh ... and Chuck-uh-Humbert." I nodded at the guy at the wrong end of my rifle. "Out of hatred, you got them to do the most outrageous thing you could think of, terrorism."

The counter read 71.

"What did you do that he had to rape you?" the idiot asked.

"Oh, come on. Really?" I blurted at him. "That's where you are?"

Nema pushed Chuck-uh-Humbert's shoulder. "Are you going to listen to his bullshit all day? Get me out of here."

"It's all true, isn't it?" he said. "You're not a virgin. You didn't save yourself for me."

Nema said, "Turn that damn thing off before we all die."

Chuck-uh-Humbert folded his arms across his chest. "There's no off-switch once it's armed. And it's keyed to the front door. If he stays, he'll kill us all. If he runs—he kills us all."

Mercury leaned into my line of sight. *Hold on, now, homeboy. I see what you're doing here. I see what you learned from me about mortals. I'm the one who told Shakespeare to write the verses you're applying.*

I said, *Which verse is that? I can't keep all your humble-brags straight.*

Mercury said, *"Thus conscience does make cowards of us all; And thus the native hue of resolution; Is sicklied o'er with the pale cast of thought; And enterprises of great pitch and moment; With this regard their currents turn awry, And lose the name of action."*

I said, *If I knew what that meant, I'd take credit.*

Mercury said, *It means the more we think about our fate, the more we become cowards. You're appealing to her conscience. But that raises the question, does she have one?*

I said, *We have to hope so.*

Chuck-uh-Humbert stole a glance at the computer screen.

The counter read 65.

"You're going to let all those young girls die?" I asked Nema. "They're just as young and innocent as you once were. You'd rob them of their future? That would be worse than your rapist. You're not that kind of woman, Nema. Tell me your password."

She turned to me. "What girls?"

I'd reached her. Maybe.

"Every church and synagogue and temple will have fifteen-year-old girls in them when your people open fire. Their heads will be split open by the bullets you're sending. Their brains and blood will splatter on the floor. Some will suffer for hours before dying. Their hopes and dreams ended because of something you can stop."

Nema moved close to me, looking up with wide eyes. Her bottom lip trembled. "You're lying. They won't kill the girls."

"You taught them to fire on full-auto, Nema. They'll aim at the thickest groups of people for maximum damage." I lowered my voice, forcing her to strain to hear me. "And you know teenage girls huddle. You're pulling the trigger. You are the one sending them to their deaths."

Nema blinked. Tears filled her eyes.

"Then they'll be spared the indignations of growing up." Her voice grew louder. Her tears began to flow. "They won't have men judging the size of their boobs. They won't have rich ladies judging their rags. They won't have family judging their sluttiness."

"They won't have the triumph of graduating high school and college. They won't have the joy of falling in love. They won't have—"

"Too bad." She shoved me hard, almost causing my finger to slip inside the trigger guard which almost cost Chuck-uh-Humbert his head. "At least those stupid girls won't suffer."

The counter read 53.

"NATO rounds tumble on impact, Nema." I grabbed her hand before she could hit me. Chuck used my split focus to back away from my rifle a few inches. "As soon as they hit tissue or bone, they tumble, sending shockwaves through the surrounding flesh. They shatter bones. They wreak havoc inside the person they hit. They're designed that way so you don't have to hit the target's center to kill someone. Can you hear those young girls screaming in agony?"

"You don't care about anyone but yourself," Chuck-uh-Humbert spat his words.

Nema faced him. "Shut up, you fucking moron."

Tania's voice broke into the comm link. "Problem. Problem. Arrianne's got a gun."

She was breathing hard. Running fast. Outside.

Something caught my peripheral vision. When my eyes tried to break through the reflected light from inside the house to the darkness beyond, all I could make out were two figures.

A three-round burst shattered the window and shredded the ceiling.

Outside, Tania threw punches at a flattened Arrianne. They were fighting for control of the weapon. Tania must have tackled Arrianne just as she pulled the trigger, which saved Nema's life.

Tania won the rifle and slammed the butt into Arrianne's forehead. Excessive but effective. Her words came over the comm. "Done being nice to assholes like you."

With my attention off him, Chuck-uh-Humbert rolled his chair back and opened the desk drawer. He pulled a pistol out just as my attention came back to him.

The counter read 47.

"I hate all of you bitches." Chuck-uh-Humbert pulled the trigger.

The bullet hit Nema square in the chest. She staggered back a step, looking at the hole in her shirt, shocked and surprised. Blood poured out. She fell on her back.

I pressed my rifle to his temple. "Put it down."

He looked at me, put the pistol under his chin, and blew his brains out.

Miguel rushed up behind me and grabbed the suicide vest and pulled it off me as I dropped to Nema on the floor. He gently set it aside. Together we checked Nema's vital signs. The bullet hadn't hit her heart directly, but the blood pumping out told us it punctured an artery. She had minutes left.

Bianca's voice on the comm. "We're contacting Air Evac units. We'll have a chopper there shortly."

Miguel and I had enough battlefield experience to know that wouldn't save her. But we kept it to ourselves.

"Nema," I said gingerly. "You want to spare the young girls. I know you do."

Her eyes fluttered. She tried to sit up. Miguel lifted her shoulders. The dying always want to see the wound for themselves. She put her fingers in the flowing blood. "Tell them not to hurt the girls."

Blood flowed down her chest and onto the floor where it pooled around her butt.

"I'll tell them. How do I contact them?"

Her eyes glazed and rolled back in her head.

"Nema." I patted her cheek. "How do I reach them to tell them not to shoot the girls?"

She sighed a long and tired sigh. As she inhaled, we could hear fluids filling her lungs.

I shook her. I looked at Miguel then around the room for something like smelling salts that might bring her back. All I saw was the computer screen.

The counter read 24.

"One, nine, six ..." Nema's voice was soft. "Three."

"You can do it, Nema. You can save their lives. What's the rest?"

"Zero, eight, twenty-three, L ..." She coughed up blood and inhaled with a ghastly noise. "Tell my mother ... fuck you."

Bianca on the comm. "Eighteen characters. You're halfway."

"I'll tell her, Nema," I said. "I'll tell her what I think of her too. What comes after L?"

"I then N and ... C." She shivered. "It's cold. So cold."

Her body spasmed violently, bile oozed out of her mouth. Her death throes. She went still. Miguel felt her neck and shook his head.

"Is that enough to work with, Bianca?" I asked. "Cuz, that's all we're going to get."

"No." She sighed.

I looked up at the computer.

The counter read 17.

Bianca continued. "But it's a start. My team's working on it. I hope it means something more than random numbers and letters." With the phone still to her mouth, she shouted at her team. "We can do this. We have to do this."

Mercury tapped my shoulder. *She been a whole lot craftier than you realize, homie. August 23rd, 1963, Lincoln Memorial, remember what happened?*

I said, *Damn it, if you know the answer, just tell me!*

Mercury said, *Not how it works. Think about that date. Famous people. People with dreams. Your little racist chose the one password none of her minions of morons would guess.*

"Holy shit, Bianca." I gathered my thoughts. "Martin Luther King gave a speech at the Lincoln Memorial on August 23rd, 1963. His 'I Have a Dream' speech. The last letters fill that in."

Her team began shouting in the background. Someone said, "That's gotta be it. Try it."

Bianca said, "Jacob, we can't do it remotely. You need to type it in. Try 19630823LincolnMem. And try it with caps and no caps."

Miguel beat me to the chair. He was the better typist. I leaned over his shoulder.

He tried it with caps. He tried with all lower case. He tried with one of each. Nothing.

"What else you got?" I asked Bianca.

"Try 19630823LinclDream."

Miguel tried it. Nothing.

An exasperated gasp went through her team on the other end. She said, "We're thinking."

The counter read 4.

Miguel looked at me. "I know what it is."

He typed in 19630823LincolnMLK.

The app opened up.

"That's it!" Bianca yelled. "We'll take it from here. Get out!"

We took off in a dead run. Through the front door. Up the driveway and across the paved road. Miguel picked me up and tossed me into the drainage ditch on the far side. He dove in behind me.

The explosion blew the mailbox over my head. Again. The shock wave pounded every square inch of my body. Again. The fireball lit up the surrounding trees. Heat singed my back. Smoke filled my lungs. Pieces of clapboard and shingles and structural beams and plumbing flew over my head. It was becoming routine.

Miguel grabbed my arms, hauled me to standing. We took off running again as the bigger objects began falling from the sky and landing around us like mortar shells.

As we ran, Miguel said, "You gotta stop pushing things to the last second."

CHAPTER 55

I WAITED IN MS. SABEL'S spare McLaren with the top down on a sunny spring day in Washington, DC. She loaned it to me for the special occasion and wished me luck. Miguel texted me a picture showing off his new threads in front of *The Kooples*, Paris. He looked *tres chic*.

Jenny strolled out of the therapist's office building at a slow and unsteady pace. It looked as if she were having second thoughts about getting in the car. She stopped and looked around, took a deep breath, put her head down, then walked straight to me. We exchanged heys. She didn't want to talk. I'd been told to expect that.

We drove down Wisconsin Avenue in silence for several blocks. Traffic stopped and started. We caught every light red.

Mercury squeezed into the tiny space between our seatbacks and the engine compartment. *You were right from the beginning, dawg. Something went wrong with your girlfriend.*

I said, *Adding "girl" to the front implies something that might not exist anymore.*

Mercury said, *Uncertainty sucks, don't it?*

I said, *You can say that again.*

Mercury said, *Imagine how your un-worshipped god feels. Who saved you from, not one, but two suicide vests?*

I said, *That's what I want to know.*

We stopped at a light.

"You wanted to meet my old friends," Jenny said. "She said it was a good idea. I mean for me, not necessarily you. Or with you. Or because you asked. I'm sorry. I'm not making sense."

"Your therapist said it was good for you to reconnect with old friends.

I get that."

We drove a couple more blocks toward the restaurant where she'd booked our lunch reservation.

"She told me to expect mood swings." Jenny folded her hands in her lap. "You noticed that, I'm sure."

Mercury said, *What is she talking about, dawg? She had wild and crazy sex with you then dumped you in the morning. Is that what she means by a mood swing?*

I said, *No need to analyze it. Remember when Thompkins got separated from the unit during a mortar attack and ended up outside the wire for twenty-four hours? He had some mood swings after that.*

Mercury said, *You mean the poster-boy for PTSD, the guy who tried to gut you? Yeah, I remember that nut job. Whatever happened to him?*

I said, *Turned into a vegan Buddhist and works for Veterans for Peace.*

"You're not saying anything." Jenny twisted in the seat to look me over.

"I'm fairly immune to mood swings. They're pretty common in war zones."

"I can imagine." She looked at the shops as we inched closer to the center of Bethesda. She went quiet again.

I tried to remember all the bullet points from the many sites I'd visited to learn about how to be supportive. Patience came up a lot. So did reinforcement. And a few other things men generally suck at.

"Would you rather not talk about it?" she asked with an edge.

"I'm trying to listen. The experts recommend listening."

"OK."

Mercury said, *Oh boy. This is worse than my marriage counseling.*

I said, *You went to marriage counseling?*

Mercury said, *I thought so. After I escorted the nymph Lara to the underworld, where one thing led to another, my wife insisted we go to counseling. Mars claimed he was a certified therapist, but he had other plans. I caught the two of them "counseling" one day.*

I said, *Ouch.*

"Would you rather I talk?" I asked. Dangerous an idea as it was, I wanted her to stay engaged. No one helped Nema deal with her trauma and she fell off the ledge into a sea of hatred. Nema choose her path. I didn't want Jenny near that precipice.

She thought about it. "Tell me what you think of our relationship."

I took a deep breath. "When we first met, you were thirsty. After a year in prison, I figured it made sense, even if it felt rushed and one-dimensional. I'm not going to pretend I didn't like it. I figured the rest of the relationship would fall into place."

"You didn't care about the rest of the relationship; all you cared about was the sex."

"Believe it or not, I care about intimacy."

"That's what I said." Her voice rose. "You got all you wanted—without any baggage."

"That's not fair." I squeezed the steering wheel tight enough to break it. "Sex is just one facet of intimacy. Intimacy is about sharing the truth. Tell me something true." Suddenly, I felt like I'd said something wrong. I added, "When you're ready."

She crossed her arms and turned as far away from me as she could in the exotic car. Which wasn't very far.

We went forward, one car length at a time, for two blocks before she spoke again. "Well. OK. Here's something true. I went into therapy today, expecting to hate it. That's why I invited you to pick me up for lunch. I expected to come out of there in a bad mood and be able to break things off cleanly with a rational explanation. Only there was a problem. I liked the session. She recommended doing things to get my life back to normal. Like reconnecting with my old friends. Facing the whispers and the rumors and the press and forging ahead with life as it is. The things she said were a lot like the things you said. She made me realize you understand the problem. So, I, um ..."

She took my hand off the shifter and held it in both of hers.

"It's not the same, but there are parallels between rape and the trauma of war."

We inched along for another block. She didn't let go of my hand.

"I'm not famous," she said. "But my father is. And Mom being the vice president makes things worse. That means anyone around me is going to have reporters and paparazzi shoving cameras and microphones in their face. They'll be asked questions about dating a convicted killer. I can't ask anyone to go through that. It makes intimacy impossible."

We made a turn onto a less traveled street. It was one-way. A construction crew blocked three-quarters of the single lane. We waited for a bored guy in a reflective vest to wave us through.

"What I'm trying to say is, dating me isn't going to be easy. I'm a long-term kind of girl. I don't have relationships of convenience. I'm not …"

She sighed.

"I knew all that before Basel-Stadt."

"I mean …" She huffed and thought and took a deep breath before going on. "I'm giving you a way out here. You don't have to help me. You don't have to worry about me. My parents and my brother are doing too much of that now. We can have lunch and shake hands, walk away as friends."

I took a long look at her. Not the supermodel type, nor bad looking, she had a different kind of beauty. The beauty that comes from determination. The kind that radiates regardless of her mood or temperament or situation.

Mercury said, *That's your cue. Get out while you can.*

I said, *What kind of heavenly guidance is that?*

Mercury said, *Now's your chance to turn over a new leaf. Make a clean break from being the whack-job-magnet you've always been. You don't see Caesars hanging around with murderers. It's bad for business.*

I said, *To the Teutons and the Gauls and the Angles, the Caesars were the murderers.*

Mercury said, *Huh. Izzat why they never liked us?*

"As long as we're being all intimate and stuff: here's something true." I squeezed Jenny's hand. "When I pulled those wires off the battery, I had no idea what would happen."

She reared back in shock and anger and fear and incredulity.

"HEY!" The guy in the safety vest blew his whistle and waved an impatient hand. "C'mon, while we're young already."

I drove around the guy.

Jenny shoved my shoulder and started laughing. "You're pulling my leg. You would never endanger me."

We turned the last corner and pulled up to *Mon Ami Gabi*, the famous French bistro. Twelve people appeared out of thin air and descended on us. Cameras flashed, phones recorded, microphones popped out.

"I'm sorry, Jacob," Jenny said. "I don't know how they found us. I made the reservations in your name."

The crowd swarmed toward my side of the car. A woman started asking questions, "Mr. Stearne, are you going to accept the French President's apology? If so, what about the key to Paris?"

A guy next to her elbowed her aside. "If you had to do it all over again, would you have worn the suicide vest on behalf of the victim?"

"Are you going to accept President Williams' invitation to the White House?"

"What about the King of Morocco's parade in your honor?"

I turned to Jenny. "I'm down for anything you are."

THE END

TO YOU FROM SEELEY JAMES

I hope you enjoyed the story and will join my VIP Readers by signing up at SeeleyJames.com/VIP. I hold a drawing every month for things like gift certificates or naming characters in upcoming books. I also give VIPs the inside scoop on things like how certain characters were named; which Shakespeare soliloquies I ~~plagiarized~~ drew from; what I'm working on next, etc.

Please remember to leave a review! Indie authors live and die by reviews. If you didn't enjoy it, that's OK, sometimes the magic works and sometimes it doesn't.

If you want to chat, please email me at seeley@seeleyjames.com or join me on Facebook: SeeleyJamesAuthor. I love hearing from readers.

EXCERPTS FROM SABEL SECURITY SERIES:

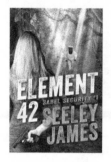

ELEMENT 42, SABEL SECURITY #1

That time you stumbled onto a mass grave and mercenaries bolted from the jungle to hunt you down.

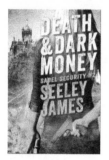

DEATH AND DARK MONEY, SABEL SECURITY #2

What if you discovered foreigners were donating to the campaigns of American politicians?

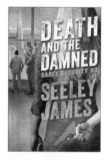

DEATH AND THE DAMNED, SABEL SECURITY #3

Why would a billionaire smuggle terrorists into the country?

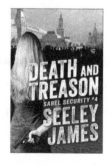

DEATH AND TREASON, SABEL SECURITY #4

What if you discover foreigners plotting to assist a political campaign?

DEATH AND SECRETS, SABEL SECURITY #5

What if DNA led you to discover your mother was the vice president—and a murderer?

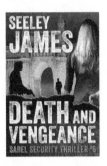

DEATH AND VENGEANCE, SABEL SECURITY #6

The president declares war based on a lie. Can Jacob Stearne stop him before the world descends into chaos?

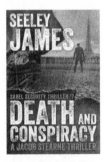

DEATH AND CONSPIRACY, SABEL SECURITY #7

Is Jacob Stearne a terrorist or a hero? Go undercover in this all-Jacob thriller.

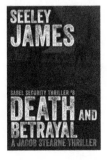

DEATH AND BETRAYAL, SABEL SECURITY #8 (FEB-2020)

Be sure to join the newsletter for more about this one due in early Feb-2020.

ABOUT THE AUTHOR

His near-death experiences range from talking a jealous husband into putting the gun down to spinning out on an icy freeway in heavy traffic without touching anything. His resume ranges from washing dishes to global technology management. His personal life stretches from homeless at 17, adopting a 3-year-old at 19, getting married at 37, fathering his last child at 43, hiking the Grand Canyon Rim-to-Rim several times a year, and taking the occasional nap.

His writing career ranges from humble beginnings with short stories in The Battered Suitcase, to being awarded a Medallion from the Book Readers Appreciation Group. Seeley is best known for his Sabel Security series of thrillers featuring athlete and heiress Pia Sabel and her bodyguard, unhinged veteran Jacob Stearne. One of them kicks ass and the other talks to the wrong god.

His love of creativity began at an early age, growing up at Frank Lloyd Wright's School of Architecture in Arizona and Wisconsin. He carried his imagination first into a successful career in sales and marketing, and then to his real love: fiction.

For more books featuring Pia Sabel and Jacob Stearne, visit SeeleyJames. com

Contact Seeley James:

mailto:Seeley@seeleyjames.com
Website: SeeleyJames.com
Facebook: SeeleyJamesAuth
BookBub: Seeley James

CPSIA information can be obtained
at www.ICGtesting.com
Printed in the USA
LVHW032058081019
633405LV00002BA/319/P

9 781733 346702